An Unmerciful Incursion

Book 6 of the Peninsular War Saga

By

Lynn Bryant

To Anya
Without you, the world would be a less interesting place.
Thank you for being my friend as well as my daughter.
I love you.

About the Author

Lynn Bryant was born and raised in London's East End. She studied History at University and had dreams of being a writer from a young age. Since this was clearly not something a working class girl made good could aspire to, she had a variety of careers including a librarian, NHS administrator, relationship counsellor, manager of an art gallery and running an Irish dance school before she realised that most of these were just as unlikely as being a writer and took the step of publishing her first book.

She now lives in the Isle of Man and is married to a man who understands technology, which saves her a job, and has two grown-up children and a black Labrador. History is still a passion, with a particular enthusiasm for the Napoleonic era and the sixteenth century. When not writing, she teaches history and creative writing, reads anything that's put in front of her and makes periodic and unsuccessful attempts to keep a tidy house.

Acknowledgments

This is the first book I've written and published in the middle of a global pandemic, and it feels like something of an achievement that I've got here at all. As always, I couldn't have done it alone.

Research is a huge part of the writing I do, and I'd like to thank various historians and writers who have helped me with the maddest questions, especially Jacqueline Reiter, Rob Griffith, Rory Muir, Andrew Bamford and many others on social media and in person. In particular, I'd like to mention Zack White who has so generously shared some of his amazing work on courts martial and patiently answered my questions. Thank you all.

As always, I'd like to thank Mel Logue, Jacqueline Reiter and Kristine Hughes Patrone for reading sections of the work and making helpful suggestions.

Thanks to Heather Paisley, my fabulous editor for showing me all the ways in which spell check doesn't help and for making me cry with laughter along the way. She's a joy to work with.

Thanks to Richard Dawson, my husband, for another amazing cover, for technical help and for endless support and patience during the writing of this book.

Thanks to my son, Jon and his girlfriend Rachael, for sharing my study during lockdown and completely ignoring my historical mutterings and to my daughter, Anya, for helping to keep me on track when I was really struggling to motivate myself.

Last but not least, thanks to Oscar and Alfie, the stars of Writing with Labradors for sharing my study and bringing me joy every day.

And in loving memory of Toby, my old black Labrador, and Joey, my old yella fella who died while I was writing this book and broke my heart. You will both always be with me in spirit.

Chapter One

Captain Leo Manson was hungry. He had been aware for some time of his stomach growling, but the sound was becoming audible now, or it would have been, if there had not been so much noise on the parade ground. The noise was rising steadily, a combination of marching feet, shouted orders and the quiet grumbling of officers and NCOs who were aware that it was past the dinner hour. The bugle had called some time ago, and the major who was theoretically supervising the drill hesitated and shot an uncertain glance towards Manson and his companion, who shook his head without speaking. Major Beaumont signalled for the drill to continue, but the interruption seemed to have affected the troops, and the manoeuvres, which had been looking considerably better, were deteriorating again.

"To the right, wheel! March!"

The men on the right of the rank stepped off, turning their eyes to the left. Manson watched, hopefully. For the first few steps, things seemed to be going well, but as the movement continued, he realised that some of the troops had forgotten to lengthen their steps. To maintain the wheel in perfect order, each man needed to pay attention to the exact length of his stride, or the wheel would fall apart very quickly. It did so, before Manson's gloomy gaze, with several men treading on those in front of them, and others scrambling in a series of quick, untidy steps to catch up. The celebrated first battalion of the 3rd Foot Guards looked like a draught of militia recruits during their first drill session and Manson gritted his teeth to stop himself intervening, silently pleading with the officers to stop the manoeuvre before it got any worse.

"Halt!"

The bellow was so loud that Manson physically jumped, even though he knew it was coming. The battalion stopped in its tracks, apart from several men caught in mid-step who cannoned into their comrades, causing a series of collisions which shoved one man out of the front rank on his own. The private froze, recognising his isolation, and looked desperately at his sergeant, who glanced at the nearest officer before jerking his head to indicate that the private retreat. The man made his way back into the line in a sideways shuffle which made Manson want to laugh aloud. Manson's companion said a word under his breath which was inappropriate for a senior officer on the parade ground and

1

strode to the front of the battalion, with the air of a man driven beyond his endurance. Manson, who had served under Colonel Paul van Daan of the 110th light infantry for more than two years, forgot about his rumbling stomach and just prayed that his commanding officer did not hit anybody.

"You, what's your name?"

The hapless soldier who had just made it back into the line, stared at the colonel, his mouth open, but no sound came out.

"Step forward."

The man did so. Paul van Daan moved closer and inspected him from head to toe with ruthless thoroughness, then held out his hand.

"Musket."

The man hesitated, and his sergeant, who seemed to have regained his wits, stepped forward. "Andrews, the officer of the 110th wishes…"

"Enough!" Paul roared, and the sergeant jumped to attention. "Andrews, give me the bloody musket before I take it from you and shove it where it will never see the sun. Sergeant Bolton, step back, I've not given you an order."

Andrews handed over the musket. He was sweating in fear, and Manson felt a twinge of sympathy for the man. Paul turned the weapon over in his hands, inspecting the touch hole, the lock and then the entire weapon very thoroughly. When he had done, he handed the musket back to Andrews who took it and returned to attention, staring woodenly ahead.

"Well, Private Andrews, it's clear you were paying attention when they taught you how to keep your musket in good order, even if you missed basic drill training. When did you join?"

"August, sir."

"When did you arrive in Portugal?"

"October, sir."

"Well, you were bloody lucky you didn't arrive earlier, you missed the worst retreat since Corunna. How much drill training have you had, so far?"

"Sir?" Andrews shot an agonised look towards his captain, who was watching the little drama with a thunderous expression. Paul followed his gaze and Manson saw a faint smile.

"Never mind, you can't really tell me you've had virtually none, can you?"

Paul turned away and walked to the front, surveying the battalion. His voice had a carrying power which any drill sergeant would have envied.

"Major Beaumont. Your officers will be missing their dinner. Why don't you go on ahead, I want a word with the battalion and then I'll join you."

There was a rustle of disquiet among the men, as the officers left. Colonel van Daan waited until they had gone, then turned back to the men.

"Sergeant-Major Clegg. Separate out the new recruits, get them lined up over there. And get a move on, I'm so hungry my belly is sticking to my spine. Private Andrews, lead them out."

2

Manson watched their faces as Paul began to shout out orders, and he wanted to smile. He had seen it happen many times before. Within minutes, the drill was running, and with only experienced troops, it ran very well. The NCOs, visibly relieved at being able to demonstrate how well their men could perform, kept the movements tight, and the companies worked well together. Paul watched, calling out an occasional order, but mostly left the NCOs to their work. Once it was evident that the Guards were moving smoothly, Paul crossed to where the new troops stood watching in miserable silence, and Manson saw Paul put his hand on Andrews' shoulder. He was speaking to him, pointing out what was happening in the manoeuvre, and Manson could see the man relaxing. Paul said something and several of the men around him laughed.

When the drill was done, Paul called the new recruits back into line. "Well done," he said. "I'd a feeling you were better than that. Don't get arsey with the new lads, we were all there once and they'll learn quicker if you work together. I'm pleased that I'll be able to report back to Lord Wellington that the 3rd Foot Guards are still the men who proved their worth at Salamanca. Is anybody hungry?"

There was a murmur of laughter and then somebody cheered. Paul grinned, and taking it as permission, the battalion yelled to a man, driven, Manson thought, not only by the thought of dinner but by an unexpected sense of camaraderie. Paul gave the order to stand the men down and walked over to Manson.

"Do you think we're going to get any dinner?" he asked.

"I'm not sure, sir. That went very well, though."

"Yes, they're good lads."

"They're good officers as well, sir."

"They might be, Captain, but if they've done more than a couple of hours' worth of work with their new recruits this winter, I'll be very surprised. Don't look at me like that. I'm going to go in there, explain his Lordship's instructions and be really, really tactful, I give you my word."

Manson watched as the tall, fair figure walked towards the solid farm building which currently housed the battalion officers' mess and felt his heart sink. Colonel Paul van Daan could manage the enlisted men and NCOs better than any officer Manson had ever seen, but his attitude towards a commissioned officer whom he suspected of shirking his duty frequently left chaos in his wake.

"Captain Manson, where the devil are you? Get in here, I'm hungry."

Manson sighed and followed, reflecting that whatever the atmosphere in the mess, there would at least be dinner.

The atmosphere was uncomfortable enough for Manson to be happy to miss breakfast the following morning. It was approximately thirty miles from Guarda, where the first division was in cantonments, to Freineda where Wellington had his headquarters. Paul, Manson and Sergeant Jenson, Paul's orderly, were travelling light and made good time. They stopped in the little village of Braga where a farmer made up for the lack of an early meal with excellent fare and a wealth of local gossip. He and Paul were clearly old

3

acquaintances and Manson ate in silence, trying to follow the conversation which was in rapid Portuguese and seemed to consist of a series of enquiries about members of the farmer's extended family. Back on the road, Paul was considerably more cheerful.

"I've known old Barboza since I was out here under Craufurd a few years ago, he was always good to us. Much better manners than the officers of the 3rd Foot Guards, I must say."

"Sir, you threatened to punch one of the officers of the 3rd Foot Guards."

"Only after he challenged me to a duel," Paul said composedly. "A challenge which I nobly resisted. I wonder if he'll complain to Lord Wellington?"

"I expect he's already written the letter, sir."

"Perhaps Wellington will be so furious that he'll remove me from this assignment," Paul said hopefully. "I'm not at all suited to the job."

Manson could not help smiling. "You are suited to the job, sir, you just hate doing it."

"I hate being away from my wife," Paul said. "She's barely out of her bed after giving birth and given what a horrendous ordeal that proved to be, she shouldn't be out of her bed at all. But we all know that she won't give a button for the list of instructions that I left for her and is probably doing something highly unsuitable without me there to keep an eye on her."

"Sir, she'd be doing that even if you were there."

"You know her very well, Captain." Paul shot him a smile. "I'm glad I asked you to come with me, Leo, it's been good to get some time with you."

"Me too, sir. It's been a mad few months."

"It's been a mad few years."

Manson could not disagree. He had arrived in Portugal with the 112th infantry, and his early introduction to army life and in particular to Colonel Paul van Daan had not been easy, but both Manson and Paul had persevered. Two and a half years later, Manson was captain of the 110th light company and enjoyed a close friendship with both Paul and his young wife, who travelled with the battalion.

Paul was currently in command of the third brigade of the light division, under its Hanoverian commander, General Charles Alten, but during winter quarters, had been given an unwelcome secondment by Lord Wellington to tour the various divisions of the army, inspecting training and combat readiness. Manson was not entirely clear about Paul's remit and he did not think that Paul was either, but after only a few weeks it was obvious that some of the officers of Lord Wellington's army were furiously resentful about his interference in the running of their battalions. Paul's friendship with Wellington, and his past record of taking on jobs that no other officer in the army wanted to do, had led to him being nicknamed 'Wellington's Mastiff' several years ago. Manson had heard the sobriquet again recently, and not in an affectionate way.

4

If Paul cared, he gave no sign of it. Manson thought that his commanding officer was more concerned with the problems he was finding with training and discipline in some of the divisions, than with his own unpopularity. Another officer might have treated this job as a sinecure, sending glowing reports back to Wellington on every occasion and making friends throughout the army but Manson knew that Paul would do no such thing. He treated each inspection as a personal quest to improve things and Manson was exasperated both with his over-conscientious colonel, and with Lord Wellington who had set him an impossible task. To make it worse, many of the officers he was dealing with, were of higher rank than he, and resented advice and recommendations from a mere colonel.

"When are your children arriving, sir?"

"Soon, I hope. I wrote to my father immediately after Georgiana's birth, asking him to make the arrangements and telling him that I want them to come here, since I'm not going to be able to travel to Lisbon this winter. My sister-in-law isn't happy about it, she's behaving as if I'm bringing them into a battlefield, which is nonsense, but I'm not sure she would be able to accompany them anyway this time, she's with child again."

"I doubt that she'll want to travel then."

"Well, we all know that my wife wouldn't hesitate, Captain, but then she's not normal. I don't blame Patience though, she's never managed to carry a child to full term, it's been a grief to both of them, so if this pregnancy is looking promising, Josh will wrap her in linen for the whole time. But I think my father will come, he enjoyed his brief visit last year, and he'll want to see Nan. I don't think he trusts me to take care of her, you wouldn't believe the letter he wrote me after he heard she'd been taken prisoner by the French last year."

Manson glanced at Paul then looked away. Anne van Daan's horrific ordeal at the hands of a French colonel shortly before Badajoz was seldom mentioned. Anne herself appeared to have made a remarkable recovery, but Manson was not sure that Paul had stopped blaming himself for allowing her to travel without him.

"Do your family know how bad it was?"

"You mean do they know she was raped?" Paul asked, and Manson heard the raw anger in his voice and wished he had not asked.

"I'm sorry, sir…"

"No, it's all right. It's good for me to say it occasionally, I'm too much inclined to pretend it didn't happen, and that's not good for either of us. No, we discussed it and agreed that they shouldn't be told the full story, it would be too upsetting for them. Even just knowing that she was held prisoner for two weeks incensed my father, he called me a variety of rude names. I think he'll want to assure himself that she's all right. I've not mentioned that she nearly got decapitated by a French hussar during the retreat, I think that might be a bit much for him."

"Let her tell him that one," Manson said. "She makes that story sound hilarious, if I'd not been there and seen it myself, I'd think she was never in danger at all. How old are the children now?"

"Grace is eleven, Francis is nine and Rowena is three. And Will, whom you have met, will be two." Paul gave him a sideways glance and smiled. "Grace is my natural daughter, although I don't intend to advertise that fact when she arrives. She's old enough to understand what that means now, and she's beginning to suffer from other people's prejudices, poor lass. And I'm not sure Patience helps. She's a very conventional woman, my sister-in-law, and although she loves the children dearly, I think she's made too much of Grace's situation."

"And your wife?"

"Leo, have you met my wife? She is the woman whose two closest female friends are her Spanish former maidservant who was once a prostitute and is now married to my regimental sergeant-major, and a Cornish miner's daughter who is living in an irregular union with the commander of my first battalion. Do you seriously think she cares whose daughter Grace is? They adore each other. I cannot say the same of Anne and Patience, mind, so it's probably just as well that Patience is unlikely to join us, it would be a strain."

"I would think so. Is Georgiana going to go home with the other children when they go back?"

"Yes. She should be weaned by then so we won't need to send a wet nurse with her, which is just as well, because I think Sergeant-Major Stewart would be indignant if we sent his wife back to England with my daughter. I've asked Nan if she wants to go with them, but she says no."

"She won't leave you, sir, and I'm thankful for it, the brigade would fall apart without her."

"I'd fall apart without her, but I try not to tell her so too often, I don't want her to feel under pressure to stay. Are you ready for a canter? I need to stop at headquarters on the way back, Wellington wants to see me. He is intending to set off for Cadiz very soon, and he wouldn't want to go without leaving me a list of impossible orders and a variety of jobs that nobody else wants to do, it would spoil his journey. Come on."

***

Paul found his chief alone in his combined sitting room and office reading letters.

"Colonel van Daan, sit down. How is your wife? And my Goddaughter? Have some wine."

Paul seated himself opposite the desk and accepted a drink with thanks. "Both thriving, thank you, sir."

"Excellent. I do not have to remind you that she should not be up and around yet? She has plenty of help, does she not? I am sure we can find extra staff in the village, should she require it."

6

Paul thought about his wife. When he left for Guarda, Anne had been organising his brigade office, getting two of his men to unpack the various regimental and brigade ledgers and files from the travelling chests and arranging furniture to be moved to her satisfaction. He decided not to mention it.

"Nan has all the help she needs, sir, she's very well, and Georgiana is in excellent health."

"Have you recovered yet?" Wellington asked, with slightly malicious amusement. "I am informed by Dr McGrigor that you found the experience rather trying."

"McGrigor has a loose tongue," Paul grimly. "I completely missed Will's birth, of course, I was on my way back from Badajoz and by the time I arrived, Nan was resting elegantly in bed. But I was with Rowena when she died giving birth and I don't think I realised how much that had affected me until Nan's pains began. I was terrified and trying not to show it. She knew, of course. I think she was frightened too."

"McGrigor tells me this was not as easy as William's birth. I am concerned about, her, Colonel. I have recently received a delivery from England, a few delicacies that it is not possible to obtain out here. I have told my servants to make up a parcel for her."

"That's good of you, sir."

"Has she found a new maid, yet?"

"She has Mrs Carter and Keren to help."

"Mrs Carter has a husband and child of her own to take care of, Colonel, and Keren Trenlow…one presumes she has her responsibilities too. Besides, it is wholly unsuitable that your wife's attendant lives in such an irregular manner. One would…"

"Why don't you mention that to my wife the next time you see her, sir?"

Wellington stopped. After a brief silence, he said:

"She would tell me to go to the devil."

"She would tell me exactly the same thing, sir."

"I am trying to help," Wellington said huffily.

Paul looked at Lord Wellington and said nothing. After a long moment, Wellington said:

"I apologise, Colonel. I have no right to question your arrangements for your wife, but if there is anything I can provide, it is hers."

Paul was touched. "Thank you, sir."

Wellington cleared his throat, an obvious signal that his lapse into sentimentality was over and he was ready for business. "Now, to work. The condition of this army needs attention, as I outlined in my recent memorandum to all officers. You read it, of course."

Paul thought about the lengthy memorandum which Wellington had circulated to his officers complaining about the conduct of the army during the recent retreat and was pleased that he was now able to do so without the urge to get up and punch his commander in the face.

"You know I did, sir," he said pleasantly. "Several times. My favourite part was when I had to read it out to my officers. Some of them are still on their sickbeds after that jolly little retreat back from Madrid and Burgos, which sounded like a summer picnic the way you wrote about it, so I read it to each of them personally just to make sure they understood. Colonel Wheeler particularly enjoyed it, I must say."

Wellington fixed Paul with a glare. "I am not in the mood for levity, Colonel van Daan."

"Nor am I, sir."

Two pairs of blue eyes locked and Paul did not look away or smile. The silence lengthened until it became uncomfortable, but Paul was fairly sure he had judged correctly. Eventually, Wellington gave a small snort and picked up his glass.

"You know perfectly well it was not aimed at you."

"Wasn't it? Well you're a bloody poor shot then, sir, because it landed right on my desk with instructions to have it read to all my junior officers."

"Did you actually read it to them yourself?"

"Yes. There are some things I don't delegate."

"There are many things I don't delegate," Wellington said, and the sally was so unexpected that Paul choked on his wine. His chief watched with wholly spurious sympathy as Paul mopped up the spill and got his coughing under control. When he could speak, Paul said:

"I thought you said you weren't in the mood for levity, sir?"

"I was unable to resist. Do you think you could set aside your peevishness to have a rational conversation? I am sorry that you were so offended by my memorandum, but it was necessary, and I could hardly provide Fitzroy Somerset with a list of those officers who were not to receive it. Besides, you needed to know what it said, because I am relying on you to help me to remedy the situation." Wellington picked up a letter from his cluttered desk. "Which reminds me, I have received a complaint," he said.

Paul regarded the letter. "That was quick," he said, sounding impressed. "He must have sent the messenger off very early, we left before breakfast. Mainly because I wasn't sure we were welcome at breakfast."

"Given the tone of this letter, I suspect he sent it off last night," Wellington said. Paul studied him and decided that he was not in trouble; Wellington sounded more pleased than annoyed. "Were you rude to Lieutenant-General Sir William Stewart, Colonel?"

"Not at all, sir. I was pretty rude to one or two of the officers of the 3rd Foot Guards though. In fact, I suppose I should tell you that Lieutenant-Colonel Armstrong called me out."

Wellington stared at him in astonishment. "Called you out? Is this another attempt to be amusing, Colonel?"

"No, sir, I promise you. There was a conversation about his battalion's drill performance and he took offence, I'm afraid."

"Did you accept his challenge?"

8

"I didn't, sir. Fortunately, I'd taken Captain Manson with me and his diplomatic skills are better than mine. But we need to talk about exactly how this is supposed to work. It's all very well for you to send me off with a letter of authorisation, but it means nothing to these officers. Half their men are on the sick list and the other half are recovering from starvation and exhaustion from the retreat. The officers are furious about the slur upon their character implied in that memorandum and when I turn up with your permission to tell them how to improve, they're in no mood to co-operate. The junior officers look to their seniors, and the senior officers aren't prepared to be told what to do by a mere colonel, especially one who is regarded as your tame monkey. Some of them will be very gentlemanly about it, others - like Sir William Stewart - are going to be very rude indeed. But none of them are going to co-operate."

Wellington was silent for a long time, frowning at Stewart's letter on his desk. "If you had their co-operation, what would you do?" he asked.

Paul thought about it. "I'd work with them at brigade level," he said finally. "I don't know how long you're expecting to be in winter quarters, sir, but it's not going to be long enough for me to take on the training of every single battalion in this army. But if I can call in the officers from every battalion in the brigade, I could work with one battalion, using a few of my officers, and show them what works and what doesn't. We could run them through all the basic drills and teach them how to set up and break camp quickly. And then we send them back to work with their own men."

"How do you know they will do so?"

"We don't. And they might not. Some of them will ignore everything I've said because they're old-fashioned and that's not how they were taught to do it when they first took up a commission. Others won't do it because they're angry at the implication that they can't do their job. And some won't do it because they're lazy arseholes, and those are the ones your memorandum was really aimed at. But if they've been taught, and we know they have, you could arrange a series of parades and inspections. That will motivate some of them. Especially if you throw in a hint of competition between the brigades and divisions. And at the very least, by the end of this, you'll know which of your officers are conscientious and want to improve and which don't give a damn. Sir, you're never going to get a perfectly trained army. But it could be improved."

"Can you do it?"

Paul studied him. "Yes, I think so."

Wellington gave one of his unexpected loud laughs and slapped his hand onto the desk, making the papers jump. Paul jumped as well.

"By God, Colonel, you are either very self-assured or very arrogant."

Paul gave a little smile. "Most people would say I'm both, sir. But if you want me to try, there are two things I'll need. I want some time to be with my family, my father is bringing the children out to visit me in a few weeks. I can't be away all the time that they're here."

"Agreed. And the second thing?"

9

"You'll need to find a way of getting them to work with me, or this whole thing will be a colossal waste of my time, and all it will achieve will be to put me in a really foul temper by the time we march out of here in the spring."

Wellington was silent again. He picked up his glass and drank then picked up a letter from his desk and appeared to read it carefully. The silence went on for so long that Paul wondered if his chief had become distracted by a new problem and had forgotten he was there.

"I will be absent for several weeks," Wellington said abruptly. "I am going to Cadiz and then to Lisbon to confer with both the Spanish and Portuguese governments. I need to assess whether it will be possible for me to accept command of the Spanish army."

"I thought you'd already accepted."

"I have. But if it proves impossible to command them, I will have to resign it. There are many things to consider, Colonel. Meanwhile, I have no quarter-master general."

"Willoughby Gordon is going home?"

"On health grounds," Wellington said smoothly.

"What's wrong with him?"

"Haemorrhoids. A sad affliction. I have told him how much I regret the necessity and how much I have appreciated his services. I am delighted to say that Murray has agreed to come back."

"That's very good news, sir."

"I want you to undertake this job, Colonel. For the time being, you should consider yourself seconded onto the headquarters staff, I will write to every brigade commander ensuring that my wishes are known. I intend to ask every divisional commander to institute an inspection of every brigade under his command, and you will be present at each inspection. I need somebody to find out which brigades and which battalions are falling short of my requirements so that we know where to concentrate your efforts."

"I don't have the authority to inspect another battalion, sir, and it doesn't go well when I try. Look at what just happened with the 3rd Foot."

"You will not be conducting the inspections, you will simply be there as an observer and you will report back on the condition of the men, their state of combat readiness, their training, their equipment."

"You get monthly returns about that, from their officers, sir."

"And if their officers happen to be a pack of idle, drunken layabouts, Colonel, how do I trust those returns?"

Paul could not immediately think of a reply and Wellington seemed to sense his advantage and pressed on.

"Once I have spoken to the Spanish and Portuguese governments, I will be in a better position to plan my next campaign. I have already written to London about new uniforms, equipment and supplies, and I want my officers and men paid every penny that is owing to them. When we march in the spring, every man of my army will sleep under canvas and will have proper food and the equipment to cook it. I have lists of all my requirements. Murray will not

10

be back for several months, and De Lancey, although a good enough fellow is an idle dog and will do nothing without my personal supervision. We need reliable transport and more horses and we need to get Cotton to realise that his troopers need more than just training in horsemanship and sabre work; half of them cannot put together a camp. I need my exploring officers out to organise their agents and bring me intelligence and I need maps. Good, reliable maps. There is so much for me to do, and I need the assurance that while I am busy, my army is making use of this time to improve its performance. I cannot stand behind every one of them myself, no matter how much I might want to."

Paul heard, with sudden painful clarity, the desperation behind Wellington's unemotional recounting of his winter plans. He wondered where, in these months, his chief would find time for rest or leisure and thought with compassion how lonely Wellington must be sometimes.

"I'll do my best, sir," he said.

"I will speak to Fitzroy and you may work with him tomorrow about the wording of the orders, to make my requirements absolutely clear. As for the reports..."

Wellington's voice tailed away and Paul understood.

"You don't want anybody to know that I'm spying on my fellow officers and reporting back to you, do you, sir?"

"I think it best that we keep that private between us, Colonel. And spying is a very strong word."

"So is bullshit, sir, but I do like to use it when it's called for."

Wellington met his gaze steadily. "Please do not think I do not know what I am asking of you, Paul. I do. I could ask somebody else to do this, but there is nobody else I trust to do it without fear or prejudice."

Paul smiled in spite of himself. "This is Yorkshire all over again, isn't it?" he said. "They'll be throwing chunks of rock at my head as I'm passing."

"No. I sent you to Yorkshire because I was still furious with you about getting yourself court-martialled in Copenhagen. I am giving you this job because I need it done, and I need it done well. And may I remind you that if I had not sent you to Yorkshire, you might never have met your wife."

"That's the only reason I've forgiven you." Paul studied his chief's tired face. "Talking of needing some time off, sir, what about you?"

"Don't be ridiculous."

"I'm not. Have you brought up your hunting pack yet?"

"Yes," Wellington said, sounding surprised. "I have set up kennels in the village. Will you join me in the chase, when I am back from Cadiz, Colonel?"

"If I ever get time between making myself unpopular and writing endless reports, sir."

"There is always time for hunting, Colonel. There is something I wish to make clear to you."

"Sir?"

"There are politics involved in this, which I know you dislike. The Duke of York has given instructions about sending some of my more depleted battalions home, to be replaced by new troops. This will involve me losing some of my most experienced men. I wish to find a way to avoid that, if I can."

"I know, sir."

"You are aware that I have just reorganised several of my most under-strength battalions, by combining them into provisional battalions, until reinforcements can be sent out. I have written to the commander-in-chief explaining my reasoning, but I do not believe that the Duke of York agrees with me."

"What are you going to do, sir."

"I will write to him, further explaining my reasoning."

"And if he still disagrees?"

"I will write again, giving my reasoning in more detail."

Paul understood, and started to laugh. "You're going to try to fob him off for the rest of this campaign aren't you?"

"Possibly for the rest of the war, if I can manage it," Wellington agreed serenely. "One should never underestimate the value of a lengthy correspondence, Colonel, handled correctly, it can make it impossible to actually do anything at all. This makes it all the more important that your reports come directly to me, however. I can argue my case far more effectively if I know the real situation. That is why I have chosen a man I trust completely."

"Thank you, sir. I hope I don't let you down, this isn't going to be easy."

"You never let me down. No, don't get up, there are one or two other matters to discuss, regarding your brigade. There will be some changes, particularly with regard to a new commander for the 115th after the sad loss of Major Corrigan. But before we go into that, I think we will refresh our glasses."

Paul did so, feeling uneasy. He was usually good at assessing Wellington's mood, but he was suddenly not sure what was going on. He sat down and Wellington picked up his glass.

"We are about to enter the usual winter quarters political wrangling about the officers of this army," he said. "I will make representation to London in the hope of getting several generals removed and they will argue with me and probably send several even more incompetent generals to replace them. I will win some of these battles and I will lose others, but I have a far better bargaining position than I had two years ago and I intend to choose my battles very carefully and make sure that they know where I draw the line. Two years ago a number of brigades were commanded by colonels or even lieutenant-colonels but that is no longer the case."

"No, sir. Apart from myself and Barnard, I can't think of any at present." Paul could feel a tingling although he was not sure if it should be hope or alarm.

"I may not be able to save both of you this time, so I will need to make a choice. There will be the usual round of brevet promotions later in the year, but I am not waiting for that. I wrote to the commander-in-chief as soon as I arrived at Ciudad Rodrigo, recommending you for a full promotion to

12

Major-General on the basis both of your exemplary service throughout this war and your current position as a temporary member of headquarters in charge of training. This is his reply. Congratulations, Major-General van Daan."

Wellington rose and saluted and Paul did the same, feeling oddly shaky. Wellington picked up his glass and raised it in a silent toast. Paul knew that his chief had deliberately chosen to break the news so unexpectedly and was enjoying his shocked reaction; there was occasionally something child-like about his chief which very few of his officers ever saw.

"Thank you, sir."

Wellington indicated that he should sit down and reached for a sheet of paper. "Now for the details," he said. "Drink the wine, General. It is possible you are going to need it."

***

Anne van Daan was writing a letter to her stepmother when she heard sounds of arrival outside, then the unmistakable voice of her husband calling for the grooms. It was almost the dinner hour and Anne had given up hope of him returning that day. She found him in the hallway, dripping water onto the tiled floor.

"Welcome home, Colonel. Is it still raining?"

Paul gave her a look and Anne laughed and came forward to help him remove the soaked riding cloak. A small figure erupted from the service quarters at the back of the house.

"I'll take it for you, ma'am, I can get it dry in the kitchen."

Paul surveyed the boy. "Thank you, Private Bannan. Have you been keeping up with your reading and writing?"

"Yes, sir. Miss Trenlow is helping me, she's a really good teacher."

"Excellent. It's too late tonight, but tomorrow morning come down to the office and read to me, I want to see how you're getting on."

"Yes, sir. Thank you, sir."

Anne watched affectionately as the boy staggered away with the heavy wet cloak. Charlie Bannan was a new and wholly unintended addition to the household. They had picked the boy up on the road during last month's terrible retreat. Charlie's mother had died on the march and his grieving father, a rifleman from the 60th, had no idea what to do about his eight year old son other than to send him home on a transport, probably into the workhouse. Anne had offered to look after the child during the remainder of the march, and by the time they arrived back at their old billet near Freineda, she had grown very attached to him and had suggested that he stay on to help out around the house and stables. She knew that Paul had agreed as an act of charity, but Charlie was proving to be a genuine asset. Paul had taken to referring to Charlie as 'Private Bannan' as a joke, but Charlie loved it and always stood a little straighter when it was used.

In their room, Paul stripped off his wet clothing and Anne found him a clean shirt and trousers. "I'm sorry I'm so late, love, I had to stop to see Lord Wellington, he sent me a message."

Anne paused in her task of bundling up the laundry, hearing from Paul's tone that something had happened. "What is it, love?"

Paul was holding his wet scarlet jacket. It was regulation, apart from a tattered white cord sewn onto one sleeve. Paul touched it. "I wonder if this will survive being removed and sewn on to a new coat?" he said.

Anne came forward to take the coat. "I don't think you'd go into battle without it, Paul."

"I wouldn't. Grogan gave me that in India, as a joke, but it's part of who I am now. Nan, I've been given a promotion to major-general."

He turned to face her and Anne dropped the coat onto a chair and went into his arms. "Congratulations, Paul. I'm very proud of you."

"You always say that."

"It's always true." Anne kissed him, then studied his face. "I'm guessing there's more."

"It's Wellington. Of course there's more. Some changes to the brigade. I've asked Johnny, Carl and Gervase to meet me in the study before dinner, will you join us? It will save me going over everything twice."

"Of course I will. But what's bothering you, Paul? This is very good news."

"It's very good news because I've been worrying that Wellington would have to replace me in charge of the brigade. It's why he's done this of course, he knew he'd be under pressure to give this command to a more senior officer, so he's used this blasted assignment he's given me, to pretend I'm on his staff and that a promotion would be appropriate. But he couldn't manage two of them, so Andrew is going to lose his brigade."

Anne felt her heart sink. "Oh, Paul, no. That's so unfair. Does he know?"

"Not yet, Wellington is going to tell him. It's bloody ridiculous. Andrew is older than I am and has served for longer and he was in temporary command of the entire division at Badajoz. He's a good man and a good soldier and he doesn't deserve this."

"I know. I'm sorry, Paul, it has rather taken the bloom off this news for you, hasn't it?"

Paul smiled and hugged her. "I'm not a hypocrite, Nan, I'm overjoyed at this promotion. But there is something else. The new temporary commander of the 115th is Major Leonard Vane."

"Vane?" Anne's eyes widened. "Do you mean…?"

"Yes. I'll need to talk to Sergeant Hammond. In the meantime, get yourself dressed for dinner and come down to the study and you can find out the rest of the news."

Three men rose as they entered the room, and saluted. Paul waved to them to sit down and went to collect a padded stool which he planted

14

unceremoniously before Colonel Johnny Wheeler who was only recently out of his bed after being badly wounded during the retreat.

"Put that leg up and stop jumping up every time I come into the room, it's ridiculous."

"Yes, sir," Johnny said amiably.

"Does that apply to us as well?" Major Carl Swanson asked hopefully.

"No. I like it when you jump up and salute me, it makes me feel important. Sit down, Gervase. I hope you don't mind my lady joining us, this is army business but given that she helps to run my brigade, I thought it would save me repeating all this. Carl, while you're still up, will you bring the wine and glasses from the shelf over there?"

When they were seated, Anne looked around at the four men, painfully conscious of who was missing. Johnny commanded the 112th with Major Clevedon as his second in command and Carl was in command of the first battalion of the 110th, Paul's own regiment, but Major Patrick Corrigan of the 115th had died at San Munoz and grief crept up on all of them at odd moments.

"It doesn't feel right without Pat," Johnny said, echoing her thought.

Paul shook his head, seeming unable to speak for a moment and Anne reached out and took his hand. Carl brought glasses and a bottle and nobody spoke until the wine was poured. Paul cleared his throat.

"You know that I saw Lord Wellington today? There are a few changes. Some of them are not wholly unexpected, one or two were a bit of a shock to me, to be honest."

"Is this bad news?" Carl asked.

"No, although I thought it might be. We've spoken before about my position as brigade commander, and it appears that it's been on Wellington's mind as well. He wrote to the Duke of York and has received confirmation of my promotion to major-general, effective immediately, which means I'm keeping the brigade."

Carl was the first to speak. "Congratulations, sir. It's well deserved, and a huge relief."

"You have no idea," Paul said with feeling, and Clevedon grinned.

"I certainly hadn't, sir, you've always behaved as though you owned this brigade and were confidently expecting to carry on in command until somebody handed you a division instead."

"I'm glad I'm convincing. Carl, if you could see the expression on your face, you'd actually laugh, it's painful, so I'm going to put you out of your misery quickly. It was a very long discussion with Lord Wellington, during which he said things about the way I organise my brigade, my regiment and my personal life that I do not intend to disclose. How I got out of there without punching him, I have no idea, except that he'd just promoted me so it would have felt ungrateful.

"None of you are losing your commands. I'm under no illusion that his Lordship has given us a Christmas gift, it's simply that the brigade is working very well and he doesn't want to disrupt it. He does, however, require that we fall into line. He's already playing havoc with the regimental system with these provisional battalions, and it is my personal opinion that when the Duke of York gets his latest letter we're going to hear him yell all the way from London. So I'm instructed to bring the 110th into line with the rest of the army and to tell you to do the same with the 112th, Johnny. This is how it is going to work.

"Both battalions will consist of ten companies, with no light company. We knew that was coming, since both the 110th and 112th became light infantry, I've only kept the light company for sentimental reasons. The old light company will now be the first company. However, I still believe there should be an elite, so I'm designating it the senior company and I'm going to order an arm badge. I suggest you do the same, Johnny."

"It's a good idea."

"We need to look at staffing. Up to now, we've tended to overcome staff problems by sharing quartermasters and medical staff, but Wellington is right, each regiment should have a proper headquarters staff and command structure. In particular, the medical staff are overwhelmed, especially with this latest episode of camp fever and with my wife unable to work at the hospital for a while. It isn't fair on Oliver Daniels. I've spoken to Dr McGrigor and he's going to write to the medical board for more staff.

"As a brigade commander, I am officially allowed one ADC and a brigade-major. It's probably not going to be a surprise to hear that I'm going to ask Captain Manson to take on that unenviable task, since he does the job anyway. I don't really need an ADC since I just yell at whoever is closest if I want something, but I've decided that if I'm doing this, I want one from each nationality under my command, so I'm going to choose Captain Kuhn from the KGL, Lieutenant Sousa from the Portuguese battalion and Lieutenant Powell from the 110th. I've chosen them primarily because none of them get on my nerves."

"That's a good reason for choosing them, sir, it'll make it easier on all of us," Johnny said.

"Don't trade on the fact that you're injured, Colonel Wheeler, I've got a long memory. This brings us to you, Major Swanson and you, Major Clevedon. I ought to have done something about this a while ago, but I was too lazy, a fact which his Lordship did not hesitate to point out to me. You'll need to move up to lieutenant-colonel in order to remain in command of your battalions, and the two senior captains in each battalion will then purchase up to major and we'll do the usual shuffle up from below. If I'm right, that will be Zouch and Barry in the 110th and Hendry and Cartwright in the 112th. I do not have to tell any of you that promotions will cost the regulation price, there will be no premiums in my brigade. If anybody doesn't have the funds, send them to me and I can work out a loan, I don't want any resentment from men being passed over, we have enough going on. The same will happen with Gerry Flanagan in the second battalion. Congratulations, gentlemen."

Carl let out a long breath. "Thank you, sir. I'm very relieved, I wasn't sure it was going to go this well."

"Nor was I, Colonel. You won't need a loan because you and Gervase are both stepping into an empty position. And now we move on to the less palatable news."

"The 115th?"

"Yes. They're staying with us for the time being, and they're short of a commander, some officers and men. I'll be honest, I want to keep them, there are some good young officers, especially Carlyon and Witham, both of whom are about to purchase their companies. Lord Wellington has a gift for me, which comes with a penalty, but I'm going to take it because it solves all our problems. He is going to give us the 117th."

"The 117th?" Carl said blankly. "They're not part of the brigade."

"They're not part of anything at all. They were blown apart at Burgos and since then, they've lost about a company's worth of men to sickness and wounds. Wellington expected them to be sent home and wasn't going to argue the point. They're a very new regiment, their colonel-in-chief, who was a crony of the Prince of Wales, has just died of his excesses, they've no second battalion, no traditions and a very poor reputation. Effectively, Horse Guards has the choice of bringing them home, appointing new officers and going through a very expensive process of building up the regiment again, or giving up. They've decided to give up and the 117th is being stood down."

"We're getting their remaining men?"

"We are. Horse Guards live and die by the regimental system, it's almost impossible to transfer men between different regiments, but if the regiment no longer exists, they have to do something with those men. Wellington has obtained permission to transfer them to other regiments as he sees fit. He is going to leave it to me to distribute them between the 110th 112th and 115th. I'm putting Manson in charge of it, he'll go through the lists, work out what's needed and allocate the men. It will mean our brigade hospital is about to fill up with their sick and wounded, mind, but that's worth it. Nan has been looking about her for a second location, since we won't be able to fit them all in to our hospital and I want a separate site for the fever patients. Some of them are still getting bouts of Walcheren fever, they were out there, poor bastards."

"That's a legacy that just keeps on giving," Carl said quietly.

"It never goes away for some of them. Some of the sick and wounded may have to be sent home, but we have the rest of winter quarters to work that out. The good news is that in place of the 117th, Horse Guards have agreed to allow a second battalion of the 112th to be raised. That means that they can do their own recruiting. There's a small cadre with a recruiting party already in barracks, but you'll be hearing directly from Horse Guards about what needs to be done, Johnny."

Johnny was studying Paul thoughtfully. "This is all good news, sir. What's the penalty? You said it came with a penalty."

"The Walcheren sick?" Gervase suggested.

"That's an inconvenience, Colonel, not a penalty. No, the penalty is that the 117th first battalion has a commander in the field who has some friends at Horse Guards, which means they won't be sending him home on half-pay. He'll be given Pat Corrigan's command in the 115th."

"Do we know him, sir?"

"I've met him, but it's more a matter of reputation, Johnny. His name is Major Leonard Vane."

Anne saw Johnny's eyes narrow slightly and Carl's lips tighten. Both of them knew of Vane's reputation. The name meant nothing to Clevedon, who asked:

"What's wrong with him?"

"He flogs his men for no good reason and has a very poor reputation with their women. Ordinarily, I would have flatly refused to allow him within a mile of my brigade, but the advantages are too great here, and Wellington has made it clear that if I want the extra troops, I have to accept him. Clearly he has friends in high places. I'm hoping he won't last, he's going to loathe how I run things and he's got money, so he'll be looking for a way out, possibly with a promotion."

"Is he not getting promotion to lieutenant-colonel?"

"No, thank God, because the 115th already has one. Lieutenant-Colonel Norton is new, he transferred in for promotion and should have joined us out here but was delayed by the death of both father and his wife within a month, poor bugger. I know nothing of him apart from the fact that he wrote me a very civil letter after Badajoz. I did wonder if he would sell out, but apparently he's hoping to come back this spring, now that he's got his affairs in order. I hope so, as it will partly solve the problem of Vane for me." Paul regarded them. "You all look a bit dazed, and I'm not surprised, it's a lot to take in. I'm going to announce the promotions at dinner. The rest, we'll deal with in time. Congratulations all of you. I feel privileged to command you and thankful that I didn't have to yell at Wellington for putting some other arsehole in command of your battalions. Finish your wine and we'll go into dinner."

Chapter Two

Since he had first taken command of the 110th, Paul had instituted the custom of officers' wives dining in the mess with their husbands should they choose to do so. He was aware that some of the more traditional officers from other regiments disapproved, and one or two had even gone so far as to complain to Wellington at such an appalling break with tradition, but Paul's own officers had long since got used to it, and competition to sit beside Anne was fierce. When no guests were present, Paul had more recently insisted that Keren Trenlow, who was Carl Swanson's very unofficial companion, join them at table. She was there today, seated between Carl and Leo Manson and Paul thought that any stranger watching the company would have taken her for an officer's young and rather attractive wife.

At the end of the meal, Anne retired with Keren in tow and Paul excused himself and went out into the damp evening air in search of Sergeant Jamie Hammond. The barracks consisted of two long barns, while a couple of derelict cottages had been repaired to house the women and children. Within the crumbling walls of an old sheep pen, a selection of tents housed the unofficial camp followers, including a number of prostitutes who had attached themselves to the brigade. Some of the women had set up as sutlers, and there was a wholly illegal grog tent run by the formidable wife of Private Gordon. Sounds of revelry floated across the muddy field and Paul changed direction and made his way between the small tents to a noisy crowd waiting to be served. Private Donahue, sheltered under a tree, was playing a dance tune on the fiddle and several couples were doing their best to dance, hindered by the thick mud of the field.

It took several minutes before the soldiers and their wives realised that Paul was in their midst and he was amused at how quickly many of those on the edge of the group melted away into the darkness. Mrs Gordon was made of sterner stuff, however, and she heaved herself off of the upturned box on which she was seated and gave a curtsey, giving Paul an astonishingly clear view down the front of her shabby gown at her very ample bosom.

"Major-General van Daan, it's an honour, sir. 'Ave you come to join us for a drink?"

"Thank you, Betty. You're doing a good trade tonight."

"It's 'cos it stopped raining, sir." Betty handed Paul a tankard and Paul raised it in a salute and drank. It was difficult to assess the contents, probably army grog supplemented with local wine, but it was well-watered. Paul surveyed her thoughtfully and Betty looked back from shrewd dark eyes, narrow in the plump flesh of her round face. "It's almost Christmas, sir."

"It's weeks until Christmas." Paul looked around and raised his voice. "Thompson, get yourself over here. And bring that cup."

Private Thompson approached warily and Paul removed the drinking cup from his hand, and gave Thompson his tankard. "Good health, Private."

The sharpness of raw spirit caught the back of Paul's throat the moment he swallowed and he coughed. Thompson was drinking the watery grog with ease. Paul set the cup down on the rough plank which served as Betty's bar.

"Any man found drunk at morning inspection is going head first into the river fully dressed, and it's bloody cold at the moment," he said, loudly enough to be heard by every man in the tent. "I'm just going over to speak to Sergeant Hammond. I'll mention that he might want to come over for a drink afterwards." Paul met Betty Gordon's eyes again. "Water it, Betty, or I'll put you out of business permanently."

"Yes, General. Very sorry, sir."

There was no sign of contrition, but Betty curtseyed again. Paul looked around the tent, collecting eyes and salutes and when he was satisfied that every man had understood, he left and made his way to the barracks. He found Sergeant Hammond seated outside on a wooden box beside a roaring fire with several other NCOs and their women, including Sergeant Major Danny Carter and his Spanish wife. The men rose to salute and Paul bent to inspect Carter's baby daughter Ana, who was sleeping peacefully in Teresa's arms.

"She gets prettier every day."

"Thank you, General."

"You need me, sir?" Carter asked.

"No, I want a word with Hammond. Although you might want to know that Betty Gordon is doing a roaring trade serving the foulest homemade spirit I've tried in years. I think I've shut her down for tonight, but maybe you could keep an eye out, before she kills half my men."

"I'll have a wander over there in a minute, sir. Just give her time to think she's safe."

Paul grinned and beckoned to Hammond. Hammond turned to the girl who had been seated beside him and spoke quietly to her and Paul was curious. She was small and dark with huge eyes in a pointed face, dressed in a shabby gown which looked slightly too big for her.

Paul led Hammond away from the barracks towards the main house. There was a faint light from several lanterns which Jenson always left burning after dark to guide late arrivals towards the stables. A fresh winter breeze ruffled the ornamental trees beside the drive.

"Everything all right, sir?"

"Yes." Paul paused by the stone balustrade which surrounded the terrace. "Well, not entirely. At ease, Hammond, this isn't a bollocking, it's a conversation between friends. Sit, if you like."

Hammond perched on the wide top of the balustrade and Paul did likewise, studying him in the faint light. Hammond was in his twenties, dark-haired and good looking, and had joined the regiment under an assumed name after deserting from the 87th. His service since then had been exemplary and Paul wished he did not need to have this conversation.

"Hammond, I've some news, and I needed to tell you because I don't want it to come as a shock. There's a new commander on his way to take over the 115th and I'm afraid you know him."

Hammond was silent for a long time, then he said:

"Captain Vane?"

"Major Vane, now. Yes. I don't want him, but I've no choice but to take him and keep an eye on him until he slips up."

"I understand, sir."

Paul studied him sympathetically. "Do you think he would recognise you?"

"No, sir. I doubt he even knew who I was, or any of the men he had flogged that badly. It wasn't about us."

There was a long silence then Paul sighed. "I know you probably don't want to talk about this, Jamie, but I need to know, it's my problem now. How did Vane work?"

"I told you what he used to do, sir."

"I know what he did. I don't know how he went about it."

"I didn't have much contact with Lieutenant Vane, sir, but we all knew what he was like. He had an eye for a pretty woman and he didn't much care if they wanted to or not. Some of the men had wives and a lot of us had girlfriends, local girls we met along the way. If he saw one he liked, he'd send Sergeant Roberts down to ask her up to his billet. Some of them said yes. It's not unknown for a woman to earn some extra money in an officer's bed, and Vane has the money to pay."

"And if they said no?"

"He'd go after their man. Get Roberts to pick on them in training and on the march. Withhold rations, pile on extra duties, send them out on picket duty in all the worst weather. And if the lassie still didn't give in, he'd haul her man up on some trumped up charge before a regimental court martial."

"How?"

Hammond smiled faintly and Paul had the sense that his sergeant thought that he was being naive. "All you need are five officers on the jury, sir, and in the field, you can get away with three. Most of them don't care, if Roberts reports a man as drunk on duty, or insolent to an officer, or if some pilfered item turns up in his kit bag, they don't ask questions or argue with the verdict. A court martial isn't hard to fix, sir."

"You could have appealed."

"To a general court martial, which has the power to give a much harsher sentence, including death. Who's going to do that?"

"Didn't anybody notice that Vane and Roberts were sending too many men for trial, and the same men repeatedly? The commanding officer must have looked at the returns. At the very least, I'd be wondering what was wrong with discipline in his company."

"He probably just glanced at the returns and signed them, sir. Not every officer does what you do."

"Well they bloody should, and then bullying bastards like Vane wouldn't get away with it. How many men were on the receiving end of this?"

"Seven or eight that I know of, sir. One of them died after being flogged."

Paul could feel his anger rising. "Why didn't the surgeon stop it?"

"Dr Lyons was old and drunk and would sign off on anything. I heard he died, sir, they found him dead in his bed with a bottle in his hand."

"Good, it's saved me wringing his bloody neck if I ever caught up with him."

Hammond gave a faint smile. "Sir, I don't think Vane will get away with it in your brigade. All you have to do is make sure that he knows you'll be studying the returns in detail. He won't have Sergeant Roberts to help him out, and even if some of the officers he brings with him aren't that good, you've got Captain Carlyon and Captain Witham and a few others who do things our way. They'll be on to him in a moment if he tries it again."

Paul thought he was probably right. "It's also true that the law has changed since then, and there's a limit on the number of lashes that a regimental court martial is allowed to impose. I'm going to speak to Captains Carlyon and Witham and tell them I want to know whenever a man is sent for court martial. I can't stop him using flogging, it's in the army regulations, although I'll make sure he knows that I don't approve. And I'm going to talk to Mrs Carter and get her to speak to the women, to make sure they know that any complaints will be taken seriously. I think you're right, Hammond, he isn't going to get away with it here. Which leaves you."

Hammond met his gaze steadily. "And you, sir."

"I'll be fine."

"You might not be. If something goes wrong, if he did recognise me, you need to say that you knew nothing about it. I'll confess…"

"Don't be an idiot, Hammond, you can confess as much as you like, my signature is scrawled all over your paperwork and it's fairly distinctive, albeit illegible. I've been talking to my wife about this, and she has an idea which I think will save us all."

"Mrs van Daan?"

22

"Hammond, you've been with me for more than three years now, you are well aware who possesses the brains in this partnership. You need to listen carefully, because I think her solution will work."

"How, sir?"

"Occasionally, if a man has a severe blow to the head, it affects his memory. According to my wife, who recently read a paper about it, it doesn't always mean he forgets everything. Sometimes, he can remember things that happened in childhood, but nothing in the past month. At other times, he can remember detailed information about his occupation but not his name. They've no idea why, but these cases are very well documented and Nan says she could produce a dozen papers written by very highly respected doctors on the effects of this."

"So if I'd had some kind of accident three years ago…"

"You might remember your first name and how to fire a musket, but not which regiment you were with, or what happened to you."

"You'd have known from the facings on my coat and…"

"You had no coat when we found you at the roadside, and no boots either. Robbed, most like. We took you back to Nan to patch up, you recovered well but never fully recovered that part of your memory, but you were obviously army, so we shoved you into the light company and waited to see if anybody claimed you. Which they didn't."

"Sir, that's a bit thin."

"It doesn't matter. If Vane claims he recognises you as Private Kingston, I'll go to Wellington. He knows me and he knows of you, and he can look at your service record. He won't want either of us court-martialled, all we need is to be able to give him an excuse to throw it out. My wife has given us one."

Watching the younger man, Paul saw him visibly relax. "It might work, sir."

"It will work. I'm hoping it will never be needed. But your job is to give it some thought and decide on what you can remember and what you can't. Just in case."

"Yes, sir."

Paul took his flask from his pocket and unstoppered it. He drank the brandy and handed it to Hammond who did the same."

"Good brandy, sir."

"I needed it after sampling Betty Gordon's poison. Who's the lassie, Hammond?"

"Lassie, sir?"

"Little dark girl, you spoke to her just now."

"Oh. Her name's Alison, sir. Alison MacDonald. Her father is Sergeant-Major MacDonald, 115th."

Paul peered at his sergeant through the darkness. He had the feeling that Hammond was blushing although it was difficult to see. "Really? I didn't see MacDonald there."

23

"He's not, sir, and I should get going, I said I'd walk her back to her billet."

Paul kept his voice deliberately neutral. "She's a pretty girl, how old is she?"

"She's sixteen, sir. Too old to count as a child any more, she's not on strength and he can't draw rations for her."

Paul understood. "What about his wife?"

"Dead, sir. Fever, two years ago. Lost three children over the past four years. Alison's a worry for him. And she's a good girl. A bit shy."

"Did he approach you?"

"We got talking on the retreat, sir. He took a shot to the leg at San Munoz, and she was helping him along. I found him a space in one of the baggage wagons and kept an eye on her for him. Nothing decided, sir. But she's a nice lass." Hammond paused. "Sir, I've been meaning to ask you, though I should really go to Captain Manson, I suppose. If there was a chance…if we did think to take it further…"

"Yes. If you decide to marry, Jamie, you've got my permission and we'll do it properly, so that she's on strength."

"Thank you, sir. It's a bit soon, yet, I want her to get to know me a bit better. It's often the way, with the girls, that they snatch at the first chance they're offered of a man to keep them, but she doesn't seem to want to do that, though her Dad would. But I like that about her."

Paul studied the young face in the lamplight. "I've not known you to show more than a passing interest in a girl in the three years I've known you, Jamie."

Hammond turned to look at him. "Last girl I had, I had to smuggle her out of the lines and back to her family before Vane got his hands on her. I'm going to be keeping a close eye on Alison while he's around, sir.'

Paul regarded him soberly. "You do that, Hammond. And if he so much as looks at either you or her the wrong way, you come to me. You can't go after him, he's an officer. But I can, and I fucking will."

***

Major Leonard Vane's transfer to the 115th coincided with Lord Wellington's imminent departure for Cadiz, and Anne announced herself recovered enough to be able to organise a reception for the occasion. Paul was not entirely happy with the decision, given Anne's recent confinement, but he knew better than to argue with his strong-minded wife. Instead, he went in search of Keren Trenlow, Anne's former maid and informal companion, to enlist her help.

Paul found Keren in the kitchen listening to Charlie reading. Paul waited by the door until the child finished, trying not to laugh aloud. There was a shortage of reading material suitable for a child, and Charlie was reading from an ancient copy of *Principles Of Military Movements*. Paul could remember Carl buying the book at a second hand bookshop in London immediately before he and Paul had travelled to Shorncliffe at the very beginning of their army careers in 1802, and he was amazed that Carl had kept it.

Charlie struggled to the end of the paragraph and Keren gave a warm smile and ruffled the boy's hair. "That's very good, Charlie, you've been practicing."

"It's even more impressive given what you're reading, I'm fairly sure I used my copy of that for firelighters," Paul said, coming into the room. "I'll see if we can find you something a bit more interesting or it'll put you off reading for life. Off you go, Private Bannan, I need a word with Miss Trenlow."

Bannan closed the book, saluted smartly and took off towards the stables and Paul smiled at Keren. "You're a good teacher."

"I only learned to read myself a couple of years ago, so I remember what I found helpful. Mrs van Daan was very patient with me then."

"It's about Mrs van Daan that I wanted to speak to you."

"The reception?" Keren looked up with a quick smile. "I think she'll be all right, sir, but you don't have to ask if I'll help her. Of course I will."

"Thank you. I have to be away for a few days on one of these inspections, and I'll feel better knowing that you're keeping an eye on her. She listens to you." Paul hesitated. "Does she seem all right to you, Keren? I'll own, I'm a little worried this time."

"She's very tired, sir, but it isn't surprising. The baby came early, and it was a difficult birth compared to William. I think that's why she's more easily upset than usual."

"If that means she's snapping your nose off as well as mine, it makes me feel better," Paul said ruefully, and Keren laughed aloud.

"She doesn't mean to, sir, she is always instantly sorry."

"I know." Paul watched as Keren tidied away Charlie's lesson books. He could remember Keren struggling over her reading when she had first come to work for Anne. Keren had been sixteen when she ran away from a humble miner's cottage near Truro to be with her childhood sweetheart who had joined the 95th in hard times. When he had died of fever before ever seeing a battle, Keren had been desperate enough to take up with Private Simmonds from the 110th, a drunkard who had beaten her regularly for eight months before Anne discovered her situation and stepped in with an offer of employment as her maid. Paul had expected the girl to use the opportunity as a refuge until she found another husband in the regiment, and he knew Keren had rejected a number of proposals.

Instead, Keren had devoted herself to Anne's interests, and Anne, whose indifference to the rules of polite society was legendary, had very quickly begun to treat her as a valued companion rather than a servant. She taught Keren how to read and write, helped her with her grammar and her company manners and talked to her as an equal. Dressed in Anne's cast-off gowns, the miner's daughter had blossomed and a number of Paul's officers had begun to show a different kind interest in Keren's dark curls, curving figure and warm brown eyes. She had taken her time choosing, and her choice had fallen on Carl Swanson, then a mere captain with no money or connections.

Paul had expected the liaison to be short-lived, but he had been wrong. Keren had been with Carl ever since, sharing his billet, managing his kit, his laundry, and his life, and despite the irregularity of their union, they shared a warm and affectionate relationship which looked happier than many marriages that Paul had seen. Two and a half years as Carl's companion had given Keren confidence, and although the rounded vowels of her Cornish accent had never left her, she looked and spoke like a lady, and was often mistaken for Carl's wife. Their mutual devotion was very obvious but Paul could not imagine what would happen when war ended and it was time for Carl to go home. What was tacitly accepted in an army camp would cause outrage in polite society, and although Carl was not wealthy, he came from a good family and would not want to hurt his elderly parents.

"Don't worry about her, sir. I can help her with the arrangements, and now that Sergeant-Major Stewart's wife is acting as wet nurse, and your wife is getting more sleep, I'm sure she'll pick up very quickly."

"You're probably right. She says I fuss too much. I'm going to leave her to you, you manage her better than I do."

The girl laughed again. "Nobody manages her better than you do, sir, but I'll do my best."

The loss of Paul's quartermaster and his assistant had come at a particularly exasperating time. There were several people who could step in to help on a temporary basis, including Anne, who had always helped with the regimental administration, but training a new man would take time that Paul did not have, and there was always the possibility that Breakspear's replacement would object to being asked to work with the general's wife. Paul hoped to find an easy solution to the problem in Captain Clinton, the long-time quartermaster of the second battalion, but a batch of letters received on the morning of Anne's reception dashed his hopes.

Paul went in search of Johnny Wheeler and found him seated on a stone bench in the garden. The white flowers of some late blooming shrub dropped petals onto the cracked paving of the path. Johnny was reading a letter but looked up at the sound of Paul's footsteps and smiled. Paul smiled back. Johnny was beginning to look more like himself after the appalling ordeal of the retreat from Burgos, when he had almost not made it back. There was still a pronounced limp and Johnny was using a cane, but he had lost the white, drawn look that he had worn for weeks. Paul had feared him dead and it had made him realise exactly what Johnny Wheeler's steady presence as his second-in-command meant to him. He was trying not to fuss over his friend like a nursemaid.

"Bad news, sir?"

"Is it that obvious?"

"You've got a scowl like a thundercloud," Johnny said, folding his letter. "What is it?"

26

"Captain Clinton will not be joining us as quartermaster, damn his eyes."

"Why not?"

"Walcheren fever," Paul said gloomily. "This morning's post brought a flurry of letters, it seems the world and his great-aunt are suddenly interested in my quartermaster problem. You know that I wanted Clinton, I remember him from years ago, and I tried to get him to come out when we were in Viseu but he'd had Walcheren fever and wasn't well enough. He recommended Nick Breakspear, though. With Breakspear getting promotion, blast him, I thought Clinton could replace him."

"Is he still ill?"

"He's never fully recovered," Paul said. It bothered him, to think of the cheerful down-to-earth Clinton still struggling with the aftermath of Walcheren fever. "He wrote frankly saying he'd like to come, but he still gets regular bouts of fever which lay him low for weeks and he thinks we need somebody more robust to be quartermaster in the field. And he's right, of course. He's recommended another man, though, but that's where it gets difficult."

"Who is it?"

"Fellow by the name of Ross Mackenzie. He's been barrack master at Melton for about four years, since before I took over. I've had no direct contact with him, requisitions and financial matters all went through Clinton or the paymaster. The only thing I will say, is he's been in charge of recruiting and we've done bloody well at that, better than most regiments."

"So what's the problem?"

"There was a letter from Gerry Flanagan in the same batch, advising me not to go near Mackenzie. Apparently, he's trouble in the mess. Argumentative, unpopular and doesn't fit in. He transferred in to command the light company just before Walcheren but he caused so much trouble out there, he was shifted over to barrack master where he's languished ever since. We know that nobody wants the job of barrack master, so if he's been stuck there for four years, my instinct is that Gerry has the right of it. But Clinton's a very good man, and he tells me that Mackenzie is exactly the man I need. And I've now received another letter, asking that I take Mackenzie as a personal favour."

"From whom?"

"Lord Chatham."

Johnny stared at him in complete astonishment. "Chatham? You're not serious? Why on earth would the Earl of Chatham be writing to you, sir?"

"Reminding me of an old obligation," Paul said.

"Obligation? What the devil...oh. Oh - Copenhagen?"

"Yes," Paul said. "He's probably the reason I'm still here, Johnny. The navy wanted my head on a platter after Copenhagen, and the Earl wrote several letters on my behalf."

"And he's written to you about Mackenzie?"

"Yes. I wrote to him to thank him after Copenhagen, once I'd got it out of young Durrell that he'd intervened. Wellington still swears they'd have found me not guilty anyway, and he might be right, but that doesn't alter the fact that the Earl put himself out on my behalf. He wrote back a very civil acknowledgement, and I thought that was the end of it, but he's popped up today, completely unexpectedly, asking me to give Captain Mackenzie a chance."

"He knew him from Walcheren?"

"It appears so. The mention of Walcheren always gives me the jitters. After what happened to our second battalion out there I could cheerfully have strung up every single one of the commanders, army and navy, but the blame landed squarely on the Earl of Chatham. He drifted off into the political wilderness and I didn't give it another thought. But whatever they say about that man's incurable idleness, and I believe every word of it, when it comes to supporting the future career of a man he likes, he's like my wife's dog with a bone, he doesn't leave it alone. His letter is a masterpiece of polite emotional blackmail."

"You don't have to do it, sir."

"No, I know. But Chatham isn't without influence, Johnny, despite the appalling mess he made in Walcheren. He's still commander of the Eastern District and he knows everybody. And I need a damned quartermaster."

"You don't need another troublemaker, sir, not with Vane on the premises. And I'm afraid I'm about to add to your headache."

Paul studied him. "Is everything all right, Johnny? Bad news?"

"How did you know?"

"I study you a lot at the moment. I want to make sure you don't disappear."

Johnny laughed. "You sentimental bastard. I am whole and recovering. But I have had some news. Rather sad news. My uncle has died."

"Oh lad, I'm sorry. I know you were fond of him."

"I was, although I'd not heard for a long time. He was very old, I think he'd been ill for a while. I feel guilty, I should have made more of a push to find out how he was. The thing is, sir, this is from his lawyer and they're asking if I can make time to go home for a spell to set his affairs in order."

"Who's the heir?"

"My cousin Susan had a child, although I'm ashamed to say can't remember his name. He must still be very young, he lost both parents to illness - typhus, I think. I'm rather guessing my uncle's will appointed me guardian."

"Go," Paul said decidedly.

"I'm sorry. I know Wellington won't like it."

"Wellington can put up with it. You were badly wounded, most men would have gone home anyway, to recover. I know you, you won't rest until you've made sure that the boy is in good hands. And the break will be good for you, take whatever time you need. I'll get the necessary travel papers organised for you. Is the lawyer in London?"

"Yes, I'll post up there first."

"I'll write to my father, you can stay in Curzon Street while you're in town. I'm sorry, Johnny."

"I'm sad, but to be honest I hadn't seen him for years. But while I'm there, I'll spend some time in barracks and I can visit Horse Guards to discuss the raising of the second battalion."

"Yes, the timing is quite good."

"Are you going to take Mackenzie?"

"I think I'm going to give him a try."

"Because of Chatham?"

"Partly. More because of Clinton. But also, he has written himself."

"Pleading his cause."

"He doesn't mention his cause, he probably doesn't know what Gerry has told me. It's an application for the post, and if I'd never heard from Gerry, I'd have taken him on that alone. And also…you're going to laugh at me, Johnny, but he's asked if his wife and step-children can accompany him, just while we're in winter quarters. Something about that…"

Paul met Johnny's steady gaze. Johnny looked back.

"You've told him he can bring them, haven't you?"

"Just through winter quarters, Johnny."

"You big, soft, sentimental bastard, General van Daan."

"Piss off to England and sort out your uncle's affairs, Colonel Wheeler. I hope it snows on you."

Paul could hear Johnny laughing as he returned to the house.

***

Lord Wellington arrived at Anne's reception looking harried and slightly distracted ahead of his departure for Cadiz. The Quinta de Santo Antonio had a series of very well-proportioned reception rooms. They had been neglected over the long years of the war, but Anne had supervised repairs the previous winter, and this year she had set several of the men to whitewashing the internal walls so that the place looked clean and bright. Winter in Portugal could often be wet, but it was a dry, mild evening so the long windows onto the terrace stood open and Jenson had organised for lanterns to be hung from the trees and around the edge of the terrace, giving a fairy-tale appearance.

Wellington's harassed expression lifted at the sight of his hostess. Anne looked beautiful wearing rose coloured silk with a lace overdress that a Madrid dressmaker had made for her. Wellington kissed her hand and remained beside her as she greeted the remaining guests, before moving to join Paul.

"Why," he asked, in blighting tones, "is there an enormous tree on the front driveway? I am not aware that we have been suffering high winds."

"Christmas, sir," Paul said blandly.

Wellington turned and looked down his long nose. "Christmas," he repeated. "General, are you quite sure that you have fully recovered from your

29

recent illness? That it has not brought on some inflammation of the brain? I have heard of cases…"

"I'm sure you have, sir, half your officers are using it as an excuse to apply for leave, hoping they won't have to come back, after your recent efforts," Paul said cheerfully, summoning Corporal Cooper, who was acting as waiter for the occasion. "Bring Lord Wellington some of the red, would you, Corporal? I want him to try it."

Cooper returned with two glasses on a tray and Paul took one and handed it to his commander-in-chief who gave a nod of thanks to Cooper. Paul surveyed his corporal admiringly. "Very impressive turnout, Corporal. Did you steal that jacket, I've never seen you look this clean?"

"Early Christmas gift from your wife, sir. She got Mrs Bennett to steal the old one while I was getting that tree cut down. I was a bit annoyed, to tell you the truth, I've had that since Vimeiro, it had a lot of memories in it."

"It had a lot of holes in it, you mean."

"That's what your wife said, sir. She told me I'd soon make this one just as revolting. It is warmer, though, I'd not realised how thin that old one had got. Excuse me, sir, duty calls."

Paul watched with some affection as his corporal made his way back to refill his tray. Cooper was one of his longest serving men, having been with him when he joined as a young officer more than ten years ago, in the 110th light company. Cooper had spent the early years of his service in constant trouble alongside Dawson, his long-term partner in crime, but age had mellowed him and since his promotion to corporal more than a year ago, he had surprised and impressed Paul with how well he had stepped up to his responsibilities. After the losses of the recent campaign, Paul was about to ask his officers to bring him their lists of promotions and he was fairly sure that both Cooper and Dawson's names were going to be on it.

"The tree, General?" Wellington said.

Paul grinned. "German Christmas customs, apparently, sir. They make a good deal more of the season than we do. We always used to decorate with greenery at home, mind, I can remember as a boy helping the farmhands cut down branches and boughs to bring in on Christmas Eve. And we used to have a Yule Log, which I believe is a very ancient custom. After my mother and my sister died, my father refused to do it any more. I missed it."

Wellington shot him a sideways glance. "How old were you?"

"I was ten. As to this, General Alten is joining us for the season and I wanted to do this for him. He misses home."

Wellington gave a snort. It was his first of the day, and it had a pleased sound to it, which boded well for the meal. "You are appallingly sentimental, General, it quite shocks me."

"That's rich coming from the man who was making sounds like a turtle dove to my baby daughter five minutes ago. Don't deny it either, I heard you."

Wellington sipped the wine. "She is my god daughter," he said huffily.

30

"She might be, but I'm not sure that has anything to do with that soppy expression you wear every time you see her," Paul said with a grin. "Don't look so defensive, sir. You must miss your boys. Why don't you get your wife to bring them out for a while, now that we're settled in winter quarters?"

"It would distract me," Wellington said. "There is so much to do, to prepare for next year. I have no time."

Paul said nothing. After a short silence, Wellington said abruptly:

"My wife is not like your wife, General. She has excellent intentions, but I know very well that she would not understand what I need to do and how little time I have to spare. We would quarrel and it would distract me. So I am afraid you must put up with me doting upon your daughter instead."

"Not a problem, sir. You know how sentimental I am, after all. I'm sorry you won't be joining us for Christmas."

"I will have no time to celebrate, I am setting out for Cadiz tomorrow. Really, I should be back at my desk now, there are some final orders..."

"Stop it," Paul said. He saw the blue eyes widen in surprise, but he was suddenly exasperated. "I know you need to go to Cadiz, sir, and I know why. I think you're bloody mad to travel in this weather, you'll be forever on the road and my sympathy lies with every single one of the men travelling with you, you will be horrible. And I am grateful that you didn't insist on me going with you. But my wife has organised this reception to give you the opportunity to have a drink with some of your officers and mend some bridges after that appalling memorandum you sent out last month. She's put a lot of work into this, and I am not having you grumbling over the champagne because there is one more rude letter to some hapless Portuguese administrator that you forgot to write. Are we clear?"

There was a long and pointed silence and Paul tried not to look as though he was holding his breath. Eventually, Lord Wellington took a long drink of wine.

"There is still time for me to insist that you come with me," he said, and Paul laughed.

"Having me with you, while you insert one of Congreve's rockets up the arse of the Spanish government sounds like a really bad idea, sir, they do not need two of us."

Wellington smiled with real amusement. "That is why I am leaving you behind to do the same to every senior officer in my army who fails to follow my instructions on the drills and training to be conducted during winter quarters this year," he said.

"I cannot tell you how much I'm enjoying it, sir. Now stop grumbling, and come with me."

Paul led the way outside and took the path towards the stables. Wellington was frowning. "Where are we going?"

"I've something to show you. In here."

One of the stalls at the end had been roughly blocked off with wooden slats. Paul stopped in front of it, lifted the makeshift barrier out of the way and bent down. "Here, girl."

The dog rose and stepped forward on long elegant legs. She was silvery-grey and smooth-coated with a long nose and a pair of arresting golden brown eyes. Paul allowed her to sniff at his hand then stroked her head. The dog nuzzled his coat and then turned and surveyed Lord Wellington with some interest. Paul looked around at his chief and suppressed a smile at Wellington's expression.

"How old is she?"

"Almost a year. She's had some training and she has a very good hunting pedigree. One of our neighbours in Leicestershire breeds hunting greyhounds and I asked my brother to bespeak one of the next litter. Her name is Pearl, but you can change it if you'd prefer, she'll learn."

"No. I like Pearl. It suits her colouring." Wellington held out his hand and after a moment, the greyhound stepped forward and sniffed. Wellington stroked the smooth head and scratched behind an ear, and the dog moved closer and leaned against his leg. Wellington was smiling.

"She's an early Christmas gift, sir. If you'd like, we'll keep her with us until you're back from your travels. Nan can work with her, she's good with dogs."

"Thank you, I would appreciate that." Wellington bent down still fussing the dog. "Pearl, General van Daan has probably paid an extortionate amount of money for a dog to keep an eye on me when he cannot do so. He is, as I have said, appallingly sentimental."

"You're talking to a dog, sir."

Wellington gave one of his unexpected hooting laughs and got up. "I am, General. Thank you very much, it is the best Christmas gift I have received in many years."

"You're welcome, sir. Come and be social, I need to find Major Vane and his officers and try to sound welcoming."

Wellington gave the dog one final pat and Paul nodded to the groom to replace the barrier and followed his chief back to the party. He found Major Vane with Carl and Gervase, who were making pained conversation with him. Vane was in his mid-thirties, a nondescript looking man, with a face that might have been pleasant had it not worn a permanently petulant expression, with the hint of a sneer. Paul found the sneer particularly irritating, and found himself wondering if punching Vane would remove it. It did not feel like a good omen for their future working relationship.

As commander in the field until the arrival of Lieutenant Colonel Norton, it was up to Vane to run his battalion. Under Major Patrick Corrigan, an effective system had been set up, and Paul had taken trouble to make sure that it was working well before Vane arrived. After the depredations of the recent campaign where a number of officers across the brigade had been killed, died of sickness or been captured during the retreat, there was the usual winter quarters shuffle up the ranks. Generally speaking, this happened within a

32

regiment, and several of Paul's favourite young officers were in a position to purchase up to captain, including Simon Carlyon, Anne's former brother-in-law and Nicholas Witham. Several promotions shifted men between regiments within the brigade, and Paul approved of this; these officers had served under him for some time and all of them knew how he worked. The officers of the 117th were an unknown quantity, however, and Paul wanted to get to know them.

"Major Vane, welcome to the brigade. I hope you've had the chance to settle into your billet?"

"My man unpacked for me earlier. Not a bad place, though the room's a bit pokey. Still, I've had worse. You've done all right for yourself here, though, haven't you, sir?"

"We've been lucky, this is our second winter here, although the first one was cut rather short by a January march to Ciudad Rodrigo. You'll find Señor Rivero a very good host, he's taken care of several officers in the past including Major Corrigan."

"Didn't know Corrigan. Irishman, wasn't he?" Vane sounded uninterested. He was staring across the room and Paul followed his gaze. "Isn't that your wife with Wellington, sir?"

"It is."

"Beautiful woman, General. You're a lucky man."

"Thank you, Major, I know it."

"Married before, wasn't she?"

"We both were," Paul said, making no attempt to keep the chill from his voice. "I was fortunate in my first marriage as well; my wife was less so, as you may have heard."

Vane's eyes widened in astonishment at his tone. Paul did not apologise. After a long, awkward silence, he said:

"Now that you're here, I'm hoping you'll do the rounds of your officers with me, I'd like to be formally introduced. I think most of them are hiding in the next room."

The former officers of the 117th had formed a group in the second reception room which led out onto the terrace and gardens. The doors were open although it was growing cooler, and several of the younger men had wandered out onto the cracked paving stones, admiring the lights.

Major Vane moved among the officers, making brief and uninformative introductions. Several of them were very young, no more than sixteen or seventeen, ensigns who had never fought in a battle and were overawed by their surroundings and their brigade commander. Paul spent some time talking to them, cracked some jokes, asked questions about their homes and families and promised dinner invitations to get to know them better. It was how he had always worked, as he had risen to command at brigade level and it had proved successful for him but Paul could sense Vane's bored contempt beside him and he knew that even without his prior knowledge of Vane's brutality, he could never successfully work with this man.

"We're a captain short, Major Vane."

33

"He's around somewhere, I insisted they all attend. Oh - over there, by the fountain. You'll be lucky to get more than a few words out of him, he's a miserable fellow."

"I'd like to meet him anyway."

The man stood alone beside the dried out fountain, looking out at the tangled shadows of trees and shrubs in the gardens as Paul and Vane approached.

"Captain Tyler, General van Daan wishes to meet you."

Vane's bored tone irritated Paul. Without looking around, he said:

"It's all right, Major Vane, I've realised I don't need an introduction. Why don't you go and find yourself another drink?"

Vane hesitated, clearly taken aback. Paul ignored him, going forward to join the solitary figure on the terrace. Tyler turned as he approached and saluted. This part of the terrace was dark, only faintly lit by the lanterns, but Paul could still see deep lines on the other man's face in the shadows. It shocked him a little. It had been seven years since he had last seen Stephen Tyler but the man seemed to have aged twenty years, although he was only three or four years older than Paul.

As Vane walked away, Paul said:

"Captain Tyler. Do you know, it didn't occur to me that you might be here, although I don't know why. How are you?"

"Well enough, sir. Congratulations on your recent promotion. All of them, I suppose. You've come a long way since Dublin."

Even the man's voice sounded different, quieter than Paul remembered, with a softer tone. He studied Tyler's tired face through the darkness.

"What are you doing out here?"

"Avoiding you, sir."

The answer was so unexpected and so close to what Paul had been thinking, that he laughed aloud. "Have you? Oh, I'm sorry, Captain. It gets cold in the evenings at this time of year, though, you should come inside."

Tyler did not move, so Paul sat down on the low stone wall surrounding the fountain. "When did you come back from the Indies?"

"Two years ago. We were back in barracks for a while, then we were sent out here, but I think we all knew the regiment's days were numbered. We were well below strength, so many deaths from fever out there, and recruiting was hopeless. Do you remember Mr Yelland, sir?"

"I do."

"He died a year into our posting."

"I'm sorry to hear that. You've been ill yourself."

"Yes, sir. It took a long time to recover. In any other regiment, I'd have been invalided out, placed on half pay. But nobody wanted the 117th, they held my place until I was fit to return."

"Would you have preferred it if they hadn't, Captain?"

"To tell you the truth, I didn't much care, sir. But I had to do something."

Paul got up. The other men had drifted inside, now that the evening had grown colder. He went to the door, looked around and signalled to Private Thomas who was acting as waiter. "Thomas, will you bring wine, please?"

"Yes, sir."

"The good wine, Thomas, not that sheep's piss that Lord Wellington sent over for the reception."

Paul returned to the wall and sat down. "What happened, Captain?"

"Nothing, sir. Nothing unusual. We were sent out to the Indies. On the voyage, the men wept below decks, and wrote letters home if they'd family, to say goodbye. They know it's often a death sentence. A third of our battalion, officers and men, didn't survive to go home. That's what happens out there. Even if you survive, if you don't get ill, it's a hell hole. I hoped I'd at least get a promotion out of it, but it turned out I wasn't that good at toad-eating the right people."

"Christ, I'm sorry," Paul said softly. The other man laughed through the darkness.

"For what, sir? It wasn't your fault we were sent out there, you did nothing wrong. Apart from to lose your temper with me in Dublin seven years ago, and let's be honest, I deserved that. I still cringe when I remember that evening. I was so drunk, and so arrogant, and you'd made me look such a bloody idiot on that parade ground earlier in the day. As if that ever mattered a damn. So I embarrassed a shy young woman and made her cry. I deserved everything I got. Is she here?"

Paul could feel an ache of misery in his chest. "No," he said. "You must have avoided the receiving line earlier."

"I did."

"Captain, Rowena died. More than three years ago, in childbirth. I married again, you'd have met my second wife if you'd not sneaked in the side door."

Paul watched the other man's face and it was painful. Tyler did not speak for a long time. Eventually he said:

"I was embarrassed to face her, so I thought I'd avoid it."

"I know. I'm sorry, Captain."

"I didn't know."

"How could you have known?"

Private Thomas approached with a tray. Paul took a glass and handed it to Tyler. "Are you all right?"

"Yes, sir. I'm just shocked. And so sorry. She was a lovely woman."

"She was."

They sat, perched side by side on the broken fountain wall, sipping wine. Paul could think of nothing more to say and Tyler did not speak either. Voices from the reception seemed muted in the distance. After a while, somebody closed the long doors.

"They've shut us out," Paul said.

"Yes, sir. Do you think they know you're out here?"

"I'd like to say no, but it might just be that somebody has seen an opportunity. I wonder if they've locked it?"

Unexpectedly, Tyler gave a splutter of laughter. "Does this happen to you often, sir?"

"More than you'd expect."

There was another long silence, but it had a different quality, as though something had shifted. Paul sipped the wine and enjoyed the rich flavour and wondered how long it would be before his absence was noticed. He was finding this quiet moment very pleasant.

"What on earth are you two doing out here?"

Paul jumped slightly. He had not heard the door open. His wife was surveying them curiously.

"Sorry, bonny lass, I ran into an old friend and it was quieter out here. Are they searching for me?"

"Lord Wellington is making grumbling noises because he thinks you've managed to sneak away and he hasn't. I think he's ready to leave, you might have to come and say goodnight."

"I will. Before I do, though, may I introduce you to Captain Stephen Tyler of the 115th, formerly of the 117th. I knew him briefly in Dublin many years ago. I've just been telling him about Rowena."

Paul had told the story of his history with Tyler to Anne and he knew she would remember. He also knew she would show no sign of it. Anne did not disappoint him. She came forward quickly to shake Tyler's hand.

"Captain Tyler, welcome. I'm sorry, the news must have come as a shock. Rowena was a very good friend of mine, I do understand."

"She was a very nice woman, ma'am."

"She was. I'm sorry, we have to go and be social, but we'd like get to know some of the new officers better, so I'd be pleased if you'd join us for dinner one afternoon."

"I'd like that, ma'am."

"Excellent. I'll send a message."

"That's very kind of you, ma'am. I think I'll say goodnight as well. It's been a strange evening."

"Goodnight, Captain Tyler." Paul studied the other man through the darkness. "Seven years ago, I insisted that you write a letter of apology to my wife. This evening, I've an apology of my own to offer. You did behave badly, no question. But so did I. I was an arrogant young show-off and I was disrespectful. I'm sorry. Let's put it behind us, we've both grown up."

Tyler saluted. "Thank you, sir. Ma'am. Goodnight."

Chapter Three

Paul had allowed himself to hope that he had been overreacting to the prospect of Major Leonard Vane joining his brigade, but after only a few days, he gloomily admitted to himself that he had not. On the day after the reception, Paul rode over for a more formal meeting with Vane. He took with him two very good bottles of brandy as a gift and gave himself a mental lecture on the way about giving Vane the benefit of the doubt.

The 115th were quartered two miles from Santo Antonio, close to the attractive medieval village of Castelo Mendo. Anne had negotiated with the owners of the Casa de Insua, a beautiful eighteenth century mansion with spreading grounds and a flourishing estate, for the use of two partly ruined barns which had originally been part of the winery. Paul's men had worked to repair the structures to be used as barracks, along with a four roomed cottage which could be occupied by the duty officers. Major Vane and his officers occupied billets in the village. The arrangement had worked reasonably well the previous year for the short time that Patrick Corrigan had commanded the battalion.

Major Vane was billeted on the top floor of the substantial house of a prosperous cloth merchant and his wife. Señor Rivero's two sons and son-in-law were all with the Portuguese army and his daughter and grandson lived with him. The room was comfortable, and Rivero had proved a welcoming host in the past.

Vane accepted Paul's gift of brandy civilly enough, but as Paul began to outline his views on discipline and punishment, Vane's lip curled and Paul had the impression that he had stopped listening. Paul stopped talking and studied Vane thoughtfully. Vane looked back.

"Is that all, General van Daan?"

"No."

There was another silence. After a while, Vane began to fidget. "Well, what else? Not sure that it's your job to lecture me about discipline in my battalion, sir, if you'll forgive the impertinence."

"I never forgive impertinence, Major, it's one of things I'm noted for. Carry on, I can see you have more to say."

Vane looked less comfortable, but managed a half-hearted sneer. "Begging your pardon, General, don't want to offend. Only I know the army regulations, sir, and I don't think what you're saying is part of them. Heard from a few friends in London before I accepted this command, you know. I wanted to know about my new brigade commander. May I speak plainly, sir?"

"That's entirely up to you, Major."

"They don't approve of your ways at Horse Guards, sir. More than a few of them think your views make you unfit for this command. Not that I agree, of course, and it's clear Wellington don't, or..."

"Lord Wellington, Major."

"Yes, of course. Lord Wellington. Thinks the world of you, I know. Even though he's as keen on a flogging as the next man. But..."

Paul got up. "No, I'm sorry. I thought I could sit through it, but I realise I can't. All right, Major Vane, we'll leave it at that. Let's be clear. My eyes are on you. I'm a stickler for paperwork, and I will check the details of every single regimental court martial or any other kind of disciplinary action in your battalion to the last letter. I will regularly walk among your men and talk to them, and ask if any of them are having any problems. And I will also do the same with their womenfolk. I know your reputation. If it isn't deserved, then you've nothing to worry about, and we'll get along very well. If it is deserved, I will be watching for you to put one foot out of line, and I will bury your career in the regimental dung heap, and you alongside it. Like you, I know the army regulations very well and I am absolutely certain I'll be able to find a few of them that you're breaking at any given moment. Showing sufficient respect for a senior officer is looking very promising at the moment. That's all we need to say for now. I'll inspect the battalion tomorrow at eight o'clock, please make sure they're ready."

Paul waited until Vane had scrambled up and saluted. He looked furious, which made Paul feel as though he had at least achieved something. He knew it was unfair to insist on an inspection on what was effectively the first day of Vane's new command, but the major's attitude irritated him, although it did not surprise him, given what he knew of the man.

The 115th was the newest of the three English battalions in the third brigade, which also consisted of two Portuguese battalions, a battalion of the King's German Legion and two companies of the 60th rifles which had recently joined the brigade, to replace several companies of the 95th which had been moved over to Barnard's brigade. The 115th was a difficult command, and Paul would have preferred to be allowed to recommend a commander himself. It had been added to Paul's brigade immediately before the bloody storming of Badajoz during the previous year, when it had been in a state of open mutiny. Savagely depleted during the battle, it had sustained more losses through the rest of the campaign, and during the retreat from Madrid. Under Corrigan, the battalion had been settling down well, but Paul did not think Vane was the right man for this command and hoped that the long-absent Colonel Norton would make an appearance very soon.

The inspection went surprisingly well, which Paul knew was largely due to several of the existing company captains, who had been working to keep the battalion running while waiting for the arrival of their new commander. He found an opportunity, as the troops marched out, to stop beside Captains Carlyon and Witham.

"Well done, both of you."

"Thank you, sir," Carlyon said, saluting cheerfully.

"How is it going? Getting to know your fellow officers?"

"A little, sir, we organised a welcome dinner. Went well, I think but it's too early to say yet. The major didn't have much to say."

Paul grinned. Simon and Nicholas had spent several weeks with Vane the previous year, travelling up from Lisbon to the lines and had been deeply gloomy at the news that he was their new commander. Paul had already spoken to them both about his concerns. He could not spend all his time supervising Vane, and he trusted Carlyon and Witham's discretion.

"I'm surprised he got promotion this quickly, sir," Simon said quietly. "He'd not long been a captain."

"Friends in the right places," Paul said grimly. "It does help. I should go and congratulate him on his battalion's excellent turnout, which will choke me, but I just wanted to assure you that I know it was you two. I look forward to seeing you both for dinner later, my wife asked me to invite you. And Simon, there's a letter from Colonel Wheeler for you, I meant to bring it and I forgot. I'm not sure the postal service has worked out where everybody is yet."

"I'm not sure any of us have, sir. He's arrived safely then?"

"Yes, he wrote to me from London. He's a bit shocked, it appears that far from being called in as his uncle's executor, he's actually the heir, the young cousin died a couple of years ago."

"Oh good Lord. Do you think he'll sell out, sir?"

"Not a chance, although part of me thinks he ought to. But he won't, he has a stronger sense of duty than any other man I know. But I'm sure he'll tell you all about it in his letter. I'll see you both later. I've had a note from Colonel Scovell at headquarters asking me to call, so I'm riding over there now."

Paul found George Scovell, Wellington's intelligence officer and chief code breaker, poring over a letter. Scovell, who was an old friend, greeted Paul cheerfully, offered drinks and asked after Anne.

"Sorry to haul you over here when I know how busy you are, General, but I've received letters from his Lordship and there is an urgent matter. I believe Lord Wellington may have written to you about it."

"If he has, I've not seen it," Paul said. "I've been inspecting the 115th this morning and I rode straight here. What's it about?"

"Captain Michael O'Reilly."

Paul stared blankly at Campbell. "I'm sorry, George, I've not a clue. O'Reilly isn't in any trouble as far as I'm aware, but even if he were, it would really be Colonel Wheeler you'd need to speak to, or given that he's in England, Major Clevedon."

"He isn't in trouble. Lord Wellington is looking for an officer to carry out an assignment and he has suggested O'Reilly. It's a long story, General, and rather an odd one.

"I'm listening."

"His Lordship has received a request from the Foreign Office. It seems that Lord Castlereagh finds himself in a little difficulty. The matter is highly confidential, and Lord Wellington has asked for your assurances that…"

"Don't be pompous, George, it doesn't suit you. What does he want?"

"He wants O'Reilly seconded to intelligence for a mission."

Paul stared blankly at him for a moment. "Michael O'Reilly is a very good officer of light infantry, Colonel, but he has no experience in intelligence."

"No, but he will be working with a man who has. Wellington has asked for Giles Fenwick.

"Giles? Well that makes more sense. Where is he now? I saw him during the retreat, but I've not seen him since."

"He's billeted in Ciudad Rodrigo, I've sent a message, he should be here in a day or two. This is urgent, General, which is why Lord Wellington has been asked to send two men. In case of accident…"

"You mean in case one of them is killed?"

"I presume so. Last year, a Foreign Office diplomat by the name of Sir Horace Grainger was dispatched on an important mission into France. Sir Horace's task was to visit several towns and cities where English prisoners of war are being held, particularly those unfortunate civilian prisoners who were caught in France when the war resumed in 1803. He travelled as far as Verdun and held discussions to sound out possible prisoner exchanges in the cases of several high-profile prisoners, including Lord Edward Paget. I believe he was authorised to extend an invitation for the French to send a similar mission to Britain later this year."

Paul frowned. "That sounds like utter bollocks. If Napoleon was going to release prisoners on exchange, he'd have done it by now. What was he really doing there, George, and why did they let him?"

"We don't know," Scovell said. "It's possible that there are genuinely men that we hold, that they'd like to see released, but the English have always been open to exchanges whereas the French seldom are. I agree with you, General, I find the whole thing very suspicious. But whatever the merits of the mission, Sir Horace Grainger has disappeared. Nobody has had word of him for a month."

"That's ridiculous," Paul said. "A diplomat doesn't just disappear. He can't have been on his own, he must have had at least a servant or two and a groom with him. What do the French say? If this was a legitimate mission, surely he had a French escort? They're not going to let an Englishman wander around the countryside at will, no matter who he is. They'll have shown him what they want him to see and then made sure he's on the right road home."

"That's exactly what the French claim they did," Scovell said grimly. "There has been an exchange of letters between Paris and London. They're being very cooperative, and Lord Wellington thinks it's because they have no idea where he is either, and they want him found."

"So why aren't they looking for him?"

"They are. But he didn't disappear in France, he'd crossed the border into Spain. He was met on his arrival in France by a small escort of French cavalry and a French diplomat by the name of Martel, who is almost certainly an intelligence agent."

"He'd have a lot in common with Sir Horace Grainger then, wouldn't he? Do you think they caught him out and quietly killed him?"

"Very possibly," Scovell said. "They've not told me directly, sir, I am not high enough up the ladder to be worthy of that kind of confidence, but my instinct is the same as yours, Grainger was spying. Ostensibly, he visited the prisoners over a period of two months. A lot of travelling. During that time, he sent regular letters home, both to the Foreign Office and to his family. Nothing unexceptionable, but then we can assume that all his letters were opened and read by Bonaparte's agents. If he managed to get any other reports out, I've not been told about them."

"Why in God's name would the French take that risk?"

"I've no idea, but they must have had a reason, they're not stupid. Anyway, Sir Horace concluded his visit in the city of Toulouse and his last letter was written from there. He set off for the Spanish border, where a Royal Navy frigate under a flag of truce was waiting off Bilbao, to take him home. Nobody has heard from him since. Naturally, when Sir Horace failed to appear at the ship, enquiries were made. It was feared he had met with some accident that had delayed him. However, it appears that none of Sir Horace's escort have returned or reported what happened. Like him, they have vanished."

"Did he have an English escort as well?" Paul asked.

"No. Sir Horace was apparently an intrepid gentleman, accustomed to travelling with only his valet and his groom for company. There was also a Spanish guide who knew the route well."

"All gone?"

"Yes," Scovell said briefly. "Our French contact tells us there is nothing more they can do. The situation along that part of the coast is very unsettled at present. You know that a naval squadron under the command of Sir Home Popham achieved some very useful victories in conjunction with the local Spanish guerrilla troops last year, including the capture of Santander. Lord Wellington's retreat meant that the Spanish garrison was obliged to withdraw from most of the coastal towns but in the countryside, the Spanish irregular troops have entirely disrupted French lines of communication along all the major roads and control whole areas."

"I know. Lord Wellington believes that the French will concentrate on trying to get control of the Spanish countryside while waiting for the new campaigning season to begin."

"Can they?" Scovell asked.

"I very much doubt it, George, they don't have the men and they won't be getting reinforcements from Bonaparte while he's off on his Russian adventure. I should think they'll concentrate their attention on the northern coast and the road through Bayonne, which is their main postal and convoy route into Spain. The partisans under Mina and Longa have created havoc these past months, helped by the navy, and Bonaparte will want Santander and those northern ports back under French control. He'll get them too, for a while."

"Did you know that Popham has been ordered home?"

"Why, what's he done now?" Paul enquired.

Scovell grinned. "I suspect it's for his own safety. By now, he's had time to quarrel with every one of the Spanish leaders along that coast."

"Sir Home Popham can start a quarrel in an empty room, George, that's not news. But I thought Lord Wellington was fairly pleased with what he'd achieved up there."

"I'm not in his Lordship's confidence, but I think he was. Fitzroy says he's written to London suggesting that it might be beneficial to send him back. Or at least to send somebody back. Perhaps not Popham, though."

"No, he tends to announce every one of his triumphs to the London newspapers before either Wellington or the Admiralty, which enrages his Lordship." Paul paused, thinking about what Scovell had said. "George, we're friends, I want you to be honest with me. Whose idea was it to send Michael O'Reilly? I understand Fenwick, it's his job. He might still be my officer on paper, but he's been working for you for more than two years now. But Michael?"

"London asked for two men," Scovell said. "We don't have two men available. Lord Wellington wants information and he wants maps, I've sent out every one of my intelligence officers and most of the corps of guides. If I wasn't busy with this code, I swear he'd have sent me as well. Another few days and Fenwick would have gone as well. Wellington gave me a list of half a dozen officers he thought might be able to do the job and told me to find one, brief him and get them out there."

"And you chose Michael."

"I can choose again," Scovell said. "I'm being honest with you, Paul. Sorry, I mean, sir."

"We're friends, George."

"Fenwick can be bloody difficult. He's one of the best agents I have, but he's happiest working alone or with his Spanish guide, Antonio. Frankly, I'd be happy just to send those two, but London isn't willing to trust the completion of this mission to a Spaniard. Running my eye over Wellington's list, O'Reilly is the best of them, and I know how good his Spanish is. He's older and he knows Fenwick. I think he'll handle him."

Paul sat quietly for a moment. Eventually, he nodded. "All right, I'll speak to him tonight."

"I'll brief Fenwick and Antonio when they get here and send them over to you, perhaps your quartermaster can see to their supplies."

"Oh very funny, George. I don't bloody have a quartermaster as you very well know. I'll get Nan onto it, she's going mad with boredom, not being able to work at the hospital with Daniels, it will give her something to do."

"Bring her over to dinner," Scovell said, getting up. "Mary would love to see her, and it will cheer her up."

"I will, thank you."

"There's one other thing. Colonel Barnard has been informed of his change of circumstances."

"Has he? Should I ask if his Lordship bothered to do that in person?"

"Does it matter?" Scovell said. "Barnard's a professional, he'll get over it, but between you and I, I'm told he's been dipping rather deeply."

"Tell me what's new. Andrew Barnard can drink me under the table." Paul studied his friend and sighed. "I'll go and see him. I might ride over there after this, my wife wants to invite the Smiths to dinner. Thanks for letting me know, George. I bloody hate army politics."

Scovell grinned. "I know you do. Which is funny really, because you always seem to come out on the right side of them."

"That's just because Wellington likes me."

"Unlike me. Oh, Paul. I should probably mention, just in case you run into him while he's here. We've an unexpected, and rather inconvenient visitor. It's…"

"Captain Sir Home Riggs Popham, Colonel Scovell," Wellington's butler intoned from the door. "Begging a word with General van Daan before he leaves."

Paul rose, turning towards the door in complete astonishment, staring at the man who was coming into the room. Scovell shuffled together his papers. "I'll leave you to it, sir. Come to dinner on Wednesday, Mary will send a note to your wife. Good day, Sir Home."

Paul watched him leave, contemplating exactly what he would say to Scovell when he next saw him, then turned to look at Popham.

Popham's eyes were on Paul's face. Paul looked back steadily. He had never in his life been more aware of the insignia of a major-general on his jacket. The last time he had looked across a room at Sir Home Popham, it had been a courtroom in Greenwich and the gulf in their ranks had loomed widely for him. Six years had passed, and their positions, in terms of rank, had been reversed.

After a long moment, Paul walked forward and saluted politely. He waited until Popham responded, to make the point, before saying pleasantly:

"Sir Home. This is a surprise, I thought you were on your way back to England."

"I am here to see Lord Wellington," Sir Home said. "I was expecting him to be here."

"I'm sorry, Sir Home, if you've had a wasted journey, since I'm guessing it's been a long one, but they'll have told you that Lord Wellington has gone to Cadiz to meet with the Spanish government, and then I believe he has some business in Lisbon. He is expected to be away for some weeks."

"But I wrote to him," Popham said irritably. He had a high, slightly nasal voice. "I specifically told him that I was delaying my departure for England to speak to him about my recall from duty. He must write to London

43

immediately to ensure that I am sent back as soon as possible; without my personal attention, all the excellent work I have done in capturing Santander and its environs will be wasted. The Spanish partisans in that area will work only with me, I am convinced of it. My presence is essential to the success of this war."

There was not a trace of irony in Popham's tone. Paul had heard a lot about Popham's activities both from Wellington and from his correspondence with Captain Hugh Kelly and he took a deep breath, trying to keep his face straight. Wellington had not been in the best mood when the last of Popham's self-congratulatory letters had arrived along with half a dozen letters from Spanish officers and administrators complaining about him and begging for his removal, and he had called Popham a number of things, but essential had not been one of them.

"I cannot understand why he is not here," Popham said. "I wrote in very specific terms about my arrival."

"Did you receive his reply?" Paul asked.

Popham stared at him blankly. "No, but I assumed that was because his letter had not reached me, since I was already on my way here."

"I think it might have been just as reasonable to assume that Lord Wellington did not respond because he did not receive your letter at all, Sir Home."

Popham glared. "It is intolerable that the army postal service should be careless with letters of such importance, Major. I have had a wasted journey and will have no time to follow his Lordship..."

"It is no longer 'Major', Sir Home," Paul said gently. "In fact, I was recently promoted to Major-General."

Popham flushed. "Yes. Of course. A slip of the tongue, no more."

"Very understandable. I am sure Lord Wellington will be sorry to have missed the opportunity of thanking you for your excellent work at Santander and wishing you well in your next appointment."

Popham's mouth was hanging slightly open. Paul wondered if he had simply forgotten his change in rank or if he genuinely had not noticed it. Popham was so self-absorbed that it could have been either.

"I am concerned that once I reach England, the Admiralty will fail to see the importance of sending me back," he said finally. "Without the firmness I am able to apply, the Spanish partisans will not hold and there is a risk that the French will take back not only Santander but other coastal areas. All will be lost."

"I think you will find that Lord Wellington is well aware of the situation, Sir Home."

"If I could just speak to him," Popham said, and Paul heard desperation in the man's tone and thought he understood why. Kelly, who detested Popham, believed that he had run out of political influence and that success on the Spanish coast was Popham's last hope of regaining the government's trust. Popham clearly hoped that Wellington might have some influence at the Admiralty. Paul knew that his chief had genuinely appreciated

44

Popham's work but was irritated by his constant letters complaining about the Spanish, the Admiralty, the weather and various other naval officers. Popham gave the impression of a man labouring under persecution and Lord Fitzroy Somerset had told Paul over a brandy that by the end of the campaign he had to intervene, to stop Wellington throwing every letter in Popham's hand directly into the fire.

"Where have you come from?" Paul asked.

"My ship awaits in Oporto. I hired a carriage at considerable expense."

Paul studied him. He was surprised at how much Popham had aged in the past six years and he looked physically exhausted. Paul knew how that felt, and was prepared to endure any discomfort on campaign but could not imagine choosing to travel over a hundred miles in miserable conditions to speak to a man who might not even be there. Paul wondered suddenly if Popham's shadowed eyes were staring at the end of his career. He could not be sorry; Popham had trampled over too many people in his relentless pursuit of influence and success and Paul had almost been one of them, but he could not help feeling a tug of sympathy for the older man's weariness.

"He's not here, and we don't know when he'll be back," he said, more kindly. "I'm sorry, you've had a wasted journey. I'd suggest you wait until his return, but I'm guessing you're expected back in England."

"Yes," Popham said. "I cannot delay by more than a few days."

"Have you accommodation?"

"Colonel Scovell's wife has very kindly found me a room for a few nights until the horses are rested. Popham was silent for a moment then looked up. "I could be of great service were I permitted to return, General."

"Perhaps that is true, Sir Home, but I'm not the person you need to convince. I don't have much influence at the Admiralty, or anywhere else, apart from on a battlefield."

"I think that you and I both know that is not true, General, or you would not still be here."

Popham could only be referring to Paul's court martial in 1807 and Paul felt his momentary sympathy evaporate. He decided that he had been tactful enough for one day.

"I don't know, Sir Home. If anybody is aware of influence used on my behalf six years ago at my trial, I should think it would be you. Why don't you try to remember who wrote you a letter suggesting that you moderate your accusations against me? Perhaps you could approach him and see if he'll put in a good word for you at the Admiralty or with the Cabinet. Although I heard a rumour that it might have been the Earl of Chatham, and I don't suppose you feel much like approaching him, after Walcheren, do you? Leave a letter for Lord Wellington with Lord Fitzroy and he'll make sure he gets it. You never know, his Lordship might just feel that you've not yet outlived your usefulness. You'd better hope so, because I'm told you've run out of friends in London. If you'll excuse me, I have somewhere else to be. Good day."

Paul saluted and turned to leave. Behind him, Popham said:

"Did you hear that from Captain Kelly, General? You may be sure that I have already sent a letter about his recent conduct to the Admiralty."

"Have you?" Paul said, looking round. "What an amazing piece of good fortune, then, that my father had already received my letter on the subject before he dined with Lord Melville last month. I think you'll find that the Admiralty had a very good grasp of Captain Kelly's contribution to the late campaign before your letter reached them. I do wonder what they'll make of your version of events, mind."

The expression of sheer horror on Popham's face made Paul want to laugh aloud. "You wrote to the Admiralty?" he gasped.

"Of course I didn't write to the bloody Admiralty, Sir Home, I'm a soldier, why the devil would I do that? I told you, I've no friends at the Admiralty. My father, however, has recently acquired a controlling interest in a major shipbuilding company and has been awarded several government contracts. He writes very favourably of Lord Melville and feels that he is going to make an excellent contribution as First Lord. They've become quite friendly."

"Is that why Kelly wrote to you? To ask your father to speak for him?"

"No, Sir Home. He knows nothing about my father, he wrote to me as a friend. I passed his letter on in the same spirit."

A calculating expression crept in to Popham's eyes and Paul wondered if he knew how easy he was to read. "If your father spoke to Lord Melville about me, you could put in a good word. I have known his Lordship for some years, of course, but I was better acquainted with his late father, and I fear the intervention of others in the Cabinet who are not so well-disposed towards me. You could explain how much Lord Wellington values my contribution. I would not forget so great a service, General, I am a man with a long memory. A man who pays his debts."

Paul did not speak for a long moment. He was so angry that he did not trust himself. Finally, he got his voice under control.

"So am I, Sir Home," he said. "And I'm hereby collecting a debt you owe to Lieutenant Alfred Durrell. Now fuck off and don't come near me again. Good day."

There was satisfaction in the absolute silence behind him, as Paul walked out of the house and went to collect his horse.

Colonel Andrew Barnard was billeted in the village of Almeida and Paul sought him first in his room, which was in a grey stone house occupied by a carpenter and his large family. There was no sign of Barnard, but Paul found his servant in his room, industriously sweeping the floor. All the windows were open but the smell of Barnard's favourite cigars still filled the air.

"I'm looking for the colonel, Griffiths, any idea where he is?"

"Not sure, General."

Paul surveyed the man and decided that he was not even bothering to sound convincing. "Don't make me start yelling, Griffiths, I've got too much to do as it is. I know he's drunk. I just want to know where he's drinking."

46

Griffiths capitulated without a fight. "The red tavern, sir, up by the fortress."

"What the devil is he doing there, the wine's terrible?"

"Pockets to let again, sir. Also, none of the officers drink there."

Paul studied him. "Is he taking it hard, Griffiths?"

"Yes, sir. He's been in command of a brigade for a long time, it feels like a demotion."

"I know. All right, thank you, lad. I'll go and find him."

Paul knew the tavern, a low two-storey building with a red tiled roof and chickens pecking in the dusty earth of the street outside. There was a substantial stable at the back of the inn and Paul led Rufus through the yard. A sleepy groom, awoken from his siesta, ambled out from a doorway and looked enquiringly at Paul. Paul noticed that Barnard's neat bay occupied one of the stalls and beckoned to the groom.

"Take care of him. I doubt I'll be long."

"You stay tonight, Señor?"

"No. Here."

The groom pocketed the coin and took Rufus' reins, looking suddenly more wide-awake. Paul made his way across the dusty yard and entered the inn through the back door. He found himself in a long room, scattered with tables and benches. It was warm and stuffy and smelled of stale wine and sweat and some kind of stew. About half the tables were occupied, some of them by groups of locals and two of them by red coated British soldiers. They were swapping stories over jugs of wine, noisy in the sleepy quiet of the afternoon. The locals looked over at them resentfully from time to time, probably wishing they would take their loud voices elsewhere. The soldiers, meanwhile, were throwing glances and sly grins at the man in rifle green who occupied a small table by the fireplace. A bottle of wine was almost empty in front of him and he was wreathed in smoke from a particularly pungent cigar that brought tears to Paul's eyes.

"He'll not be able to stand by the day's end," one of the sergeants commented in a rich Irish accent which he did not bother to lower. "Wonder if he'll find his way home or fall asleep under the table."

"Wonder what he's got in his pockets, then."

"Who is he?"

"Barnard of the light division."

"It's Barnard of the 95th now," the sergeant said gleefully. "Lost his command to a richer man, I'm told. Won't be much in his pockets to pinch, the way he's drinking."

"Wonder if he…ow!"

Paul had reached the table and smacked the private smartly across the back of his head. "You don't have enough brain in there to wonder much. Get to your feet, the lot of you, there's an officer present."

They scrambled to attention, saluting. Paul let them stand for a long time, surveying them. "It's good to see the men of the 71st are keeping up their reputation as a pack of drunken bastards who don't have the sense to keep a civil tongue in front of a senior officer. Which company?"

"Third, sir."

"Thank you. I shall be sure to mention to Colonel Cadogan how well you conduct yourselves when you're off duty, he'll be delighted, I know. Are you billeted here?"

"No, sir. Marching down to Coria, detachment of sick returning to duty."

"And stopping off to get drunk on the way. I hope you've got the money to pay your shot, or you'll be on a charge for looting as well. Pay up and get moving."

Paul watched them file out then turned to survey Colonel Barnard. Barnard was holding the glowing end of his cigar in one hand and the bottle in the other. "It's all gone," he said, in surprise.

Paul walked across, took the cigar and stubbed it out. "You'll set fire to yourself in a minute," he said. "You're foxed, Colonel Barnard."

"Lieutenant-Colonel Barnard," the Irishman said, enunciating the words carefully. "I am a lowly Lieutenant-Colonel and not worthy to drink in the company of the esteemed, the mighty, the overweening majesty of the commander of the third brigade of the light division."

"Well we're certainly not drinking here," Paul said grimly. He glanced over to the landlord. "Can you send to the stables to get both horses saddled?" he asked in Spanish. "And I'll pay the bill."

"I understood that," Barnard roared. "I'll pay for my own wine. You save your money for your next promotion, General."

Paul counted to ten in his head. He nodded to the landlord who scuttled off. There was some muted laughter from some of the other tables. There was no point in trying to have a conversation with Barnard here. Paul needed to get him back to his billet and preferably sober first. He watched as Barnard rose, putting the bottle down heavily on the table. He tried to step over the wooden bench, misjudged the height of it and would have crashed to the ground if Paul had not caught him. He hauled Barnard upright.

"Come on, outside, you can wait there, while I bring the horses round."

Barnard shrugged his supporting arm away. "Fuck off, Van Daan."

Paul ignored him, took a firm hold and steered him outside. There was a rickety wooden bench against the wall. Paul lowered his friend onto it and went back inside to pay the bill. He went out the back door to find the groom leading both horses across the yard. Paul gave the groom another coin and beckoned for him to bring them round to the front, wondering how he was going to get Barnard onto a horse. He rounded the corner of the building and stopped.

Barnard lay on his back in the dust. The wooden bench was standing on one end, precariously threatening to crash down on top of him. Paul swore under his breath and ran to grab it, lowering it safely down. He looked down at Barnard. The Irishman looked up at him.

48

"It tipped up," he said.

"So I see," Paul said gravely.

Barnard began to laugh. He laughed softly at first, then harder, his whole body shaking. Despite Paul's exasperation, there was something very infectious about it. After a moment, Paul started to laugh as well. He reached out his hand and Barnard took it, allowing Paul to pull him to his feet. Paul sat him cautiously on the bench and sat next to him. The bewildered Spanish groom stood watching, holding the two horses, and Paul and Barnard laughed until tears ran down their faces.

"I'm sorry, Paul," Barnard gasped finally. "It's not your fault. You're bloody good, better than me."

"No, lad, you've got the right of it this time. If I hadn't been able to afford promotions when I did, it'd be me out on my ear, not you. It's about seniority and that comes from money. I'm so sorry."

Barnard wiped his eyes. "You know what's worse? It's Kempt."

"I know, Wellington told me." Paul eyed his friend curiously. "You don't like him?"

"Of course I bloody like him. Who doesn't? And he's bloody good at his bloody job. I can't even bloody well say he's useless. So bloody annoying. I keep saying bloody, don't I?"

"A fair bit, yes."

"I wonder if I can ride?"

"Well we're going to have to find out, Colonel, because you're coming back to dine with us. What on earth made you ride out here to get drunk?"

"I didn't want my officers to see me like this."

"Jesus Christ, Andrew, all your officers have seen you like this. More than once."

"Not for this reason. That wine was terrible."

"What did you expect in a Spanish tavern in the arse end of nowhere? Come on, let's get you up. All you need to do is hold on, we'll take it steadily. If you still want to drink when we get back, I've got a very good Portuguese red."

"You have an excellent palate, Colonel van Daan."

"Thank you." Paul watched critically as Barnard made it into the saddle. He clutched the reins of his surprised horse and swayed for a moment, but seemed to steady himself.

"It is one of the things I admire about you."

"I'm touched, Andrew." Paul mounted, nodding his thanks to the groom.

"You have never offered me a bad wine."

"It is one of the many advantages of coming from wealth, Andrew. Fortunately, it's one I can share with my friends." Paul eyed the Irishman as they made their way slowly up to the road. "Look, Wellington is genuinely upset about this. You know how ruthless he is with his officers and mostly he doesn't give a damn, but this is bothering him."

49

"He didn't show it. He has told me to put up with it and shut up."

"He didn't say that, Andrew."

"He almost said that."

"Kempt has recovered from his wounds and wanted to come back. He's a major-general now, it had to be at least a brigade. And you…"

"And I'm a lieutenant-colonel who only ended up as a brigade commander by luck," Barnard said. "It's all right, sir, I understand."

It jarred Paul to hear Barnard call him sir. Although Paul's army rank was senior, as fellow brigade commanders Paul had always treated the Irishman as equal in rank. Barnard was older than him by seven years and had eight years longer service.

"Don't," he said. Barnard shot him a crooked smile.

"I need to," he said. "It's a habit, I'll get used to it again."

"Not for that long, I hope. He told me, very specifically, that he is going to find an opportunity to promote you as soon as he can. He says he told you the same thing."

"I thought he was just being nice."

"Jesus, Andrew, you really are drunk, this is Wellington we're talking about, he's never nice. Just wait, it will come."

"Well if it does, I hope to God it's not over the dead body of one of my friends," Barnard said bluntly. "Paul, thank you. I can see this really bothers you. Don't let it. I'll go back to my battalion and I'll do a good job. It's how the army works."

"It is. It shouldn't be. It could have been me."

"It was never going to be you," Barnard said. He sounded more sober. "It's different with you, Paul, we all know it. And that's not a complaint, it's a fact. He'd fight tooth and nail to keep you where you are, that's why he promoted you to major-general."

"Thank God, because otherwise he'd have offered me a staff post and we'd kill each other. But when I heard about you, I tried to imagine what it would be like to go back to commanding the 110th and I was surprised to find that once I got past the hurt pride, it didn't feel so bad."

"Really?"

"I'm where I belong and I'd miss it, I know I would. But things were a lot more simple then. I had time to spend with my officers and men, instead of constantly playing army politics and arguing Wellington's case for him with officers who will never understand because they don't want to. When I first married Nan, I can remember sitting with my friends in the evenings, drinking wine and holding her hand and not drowning in paperwork."

There was a long silence. When Barnard spoke, his voice was clearer, as though the fresh air was blowing away some of the wine fumes.

"What a pile of horse dung," he said cheerfully. "I am reliably informed that you drilled those poor bastards into the ground, three junior officers left because they couldn't stand the pace and you had to apologise to both Craufurd and Picton for bawling them out about their mistakes when you were still only a major."

Paul looked at him and started to laugh again. "It's true," he admitted.

"Enough of this maudlin sentimentality. I am over it, General van Daan. Also, I'm developing a headache, for which good wine is the only remedy. Speed it up a little, will you, I'm getting hungry."

"You drunken, Irish bastard, Barnard, you will have the hangover from hell tomorrow and no sympathy from me. Come on then. Don't break your neck, falling off that horse."

Chapter Four

Captain Michael O'Reilly of the 112th arrived back into his room after three hours of drill and bayonet training with his company, to find his servant sitting cross-legged on his bed mending a stocking. Michael paused in the doorway to admire the view. Several days ago, he had hauled Brat over to Ciudad Rodrigo and invested in a new suit of clothing, a haircut and a pair of boots. The boots stood neatly beside the bed with a shine that Lord Wellington might have envied and the bright chestnut curls caught the late afternoon sunlight through the window as Brat's needle flew in and out. Michael, who was used to a rather more casual attitude to clothing, boots and kit, was beginning to feel that he could not put anything down without it being cleaned, mended or tidied away.

"Afternoon, Brat."

Brat jumped, having been engrossed in her work. She scrambled off the bed and gave a little bow. "Captain, I did not hear you. I will fetch hot water."

She headed for the door, snatching up her boots on the way and Michael watched her go with a little smile, then went to sit on the edge of the bed to remove his own boots.

Michael had managed for his first fourteen years in the army without a servant of any kind. The first eleven years had been spent in the ranks, rising to sergeant-major in the 110th before he had unexpectedly been given a commission. It was not unheard of for long serving NCOs to be awarded a commission for some piece of conspicuous heroism, but Michael knew it was often not a success. The officers' mess was a place for gentlemen and it was not difficult to freeze out an officer raised from the ranks.

It had not happened to Michael, partly because he had been born a gentleman, however far he had fallen after his dabbling in rebellion in 1798, but mostly because his commanding officer ran his mess, like his battalion, with a rod of iron. The usual squabbles and internal politics were not permitted in Paul van Daan's mess and new officers quickly learned. Michael had settled easily into his new role and two years later, newcomers often did not realise that he had begun in the ranks. The 110th and 112th were not wealthy regiments, and Michael was not the only officer living on his pay. He paid the camp women to do laundry and mending and managed his horses himself, paying a small sum to the ten year old son of one of his men to lead his pack mule on the march.

The arrival of Brat the previous year had changed all that. Her name was Ariana and Michael had found her in a dark alley in Madrid, raped and beaten and half-starved. She was an orphan from an outlying farm, surviving on the streets of the capital, doing odd jobs for a crust of bread, and selling herself to the troops of either side when she grew hungry enough. It had been an act of casual kindness to take her back to brigade headquarters, get her patched up and find her work in the palace while the brigade was there.

Michael had been horrified when she had appeared in camp during the retreat, soaked and shivering and hungry, having followed the army in search of him.

"I feel safe with you."

Michael was both touched and exasperated, but since he could hardly abandon her, he had taken her with him. She marched with the women, and had taken over management of his kit, his horses, his baggage mule and his life with single-minded determination. Back in Ciudad Rodrigo, Anne van Daan had bought her women's clothing and found her lodgings and work in one of the convents and Michael had thought that he had seen the last of her until he discovered her wet and exhausted, back in her boys' clothing, waiting on the doorstep of the quinta in December.

"What in God's name are you doing here, Brat?"

"I feel safe with you."

The enormity of her terror of being left unprotected, to the mercy of the passing armies, made it impossible for Michael to send her away. He was not sure how he would have enforced it anyway. Although she was dressed as a boy, it was impossible to disguise her sex and Michael was aware of the sniggers of both officers and men, many of whom assumed that Brat was sharing his bed. He had told her, kindly but firmly, that this arrangement must end when the new campaigning season began and planned to ask Señora Mata if a place could be found for her to work on the farm. Brat was strong and hard-working and there was a chronic shortage of labour.

The door opened and Brat reappeared with a heavy jug of hot water. Michael got up to take it from her and she dodged him neatly and set it on the wooden wash stand, then poured into the basin.

"You have soap and towel. Do you wish that I should shave you?"

Michael was trying not to laugh. "Out," he said firmly, although he knew that she could see it. "You're not my valet, Brat, and I've been shaving myself for twenty years."

"I did not think you were so old, sir."

She had gone before he could reply. Michael went to wash, still smiling. Brat's English was improving daily, and in the security of her new life, the terrified child was turning into a young woman with a quick wit and an impudent tongue. Michael had asked Jenson and Sergeant George Kelly to teach her her duties, and she was an apt pupil, who learned quickly and teased both her mentors unmercifully. Kelly had found her a place to sleep, just off the kitchen, and Brat had fashioned curtains to give her some privacy. She was settling into safety and comfort like a feral cat becoming domesticated, but with one suspicious eye on the cold world outside.

Michael had just finished dressing when Brat reappeared. "Captain, General van Daan wishes to see you," she said. "He is in the office."

"Thank you, Brat. Any idea what it's about?"

"No, Charlie brought the message. Perhaps you are in trouble."

"Perhaps you should mind your own business, urchin. All right, I'll go down. Will you speak to the grooms about..."

"Sligo's left front shoe. I have done so. Wait. Hold still."

Michael obeyed, and she stood on tiptoe to untie and retie his hair ribbon, then straightened his neck cloth and brushed an imaginary speck of dust off his shoulder, making Michael feel like a child on his first day of school. Apparently satisfied, Brat stepped back with a nod. Michael gave an ironic salute and went to find Paul.

"You wanted to see me, sir?"

"I do. Come and sit down, Michael, and have a drink. How are the new recruits coming along?"

They talked for a while of training and recruitment and brigade matters. Michael was enjoying himself, but he had a strong sense that Paul was skirting another subject, and as he thought it, the general sighed and put down his glass.

"I could sit here until dinner doing this, but I can't. I've something to tell you, and it won't wait, I'm sorry, Michael."

"Am I in trouble, sir?"

"Not unless you've done something that I don't know about. I had a long conversation with Colonel Scovell yesterday and an even longer letter from Lord Wellington when I got back here, and I'm sorry to say you feature very heavily in both of them. I'm going to tell you the whole story, and then you've a decision to make, Michael."

Michael listened, in growing astonishment as Paul laid out Wellington's assignment for him. When Paul finally fell silent, he said:

"Sir - I don't really understand why I'm being asked to do this. I've never worked in intelligence."

"I know, but they've nobody else, and London has asked for two men to be sent. To be honest, there's no training for this work, Giles was completely green when they first sent him out there. He proved to have a flair for it. Scovell thinks you might too."

"Or I could end up dead."

"You could. Equally, I could get you killed on a battlefield in a few months' time, I've had a good go at it before."

"You have, sir. Alba de Tormes, for example."

"We don't talk about that, Michael. Not if you want dinner."

"What does Fenwick say about this?"

54

"I don't know, I've not seen him yet, I think George was hoping to speak to him today. He'll accept it, Michael, he's a professional. So are you, but you're not an intelligence agent. You need to give this some thought, because if you really don't want to do it, I will tell George he needs to find somebody else."

"Who were the other choices?" Michael asked. He felt slightly off-balance. "Any of our men?"

"I don't know, to be honest, Wellington drew up the list."

"I don't understand that, sir. Lord Wellington barely knows me, and the little he knows, he doesn't approve of. He'll speak to me if he has to, but the fact that I came up from the ranks sticks in his gullet. Especially because he said it would be a disaster and you told him it wouldn't and he can't stand it when you're right and he's wrong."

"That's so true, it's genuinely funny."

"So why me?"

"Because he's done his homework. He knows that you're intelligent, your French is good and your Spanish is better, you're an excellent horseman and you're courageous. He knows that you're one of the men I would trust above most others. He also knows that you're unmarried, with no obvious responsibilities."

"And I can see why that would matter." Michael was silent, thinking about it. "Who would be in command?"

"Giles. That has nothing to do with seniority or the date of your commissions, it's about his experience in this field. He'll have his Spanish guide with him as well, so there'll be three of you."

"So why am I needed?"

"Because he's Spanish, and they're arseholes, so they think he doesn't count."

Michael smiled and sipped the brandy. "Lucky him."

"If you don't want to do it, I'll get you out of it, Michael."

"I'm not sure how."

"George Scovell is a friend, and unlike Wellington, he does know you, and he's chosen you because he thinks you'd be good at this. But if I tell him no, he'll accept it. He'll have other options."

"One of which might be Leo Manson. If Wellington has been looking at your officers for this, don't tell me he's not on the list."

Paul's silence told Michael that the thought had occurred to him. They sat quietly for a while, as the late afternoon shadows spread across the floor and there was sound of movement in the big old house as the officers of the 110th clattered up and down the stairs getting ready for dinner and making their way to the big mess room for drinks. Michael always enjoyed the comfort of winter quarters for at least a month, and then boredom would set in and he would find himself restless, waiting for orders. He knew that Paul was the same, except that he was bored within a week.

Michael tried to imagine what the next months might bring should he agree to go. He was used to the structure of regimental life, the companionship of his friends and the order of drills and training and marching with the army. He had seen Giles Fenwick come and go over the years without ever really thinking about what his life might be like. Michael had never had reason to question his own courage, but he felt a sudden twinge of discomfort, wondering if his hesitation was because he was afraid.

"I'll need your wife to take care of Brat for me," he said quietly.

"You know that we will, Michael."

"I thought that through winter quarters, she'd have time to settle down a bit. Without me here, I don't want her to go running off..."

"Michael, if you decide to do this, I promise we'll take care of her."

"All right. Tell Colonel Scovell I'll do it, sir."

Paul studied him without speaking for a moment and when he did, Michael had the sense that he was trying to keep his voice light. "If you get yourself killed out there, Michael, I'm going to nail Scovell's balls to the doorframe right alongside Wellington's for this. So for the sake of success in this war, it's your duty to stay alive. Let's go to dinner. I've yet to tell my wife about this, and I'm telling you that's a job I'm not looking forward to."

***

Paul's new quartermaster arrived the following day in the middle of a winter thunderstorm. The weather had been threatening all morning and at noon, Paul took a long hard look at the sky and decided to postpone his visit to the second division. He rode out to the abandoned village a mile to the north where the 110th and 112th were working on skirmish training and found his brigade-major along with Carl and Gervase, in the process of calling the men in.

"I'm guessing you're not going, sir?" Manson said.

"Not a chance, this is going to hit at any moment and I'm not riding through a storm unless I have to."

As Paul spoke, there was an ominous rumbling. The sky was growing rapidly darker, and one or two of the men were looking uneasily towards the sky. Sergeant-Major Carter bellowed at dawdlers to get a move on, and the two battalions were in marching order when an enormous crash of thunder made the officers' horses start nervously. Rufus sidestepped a little and Paul reined him in, talking quietly to him. The big roan stilled under his hands, reassured, and immediately started up again as a vivid flash ripped the dark sky in two.

"Jesus Christ, that sounded close," Carl said.

"Too close, let's get them back and under cover. Quick time, Carter."

"Yes, sir."

Rain began to fall as the troops set off at a fast pace, and Paul observed with amusement that there were no dawdlers now. Leaving the retreat to the subalterns, who were on foot anyway, he turned Rufus towards home, indicating that the mounted officers should follow. Rufus had been under fire more than once and was steady in most circumstances, but no horse enjoyed a thunderstorm, especially one as noisy as this, and Paul was keen to get him into his stable.

He arrived with Carl and Manson, a little ahead of the other officers, to find a covered wagon pulled up on the driveway along with several horses. Grooms came running as a small, bedraggled party clambered down into the deluge. To Paul's exasperation, the grooms made their way immediately to the arriving officers of the 110th rather than to the shivering woman and children. He took a breath to bellow, but another voice was raised ahead of his.

"Fry, Bolton, what on earth are you doing? Our officers are more than capable of stabling their own horses, see to our visitors. This way, ma'am, bring the children."

Anne was on the steps, waving, and an officer who must be Captain Mackenzie, handed his reins to a passing groom and shepherded his wife and children towards the door as Paul took Rufus to the stable. He was very curious to meet the man who had divided opinion in the second battalion so sharply, and who had somehow managed to arouse the interest of the notoriously idle Earl of Chatham.

Paul found Mackenzie alone in the study, gently steaming before a fire in the grate. Mackenzie was a few years older than Paul, his dark hair sprinkled with early grey. A pair of wary dark eyes studied him. Paul returned his salute and collected madeira and two glasses.

"Welcome to Portugal, Captain. What a day to arrive."

"Thank you, sir. It's been difficult the whole way, to be honest. I wanted to hire a carriage, but there was nothing available in Oporto. The wagon leaked and the horses were lame more often than not. Luckily my wife is very calm, nothing seems to put her out."

Paul poured the wine. "She'll get on very well with Nan, then, she displays the most astonishing sang froid through the worst circumstances. As it's warm in here, I suggest you dispense with formality and take that wet coat off. Has my wife kidnapped your family?"

Mackenzie smiled. "Yes, sir, I think they are in the kitchen. She suggested I join them, but you'd just ridden in and I wanted to introduce myself."

There was painful uncertainty under the other man's calm exterior, and Paul was very sure now that Mackenzie knew exactly what Lieutenant Colonel Flanagan had written about him. It made Paul's job either easier or more difficult, depending on whether Flanagan had got it right or wrong but it seemed that Mackenzie did not want to shirk the issue which was a good sign.

"Hang your jacket over that chair by the fire and come and sit down, Captain. Has my wife explained the billeting yet? We're not short of space here, but as your family is with you, we've given you your own quarters in one of the farm cottages. It's simple but you'll be comfortable there. I'll leave it to Nan to go over all the arrangements with you."

"Thank you, sir. It was very good of you to agree to allow Katja and the children to join me, I wasn't expecting you to say yes."

"I couldn't really say no, given that my own children are coming out for a couple of months. We're very secure here, and as you can see, very well provided for. I think..."

There was a knock on the door and Paul sighed. "There is no peace. Come in."

"Sorry sir," Jenson said. "Captain Fenwick is here."

"Oh. All right, send him in, Jenson." Paul rose. "Will you excuse me, Captain Mackenzie, this will only take a moment.

The officer who entered dripped water from his bicorn hat and shabby great coat. He removed the hat and saluted. "I'm sorry to interrupt, sir, it's just that I've orders regarding O'Reilly from Colonel Scovell, and..."

"No, it's all right, Giles, my new quartermaster has just arrived. Come in for a minute."

Giles Fenwick came fully into the room and placed the hat on a small side table. His eyes were on the other man and Paul saw Ross Mackenzie smile broadly, transforming his rather intense face. He moved forward and Giles did the same, his hand outstretched.

"Giles Fenwick, it has been far too long."

"Captain Mackenzie. I must owe you about eight letters, I am sorry. What in God's name are you doing here, I thought you chained to Melton for the rest of your life."

"So did I," Mackenzie said. "It's as the general says, I've been appointed quartermaster. On a trial basis, I understand."

Giles gave an expressive snort which Lord Wellington would have been proud to produce. "Trial basis, my arse. Is that what Flanagan told you?"

Paul regarded him in mild disbelief. "That would be Lieutenant-Colonel Flanagan to you, Captain Fenwick, and it was I who suggested a trial period through winter quarters. There's a big difference between barrack-master and quartermaster in the field, and it's been four years since Captain Mackenzie had any campaign experience."

"Sorry, sir," Giles said. "But that doesn't make a difference when they want to appoint an influential general who hasn't been in the field for ten years and has virtually no command experience to..."

"Giles, for God's sake," Mackenzie said sharply.

"That will do, Captain," Paul said mildly. "I'd forgotten you were at Walcheren. I presume that's where you two met."

"Yes, sir," Giles said. His expression of slightly belligerent protectiveness made Paul want to laugh aloud, but he restrained himself.

"At some point before you leave, I'd like to ask you about that campaign, but not right now. Apart from anything else, you're creating a small pond in the middle of my brigade office. Go and find out where you're billeted and get dried off, I think you'll find my wife in the kitchen with Captain Mackenzie's family."

"Katja is here?" Giles said, his face brightening. "That's..."

"Enough, Giles!" Paul said, raising his voice. "I'm trying to speak to my new quartermaster, not organise your social life. When do you have to leave?"

"Two days, maybe three. It depends on how long it takes to get supplies organised. I was hoping…"

"Talk to Nan, she'll help. You'll find Michael drying out in his room, I imagine. Is Antonio with you?"

"Yes, sir. He can share my billet."

"As long as he doesn't talk as much as you do, he's very welcome. Now get out of here and I'll see you at dinner."

Giles grinned, saluted and left. Paul turned back to Mackenzie, who was regarding him with a slightly worried expression. "I'm sorry, sir. It's been a long time. And Giles…Captain Fenwick…"

"Sit," Paul said. "Don't worry about Captain Fenwick, I am entirely accustomed to his inability to keep his mouth shut when he ought to, it's been getting him into trouble for years. I'm rather more interested in what happened in Walcheren in 1809 to set him off like a rocket at the mention of it."

Mackenzie sat obediently, the wary eyes studying him. Paul went to his desk and picked up Flanagan's letter. "Belligerent, disruptive and prone to causing arguments in the mess, which caused his fellow officers to ostracise him for the duration of the Walcheren campaign," he quoted. "Is any of that true?"

Mackenzie flushed a dark red and his jaw tightened. "Lieutenant-Colonel Flanagan is my senior officer, sir, it isn't my place to question his opinion."

"Well I'm Captain Fenwick's senior officer, but that doesn't seem to stop him."

Unexpectedly, Mackenzie's face softened into a singularly attractive smile. "It never did, sir. It worried the life out of me that he'd get himself cashiered speaking up for me, but even a direct order couldn't stop him."

"That is one of the things I like about Giles," Paul said, returning the smile. "Drink your wine, Captain, and tell me what happened, would you? You may as well, because he's definitely going to."

***

Michael found Giles Fenwick after an exhaustive search, occupying a room in one of the farm cottages. He had come prepared for a briefing on their proposed mission, but found Giles seated cross-legged on his bed in shirt sleeves and without his boots on, telling three wide-eyed children the story of the retreat from Burgos. Michael leaned his long form against the doorpost, folded his arms and prepared to listen. Giles was a good storyteller and managed to convey something of the difficulties of the retreat without going into too many details of the death and misery. His audience were spellbound. Michael studied them with interest, two fair-haired boys, probably in their early teens and a girl who was slightly older and very pretty.

Giles reached the end of his story and stood up, reaching out to ruffle the hair of the younger boy. "Right, I need to speak to Captain O'Reilly here, so get yourselves off and get ready for tea."

"Will you have tea with us, Captain?" the girl said. She spoke with an accent that Michael could not identify, but he realised that these must be the step-children of the new quartermaster.

"If I can. I'm only here for a few days, so I'd like to see as much as I can of you all. I'm still reeling at how much you've all grown, you'll be as tall as me before long, Cornelius. Go on, off you go."

As their footsteps clattered down the stairs, Giles reached for his boots. "Sorry about that. I was looking for you earlier, but…"

"I needed a word with my company. I'm handing them over to my senior lieutenant, I wanted to say goodbye to them, in case…is this where you're billeted?"

Giles looked around. "Yes. It was Mrs Mackenzie's idea, they're staying here. I've not seen them since I left England, it will be good to have a bit of time with them. But you're not here to talk about my billeting arrangements, are you? I'm told you'll be joining us on this bloody stupid expedition."

"That's reassuring from my new commanding officer," Michael said. He had not intended to say it, but he was not sorry. The issue of their respective positions was nagging at him, and while he knew it was not Fenwick's fault, he did not want to set off without having had the conversation. Giles surveyed him with blue eyes which looked faintly amused.

"Is that a problem, Captain?"

"It can't be, can it? I've been told to report to you. I'm reporting. What happens next?"

"Well if you take that attitude into northern Spain with you, Captain O'Reilly, I'll be leaving you at Corunna, I don't have time for it," the younger man said unemotionally. "What is it, the age difference, the length of service or the date of commission? I don't know when you were made captain, by the way, but I know I made lieutenant a long time before you did. You were in the ranks at that point, I believe."

"Here we go."

"No, that's exactly where we're not going. I'm glad you raised it, because we won't be discussing it again. I don't give a damn where you started out, O'Reilly, or how you got to where you are. When we disembark at Corunna, you're in my territory, and I need to know now if you're capable of taking an order, because if you can't, you're not coming."

For some reason, Fenwick's unmistakably upper class accent infuriated Michael even more. "You jumped-up, arrogant young bastard. How dare you speak to me like that. I was fighting in India when you were still a snotty brat attached to your mother's apron strings, and if you…"

"It's unlikely, O'Reilly, I was very young when she died. Stop frothing at the mouth, I'm not trying to insult your courage or your ability, if you didn't possess both they wouldn't have proposed you for this mission. I'm

60

just telling you that it's going to be different out there. I know what I'm riding into. So does Antonio. You don't. That's all right, we were all green once. But..."

"Green? Christ alive, are you trying to get me to punch you?"

There was a long silence, while Michael tried to get his temper under control. Suddenly, completely unexpectedly, Giles said:

"Possibly. It would give me a chance to hit you back and I've been wanting to do that since you spent weeks humiliating me on the parade ground in Lisbon just over two years ago."

Michael froze, remembering. He stared at Giles, realising suddenly how neatly their positions had been reversed and his anger died abruptly. "Oh. Oh shit, I'd forgotten that."

"It appears I haven't," Giles said wryly.

Neither of them spoke. After a moment, Giles crossed the big, bare room and took a bottle from his pack along with two pewter drinking cups. He set them on a brass bound chest and poured two generous measures, then handed one to Michael. Michael took it with a nod of thanks and drank gratefully, his eyes on Giles and his thoughts two years in the past. He wanted to defend himself, to assert that he had only been doing his job and that he had not treated Giles any differently to any of the other new officers but he knew it would be a lie. Giles still did not speak.

"I'd been made lieutenant about six weeks when you arrived in Lisbon," Michael said finally. "I'd been in the ranks since I was twenty, never had any hope of a commission, and suddenly there it was, tied up with a ribbon. And not the usual, 'here's an ensign's commission, my good man, and a job in the stores for the rest of your career.' It was a combat posting under a captain I liked and admired, and an immediate brevet promotion to lieutenant. I can't imagine how he managed that."

"Neither can I. So why me?"

Michael picked up the brandy and poured again, then put the bottle on the floor and sat down on the chest. He thought about prevaricating but decided to tell the truth. He was only just beginning to realise that he actually wanted this posting, was fascinated by the idea of working within touching distance of the enemy, without the safety net of his company and his friends, but he knew that Giles Fenwick was right. They could not work together in such dangerous conditions when both were clearly nursing their own resentment.

"Several reasons," he admitted. "You were - how old?"

"I'd have been twenty three, I think."

"Twenty-three and you'd already been lieutenant for years, you'd have been captain if you could have afforded it. You were an arrogant little shit, you walked onto that parade ground as if you owned it, but you didn't. You weren't bad, but you weren't that good, which wasn't your fault. Any officer who'd served under bloody Longford was bound to have picked up bad habits, it was easy to fix, but unlike Zouch and the others, you hated to be told and you made it obvious. You had that voice, which sounds as if you can't be

61

bothered to finish a sentence and when you heard I'd recently been made up from the ranks, you looked at me as if I was something you needed to scrape off the bottom of your shoe. And I was put in charge of bringing you up to scratch. I'd been ordered around by the likes of you for more than ten years and flogged by a few of them as well. Of course I bloody made the most of it. What's your excuse?"

Giles reached for the bottle, topped up his cup and sat on one of the bunks. "I was serving under Longford, I'd spent years along with Zouch, doing his job for him and watching him get the credit for it. I hoped for more out here, but for those first weeks, all I got was an earful of grief from a jumped-up bog-trotter who'd only been an officer for five minutes, and to make it worse, was on first name terms with my commanding officer. I thought I'd jumped straight from the frying pan into the fire. I was permanently pissed off because I thought I was going to get passed over again."

Michael studied the younger man and Giles looked back steadily. After a while, Michael drained his cup. "Well wasn't that a load of bollocks to be sitting on for two years, then?" he said conversationally, and Giles started to laugh.

"Utter bollocks. Do you still want to do this?"

"Yes."

"Good. I've been talking to Mrs van Daan and we're not taking our own horses. We're going over the mountains in winter, we'll do better with local ponies, they're suited to the territory. We'll ride as far as Oporto with a couple of the grooms, and they can bring our mounts back here when we sail. I've a contact in Corunna, a local priest, I've written to ask him to hire mounts for us, he'll have them ready. Let me call Antonio, he's flirting with Katja Mackenzie in the kitchen, and I'll show you the route we'll be taking. Dig in that pack, there's a map."

Michael obeyed, unfolding the map on one of the beds. Giles yelled down the stairs for his Spanish guide then came to Michael's side. "We'll take this road out of Corunna."

Michael shot him a glance. "Do I need to call you 'sir'?"

Giles looked revolted. "Not unless you want a punch. I answer to Captain or Fenwick. But my friends call me Giles, and we're going to be spending a lot of time together."

"Giles it is then. You can call me anything other than Mick."

His companion gave an unexpectedly mischievous grin. "You shouldn't have told me that," he said, and bent his fair head over the map again.

***

The quinta de Santo Antonio boasted a series of excellent reception rooms, the biggest of which served as the officers' mess for the 110th, with an attractive square parlour leading into a large dining room. The parlour was furnished with wooden chairs, benches and assorted tables and a few armchairs

62

and the officers used it as a sitting room. Anne usually dined in the mess but there was a smaller room at the front of the house which she used on those occasions when Paul wished to entertain privately.

The meal was intended as a welcome dinner for Paul's new quartermaster and his wife, but at the last minute, Paul had decided to include Giles Fenwick and Anne suggested they add Michael O'Reilly to the party. She had also suggested that Antonio Ortega, Giles' Spanish guide be included, but Giles grinned and shook his head.

"He won't come, ma'am, he'd feel as though he was intruding. Besides, I believe he has another engagement this evening. But thank you."

"What's her name, Captain?"

"He won't tell me, he says he doesn't trust me."

Anne laughed. "Well please tell him that when you get back, I would like him to dine with us. I wasn't at my best the last time we met, but he managed to make me laugh even then."

The party convened on the long terrace at the back of the house in pale winter sunlight, and Señora Mata's thin-faced daughter, Renate, served champagne. Katja Mackenzie was dressed in deep blue with white lace trimmings and a delicate blue and white lace headdress pinned to her fair curls. Katja was some years older than Anne, probably in her early thirties, and very attractive. She did not seem at all overawed by the very masculine environment of Paul's headquarters, but Anne supposed that as wife to the barrack master she was used to it.

"I hope the children have settled in well. You must let me know if there is anything you need."

"Thank you, you've been very kind. I left them badgering poor Louisa, my companion, to take them out for a walk before supper, they're so curious. General van Daan tells me he has managed to find some ponies for them."

"We have. We've been on the hunt for something for our children to ride when they arrive, and Captain O'Reilly found a breeder who specialises in pack animals for the army. It's very enterprising of him, I must say, there's a chronic shortage of good horses out here. Most of the officers wouldn't ride these local ponies, but they're ideal as pack horses, so we've bought up his stock to use during the next campaigning season. He was delighted with the price, we are delighted to have stolen a march on the rest of the army and in the meantime, the children can use them. I'm sorry Michael is going to be away for a few months, since he's the best horse trainer in the regiment, but Isair, my groom is very good and has offered to help the children to get to know them."

"They'll be very excited. None of them could ride when we first moved to England, they were very much raised in a town, but they have their own ponies now and they love riding. At least the boys love riding and Margriete loves the way she looks in the saddle."

Anne laughed. "I don't blame her, ma'am, she is very pretty. How old is she now?"

"She is fourteen. Cornelius is twelve, Hans is eleven and my little Catriona is almost three. They are looking forward to meeting your children when they arrive. How old are they?"

The conversation remained domestic until the party was seated, and then became more general. Paul and Ross were talking about supplies and billeting, and Anne was quickly drawn into the discussion, with plans to introduce the new quartermaster to the existing system on the following day, along with the regimental commissary officer, Lieutenant Sinclair. Giles and Michael were quickly included, talking about the unique problems of supplies faced by an intelligence officer. Renate Mata brought through trays of covered dishes, assisted by Charlie Bannan. It was Charlie's first experience of helping to serve at dinner and somebody, presumably Jenson, had ensured that he was scrubbed thoroughly clean for the occasion. Charlie looked very pleased with himself, and Anne tried not to smile openly at his solemn expression as he helped Renate to arrange dishes and serve wine. As he followed the young woman to the door, Paul said:

"Private Bannan."

"Sir?"

"Well done. Excellent turn out, I'm proud of you." Paul smiled at the girl. "Thank you, Renate. Go and get the children their supper, we'll call Charlie if we need anything else."

"Yes, sir."

Paul turned back to Ross. "Talk to me about recruiting, Captain Mackenzie. You've been doing it spectacularly well, we seem to be one of the most successful regiments in the army for attracting new recruits, and they're not all coming through the courts. Colonel Wheeler is currently in England setting up a second battalion for the 112th and he is going to want to know how you do it. As do I."

Anne smiled inwardly, watching the Scottish captain visibly begin to relax. Paul had a gift for managing people, both officers and men, and it was the real secret behind his extraordinary success. Other officers were sometimes scornful about Paul's personal fortune which had enabled him to buy his way up the promotional ladder, and could be spiteful about his friendship with the commander of the forces and Anne knew that both of these had played their part. But watching him talking to Ross Mackenzie, she felt a little rush of pride, not in his achievements but in who he was.

"Your husband is a very good commander, Mevrou. I have not seen Ross this excited about his work for a long time."

Anne turned, surprised to realise that Katja had been following her own train of thought. "Yes, he's good at this. He is also very good at selecting the right man for the job, and I can tell that he thinks he has struck lucky with Captain Mackenzie."

"He has," Giles said. "I know it's going to be hard for you, Katja, being without him. But I'm glad for him. He should have been back in the field a long time ago, it's a disgrace that he's been kicking his heels in barracks for three years because he had the courage to do the right thing."

Katja glanced at Anne, and Anne understood. "The general told me a little about it, ma'am. I gather his career was held back because he reported a fellow officer for going into battle drunk. It is appalling, I wish we had known sooner."

"I wish I'd said something sooner," Giles said grimly. "I was an idiot not to realise that nobody had told General van Daan, ma'am."

"You're not with us that often, Captain, it's not surprising the topic didn't come up."

"It is not all bad, Mevrou. We have had three very happy years together in Melton Mowbray, and we have had time to settle and for my children to become his family. That would have been more difficult if he had been away all the time. We will miss him very much when it is time to leave, but we feel at home there now, and I have so much to do, I shall not be bored."

Paul had caught the end of the conversation. "I gather you're rather like my wife, Mrs Mackenzie, you're never without occupation. What's this I hear about setting up a school in barracks?"

"Ja, it is my favourite project, General. It began with one or two of the new recruits who could not read or write but hoped for promotion to corporal or sergeant one day. In those early days I was very new and had no friends in the area, so I had little to do. I began to give some lessons, and it grew from there. Last year, we raised some money from local subscriptions to build a schoolroom, and now we teach not only those men who wish to learn but also the children. We have three teachers, one who is a paid schoolmaster and two ladies who give their time for free."

Paul's expression was intent. "That sounds very impressive, ma'am, and I'd like to know more. We've helped one or two of our lads when they've approached us individually, but I've been talking for a while of something more formal out here. It's difficult to do much on campaign, but during winter quarters they'd have time to study. As for the children, we have our own project in Charlie there, and he's coming along very well, but I'd like to do more. How did you raise the money?"

Katja Mackenzie was passionate about her subject, and Anne found herself quickly caught up in her enthusiasm. Paul listened intently, asking an occasional question. The topic moved from education to conditions in barracks and on to the health of the men and Anne was able to join in, explaining her own work with the medical services. By the time the table broke up, it was late and Anne was tired. Before going to bed, she slipped in to the temporary nursery, where Sergeant Stewart's wife Sally, who was acting as wet nurse to Anne's tiny daughter, snored peacefully beside her charge. Anne bent over the crib and kissed Georgiana very gently, then joined Paul.

"I think that went well."

"I think we've struck gold with Ross Mackenzie," Paul said, with a jaw-cracking yawn. "As for his wife, it's a shame she has to go back home, what an extraordinary woman."

"She is. I'm looking forward to getting to know her better." Anne seated herself to allow him to unbutton her gown. "Where is she from?"

"She was born in Middelburg but lived in Vlissingen and Antwerp. I think her first husband was a good deal older than her, and when he died she ran his businesses single handed before she married Mackenzie, and she still holds a controlling interest in them. I can't wait to introduce her to my father, she knows all the places he knew as a child, it's possible they've some acquaintances in common, the mercantile communities in those little Dutch towns are very small. He may even have known her parents."

Anne slipped into bed. She was aware suddenly of a faint sense of unease, although she could not explain it to herself. "How funny. I never really think of you as Dutch."

Paul got in beside her and blew out the candle. "I'm not really. We were raised as good English gentlemen. I can remember going to Holland a few times when I was a child, but then the war made it impossible. I went again just before I joined up in '02 - everybody else in London was going to Paris and I went to Vlissingen and Antwerp. I'm glad I did, actually, from what I've heard, we didn't leave much standing in Vlissingen when we bombarded it in '09, including poor Katja's dye shop."

"Katja?" Anne said.

Paul drew her into his arms. "She suggested I call her that. You don't mind do you? You're not usually that formal."

"No, of course not," Anne said. "I was talking to Giles and Michael so I didn't hear all your conversation. You've taken a liking to her, haven't you."

"To both of them," Paul said, with another wide yawn.

"She reminds me a little of Rowena," Anne said. She was still probing her own discomfort, not sure what was causing it. Paul brushed her ear with his lips. It tickled and Anne giggled. "Stop that, you're too tired."

"I probably am. I wouldn't have thought of Rowena. Actually, she reminds me more of you. Kiss me goodnight, girl of my heart, before I fall asleep and miss the chance. I love you."

Anne kissed him for a long time. "I love you too, Paul. So much."

Paul shifted slightly, suddenly sounding more awake. "Are you all right?"

"Yes. Yes, of course. I think I'm tired as well."

"You're sure."

"Very. Go to sleep."

He was asleep very quickly, but Anne took longer. She lay awake, telling herself that she was being ridiculous. She had never suffered from jealousy and knew that she had no reason to. The odd little pain in her heart caused by Paul's obvious affinity for Katja Mackenzie was an extension of her unusually low mood since the birth of Georgiana. It would pass, and Anne had no intention of allowing it to get in the way of making a friend.

Anne moved to turn over and realised that Paul was lying on her hair. She freed it very carefully and closed her eyes, wishing that her mind would stop racing.

"You have precisely ten minutes to either tell me what's wrong or go to sleep, Anne van Daan. After that, I'm going to beat you."

Anne froze. "I thought you were asleep."

"I would love to have the opportunity, it's like trying to sleep through a cavalry charge the way you're fidgeting."

"Oh, I'm sorry, love."

Paul rolled over, pushed himself up onto his elbow and kissed her very thoroughly. "Well, I'm awake now," he said. "And given that it's your fault, I think you have a duty to entertain me."

Suddenly the pain was gone, and Anne reached up and drew him closer. "I will do my best," she said seriously, and kissed him again.

Chapter Five

Michael had not been to Oporto since he had fought there in 1809 and there had been no time for sight-seeing. He had not expected to spend any time in the city, but *HMS Collins,* the Royal Navy frigate which was to transport them to Corunna was not ready to sail. Her commander, a fresh-faced lieutenant who did not look old enough to have his own command, was apologetic.

"It will only take a couple of days, Captain Fenwick, but I can't sail like this. We ran into a storm coming up from Lisbon and there's damage to the sails which means if we get into trouble, we'll be a sitting duck. The French navy shouldn't be a problem on this voyage, but there's always the possibility of a lone ship looking for trouble. I'm not risking either my ship or your mission, since I'm told it's important. Two days, and we should be able to sail with the tide on Tuesday. I can offer you accommodation aboard ship or recommend an inn."

"We've stabled our horses at an inn, we'll stay there," Giles said decisively.

"Horses? I wasn't told I'd need to accommodate horses."

"You won't. We rode with three army grooms, they're going to take the horses back to headquarters and we're hiring local ponies in Corunna. And if they lose my horse to brigands on the way, I am going to shoot them when I get back, so they'd better be alert. How long will be be at sea?"

"It depends on the wind. Two days, I would think, but we could do it in less."

"Thank you. Will you send a message when you know you'll be ready to sail?"

The inn was shabby, but dry and reasonably quiet, in the Ribeira district close to the river. Giles, Michael and Antonio walked through the town, which both Giles and Antonio seemed to know reasonably well.

Oporto was on the sloping banks of the Douro, with a jumble of houses, shops, churches and public buildings rising up on both sides of the river. The main town was on the north bank, and narrow cobbled streets twisted past huge merchants' houses and a bewildering variety of churches, many of them set in small, leafy gardens. From the cathedral, there was an excellent view over the town, with buildings tumbling down towards the river. Sunlight glinted off window panes, and balconies and gardens were a riot of colour. Below, the Douro wound its stately way to the sea, with a variety of boats and barges tied up along the banks or moving like toys on the silvery surface.

"It is very beautiful," Antonio said.

"It is," Michael admitted. "I barely noticed what the place looked like last time I was here."

"You were here in '09?" Giles asked.

"Yes. Five or six companies joined Wellesley in Lisbon and marched up here a week or so later." Michael turned and surveyed the view. "Just up there was his headquarters in the monastery, and over there was the Bishop's Seminary where we fought the French. We crossed in some wine barges just down there, and climbed up that slope opposite." Michael looked over the hillside. "I can't see it from here, it's behind those trees, but I think that must have been the convent where one of the hospitals was, where the very lovely Mrs Carlyon was helping the surgeons, and Major van Daan spent all his spare time hanging around the place."

"We didn't lose many that day."

"No, it was an easy one. Paget lost his arm, of course. He was in command of the Seminary, was shot down and handed command to the major. But he was bloody unlucky, most of us hadn't a scratch. Brilliant tactics." Michael glanced at Giles. "Where were you at that time?"

"When was that, May? I'd have been in barracks at Melton Mowbray, serving under Captain Longford. Very soon afterwards, of course, we went to Walcheren. My men died of fever while you were winning glory at Talavera."

"Talavera wasn't glorious, Captain, it was a fuck-up from start to finish. We weren't ready to fight them then, we were lucky to get away with it. And we almost lost General van Daan."

"I remember hearing about it. Have you admired the view enough? There's a tavern two streets away with very good food, excellent wine at reasonable prices and a rather attractive barmaid called Lotta whom I've not seen for a while."

Michael laughed aloud. "You make a fine town guide, Captain Fenwick. Does Lotta have a friend?"

Antonio clapped him on the shoulder. "She has several friends, Captain. I know them well. Come, we shall buy them supper, and then, who knows?"

It was a good evening, filled with laughter, and Michael approved Giles Fenwick's choice. He was fairly sure that he was being managed, but he appreciated the fact that his new commanding officer seemed willing to make the effort. Evenings like this mattered on a battlefield, when the man standing beside you in the square felt like a friend, and Paul van Daan had always been very serious about fostering camaraderie among his men. On this mission, with only three men, it was important that they trusted each other.

Michael was pleasantly drunk when he left the tavern. Antonio had elected to remain for the night, but Giles appeared just as Michael was standing outside, inhaling the cool night air and trying to clear his head.

"Drunk on duty, O'Reilly?"

"More than a little, sir. Yourself?"

"Definitely jug-bitten. Antonio is still closeted away with the lovely Maria and let out a stream of Spanish abuse when I banged on the door. He'll be back when he's sobered up, she'll look after him. Jesus, it gets cold at night at this time of year, I should have brought my cloak. Never mind, we shall march, Captain, although possibly not in a straight line."

He offered Michael his arm, and Michael took it. They made their way carefully down the cobbled streets, stumbling over raised stones and bumping into each other when they fell out of step. Michael grew warm with the walk, and thought about the evening. The woman had been attractive, older than Michael, with a mass of dark, untidy hair and a generous smile. She had shared supper and wine and then her bed with uncomplicated friendliness that probably earned her a fortune with lonely soldiers far from home. Michael added a generous tip and was thinking of her, still smiling, as they staggered finally into the narrow street where their billet was located.

"We did it," Giles said, in pleased tones.

"By a bloody miracle. Couldn't tell if you were holding me up or tripping me up there."

Giles started to laugh and after a moment, Michael joined him although he could not remember what was funny. After a few minutes, a shutter above banged open, and a man's voice yelled in furious Spanish. Giles called up apologies, his voice still shaking with laughter and the shutter closed with an indignant crash.

"Making friends with the locals," Giles said. "Oh Jesus, I'm drunk. Thank God we don't have to sail tomorrow, I'd die."

"We've still got to get up those stairs," Michael pointed out. "They're very steep."

"Might end up doing it on hands and knees," Giles said seriously and Michael started to laugh again.

"I need a piss first. And I'm going to check on the horses."

"You're a very cons...cons...a good officer, O'Reilly. I shall come with you. It's my duty."

"Well done, sir."

"Need to stop calling me sir," Giles said earnestly. "Keep looking behind me for the general, 's making me nervous. Name is Giles. I shall call you Michael. Don't need a pissing contest about who's in charge unless it's an emergency."

"Too drunk for a pissing contest."

"Good time to have one."

They were laughing again as they rounded the edge of the stable door. All three horses were in their stalls, dimly outlined in the darkness. Michael relieved himself against the stable wall and waited for Giles to finish doing the same. At the last moment, Michael turned back towards the stalls.

"Where're you going, Michael?"

"Just checking, sir. Giles. Got a suspicious mind when it comes to Sligo."

"Good Irish name. Mine's Boney. After Bonaparte. Thought it was funny in England. Not so funny out here."

Michael was laughing again. He went into the stall and looked around, then went to his horse and ran a hand down the sleek neck. One of the lads must have groomed the horse after the long ride, brushing out his silvery mane and tail, and he reminded himself to tip the groom in the morning. In the next stall, Giles was leaning against Boney, talking softly to him. It sounded like gibberish to Michael, but he supposed the horse did not care. He was fiercely grateful for this evening and when he was sober enough, he would tell the younger man so. Whatever the following weeks might bring, he felt considerably better about his relationship with his companion.

Eventually, Giles heaved himself up. "Right. Just the stairs, and then I can sleep until noon. Michael, you're excused all duties until I wake up and think of some."

He moved towards the stable door and Michael followed. Suddenly, Giles froze. "Did you hear that?"

Michael had not, but the other man's manner cleared his head abruptly. He stood very still. Giles did not move, but stood listening intently. After a moment, he turned to Michael and pointed to the far end of the stable. There was a second door there. Michael nodded and slipped past Giles out of the stable. Suddenly he was more sure footed and he ran around the outside of the long wooden building to the other end and stood guarding the door as Giles made his way down the aisle between the stalls, searching each one. Michael could hear him moving and wondered if his companion's drunken imagination had got the better of him, when he heard Giles speak in fluent Spanish:

"There you are. Out, you little bastard, let's see what we've got."

There was a scuffle and the thump of something hitting the wooden wall, and Giles gave a yell of pain. Michael opened the door and moved inside just as a slight figure emerged from the end stall and headed towards him. Michael stood ready, but the emergency had sobered his companion, and Giles was on his feet, scooping up the boy into strong arms before swinging him around and throwing him back into the stall. There was a scream of pain and then silence. Michael felt a sudden chill. He closed the door behind him and moved forward.

"Giles, who is that?"

"God knows, probably a horse thief."

The crumpled figure lay at the back of the empty stall among the hay. Michael moved forward cautiously, cursing the darkness and his own drunken clumsiness. "How hard did you hit him, Giles?"

71

"I don't fucking know, Michael, I'm drunk and he rammed his head into my gut. I was just trying to stop him. Is he all right?"

There was anxiety in the other man's tone that reassured Michael. He knelt down beside the unconscious figure and felt his head, waiting for his eyes to adjust to the darkness. A pale face, framed by curly hair gradually became visible. Michael could feel the stickiness of blood in the hair. He blinked and then blinked again and forced himself to focus and suddenly he knew why that scream had bothered him so much.

"Is he all right?" Giles said again.

"No, he's unconscious. And it's not a boy."

"Of course it's a boy…"

"It's bloody not, but I don't blame you for thinking it is. It's Brat. It's my servant."

Michael carried Brat up the steep stairs to the room he was sharing with Giles. He was abruptly sober, with a throbbing headache and a sick feeling in his stomach. Giles trod behind him silently. Michael laid her on his narrow bed and bent over her feeling through the unruly chestnut curls for the wound. There was a definite bump but the bleeding had stopped.

"Is it bad?"

"I don't think so, she's got a fair bit of hair to cushion the blow. Pass me that washcloth, will you?"

Giles did so and Michael wiped the cold cloth over Brat's face. To his relief, he saw her eyelids flicker and then she opened her eyes, looking up at him confusedly.

"Captain."

"Welcome back, Brat."

"I hit my head," Brat said, lifting her hand to feel the bump. "I don't remember…oh."

Michael stepped back, his eyes on her face. He watched memory return, and with it a flood of colour to her face. Silently, he returned the cloth to the wash stand then turned and looked at Brat who was sitting up cautiously.

"Captain, I am sorry."

"You had bloody better be," Michael said furiously. "What in God's name are you doing here, hiding in a stable on your own? How many times have we talked about this?"

"I cannot count the times, sir."

Michael heard what he suspected was a snort of laughter from Giles, which did not help his bad temper. "What are you doing here?"

"I followed you."

"How, for God's sake? We rode here, and we rode fast, your mule would not have got you here that quickly."

There was a long silence. Brat's pale face was scarlet and she looked as though she was going to be sick. Michael was torn between concern and fury, but he folded his arms grimly and waited.

"I borrowed a horse. I am a good rider, I told you."

"You stole a horse?"

"Borrowed. I will return it, of course," Brat said, with great dignity. "My head aches."

"So does mine."

"That is because you have been drinking. My head struck the stable wall."

Giles made another snorting sound. "I'm very sorry about that, lass, I thought you were a horse thief. Look, Michael, I'm sorry to be difficult, but I really need to sleep. I've no idea what your arrangement is with your er…servant, but could you…"

"She's my servant, nothing more," Michael growled. "Brat, I've no idea what you're doing here, and I'm telling you that you're going straight back, but right now we need to sleep. Get yourself into that bed over there, Antonio won't be back until the morning."

"I can sleep in the stable, sir."

"Do as you're bloody told. I'll deal with you in the morning. Christ, my head aches."

Giles was laughing. "Mine too. Have some brandy and water, Michael, it'll ease the worst of it."

Michael took the glass and drained it. "I'm sorry about this."

"Don't be. I'm just relieved she isn't worse hurt, I'd no idea." Giles looked over at Brat. "You'd best get yourself under the blankets and hide your eyes, Brat, because I'm not sleeping in my clothes when I don't need to. In the morning, when he's sober, Captain O'Reilly will bend his mind to getting you back to where you're supposed to be. Good night."

***

Giles woke to sunlight falling directly onto his face, and groaned aloud. They had not closed the shutters and there were no curtains or blinds at the windows. Giles lay still, his arm over his eyes to blot out the light and tried to pretend that he did not need to move, although he knew that he was going to need the chamber pot.

There was a movement across the room and then a retching sound. Giles grinned, despite his pain, reflecting that it was clear that Captain O'Reilly was in a worse case than him. It probably meant that he would have to go outside to use the latrine, though, so he sat up, looked across the room and blinked in surprise. Michael's bed was empty but the figure bending over the pot was not the Irishman, but a leggy girl with short auburn curls, dressed in trousers and a loose shirt. She was vomiting distressingly, holding on to the bedpost for support, and Giles swung his legs over the bedside and reached for his trousers, pulling them on quickly. He padded barefooted over the rough boards.

"Are you all right?"

The girl looked round, wide-eyed and Giles winced at the sight of her face. One side was sporting the beginnings of a darkening bruise and she was white, with dark circles under her eyes.

73

"Oh bloody hell, did I do that?"

"My head hurts. It hit the stable wall, I think."

She was shivering, and Giles surveyed the room then picked up the enamel bowl from the wash stand, went to the window and emptied it. He returned to the girl. "Up onto the bed, you're going to fall over in a minute. Have you a cloak with you? Never mind, put mine round you for now, you need to keep warm. Here, under the blankets and hold the basin on your lap in case you're sick again. I'm going to find Michael."

Giles found the Irishman in the dining room, drinking mild ale and eating bread and cheese. He rose as Giles entered.

"How's your head?"

"Hurting. But not as badly as your brat, Michael, she's casting up accounts in the washbasin at present."

Michael froze. "She's ill? She was still asleep when I came down. What in God's name...?"

"I've seen it happen before with a blow on the head. Don't look so panicked, Michael, it's not serious, but she should rest for a day or two before she attempts the journey back. Finish your meal, I've asked the landlord's wife to go up to her, she'll get her cleaned up and make her comfortable, she needs a woman."

Michael sat down again. "God only knows what I'm going to do with her," he said. "Bad enough that she rode here alone, anything could have happened to her."

"Don't worry about it. The landlady here can look after her for a few days while the horses are resting and then she can travel back with the grooms and our horses, to explain herself to whoever she stole that horse from."

"Borrowed, Giles," Michael said seriously, and Giles laughed aloud and reached for the bread.

"Do you know who it was?"

"I do, I went into the stables for a look this morning. I can't believe I didn't see him last night, but of course I was seriously castaway and wasn't looking. It's Mondego, Colonel Wheeler's second mount."

"The piebald gelding? Jesus Christ, he has to be too strong for her, I'm surprised she didn't break her silly neck."

"She can ride," Michael said. "But it was a mad-brained thing to do, and not for the first time."

Giles summoned the waiter for more ale. "What in God's name is the story with this girl, Michael? You do know what army gossip says, don't you?"

"I can guess," Michael said. "The general tells me it's a judgement on me for too many years of womanising. Although how he can say it with a straight face, given his younger days, is a mystery to me."

Giles grinned. "I've only ever known him since he was married to Mrs van Daan, Michael, it's hard to imagine him looking at another woman."

"Well trust me, he did a lot more than bloody look before he met her. His poor first wife. As for me, I'm single and likely to stay that way, and yes, I like the women. But Brat isn't one of them. I picked her up in Madrid last year, she'd been raped and beaten bloody in some alley."

"Oh Jesus."

"She'd been living on the streets, she came from a farm outside the city until the French killed her father. Begging, finding work when she could and selling herself to the soldiers of both sides when she grew desperate enough. Mrs van Daan patched her up and we found her work at headquarters. When we marched out, I thought I'd seen the last of her, but she followed the army, showed up in some filthy little village in the rain. I couldn't turn her away, she'd have died. She was terrified to stay in Madrid when the French returned."

"I don't blame her."

"Mrs van Daan tried to help, but she'd latched onto me, I don't know why. The general said he thought it was because I was the first man who'd tried to help her without expecting payment in kind. It was nothing to me, a casual act, but it meant everything to her. She trusted me, I suppose. Anyway, she stayed with me for the retreat, took care of my baggage mule, acted as my servant. When we got to Ciudad Rodrigo, Mrs van Daan stepped in again. Bought her women's clothing and found her work in one of the convents, in the kitchen."

"And?"

"She turned up a few weeks later on the doorstep of the quinta, back in boys clothing and soaked to the skin, she'd walked from Ciudad Rodrigo to find me. She didn't trust the nuns to protect her, she said they wouldn't be able to protect themselves. You'll think I'm mad, Giles, but she was so bloody desperate. I gave her a job through winter quarters. I thought that a few months of security would give her a chance to settle. I knew it would take time, but I didn't expect this."

Giles could not help smiling at the other man's expression. "I'm impressed, Michael, I've never had a servant that devoted to me. Does she have a name? Other than Brat?"

"Ariana."

"Very grand."

"I called her brat at the start, and it sort of stuck. To be honest, I wasn't keen on yelling 'Ariana' every time I want my boots cleaned. Not that it matters, because I know what people think. It's probably what you're thinking."

"You couldn't make up a tale that unlikely. Poor lass, she must have been terrified beyond reason. God knows what happened to her to make her that scared."

"I prefer not to think about it too much."

"Or me. She'll be all right. I'll speak to old Lopez and leave him some money for her keep for a few days until they're ready to ride back to Freineda. I doubt Colonel Wheeler will be back by then, but she's going to get an earful from the general for taking that horse."

"I'll write to him." Michael shook his head. "She's a bloody responsibility."

"How old is she?"

"I'm not sure I've ever asked. Older than I first thought, she was half-starved when I found her. Seventeen or so, maybe?"

"She's going to make a very attractive girl when she finally gets back into skirts."

The Irishman glared at him. "That's not how I see her."

"It's how the rest of the army is going to see her, Michael."

"Do you think I don't bloody know that? It's the reason I dread her going off on one of her madder exploits. Anybody could have found her hiding in that stable." Michael rose, draining his tankard. "I'm going to see how she is, and try to talk some sense into her. Do you need me for anything?"

"No. I'm going down to see the district commissary to arrange supplies for the next part of the journey. Once we arrive in Corunna, we're very much in Spanish territory and they'll fleece us for everything we need, so I'd rather carry as much as we can."

"Thank you. I mean really, thank you, Giles. You've been bloody good about this, you must think I'm mad."

"Servant or not, Michael, she's clearly your responsibility. We'll make sure she gets back safely. I'll see you later."

***

The port of Corunna sat neatly on a promontory on the coast of northwest Spain. Michael had never been to the town and stood at the ship's rail as the *Collins* approached, watching the shore grow closer. Lieutenant Greene, with one eye on his crew as they brought the ship in, pointed out the tall tower of the old Roman lighthouse which commanded impressive views along the coast.

"You weren't with Moore at the battle?"

"No," Michael said. "Captain Fenwick was still with the second battalion then. Most of our first battalion was there, and I've heard the stories, it must have been hell on that retreat. How they managed a victory that day, the condition they were in, I've no idea. As for me, I was in Lisbon with several companies badly afflicted with camp fever. We thought we were missing out at the time. Now, I'm just grateful."

"We'll dock in about an hour."

"Thank you," Giles said. "We'll be staying at the inn at the corner of the Rua San Benito, they know me there and our hired horses should be waiting for us. You've been very helpful, Lieutenant Greene, I appreciate it."

"Always happy to help out the army," Greene said, with a hint of irony. Giles responded with a warm smile.

"In my experience that's very true, Lieutenant, I've one or two good friends in the navy. Thank you."

76

"You're welcome. I'm hoping that if we can unload quickly, we can make this evening's tide, I've orders to join my squadron as soon as possible."

The quayside was bustling with activity as Michael, Giles and Antonio scrambled up from the ship's boat. Giles thanked the sailors who had rowed them ashore and slipped them several small coins, then led the way through the crowd, with Michael lengthening his stride to keep up.

"I'm learning a lot from you," he said. "Is this how you manage your Spanish allies?"

Giles shot him a surprised look. "Pretty much. Nobody here needs to do anything for me at all. I'm not their senior officer, they don't owe me obedience, and at times they're putting themselves in danger to help me, shelter me or provide me with information. So being pleasant, saying thank you, and tipping generously is the only way I get anything done. It becomes a habit."

"It'll never catch on in the army, Giles."

"That's why I'm better off out here."

The inn was in the heart of the medieval quarter of Corunna, a maze of narrow cobbled lanes, opening out onto impressive squares, and beautiful churches with soaring spires. The landlord was thin, long faced and bespectacled, and greeted Giles with a silent nod then led the way up three flights of stairs to a long attic room with four bunks and a sturdy lock on the door. Michael dumped his kit bag onto one of the bunks while Giles held a brief, low voiced conversation with his host. When the landlord had left, Giles joined Michael and Antonio.

"Father Cordoba has done his job, the horses are in the stable and we can eat here later. I'd like to set off tomorrow if possible, the horses will be well rested and ready to go. In the meantime, we're going to visit Father Cordoba who is the priest at St Tomas Church in the old quarter. He's a mine of useful information and he has a chain of informants in the villages eastwards towards the hills. I'd like to catch up on the gossip before we set out." Giles studied Michael for a moment. "Are you nervous?"

Michael opened his mouth to refute the suggestion and then paused. "Yes," he said. "It's new to me."

"Good. Personally, I'm bloody terrified every time I set off into those hills without knowing what the hell I'm riding into. Come on, I need a drink, and you can guarantee Cordoba will have more than communion wine stashed away in his study."

Father Cordoba greeted Giles and Antonio as old friends, and led them through into his study where he produced an excellent port and looked enquiringly at Michael.

"Father, this is Captain Michael O'Reilly. He's new to the work but he's not new to the army and his Spanish and French are both very good. Michael, I think you'll keep up, but if you've a question, just ask. Father Cordoba speaks some English, but he isn't fluent so from now on, we'll speak his language."

"Thank you," Michael said, and Giles turned back to the priest. "What news, Father?" he asked, in Spanish.

The conversation lasted an hour, and Michael's only part in it was to listen intently. Michael had come to languages late. His studies at Trinity College in Dublin had given him a good working knowledge of Greek and Latin but nothing else. He had picked up a smattering of one of the local Indian dialects and a few words of Danish during his early career but had been too lazy to really try until he found himself briefly prisoner of the French in a barn in Portugal and realised the advantages of knowing the language. His French had improved rapidly with Anne's help and his Spanish was very fluent after his months in Madrid last year, where he had made friends in the city. Following Father Cordoba's rapid conversation took all Michael's concentration, but at the end of the hour, he felt far better informed about the current situation in these northern provinces of Spain.

The northern lands, which included Naverre, the Basque provinces and the mountains around Santander and Burgos, were of vital importance to the French, because the great road from Bayonne to Madrid was the main communication route. For several years, Spanish partisans had been making life difficult for the French in this area, led by Mina to the west, Jauregui in Biscay and Porlier to the west around Santander, while Longa, under the theoretical command of General Mendizabal and the Spanish seventh army, had proved a serious problem with a series of lightning raids on French convoys, which disrupted post and supplies for weeks at a time.

The previous year, the guerrillas had received substantial help from a British navy squadron under the command of Sir Home Popham. Popham had worked with the Spanish irregular forces along the coastline to attack the much depleted French garrisons, and with guns and additional men provided by the Royal Navy, and the French stretched to their limits by Wellington's successes further south, a number of small ports were taken by the combined forces, culminating in the taking of Santander at the beginning of August.

With the enforced retreat of Wellington, the Spanish garrisons had been obliged to withdraw from most of the coastal strongholds and the French had returned, but the area was far from pacified. For a time, during that year, Mina had held full possession of most of the countryside and had raised taxes, established courts of justice and even set up a customs border for trading non-military goods with France. Michael was astonished at how far the Spanish irregulars had come in their attempts to take back their lands from the French.

"So where are we now, Father?" Giles asked, when the priest finally stopped speaking.

"Our tide has gone out it is true, but nothing has been swept away, merely left dry for a little. We hear that the Emperor is unhappy and has demanded that the Army of the North does its job and chases these Spanish peasants back into hiding again. Caffarelli managed to regain possession of the great road, and drove our men from Bilbao and all of the coastal towns except Castro Urdiales, which still holds. He raised the blockade of Santona, but as soon as he moved on, Longa's men returned to their positions around the town.

Now the great road is once more at a standstill because of Spanish raids, many of Caffarelli's men are tied down in garrisons and Bonaparte is furious and has appointed a new commander."

"Do we know who?"

"Clausel. He has been in France, but will be returning very soon, with orders to achieve what Caffarelli could not."

"Which is?"

"To slaughter us, Captain Fenwick," the priest said, and his voice was hard. "And to prevent that, we must slaughter them first."

"And you know nothing of this English diplomat?"

"I have heard nothing, but the border with France is many miles away, news takes time to reach me. Where do you begin your search?"

"I want to make contact with Porlier, if I can. I know him personally, and even if he knows nothing of Grainger, he'll be able to put me in touch with Longa's forces."

"It is a long and hard journey in the mountains in winter. Is it worth it, Captain, for a man who is probably already dead?"

"My government thinks so, Father, and I go where they send me."

Outside, the shadows had lengthened and the air was becoming cooler, although the sky was still clear and blue. They walked in silence down the steep road, pausing to allow a contingent of Spanish troops to march across their path. The Spanish officer, noticing their uniforms, called his men to salute and Giles and Michael returned it. When the way was clear they resumed their walk back to the inn and Giles led the way through the tap room into a small private room at the back. The landlord brought a jug of wine with cups and set it on the table between them.

"Have the horses been fed, Gonzalez?"

"They have, Señor. My groom fed and watered them."

"Thank you, we'll check on them after we've eaten."

Michael was pouring the wine. He looked at Giles. "Are we expecting a guest, Giles?"

"A guest?" Giles appeared to notice the fourth cup. "Oh - no. A mistake, I suppose. You can take it away, Gonzalez."

"Your pardon, Señor, I thought your friend would join you."

Suddenly Giles was alert. "Friend? What friend?"

"The boy, Señor. He arrived while you were out."

"From where?"

"From the ship, Señor," the landlord stammered. "I do not understand, he said he was with you. A Spanish boy."

Michael could not bring himself to look round at Giles. "I see. Thank you. Where is the boy now?"

"I sent him to the kitchen, Señor, for some food. He was not well, he had been sick at sea, he said, being down in the hold the whole voyage."

Michael turned on his heel and walked through the inn. The kitchen was at the back, a wooden lean-to which smelled strongly of stew and spiced sausage. There was a rickety table with benches, and at one side, Brat was

79

seated, mopping up the remains of her meal with a piece of bread. She looked up as Michael, Giles and Antonio entered the room, crowding the small space, and got to her feet, stepping away from the bench. Michael stood looking at her, and she looked back steadily, head held high, her eyes full of apprehension. Michael wished wholeheartedly that she was the boy she seemed, because he very much wanted to box her ears for her. He also thought, with a sudden sense of panic, that she looked nothing like a boy at all.

"How did you get Lieutenant Greene to let you on board?" Michael asked.

"I did not. I simply waited until they were busy and hid."

"And this end?"

"When we docked, I waited until you left the ship and then came out of hiding. The sailors did not know you had no servant with you, they thought my sickness had delayed me and told me how to find this inn. They were in a hurry to unload."

Michael looked over at the landlord. "Is the ship still in port?"

"No, Señor, I could see the sail from my window, they only stayed to unload and to take on water and supplies."

"This is bloody ridiculous!" Giles exploded. "What in God's name are we going to do with her now? Don't you have any control over her at all, O'Reilly? Bad enough to have to leave her in Oporto, but at least she had the grooms to get her back where she should be. Who the hell are we going to leave her with in Corunna?"

Michael's eyes were on Brat's face. He could read, with absolute clarity, her desperate terror and see the pleading in her eyes.

"Brat, you should have stayed," he said softly. "I know how frightened you are, but Mrs van Daan and Miss Trenlow had both agreed to keep an eye on you, and Jenson would never let anything happen to you. You were safe there, and now you're in danger, whatever we decide."

"I am sorry, Captain."

"You're always bloody sorry, Brat, but it doesn't help."

"I can be useful."

"Useful?" Giles bellowed. "You've no bloody idea what we're going into, you stupid girl! We're riding hard and fast and we'll be dodging French patrols and living rough and probably dodging a few of the Spanish as well. I need men I can trust, not a leggy brat who can't work out if she's a boy or a girl, and has no idea..."

"Me, I have an idea!" Brat shouted suddenly, and the change from apologetic meekness, to spitting fury, was so shocking that it silenced even Giles. "It is I who am Spanish, not you. It is I who came from these villages, where men fight and die, and whole families are killed by the French because one man stood up to them. My father was such a man and I watched him die. You have never stood in your own home and seen the blood of your father on the ground and known what they were about to do to you. Do not tell me what I know and do not know, and do not tell me where I can be and not be, I am tired of it. This is my land, not yours. Also, I can ride as well as you can, and I am willing to prove it."

Nobody spoke for a long moment. Brat looked at Michael. "I will answer to Colonel Wheeler for his horse when he returns, and if he wishes to flog me for the theft, he has the right, but the grooms will take the horse back with the others, it will be safe. I could not stay. I could not stay where they watch me and they smile behind their hands, and they think that you keep me with you because I share your bed. Because they also think that when you are gone, I will share theirs, and I will not. Nor will I hide behind doors, like Miss Trenlow, when the officers of other regiments treat her like a prostitute because she is not married and the others do not care. I do not trust those men, and I do not trust other women to protect me, because they cannot protect themselves. I am here, because I am your servant, and where you go, I go. And there is no hardship or danger that I cannot accept."

The silence lengthened in the room. Michael could not take his eyes from her. She had grown up before his eyes, and he had no idea what to say or do.

Inevitably it was Brat who spoke first. "If you will not take me with you, I will remain here until you return. I can find work."

"No," Michael said.

"O'Reilly, don't be an arsehole," Giles said furiously.

"Sorry, sir, I can't help it. She's right. I wish to God she hadn't come, but she's here now, and I'm not leaving her unprotected in a town she doesn't know. I do apologise for putting you in this position. If she comes with us, she's right. She won't hold us back, she'll make herself useful and I'd trust her with my life. If you can't agree to that, I wholly understand, but I'm not leaving her here alone. I'll stay with her and get her back safely."

"Are you out of your mind? You don't get to make that choice, you're an officer of this army and you've been given a job to do. If you don't do it, you'll have deserted your post, and you'll be up before a court martial and they'll bloody cashier you."

"Very likely, sir, but it won't cost me anything since I had my commissions without purchase anyway. And if they take my commission away…well, I was a damned good sergeant."

"Michael, for fuck's sake, act your age."

"I'm sorry, sir. I really am. But I can't leave her here alone."

Giles rolled his eyes and made a faint growling noise in his throat. "Stop bloody calling me sir, I thought we'd dealt with that?"

"We have. Giles, just one question. If I'd turned up here with a servant, a Spanish boy of this age, who'd lost his family to the French and had proved his loyalty and his courage on that retreat back from Madrid, would we be having this conversation?"

Giles glared at him. "No," he said finally. "But it is not the same thing. She is not a boy, and she doesn't even look like one. Look at her, for Christ's sake! I can't believe the general has let you get away with this."

"The general doesn't think it's his business as long as I do my job. I'm willing to do my job, Giles. Give me a chance."

"She is not bloody well coming with us, it's ridiculous."

"Well, I'm not leaving her here alone. Anything could happen to her."

"Good. She bloody deserves it."

"If I thought you meant that, we'd be having a different conversation."

"Oh dear God, tell me you aren't intending to challenge me over a Spanish peasant girl whose reputation must be so far beyond defending that…"

"You keep this up, boy, and I'm more likely to punch you than challenge you, I wouldn't waste the effort. Is that the attitude you usually take with the local women?"

Giles moved forward and seeing his expression, Michael shifted his weight slightly, ready to defend himself, but they were interrupted by a crash, which made both of them jump. Michael turned to see Antonio, holding a cooking skillet in one hand and an iron poker in the other. The Spaniard hit the skillet again and the sound reverberated through the room. The quarrel had driven the inn staff out of the kitchen and only Antonio and Brat remained. Antonio put down his improvised drum and raised the poker menacingly.

"If you continue to argue like *niños traviesos,* I will strike you instead of this pan," he said flatly. "This is not a quarrel about this girl, it is a quarrel about who is the bigger man, and I tell you both that I will not travel through enemy country with two such big men, for they make so much noise that the French will hear them coming for miles. Me, I think it will be better if you both go back to Oporto and I will take this Spanish girl, to find this Englishman, for she may be more use."

"I will be more use," Brat said mutinously, and Michael glared at her and then at Giles. Giles was looking at Antonio. To Michael's surprise, he sighed.

"Put the poker down, Antonio, before I shove it up your arse."

"You are welcome to try, Englishman."

"Put it down. I'm over it."

Antonio surveyed him thoughtfully for a moment, then returned his weapon to the fireplace. Giles turned to Michael. "I'm sorry. I didn't mean that. Of course…"

"It wasn't me you insulted."

Giles looked as though he was restraining himself with an effort, but he turned to look at Brat. "I'm sorry, that was a stupid and thoughtless thing to say, I was angry. I'm still angry, but of course I don't wish harm to you. I just don't want to take responsibility for you either."

The apology surprised Michael and Brat seemed taken aback as well. After a brief silence, she gave a dignified nod. Giles turned back to Michael.

"What I ought to do, is leave you behind to face the consequences of this piece of idiocy."

"It's entirely up to you. You didn't want me to come anyway."

Giles shot him a surprised glance, then gave a twisted smile. "No, I didn't. But I've revised my opinion, I think you might be useful."

"I have an idea," Antonio said.

"Go on."

"On the route we have chosen, there are two - no, three convents, where we will spend the night. They will offer safe haven to a young girl."

Michael glanced at Brat and read her expression with disastrous clarity. "I hate to break it to you, Antonio, but I've tried leaving Brat at a convent before. It didn't go well."

"She may feel differently on this journey, for as Giles says, it will be very hard, and in winter conditions. Take her with us, Giles. I will find another pony for her. If she is as strong as she says, and does not slow us down, then what harm to take a Spanish servant with us. If it proves too much for her, she can remain with the nuns, until Captain O'Reilly can arrange to have her escorted back to the army. At least with them, she will be safe and protected, more than in a strange inn in an unknown town."

Nobody spoke. It was a simple solution, which saved face on all sides. Michael watched Giles' struggle between seeing the sense of it and wanting to assert his authority. Reassuringly, common sense won, and Giles gave a curt nod of agreement.

"All right, we'll try it. It's your job to supervise her, Michael, and if she's holding us back, she stays behind with the nuns, I can't have her risking this mission."

"I will not," Brat said.

"We'll see. Michael, you've a day to get her properly equipped and supplied and I'm not bloody paying for it."

Giles was scowling at him and Michael felt suddenly very sorry for the younger man, who had enough on his plate and should not have had to deal with this. "I'll see to it, sir."

"I can't believe you're going to risk losing your commission over a skinny Spanish brat when you're not even sleeping with her."

Michael felt a flash of anger and suppressed it firmly. He knew perfectly well that in Giles' position he would have thought the same thing. "Well I'm not, Giles. As for the rest, wouldn't you risk your commission for Antonio?"

"Antonio has proved his worth, Michael, many times over."

"Let me prove mine, Captain," Brat said, and Giles rolled his eyes then turned his ferocious scowl onto her.

"You're not going to make it beyond the first few days in those conditions."

"And you, do not know very much about women," Brat said, with alarming composure. "You think we are weaker than you because we do not carry swords and shoot guns. And I think we are stronger than you, because if you watch the women in camp, they are carrying children and baggage so that their men may swagger with their swords and their guns. And sometimes they carry those also when the poor men get too tired. I will not slow you down."

"See that you don't," Giles said, and there was a suspicious gruffness to his voice which made Michael wonder suddenly if he was trying not to laugh. You'll have to sleep down here tonight."

"I will sleep by the fire, I am used to it."

"Good. Is there any chance I can get some food now? It's been a long day and I'm bloody starving."

Michael put his hand on the younger man's shoulder. "Lead the way. I am sorry, Giles. And thank you. You're not going to regret this."

"I probably am," Giles said grimly. "The drinks, by the way, are on you, Captain O'Reilly."

He stalked out of the kitchen and Michael looked at Brat. She gazed back steadily. "I am sorry that he is angry with you, Captain, and that it is my fault."

"You are going to cost me a commission's worth of favours before this campaign is over, Brat, I swear to God. Finish your meal and get some rest. In the morning, we'll see to some supplies for you. And you'll need something warmer to wear, it's going to get bloody cold up in those mountains."

"I will take her, Captain."

Michael looked around in surprise at Antonio. The Spaniard smiled. "A red coat in a Spanish market with a young girl, they will think she is your woman and fleece you. Me, they will see I have no money and feel sorry for me, that this girl takes advantage of me. Give me a good price."

Michael gave a splutter of laughter and Brat turned furious eyes onto the Spaniard. "They will think nothing of the sort, Señor Antonio," she said scornfully. "They will look at your face and think that no girl would take up with a Cantabrian with a face like a monkey, so they will think you are my father and be sad that you are so old and so grumpy."

"They will look at my face and think that no man so good and so wise could have such a daughter, with the tongue of a viper and the sense of a wood pigeon."

"And then they will laugh, because while you preen like a peacock of your wisdom and your goodness, they will have picked your pocket and left you penniless." Brat turned back to Michael and unexpectedly gave him one of her sunniest smiles, which always left him slightly breathless. "Do not fear, Captain. You shall help Captain Fenwick tomorrow, and I will go with this poor, foolish Cantabrian pig farmer to show him how to barter in the market and keep him safe."

Antonio was grinning broadly. He opened his mouth and Michael held up a hand firmly. "Enough, both of you. I'm going to get my dinner. If you want to stay and trade insults with her, Antonio, you're very welcome, but I'm warning you, you'll tire before she does. Goodnight, Brat. Stay inside and behave yourself."

Chapter Six

Lord Wellington returned from Cadiz and Lisbon towards the end of January and surprised Paul, arriving at Santo Antonio on a bright winter morning to find Paul scowling over the mail while his quartermaster filled out the monthly sick return and Anne was writing to her sister. Wellington paused in the doorway as the two men saluted, and Anne put down her pen and came forward, hands outstretched.

"Welcome back, my Lord. How was your journey?"

"Unpleasant," Wellington said, raising her hand to his lips. "Good morning, ma'am, how are you? And how is my god daughter?"

"Growing fast. Come and see."

Wellington moved to the basket, his expression softening as he studied the sleeping baby. "She is very pretty, ma'am. I hope the wet nurse is proving satisfactory?"

Paul glanced at Ross, suppressing a smile at the Scot's expression at the sight of the commander of the forces discussing Anne's nursery arrangements in painstaking detail. He waited until Wellington had satisfied himself that both Anne and Georgiana were well, then moved to bring a chair for Wellington.

"It's good to see you, sir, it's been very quiet around here. May I introduce you to Captain Ross Mackenzie, my new quartermaster?"

Ross saluted and Wellington regarded him affably. "Very good to meet you, Captain. I believe I may have seen your wife and children on my way in, Sergeant Jenson informs me they're spending the winter with you."

"Yes, my Lord, I was grateful to General van Daan for allowing it."

Wellington snorted. "You will be fortunate if General van Daan does not co-opt them into service, sir, he should really pay his wife a salary for the work she does."

Anne laughed. "I'm very idle at the moment, sir."

"As you should be, ma'am, you need time to recover. You must be eager for the arrival of your other children."

"I cannot wait, although I am enjoying Captain Mackenzie's in the meantime. I am sure you wish to be private with General van Daan, so I will take Georgiana to her nurse and then Captain Mackenzie and I will join the children in the stables, they are getting to know the new ponies."

Wellington waited until the door closed and then turned a suspicious eye onto Paul. "Where did those ponies come from, General?"

"I looted them from the local population, sir. Told the lads to take the lot but only to shoot if they fought back. Would you like a drink? How was Lisbon?"

"Oh for God's sake, I have not missed you at all."

"Yes, you have, they've been toad-eating you for weeks and you can't stand it."

Wellington glared at him for a moment, then sat down and accepted a glass of madeira. "If only that were true," he said with a sigh. "Neither the Spanish nor the Portuguese government showed the least tendency to toad-eat. In fact at times, they appeared to struggle with basic courtesy. Still, the visit was useful and I think I have clarified my position. The ponies?"

"Pack animals, sir, bought and paid for, fully receipted and entered into the regimental books. He has some promising youngsters as well, but they'll not be ready until next year. I have spoken to him about your needs for the campaign and he is going to see what he can buy in. I've given Colin Campbell the details."

"After you have taken all the best stock."

"Yes, sir."

"There are rules about this, General."

"Really? Did you write a memorandum about it, sir?"

"If I did not, I shall do so immediately." Wellington looked down his long nose for a moment, then set down his glass and gave a reluctant smile. "I have missed you," he admitted. "I have also come to collect my dog."

"She's ready for you, sir, I'll get Jenson to bring her over. I'm glad your trip was worthwhile."

"Sit down and I will bore you with the details."

Paul poured himself a drink and did so. He was not bored, but even if he had been, he would have encouraged Wellington to talk. Paul was not an expert on the complex politics of the Portuguese and Spanish monarchies, but he knew that away from the careful language of letters to London and diplomatic dispatches, Wellington needed to be able to speak freely and occasionally indiscreetly to somebody.

An hour passed quickly and Paul got up to refill their glasses. Wellington gave a faint smile. "Talking politics to you is very soothing, General, it is the one time you never interrupt."

"That's because I don't know what you're talking about half the time."

"Liar," Wellington said amiably. "I received a letter from Captain Fenwick, telling me that they have arrived safely in Corunna."

"I'm glad to hear it, sir." Paul studied Wellington thoughtfully and decided not to mention the letter he had just received from Michael O'Reilly regarding the safety of his infuriating servant and the imminent return of Johnny Wheeler's spare horse.

"You are worried about O'Reilly, aren't you?"

"Yes," Paul said. "I'm worried about both of them actually, but Giles is used to this. I'm concerned that the diplomat they're looking for is actually a spy."

"Of course the damned man is a spy," Wellington said. "They would never panic this much over a diplomat. I don't know what information Grainger was carrying, but they're desperate to know if the French have him or if he's dead. And I will be honest with you, it is possible they would be happier with the latter."

"Poor bastard." Paul was silent for a long moment. He could feel a knot of sheer misery in his gut thinking about Michael. "Why Michael, sir? I understand Giles, it's his job and he's very good at it. But why O'Reilly? Was that your choice?"

"Yes," Wellington said coolly. "I told the truth, General. London wanted two officers sent as a precaution, and time is of the essence. As it happens, I had already sent out all my regular intelligence officers to scout French deployments and to map the countryside ahead of the new campaigning season. Another week and Fenwick would have gone as well, I had his assignment in mind. Given that I had to choose, I wanted one of your officers, because I trust them. I thought about Manson, but O'Reilly is older and more experienced."

Paul gave a twisted smile. "And you don't like him as much."

"I don't know him as well."

"What have you sent him into, sir?"

"I have no idea, General, that is why I am trying to be honest with you. I know he is your friend. I also know that you think I value him less because he was raised from the ranks. I find myself quite insulted by that idea. I put his name forward because I thought that a successful conclusion to this mission would open doors that might otherwise remain closed to a man from his background."

Paul stared at him in complete astonishment. "Is that why you did it?"

"Yes," Wellington said huffily.

"Jesus. I misjudged that rather badly, I'm sorry, sir."

"I accept your apology. I can see why you might have thought otherwise."

Paul could think of no reply. They sat quietly for a moment, sipping the wine. Eventually, Paul said:

"Is that everything, sir?"

"Not entirely. I wished to share something with you. The news will make its way through the army in its own time, as usual, but I know I can rely on your discretion. This reached me when I was in Lisbon, I am awaiting further details. It concerns Bonaparte's defeat in Russia."

Paul took the letter, his eyes on Wellington's face. He realised suddenly that behind Wellington's cool exterior, there was a sense of coiled excitement. "Russia?"

"Read it."

Paul read, and then read faster, skimming over one or two paragraphs to reach the conclusion. He looked up into Wellington's eyes, then looked back at the letter and read it again more slowly then handed the letter back to Wellington.

"How reliable is that information?"

"As to exact numbers, I have no idea. But I think we may trust the essence of it. Bonaparte has left the best of his army dying by the roadside in Russia."

"Do you think Joseph Bonaparte knows that?"

"I imagine he knows something by now. Certainly, I think we may expect some movement within his army very soon."

"Do you think they'll withdraw from Spain as this suggests?"

"Good God, no. Above all, I must continue to disabuse the government of that idea, it would be folly to plan our campaign based on that assumption. I think we may well look for the withdrawal of some troops, which will mean that the French will be even more over-stretched than they are now, but I intend to be very clear that we must continue to assume that Bonaparte will fight for Spain. All the same, this changes everything."

"Yes. Sir, do you think it could be the beginning of the end?"

Wellington gave an impressive snort. "What a ridiculous question, General. I have seldom heard such a foolish phrase, we will know it is the end when he is defeated. It is our job to beat him, we will leave it to historians and storytellers to make up fantastical tales about where the tide turned."

Paul could not help smiling. "You'll never lay odds on it, will you, sir?"

"I gamble my army, Paul, every time I take the field. Fenwick and O'Reilly - can they work together?"

"I think so, sir. Might be a few moments along the way, but it'll be good for them."

The door opened and Anne entered with the silvery grey hunting dog on a leash. "Here she is, sir."

Wellington snapped his fingers and Pearl trotted forward to be stroked. "Thank you, ma'am. I've been looking forward to working with her. If the weather is fine, I hope to take my pack out tomorrow, General. Will you have time to accompany me? And your wife, of course."

Paul thought about the pile of notes from his last inspection visit that needed to be written up then looked at Wellington's face. "I'd be glad to, sir," he said. "It's good to have you back."

***

Lieutenant-Colonel Carl Swanson was enjoying the rare luxury of a bath after a full day of training in miserable weather. Baths were usually taken in the huge wooden washtub belonging to the wife of Corporal Bennett, a monstrous item which was transported on campaign on the back of Mrs Bennett's long-suffering mule and which had survived numerous battles and retreats. Heating water for a bath was a long and laborious process, and most of the officers preferred to save their money and their servants' backs and make do with a daily wash and a bath in the river when possible.

The bathtub at the quinta de Santo Antonio was enormous, and took forever to fill, but was long enough to sit up with legs fully stretched. When he had arrived back in his room, soaked and muddy and miserably convinced that the new recruits taken on from the 117th were never going to learn to form square in less than twenty minutes, Carl found the bath filled, with a glorious aroma of rosemary and lavender floating up from the water and his lover awaiting him with clean towels and a glass of wine. Carl sank into the heat of the water and lay back, sipping the wine and trying to remember how he had ever survived without Keren Trenlow to take care of him.

"Is that better, Colonel?"

"It's perfect." Carl opened his eyes and found her seated on a wooden chair near the tub, sipping her own glass of wine. "You're perfect. How did you know?"

Keren laughed. "I walked out there this afternoon to watch for a bit. The rain came down, so I'm afraid I beat a cowardly retreat, but I could see it wasn't going well, and I thought you might need cheering up."

"What can I give you as a present, darling girl? There must be something."

Keren leaned forward, her dark brown hair curling in the steam rising from the bath. "I'll settle for a kiss."

Carl kissed her for a long time. The hot water was soothing, but he knew that Keren herself soothed him. There was something very peaceful about his gentle, Cornish lover that could make him feel better no matter how bad the day had been.

They had been together for almost two years now, and occasionally, when Carl allowed himself to think about it, he marvelled at how quickly the time had passed and how easily she had fitted into his life. Socially, they were worlds apart; Carl was the only son of a poor but well born country parson and his wife while Keren had been born in a miner's cottage near Truro. When her childhood sweetheart joined the 95th, Keren chose to follow him, but she had no official position and his death of fever before he ever saw a battle left her easy prey. She had accepted the protection of a drunkard, who beat her regularly until Anne van Daan had intervened.

Carl's first memories of Keren were of a shy eighteen year old, self-conscious in her borrowed clothing, acting as Anne's maidservant. Carl had always thought her pretty, but she had grown up quickly in her privileged position, learning to read and write, gaining confidence and moving gradually from maid to companion in Anne's easy-going household. Her development had been noticed by a number of Paul's officers, and there were bets being laid in the mess as to which lucky man would manage to persuade Keren Trenlow into his bed. Carl did not think his name had been on the book, but in the heightened tension of battle he had acted on impulse and Keren, to his surprise, had welcomed him. Liaisons such as theirs were common in the army, but did not last and could not be taken seriously. Carl knew that the growing and lasting attachment between the commander of Paul's first battalion and a common miner's daughter must be an exasperating social problem for his commander and his wife, and was very appreciative of the efforts they made not to show it.

As Carl relaxed, soaking away the frustrations of the day, Keren moved about the room, collecting his laundry, and setting his boots outside the door for Ned Browning, his orderly, to take for cleaning. It was difficult to imagine life without Keren now and Carl no longer tried. One day, he supposed, the long war would end, and if he survived it, he would return to England, with the boredom of barracks life and regular visits to his gentle father and eagle-eyed mother. Carl had no idea what he would do about Keren then, and the thought appalled him. He had no wish to lose her, but he could not bear the thought of hurting his very respectable parents by arriving home with an attractive mistress and possibly, by then, an illegitimate child. Keren had been briefly pregnant the previous year, although she had lost the child before she even knew that she carried it. Carl was shocked at how upset he had been, and since then he found himself watching Anne van Daan with her tiny daughter, imagining Keren with his child in her arms. Thoughts of the future bewildered him, so Carl chose to focus fully on the present. She was here with him, and that was enough.

"Are you ready to come out now, before you're as wrinkled as a prune?" Keren asked.

Carl grinned. "Too late for that. It was worth it, though, I feel much better. I'm very tempted to ask if you'll join me, but we'll be late for dinner if we do. Later though…"

"I'll hold you to that, my lover. Come on, I'll hold the towel for you."

Carl was dressing when the knock on the door surprised him. "Who is it?"

"Browning, sir. Begging your pardon, but there's a problem in the kitchen."

"The kitchen?" Carl said, baffled. "What the devil has that to do with me? Isn't Kelly there?"

"Yes, sir. He don't want the General or Mrs van Daan involved, sir. It's Mrs Stewart. She's had a bit of an accident."

Carl looked at Keren, who was frowning. Sally Stewart was married to Sergeant-Major Rory Stewart, a taciturn Scot from the 110th who had recently returned from an unofficial attachment to the 112th. The couple had two children and Sally had recently lost a young baby after the privations of the retreat from Madrid and was being employed as wet nurse to Georgiana.

Carl was sure that both Anne and Paul would want to know if something was wrong with Sally.

"I'll go," Keren said. "Come down when you're ready."

Carl finished dressing quickly and went down to the big square kitchen where Sergeant George Kelly, Paul's cook, was supervising the preparation of dinner along with several hired maidservants, and Renate Mata. Carl looked enquiringly at Kelly who grimaced.

"She's in the scullery and she's a mess. She's not going to keep this quiet, so she isn't."

Carl went through to the narrow utility area and stopped, appalled. Sally sat on a wooden kitchen stool while Keren bathed her bruised face. One eye was already beginning to blacken and Sally's lip was cut. She looked up at Carl from worried eyes.

"What the hell happened?"

Sally shook her head. "It's nothing, sir. Just a silly accident. Nothing."

"Me Da hit her," a voice said. Carl had not seen the children, sitting at the back of the room on the stone floor beside a big milk churn. "He hit Callum too."

Carl beckoned. "Over here, Callum."

The boy got up, shooting a furious look at his sister. Callum was nine, tall for his age, with his father's long bones and his mother's soft grey eyes. "It's nothing, sir. Just a smack, for talking back, like."

Carl examined Callum's face and decided the boy was probably right, although Stewart had clearly hit too hard, with finger marks still visible on Callum's smooth, slightly grubby cheek. Carl tactfully ignored the tear streaks and put his hand under Callum's chin, lifting his face for examination. "Did you talk back?"

"Yes, sir."

"And your Mother?"

Callum hesitated, clearly torn between wanting to defend his mother and protect his father. Carl gave a faint smile. "Out with it, lad, I'm going to find out anyway."

"Da's been drinking, sir. He can get a bit this way when he's drunk."

"I know it well," Carl said grimly. "There's a difference between getting a bit belligerent in the drink and beating your wife, though. All right you two. Your mother will be staying here tonight with the baby anyway, but how would you like to sleep in the kitchen for the night until your father sobers up?"

Rosie's tear-streaked face brightened. "Can we, sir?"

"Yes, as long as you don't get in Sergeant Kelly's way. I'll get Browning to fetch your bedrolls in a bit." Carl glanced at Kelly who had come to stand in the doorway. "That all right, George?"

"Aye, they can lend a hand and earn their supper. Come on, you two, come and wash your faces and I'll give you a job to do."

When the children had gone, Carl turned back to Sally Stewart, studying her compassionately. Sally was thirty-five and had borne five

91

children, only two of whom had survived. Carl could remember her from his first days with the regiment, the prettiest barmaid at the *Boat Inn* in Melton Mowbray who had married Rory Stewart and travelled the world with him. Time and childbearing had taken its toll on her slender frame and the peaches and cream complexion was tanned from years on the march, but Sally was still an attractive woman and she and Rory had always seemed a devoted couple. Stewart was known as an aggressive drunk and successive officers had warned him about fighting when he was inebriated, but Carl was not aware that he had beaten his wife or children before, and Sally's white, shocked face suggested that it was new to her as well.

"What the hell happened, Sally?"

"It's like Callum said, sir. He's been on the drink, and it's worse than usual. I was sharp with him, like, giving him a piece of my mind. I shouldn't have spoken so, I know what he's like."

"We all know what he's like, but if he's used you as a punching bag before, I've not heard of it. Are you sure there's nothing more I should know?"

"No, sir."

Carl eyed her doubtfully. "I'm not sure I believe you, Sally, but I can't force you to tell me, it's your private business. I'm going to need to tell General van Daan."

Sally looked up in alarm. "No, sir, please don't. He'll be furious, you know what he's like about this. Especially with me."

"That's exactly why I need to tell him I've dealt with it. Rory's the sergeant of Elliott's company, so I'll speak to him, but I'll deal with Rory myself. You can't hide this, Sally, Mrs van Daan is going to notice the minute she sees you, and you really don't want her getting hold of your husband, she'll geld him." Carl paused, thinking about it. "Does this have anything to do with coming back to the 110th?"

"A bit, sir. He was sergeant-major in the 112th and now he's back to company sergeant. It's a come-down."

"He's still sergeant-major, Sally. We couldn't leave him with another regiment indefinitely, but he's not lost rank."

"No, sir, but you've two sergeant-majors in the 110th now, which isn't right, and Sergeant-Major Carter is treated as senior although he's younger and was promoted later."

"I know. It was awkward for Rory, and I'm sorry for it, but we couldn't leave him with another regiment forever. Informally, Carter is seen as Brigade Sergeant-Major, and Rory as Regimental Sergeant-Major."

"There's no such thing, sir, apart from in this brigade."

"That's all that matters."

"You're not going to put him on a charge, sir? I don't want that."

"Not this time. I am going to deal with him, though, and make it very clear that if he does this again, he'll be back in the ranks in a heartbeat, I'm not bloody having this in my battalion. Are you all right?"

"Aye, sir, it looks worse than it is."

"Right. Have some dinner and get yourself up to the nursery. When Mrs van Daan sees you and shrieks, tell her I'm dealing with it. She'll accept that, and I'll talk to the general myself."

"Yes, sir. Thank you, sir. I'm that sorry."

Carl watched her go. Keren tidied away the water and cloths then joined him. "Are you going to speak to him now?"

"I need to, before Paul gets to him. I'm sorry, darling girl, I'm going to be late in for dinner. Save me some food, will you?"

"I will. Do you believe her, Carl?"

"Not entirely. I believe that Stewart is blind drunk and I believe that he feels a bit put-out about what he perceives as loss of status. But I don't believe that's why he hit her. I'm not aware that he's hit Sally before and it's my job to make sure he doesn't do it again."

Carl found Sergeant-Major Danny Carter finishing his dinner with his Spanish wife and small daughter. Carter's long face grew increasingly grim as Carl explained, and he reached for his coat. "Best deal with him before General van Daan comes after him, sir. I'll get Sergeant Hammond to give us a hand."

Rory Stewart was asleep, snoring loudly on his wooden pallet. The men of the 110th were housed in two long barns on the Santo Antonio estate. Paul preferred to keep the women and children out of barracks, but had allowed a family camp to be set up in a nearby meadow, where wives, children and camp followers were allowed to take over several crumbling farm buildings or to pitch tents and build wooden huts. An exception was made for the NCOs who had families, and Stewart occupied a partitioned area at the end of one of the barracks. Sally was a conscientious housewife, and the room was usually clean and tidy, but presently it stank of cheap grog and tobacco. Stewart's pipe lay on the floor beside him, a few glowing embers on the floor and Sergeant Hammond swore and stamped it out.

"Surprised he's not set himself on fire, the silly bugger. Look at the state of him."

"Let's wake him up, then."

Stewart grumbled as they hauled him up, and began to curse as they carried him outside into the rain. Nobody was about in the muddy yard, and Carter and Hammond dragged the Scot towards the stables, where the heavy rain had filled the big, iron water trough to overflowing, held the back of his head and dunked him several times in the brackish water.

By the third dip, Stewart was struggling violently, ready to fight. Carl nodded to his two NCOs, and they released him, so suddenly that Stewart staggered backwards and sat down in the mud. He sat for a moment, shaking his head to clear it, water spraying off him like a wet dog shaking himself, then surged to his feet, fists up. Carl waited until Stewart was close enough to touch, then punched him once, very hard. Stewart was a big man, some inches taller than Carl, but he was not sober enough to keep his feet and he fell again, measuring his length on the ground. Carl did not wait for him to get up again. He went forward, crouched down, and put the muzzle of his pistol against

Stewart's head. The gun would never fire in this weather but Carl did not think Stewart was sober enough to know it.

"Were you about to strike an officer there, Sergeant-Major Stewart?"

Stewart coughed up water. "No, sir."

"I'm glad about that, because if I thought you were, I'd put a bullet in your brain as soon as look at you. Now on your feet and let's see if we can manage a salute."

Stewart managed it, and stood swaying, with rain running down his face. Carl surveyed him with considerable distaste. "Look at the state of you. You're soaked, you're filthy and you stink. You're a disgrace to those stripes, Sergeant-Major Stewart and it would serve you bloody well right if I relieved you of them."

"Sir."

"I've just been helping my girl to patch up your wife in the kitchen, and I'm told you hit your son as well, when he tried to defend his mother. That must make you feel bloody proud of yourself, beating a woman and a nine year old boy."

Stewart did not speak. Carl walked closer. "I hope you can hear me, Stewart, because you are not getting another chance after this. You need to pull yourself together and sober up. I've no idea what your problem is and I do not care, when General van Daan sees what you've done to your wife, he is going to be bloody furious, and we both know that doesn't end well. I'm going to report this, and I'm going to tell him I've dealt with it informally. The rest is up to you. You need to prove that I've not made a mistake in trusting you this time, because if I catch you laying one finger on her again, your long years of service aren't going to matter a damn, you'll be back in the ranks and on the shittiest duties I can find for the rest of your time in the army. Are we clear?"

"Yes, sir. Sorry, sir."

"You'd bloody better be. Now get yourself cleaned up, clean that room and sleep it off. Your family is staying up at the main house for the night. I'll be conducting an inspection of your quarters before morning parade and if I find one thing out of place, you're on a charge. Dismissed."

Carl, Carter and Hammond watched his erratic progress back towards the barracks. "Think he'll find the right door, sir?" Carter asked.

"Just about. Not sure he'll remember what to do when he gets there, mind."

"Bloody idiot. Is Sally all right, sir?"

"She will be. Thanks for your help, Danny. You too, Jamie. I'd better go, I need to catch the general to tell him Stewart has been dealt with, and to persuade him not to shoot him in the head, he's got a soft spot for Sally."

"I remember that, sir," Carter said with heavy irony.

"Shut it, Carter, we do not mention that. Particularly in front of Mrs van Daan, who probably has no idea that her daughter's wet nurse went to bed with her husband many years ago. I don't think I want to be the one to tell her."

"Good idea, sir. As for Rory, I'll keep an eye on him, and Teresa can have a chat with Sally regularly to make sure things have settled down. It probably won't happen again, he's an aggressive bastard when he's had a few, but he's never been rough with Sal or the brats as far as I know. God knows what brought this on."

"I don't care as long as it doesn't happen again. I need to get over there and get to him before somebody else tells him about it. I'll see you tomorrow, Sergeant-Major."

"'Night, sir."

The dinner gong had just been sounded and the officers were making their way into dinner as Carl arrived, brushing raindrops from his coat. He found Keren awaiting him, looking charming in simple sprigged muslin. The sight of her lifted his spirits again, and he took her hand and kissed it with a formality that made her giggle.

"Heavens, you'll be bowing to me next, Carl."

A hand landed firmly on Carl's shoulder. "Lieutenant-Colonel Swanson," Paul said jovially. "You're a little damp. Been for an evening walk to check on the barracks, by any chance?"

Carl sighed. "I take it you've seen Sally?"

"My wife has seen Sally. She has sent her to bed with a cold compress on that eye, and has arranged for Callum and Rosie to spend the night in the nursery with her in case she needs help. How is Sergeant-Major Stewart, by the way?"

"Regretting his drinking habits," Carl said, leading Keren into the dining room. "Carter and Hammond gave him a bath in the horse trough and I gave him a thump and warned him this is the last chance."

"He's lucky you got to him first," Paul said grimly. "Did you find out what his problem is?"

"No. Neither he or Sally would tell me what the quarrel was about. I've taken the position that I don't care, he is not allowed to beat his wife while he serves in my battalion."

Paul clapped him on the shoulder again. "Good man, I approve of that position. Next time you speak to him, mention that if he touches her again I'm removing his stripes along with his bollocks, will you?"

"I'll remember to mention it, sir," Carl said. "Now if you'll excuse me, I need a drink and my dinner. It's been a difficult day."

"I'm afraid it's not going to get any better," his commander said apologetically. "I'm not sure if I remembered to tell you, but I'm off to Bejar the day after tomorrow, to annoy the second division, so I'm leaving you in command again. The good news is it'll keep you off the training ground in this weather. The bad news is that the monthly returns are due in, and I want you to go over Vane's books from the 115th with a very fine tooth comb. I'm not happy about the number of regimental courts martial he's held this month, I want to find out what's going on, so talk to Carlyon and Witham about it will you? And get Tyler over to dinner. I want to know what he makes of Major Vane, and I think he'll talk more easily to you than to me. In fact, Keren, you could act as hostess, I think he'd like that."

95

Carl regarded him, stunned. "Remind me again what the good news was?"

"I won't be here," Paul said soothingly. "Think of how peaceful that will be."

***

Paul had decided to take his wife to Bejar with him and Keren Trenlow approved the idea. She had come to know Anne very well, and knew that all was not well with her former mistress. Anne had recovered physically from the retreat and the birth but suffered from occasional low spirits which was very unlike her. Keren suspected boredom played a part. Anne was used to being frantically busy, and being unable to work in the hospital left her with a lot of free time on her hands. The arrival of another officers' wife had alleviated some of that, but Keren was puzzled by a slight reserve in Anne's manner with Katja Mackenzie.

Carl moved himself into the office in gloomy resignation and Keren tried not to laugh openly. Her lover loathed paperwork, and over the years of his command had developed the art of delegating as much as possible to his subordinates, but with Captain Mackenzie relatively new in post and no official quartermaster's assistant, Carl could not avoid it.

Keren had promised Anne she would watch over Georgiana, but she knew it was unnecessary. Sally Stewart was taking her duties as wet-nurse very seriously, and when Keren looked in on the nursery, she found Georgiana sleeping peacefully while Sally sat beside the crib with some sewing. Keren suspected that Sally was using her duties with Georgiana as an excuse to avoid her husband until his current bout of drinking subsided and Keren did not blame her. During her first year with the army, she had experienced the misery of living with a drunkard who was free with his fists and she was worried about Sally.

With nothing essential to do, Keren collected her market basket and set out for the village. With the frontier villages more settled, and the presence of Wellington's army as customers, pedlars and travelling salesmen were once again beginning to tour the area, bringing stocks from Lisbon and Oporto to local shops and markets and selling directly to customers where they could. Keren had received a message from the young wife of Captain Smith of the 95th to say that such a pedlar was currently staying at the tavern, and with an eye to her depleted stocks of sewing materials, she wanted to be among his earliest customers.

It was barely three miles into the village and Keren decided to walk. She had only learned to ride a year earlier, but long hours in the saddle during the last campaign had turned her into a very confident horsewoman. What she lacked, was the confidence to walk into the stables and ask the grooms to saddle up her horse. Carl had bought Lily as a gift for her, but Keren still found it difficult to see the horse as hers, to be ridden as and when she chose. She supposed it was the difference between a lady born to wealth and privilege, and

96

a girl raised in poverty in a miner's cottage. It was a fine dry day, and Keren preferred to walk than struggle with her discomfort.

It was not market day and the village was quiet. One or two officers stood around talking outside Lord Wellington's house and at the church opposite, the priest was discussing something with his sexton in the churchyard. As Keren approached the tavern, a collection of soldiers were sitting at one of the tables, and at the sight of her, several of them scrambled to their feet. Keren nodded to them and went into the dim tap room, smiling to herself. Outside of the brigade, few of the enlisted men knew who she was or anything about her circumstances, but the quality of her clothing suggested an officer's wife and she was always treated with respect.

Keren found the pedlar in a back room and was delighted with the range of his stock. She bought needles and thread and a supply of pins, and with the essentials chosen, indulged herself with a glorious range of embroidery silks. Keren loved embroidery, and as a girl, had assisted her mother who sewed up at the big house through the winter months. She bought silks and several lengths of fine lawn and cambric to make shirts for Carl and some new undergarments for herself. There was some very good white linen and Keren thought she might embroider a set of handkerchiefs for Anne, who could never find such a thing.

Haggling over the price took some time, and Keren kept a straight-face at the pedlar's chagrin when he realised that the elegantly dressed officer's lady could not be fleeced. She left with her basket full, and thought as she crossed the main square, that if she had known she would be buying this much, she would have been brave enough to ask for Lily to be saddled. It had grown warmer through the morning, with the unpredictability of late winter in Portugal and Keren hoisted the basket over her arm and set her face resolutely towards the quinta.

She was overtaken on the road by several officers on horseback, none of whom she knew. They raised their hats in some puzzlement, clearly unsure of her status. A farm cart passed, going in the opposite direction, and then another horseman came up beside her and a voice said:

"Miss Trenlow. What a delightful coincidence."

Keren's heart sank as Major Vane dismounted and fell into step beside her, leading his horse. "Major Vane. Are you on your way to Santo Antonio, sir?"

"Yes, I've some business with the officer in charge of the brigade. Who happens, I believe, to be your lover at present. How proud you must be."

Keren fixed her eyes on the road ahead and did not look at him. "You'll find Colonel Swanson in the general's office, I believe, sir. Please don't feel you need to keep me company, you may ride on."

"I don't wish to. As a gentleman, I wish I could offer to carry that very heavy looking basket, but I don't think I can manage that and my horse. What have you been buying? Surely he can at least afford a servant so that you don't have to do his marketing for him? Or is he saving money by getting you to combine the roles of maid and mistress?"

97

Keren knew that she was blushing furiously. She flashed him a look of dislike. "You're very impertinent, sir. Don't think I won't speak of it to Colonel Swanson."

"I hope you do, Keren, I'd like to hear what he's got to say to me about it. It's not as if he can challenge me to a duel over a pretty camp follower, is it?"

Keren did not reply. She could feel tears pricking behind her eyes and she blinked hard, determined not to shed them.

"Or do you think he will?"

"Why don't you ride on, Major, you've had your fun."

"You think this is the kind of fun I want to have with you? Oh, Keren, you're not that naive. Think about it. I can buy him out twenty times and not notice the dent in my pocket. He's done very nicely out of you, but it's time to trade up. I promise you, you'll have a boy to carry the basket and a maid to do your sewing for you. Just say the word."

Keren glared at him. "I'd rather do my own sewing, and I don't need a servant. Or anything else you could offer me. I'm happy, I'm where I want to be, and I would ask you to desist from pressing me with attentions that I don't welcome, sir. It's not the act of a gentleman."

"But then you're not a lady, are you, Keren?"

"Miss Trenlow."

The voice startled Keren. Locked in her own distress, she had not noticed the horseman approaching from the direction of the quinta, but she knew the voice and she looked up to see Captain Manson dismounting. Manson saluted punctiliously to Major Vane and smiled at Keren.

"Your servant, Miss Trenlow. I'm glad I met you, Colonel Swanson asked me to look out for you. He was worried about you walking back from the village, with that foot of yours barely healed, and I'm warning you he's going to ring a peal over you about not taking Lily."

"Captain Manson." Keren studied the other man and was very sure that Carl had said nothing to him and had no idea that she was walking anywhere. She wondered how much of the exchange Manson had seen as he rode towards them, and what had made him intervene, but she was passionately grateful. "Yes, it was a little silly."

"And that basket looks heavy," Manson said cheerfully. "Never mind. You shall ride, ma'am, with the basket across your knees and I'll lead him back. It's only a mile and a half."

"Oh - are you sure…"

"I'm under orders from the colonel, ma'am. Major Vane, will you ride with us?"

Vane was scowling, his eyes narrowed as he studied Manson. "No, I've wasted enough time on your commanding officer's mistress. I'll ride on and conclude my business, it won't take long."

"Capital," Manson said, with wholly false good cheer. He watched as Vane mounted, and gave a smart salute. Vane responded reluctantly and rode off and Manson turned to Keren.

"What was that bastard saying to you?"

Keren took a deep breath, trying not to cry. "Please," she said. "Captain, please, don't. Thank you so much for your assistance, but please do not mention it to Colonel Swanson. It would be so awkward for him."

Manson studied her for a long moment. "Ma'am, I don't think shoving that man's teeth down his throat would give him more than a moment's difficulty, I am not sure what the problem is. I will be bound by your wishes, of course I will. But you should tell him. Or you should tell Mrs van Daan, if you are worried about him. In fact, it would be better to tell her, since she would undoubtedly tell the general, and I would very much like to see that."

Keren smiled as he took the basket from her and set it on the ground to help her into the saddle. "Captain, I have no wish that my awkward situation should cause any of my friends embarrassment."

Manson helped her arrange herself comfortably, then passed up the basket. "I'm not going to say any more, ma'am," he said evenly. "Other than to say that your awkward situation ought to cause at least one person embarrassment. Hold on tightly, it won't take long."

Chapter Seven

Giles had ridden through the Galician and Cantabrian Mountains before, and would not have chosen to do so in winter, if choice had been given. Even in summer, the heights could be cold. In February there was still snow on the peaks and a biting wind with showers of rain, snow and sleet dogged their steps as they made their way up the foot hills into the high passes.

The weather made it difficult to sleep out in the open for more than a night at the time, but Antonio knew the countryside very well and guided them steadily from village to village. Most of the time they found a barn or stable to sleep in, curled up with the horses, with whatever food their host could spare for them. Sometimes they found a monastery or convent, and spent the night on hard beds in a dormitory, but with proper food and news from the Abbott or Abbess who was often very well informed of developments in the outside world. Giles was silently amused at Michael O'Reilly's visible surprise at how many churchmen were part of the guerrillas' information networks.

Giles was known in many of these places, either personally or by reputation, and he felt relatively safe up in the mountains. Even if there were French troops in this part of Spain, they would stay well clear of the high passes. Local knowledge was crucial to keep safe in these areas. Antonio, and to some extent Giles, knew which roads would be impassable in the snow, which rivers were likely to be unfordable in winter flood, and which passes were subject to regular rock falls as the winter ice began to melt. A small band of guerrillas could find their way through the mountains even in the worst weather, especially when every village was a sanctuary for them, and it was even easier with Giles' small party. A French scouting troop would have been slaughtered within hours.

After ten days, Giles stopped watching his new recruits for signs of weakness. Michael O'Reilly did not surprise him that much. The Irishman had spent years in the ranks before being commissioned, and was used to hard travelling and harsh living conditions. Giles found him an easy companion, who asked intelligent questions and appeared to have forgotten his resentment of not being placed in command. Giles thought, after two weeks travelling with Michael, that the Irishman would make a good intelligence officer and wondered if, after this, Wellington would offer Michael more work of the same kind.

Giles did not expect the girl to last two weeks and he was exasperated with Michael's insistence on bringing her but he was sure she would be a short term problem. Before leaving Corunna, he had spoken quietly to Antonio and they had deliberately mapped out a route which included four convents, any of which would be willing to take Brat for a small fee, when she finally acknowledged that she could not keep up. Giles watched her during the first days, eagle-eyed for signs that she was slowing them down, or that Captain O'Reilly was devoting attention away from his mission to ensure the comfort of the Spanish girl.

They passed through two convents and Giles did not make the suggestion although he knew he ought to have done so. Brat was indefatigable. She slept in the open when necessary, wrapped in the thick grey cloak Antonio had found for her, or curled up on a bunk beside the men in the monastery dormitory without a trace of embarrassment. Giles could see no sign of any sexual relationship between her and Michael. The Irishman treated her exactly as he might have treated a young and trusted servant and Brat repaid him with a quick attention to his interests that Giles found rather enviable. There was nothing Brat would not turn her hand to. She proved to be a very good camp cook, foraging for herbs to add flavour to whatever the men managed to shoot for the pot, and she quickly took on the role of groom to all four ponies. She never complained of being tired, or cold, or uncomfortable although Giles knew at times she must have been all three; they all were. She rode through the worst weather, gathered firewood, fed and watered the ponies and rapidly made herself so much a part of the group that Giles sometimes forgot that she was not supposed to be there.

Giles enjoyed Brat's relationship with Antonio. The Spaniard was unmarried, a stocky dark man in his forties. He had been recommended to Giles after his band had been ambushed and almost wiped out by the French and Giles had accepted his services cautiously but quickly found that there was no hint of past tragedy in Antonio's twinkling dark eyes. He was good humoured, intelligent and enjoyed a joke and he and Giles had developed a comfortable friendship over the past two years, but Giles had never known him as talkative as he was with the young Spanish girl. Brat teased him unmercifully and he repaid her in kind.

Snow began to fall heavily as they crested the mountains above San Isidro and began to make their way cautiously down the narrow track. Giles thought gratefully of Father Cordoba as his pony picked a sure-footed route through the crisp white snow. He had a suspicion that his big, raw-boned grey might have ended with a broken leg in these conditions. The snow muffled sound, and all he could hear was the crunch of the horses' hooves and the rattle of harness. Even the irrepressible Brat had fallen silent. Giles turned to look behind him. She was riding beside Michael, the hood of the cloak pulled up over the unruly chestnut curls and a thin layer of snow lay across her shoulders. Giles slowed and dropped back, allowing Antonio to overtake him.

"Are you all right, Brat?"

"Yes, Captain."

"It's about twelve miles to the convent, Antonio knows the path well. Just let your horse find his way, don't worry about guiding him. He's better at this than we are."

She turned her head and flashed him a quick, uncertain smile. "Am I slowing you down?"

"Are you…Jesus, no, Brat, this bloody weather is slowing us down." Giles studied her for a moment and gave a reluctant grin. "Stop worrying about it, I'm not going to send you back now, although if you've any sense you'll stay with the nuns."

"I do not wish to, Captain. I will work hard, I promise."

Giles was unwillingly touched. He looked ahead to where Michael was riding beside Antonio, his cloak wrapped about him and his hat pulled down low to protect his eyes from the swirling snow. "You've done remarkably well, Brat. Don't think I don't know you have a point to make."

"I do not," the girl said, turning the blue-green eyes to his. "If I am here, it is right that I do my share."

A gust of wind caught the hood of her cloak, dragging it back off her head. Brat swore under her breath, and pulled the hood back up fiercely, making Giles laugh.

"You're doing your share, Brat. Just hold on. There'll be a fire and hot food tonight."

It was a long and miserable day. Giles was soaked through to his underclothes and knew that every item of clothing in his pack would be equally drenched. There was no way of going any faster, and he tried to detach his mind from his discomfort, allowing the sturdy little horse to make its way steadily down the steep slope. As the slope began to flatten out into the foothills, they were wading through snow almost a foot deep and Giles suspected that once they gained shelter, they might have to remain there for a few days until the storm passed.

The convent buildings were at the edge of a village, and loomed up unexpectedly, just as the gathering darkness was beginning to worry Giles. Lights gleamed through the swirling flakes and Antonio pushed his tired pony into a trot to arrive at the gatehouse ahead of them, to ask for shelter. By the time Giles, Michael and Brat joined him, the gate had been opened and two grooms waited in the courtyard, up to their calves in snow, to take the horses. A nun wrapped in a thick cloak stood waiting in the doorway holding a lighted torch and Giles followed her into the convent.

He found himself in an echoing hallway, lit by torches set in wall sconces. Four nuns and a priest stood waiting and Giles removed his hat, which immediately poured water onto the stone flags, and bowed.

"Reverend Mother, thank you for admitting us."

"Our allies are always welcome here, Captain Fenwick. We look for news from Lord Wellington's army, and may have news of our own to share. Sister Juliana will show you to the guest hall and your clothing will be

102

laundered and dried. I am afraid we have only robes until your clothing dries, Father Luis will bring them to your room."

"Thank you, ma'am."

"When you are ready, Sister Juliana will escort you to my dining parlour."

The guest hall was a long flagged room with a dozen bunks lining the walls. Two young novices were making up the beds while an older nun knelt before the fireplace, patiently coaxing a fire into life. As they waited, shivering in wet clothing, a groom brought their kit bags and saddle bags in from the stable and Father Luis arrived with an armful of plain black woollen robes and linen shirts. Giles smiled his thanks as the women left, noticing that one of the younger girls was very pretty. The older nun paused at the door.

"If you will leave your wet and soiled clothing beside your beds, Captain, we will collect them while you dine and have them laundered and dried. Also your shoes. There are rush sandals with the robes."

"Thank you, sister."

The woman surveyed them, and her eyes rested on Brat. "There, at the end, is a private chamber. Sometimes we have guests who do not wish to sleep in the guest hall. Sister Inez will make up the bed while you dine, child."

Brat blushed scarlet and bowed her head.

There was a moment's silence after the nuns had left. Antonio went to bolt the door and then turned, the dark eyes bright with amusement. "It would seem that your disguise does not fool the good sisters, little fox. Come, I will carry your things to your chamber, find yourself some clothing in that pile."

Brat obeyed with unusual docility. When she had gone, Giles looked around the room. "Sometimes, I'm just grateful for the little things," he said. "Do you ever wonder if England might have been better not to have wiped out the religious houses under Henry all those years ago, Michael? This is much better than an overpriced coaching inn."

"You'd not have found an overpriced coaching in out here in the first place, and there's a few things I wish the English hadn't done over the years," the Irishman said. He had removed his boots and was regarding them gloomily. "I spend half my pay on footwear and it's still not enough. Look at the damned things, these were new two months ago, I ruined the last pair on that retreat."

"They'll dry out." Giles took off his red coat and hung it over the back of a wooden chair, then sat to remove his own boots. Michael was investigating a plain wooden wash table.

"Warm water," he said, in pleased surprised. "I've forgotten what it's like to be clean."

"I've forgotten what it's like to care. I've done that journey more than once before but never in the winter. Thank God for old Cordoba and his Catalan ponies, my poor Boney wouldn't have survived that."

Antonio had returned and was sorting through the monks robes. Michael poured water and stripped off his soaked shirt, reaching for a dish of soap. "Is the rest of the route as bad?"

"It depends on which road we take," Antonio said. "I would wish to skirt the foot of the mountains, keeping close to the coast, there will be less snow and the road is better. But we need to know more about where the French are."

"And where the hell we're heading for," Michael said, his voice muffled by a towel. "I feel as though I'm walking blind here, into God knows what."

Antonio laughed aloud. "Welcome to the life of an intelligence officer, Captain O'Reilly. These robes smell a little musty, but they are clean and I do not think they have lice."

"As I said earlier, the little things," Giles said. "You're clean enough, Michael, shove over. I must say I am looking forward to the sight of you dressed as a monk, it's a shame the general can't see it."

"I've always admired the general's sense of humour."

Giles washed quickly, and pulled on one of the rough linen shirts, a rusty black robe and a pair of woven sandals. There was no mirror but he could see the gleam of amusement in Michael's dark eyes and Antonio was laughing openly. Giles hair was drying, and he combed it through roughly with his fingers, thinking that it was getting too long. Going to his pack, he dragged out his soaked, dirty garments and left them in a pile on the floor, as Michael and Antonio did the same.

"Ready?"

"Yes." Michael raised his voice. "Brat, have you died in there, you're awful quiet? Come and get dinner, I know your appetite and you'll be eating the furniture if we don't feed you soon."

"I am here."

Giles looked up, surprised at how easily he could recognise her discomfort from her tone. She had emerged from the doorway at the end of the room, dressed in a black nun's habit. The chestnut hair had dried in a mass of little ringlets for which a London debutante would have willingly spent tedious hours in curl papers and there was something ethereal about the pale face above the stark black of the garment. Giles heard Michael catch his breath and he was not surprised. The transformation was so surprising that Giles wanted to say something, to compliment the girl, as if she had appeared ready for a ball or a party, but he bit back the words just in time.

"Ha. Little fox, you are a very unlikely nun," Antonio said cheerfully, and the girl gave a tentative smile. Giles realised suddenly, what he should have understood before, that Brat's boy's clothing was not a convenience, but a defence, and she wore it like a suit of armour. Arrayed as a girl, even in the shapeless habit of a nun, she was vulnerable and a little afraid.

"Well at least we're clean," Michael said. "Come on, Brat, lets find some food."

She came forward quickly and Giles stood back to allow Michael to put his hand on her shoulder and steer her to the door. Giles had begun to believe that he understood his companion's odd relationship with this girl, but he decided that he had been wrong and that he did not really understand at all.

The Abbess greeted them in a warm dining parlour where a variety of hot dishes were being set out along a polished refectory table by the two novices. She had clearly been prepared for Brat, and pulled out a chair for her with a reassuring smile that gave Giles a very good opinion of her. Like most of the English officers, Giles had initially taken a negative view of the many religious houses that flourished through Portugal and Spain, but during his time as an intelligence officer, he had met with a great deal of kindness as well as receiving a lot of help from priests, monks and nuns.

Abbess Maria Agnes was probably in her forties with a patrician nose, a decided jawline and a pair of shrewd grey eyes. Many British officers saw Spanish convents as prisons, where young girls were locked away, forced into a religious life by uncaring families. There were undoubtedly such cases, but Giles had talked to a number of women in religious houses by now, and knew that the convent could also be a refuge, for both unmarried girls and widows. For others, it was a career, one of the only ways that an intelligent ambitious woman could rise to a place of prominence in her own right, and Giles suspected that the Abbess was one of these women.

The food was hot, well-cooked and plentiful and for twenty minutes, the Abbess kept up a flow of small talk which was clearly designed to allow her hungry guests to eat. They had been subsisting on basic rations, plus anything they could shoot for the pot, for several weeks, punctuated with the occasional scratch meal from a villager or local priest. The previous convent had been a small foundation and the nuns had shared what they had generously, but Giles had not eaten like this for a while.

Eventually, with his hunger satisfied, Giles took an apple from a dish of fruit and smiled at his hostess. "My thanks, Mother Abbess, for the meal and your patience. You must think you have been invaded by starving wolves."

The Abbess laughed. "You have had a long and difficult journey, Captain, and you will speak more freely with a full belly. And we are hoping for news, Father Luis and I."

"I am hoping for the same," Giles admitted. "You'll have heard of Lord Wellington's retreat last year, I am sure."

"I believe it was very difficult."

"It was, and it has left his Lordship with an army needing rest."

Giles talked, and his companions allowed him to do so. He had no fear, in this setting, of a Bonapartist agent, but he was careful anyway not to share information that was not likely to be generally available to the enemy. By now, the French would have scouted Wellington's lines as well as they could, and would know that the Allies, like the French, were recovering from the previous year's campaigning. There was nothing new, but Giles gave as much information as he could, and supplemented it with news from London. The Abbess listened and asked an occasional intelligent question.

"Thank you, Captain. I am glad to hear that Lord Wellington has accepted command of the Spanish army, although he has taken on a challenging role. You have no doubt had news from your friends in Corunna, about what is happening here?"

"I am told that General Clausel is to take over the Army of the North?"

"Indeed, although he has not yet arrived from France, so Caffarelli still commands. We have scouting parties through the region, reporting to General Porlier and General Longa. Sometimes we receive their wounded here, which is why the guest hall is always ready for occupation. We are very much out of the way here, and the French do not venture this high into the mountains."

"Do you know where General Porlier is to be found at present, Mother Abbess? As I explained, we are trying to trace the movements of Sir Horace Grainger after he crossed the French border. The French tell us that his escort had instructions to take Sir Horace along the main road towards Bilbao, where a Royal Navy gunship would be allowed in under a flag of truce to collect him and take him home."

"Do we know if he reached Bilbao?" Father Luis asked.

"The French say he did not. He spent a night in San Sebastian, which is about seventy miles from Bilbao, and according to the French, nobody heard from him or his escort again."

"It is a dangerous road, Captain, especially for a man travelling with the French."

"It should not have been, they carried a flag of truce."

"Would the French have heeded that, I wonder?"

"Would Mina's irregulars heed it?"

"Perhaps not," the priest concluded. "It has been many weeks since this man disappeared, Captain. I must tell you that it is entirely possible that he was killed in some skirmish, quite accidentally."

Giles had wondered about Father Luis from the start and he was rapidly coming to the conclusion that although Luis might be a real priest, that was not his only job. He studied the other man thoughtfully. Luis was about his age with weathered skin and a thick black beard which had the effect of concealing some of his expression.

"Was he?" Giles asked bluntly.

"I do not know, Captain."

"Then my journey is not over. It would be helpful to know where I can find General Porlier, Father, I don't like the thought of combing these mountains in this weather in search of him."

"Captain, I think you must resign yourself to remaining for a few days at least," the Abbess said, glancing over at the windows which were covered with dark drapes. "I know you had the news from Father Cordoba, but you will not have heard the latest. General Mina has had some success in Naverre, his men had been besieging the French outpost at Tafalla, and the garrison surrendered. Also, General Palombini's Italian division, which was sent to join the Army of the North, was attacked by General Longa's men at Poza de la Sal and lost supplies and many prisoners in fighting them off. All across the region, our men are holding off the French, making it impossible for them to consolidate any gains they make."

"And Porlier?"

"I believe his men have returned to blockade Santona."

"Caffarelli must feel as though he's swatting at a swarm of bees," Michael said.

"He has been stung many times, Captain."

"If you'll have us, Mother Abbess, we will wait out the storm here and then head towards Santona. With this much fighting throughout the region, it was no time for a diplomat with a French escort to be travelling on the high road. It's possible that Sir Horace and his escort were attacked and killed in a skirmish."

"If General Longa or General Porlier knew of this, they would have written to Lord Wellington or to London, Captain."

"If they knew of it, Father Luis. If the attack was carried out by a smaller band, they may not have reported it. They may not even have known who he was. Lord Wellington will attach no blame for what may have happened by accident in wartime, but for the sake of Grainger's employers in London, and even more so for his family, we should know the truth."

Father Luis gave a sardonic smile which suggested that he knew very well why the English government was so keen to know the fate of Sir Horace. "That is a noble sentiment, Captain."

"I think so, Father," Giles said gravely. He glanced down the table and smiled. "Mother Abbess, with your permission, I think we should chase our youngest recruit off to her bed, she is falling asleep at your table."

Brat, whose head had been nodding over her empty plate, jerked upright, blinking. Michael laughed aloud and rose.

"I'll escort her, if you'll excuse me, Mother Abbess, I'm tired myself. Thank you for your hospitality and for all the difficult questions you have not asked me. With your leave, I'll present an account of myself privately tomorrow."

"I would be glad to talk with you, Captain O'Reilly. I will bid you all good night. I am afraid our bells call us to worship at times that may disturb you, and you have no need to join us in our prayers. All the same, should you wish to, we would welcome you, no matter what form of worship you generally follow. Rest well."

***

The small party was snowbound at the convent for four days. Michael could sense Giles' frustration and to some extent he shared it, but he was relieved when the younger man studied the weather, talked to one of the convent's tenant farmers and shook his head.

"We've no choice. The Lady Abbess has found a man willing to take a letter to General Porlier. He's local and he knows the roads, even in this weather. I'm hoping that by the time we can travel, we'll have news of where to find him."

"Do you know him personally, Giles?"

"Yes, we've met a few times. I've no idea if this is a fool's errand, to be honest. We may never find out what happened to Grainger, he might be rotting in some roadside grave along with half a dozen French troopers. But if he was involved in a skirmish, and I'm beginning to think that's increasingly likely, the guerrillas are more likely to have reported it to Porlier or Longa or Mina than they are to the English authorities."

"You think he's dead?"

"Yes," Giles admitted. "I think if he was still alive, he'd have found a way to get a message out. He's not new at this, Michael, he's been running these so called diplomatic missions for years."

"Could the French have worked out that he's a spy and taken him prisoner or killed him?"

"Definitely. In which case, any useful information he was carrying is lost to us and anything he knew, they probably know as well. I wish I knew more about what he was doing in France."

"Not, you think, negotiating prisoner of war exchanges, then?"

"No," Giles said. "Where are you off to, Michael, dressed like a monk?"

"It's all I have until my laundry reappears. Brat doesn't trust the convent laundress, she's prowling outside the scullery like a caged wildcat waiting for them to make a mistake with my woollen stockings, I fear for their lives. I'm going to speak to the Reverend Mother, Giles."

"About Brat?"

"Yes. She accepted the situation yesterday without the least sign of disapproval, but I owe her an explanation."

Giles studied him for a moment then smiled. "I suppose so. I hadn't really thought about it, Michael, but I imagine this is making you squirm a little, isn't it? Antonio was up for early prayer this morning, and he informs me that he wasn't the only one."

"He wasn't," Michael said, without smiling. "It's not something I have the opportunity to do very often, Captain, I hope it doesn't trouble you?"

"Why would it? To tell you the truth, I'm not one for praying much in any form of religion, Michael. Where I grew up, going to church was a matter of duty and it was more important to understand who sat in which pew and what that meant for their position in local society. Have you not found the Test act a mite inconvenient?"

"Not so far, as nobody's asked me to take it. We all keep very quiet on the subject of my religious preferences and I suspect that's the way it works for most Irish officers." Michael gave a wry smile. "I'd not been to mass for years until I came out to Portugal and Spain. From time to time now, I go, very discreetly."

"Go as much as you wish while you're under my command, Michael, and you've no need to be discreet about it."

Michael was touched. He had not thought Giles Fenwick as a particularly sensitive person, but during these past weeks he had seen a different side to him, and he had been surprised by a number of small but

108

significant kindnesses, particularly towards Brat, which seemed at odds with Giles' tough exterior and affected aristocratic disinterest. Three years learning to ignore the snubs and rudeness of other officers who disapproved of men promoted from the ranks had taught Michael a lot about wearing a mask but he had only just begun to catch glimpses behind the one Giles Fenwick wore and he liked what he saw.

"Thank you, Giles. I appreciate it."

The Abbess received Michael in her sitting room with grave courtesy, and offered him a seat. Michael seated himself somewhat apprehensively on a wooden settle opposite her. The fire was lit and the room was pleasantly warm, with the scent of pine logs.

"I was pleased to see you at Mass this morning, Captain, although a little surprised. Your Spanish is very good, but we can converse in English if you wish."

"Thank you, Reverend Mother," Michael said, in some relief. He had got used to speaking in Spanish for most of the time, but for this conversation he would be glad to use his own language. "My religion cannot be a surprise to you, although you are right, I don't generally practise it openly. It is not permitted for an officer of his Majesty's army to belong to the Roman church."

"And yet, you do."

"There are ways around it, ma'am. These days, there's nobody chasing us to take the oath, they don't want to lose experienced officers. If we stay quiet, they'll leave us alone."

"And Captain Fenwick?"

"Captain Fenwick is my commanding officer on this mission and has explicitly informed me that I can go to Mass as openly as I like."

"He seems like a good man."

"He is."

"I hope you will take this opportunity while you are with us, Captain, and Father Luis is available to hear your confession at any time you wish."

Michael smiled. "I'll definitely avail myself of that opportunity before I leave, ma'am. But it's not really confession that I wanted to speak to you about. I was very grateful that you were so accepting of my rather unusual servant yesterday, and I wanted to thank you for your kindness in providing a separate chamber for her. You are owed an explanation."

The older woman gave a singularly sweet smile. "You have no need to make your confession to me, Captain."

"I've nothing to confess with regard to Brat, although poor Father Luis might find himself quickly bored with some of my other sins. There's nothing between Brat and I, although most people don't believe it. I find it matters to me that you know the truth, for your kindness, and I think it would make Brat happier as well."

"What is her real name?"

"Ariana Ibanez. I found her in Madrid last year, we took her in as an act of charity. She stayed rather longer than I expected."

Michael told the story in more detail than he had told it to Giles and Antonio. With other men, he felt very protective of Brat's dignity and he knew she would hate them to know that she had been prostituting herself for little more than a crust of bread when he found her in Madrid. The Abbess's steady gaze told him that Brat's story saddened but did not shock her.

When he had finished, the Abbess rose and went to a tall cupboard in the corner of the room. She brought wine and two delicate Venetian glasses that made Michael smile. He touched the intricate design.

"Beautiful. I'm not used to anything this fragile in an army camp, Mother Abbess."

"The wine is French, Captain, but I think you will enjoy it. Will you pour? Thank you for explaining about Ariana, I am happy to have heard your side of the story. Would it surprise you to hear that she came to see me herself earlier today?"

"Did she?" Michael laughed and sipped the wine. "I didn't know, but it doesn't surprise me that much."

"She told me that Captain Fenwick has been hoping that she would agree to remain at one of the convents along the way."

"Captain Fenwick is under the charming misapprehension that it's possible to send Brat anywhere she doesn't want to go, ma'am. I no longer share his optimism. I wish I could, it's been a hard journey so far and it could get much more dangerous. I'd rather she was safe. She should have stayed in Freineda, my commanding officer's wife would have taken care of her."

"She wants to be with you, Captain."

"She says she feels safe with me," Michael said ruefully. "I've been hoping, with time, that she'll learn to trust other people."

"I think she is beginning to do so," the Abbess said, sipping the wine. "Captain O'Reilly, I will tell you the same thing that I told Ariana this morning. I would be very happy for her to remain with us for as long as she wishes, and there would be no requirement to take orders. Unlike some other foundations, I have always insisted that my novices enter the convent of their own volition. This means that we are not a particularly wealthy house, but I will not have my convent used as a means of ridding families of their unwanted daughters, nor will I imprison a young woman for no other reason than that she has refused an undesired marriage."

"There are plenty of other convents who will do both of those things for the right price, ma'am. My faith doesn't blind me to the abuses of the church at times, I saw it growing up in Ireland and I've definitely seen it here."

"So have I, Captain. I am unable to control the entire church, but within these walls, my writ is law, and you will find no such abuses here. If Ariana chooses to remain with us, I ask nothing other than that she help with the daily work of the convent."

"Do you think she will?" Michael asked. He was not sure what answer he was hoping for.

"No, I don't. I think she will give it serious consideration, she is a very thoughtful young woman, but I think she will choose to go with you. She is wholly devoted to you, Captain, you must see that."

Michael smiled, shaking his head. "Not in the way I think you mean, Reverend Mother. Brat's very young, and despite her appalling early experiences - or perhaps because of them - I don't think she sees me or any other man in that way."

The Abbess frowned. "How old do you think she is, Captain?"

"I'm ashamed to say I don't know for sure."

"She is nineteen. She told me that she deliberately gave your colonel's wife the impression she was younger, because she thought it might make her more inclined to help her."

"It wouldn't have made any difference, but Brat can't have known that. What does it matter?"

The Abbess sighed. "It matters because you treat her rather like a young brother, Captain, and I think she has fallen into the habit of behaving the same way, but she is not a boy and she is not a child. If her father had not died as he did, she would undoubtedly be married by now, probably with a child of her own, our girls marry younger than yours. I mention it, not because I believe there is anything wrong in your dealings with her, I think you have been very kind. And it seems your own officers have accepted this rather odd master-servant relationship. But out in the world, men are going to see Ariana very differently. She is not naive, she understand this, and is willing to accept it in order to remain at your side. For the duration of this mission, I think you have no choice but to carry on as you are. But when you return to your regiment, I think you need to talk to her, Captain. You should be honest with each other."

Michael was silent. He felt rather as though this gentle woman had punched him hard in the gut, taking his breath away, and he could think of nothing to say. The Abbess did not seem to require anything more. They drank wine in slightly awkward silence and then Michael set his glass down carefully and rose.

"Thank you, Reverend Mother, for your candour. I'm not sure I agree with you but you've given me a lot to think about."

The Abbess rose and walked across to the window, and Michael followed her. Some of the nuns and one or two servants were outside. The snow had stopped although the sky with heavy with the promise of more, and they were carrying brooms and spades, taking the opportunity to clear drifts from doors and pathways between the convent buildings. Brat was with them, wearing her cloak and boots over the habit. She was talking to one of the young novices and Michael heard her laugh as she began to wield the spade outside the stable door. He thought that it was good to see Brat laughing with another girl.

"I wish she'd stay," he said abruptly. "I worry about her."

"I will talk to her again, Captain. In the meantime, there is little you can do. I have told Captain Fenwick and Señor Ortega that they are welcome to use our library, it is small but there are works of literature and history as well as religious books. Also, if you have letters to write, I can arrange for them to be sent with ours to Corunna and onwards."

"Thank you, Reverend Mother."

It was instinctive, and wholly a product of his early years, to bow his head for her blessing. Outside in the cold, crisp air, Michael hesitated, then went to join Brat. She threw him a broad grin.

"Have you come to help, Captain?"

"Not in these clothes, urchin, I'll freeze. I'm surprised you're not."

"It is not cold when you work, and they have lent me gloves. But I will come now, to see if your laundry is dry and…"

"No, stay, you're enjoying yourself and the fresh air is good for you. I can find my own laundry."

Brat lifted her eyebrows expressively. "Are you certain of that, Captain? I have known you to lose it, even in a small room."

Michael did not deign to reply. After half a dozen steps towards the guest hall, he turned, scooped up a handful of snow and threw it accurately so that it struck Brat on the back of her head. She gave a little shriek and turned. Michael began to run, hampered by his long robe and the ridiculous rush sandals, but he still made it inside the door in time and her snowball hit the outside of the door just as he was closing it. He could hear her calling out grisly threats as he made his way up to the guest chamber in search of warmer clothing.

Chapter Eight

Bejar was an ancient walled town, and the furthest eastern outpost of Hill's second division, which was sprawled over a large area stretching from Brozas to the south to the high passes of Sierra de Francia and Sierra de Gata to the north. Hill had established his divisional headquarters in the old Roman city of Coria which was approximately in the centre of his lines, and had placed the 50th foot in Bejar. Paul had visited before, but it was Anne's first time and as they rode through the partly ruined gates of the town, she looked around her in delight at the old medieval streets.

Bejar enjoyed an elevated position on a craggy range of hills and could be seen from a long way off. The road narrowed as it approached the town, circling the rocky precipice and running through ruined city gates and up a long street to the main Plaza. It was lined with elegant houses, all of which had wide balconies. The town seemed in fairly good repair, although there was a selection of older buildings which were partially ruined and the city walls and gates were in need of some work.

They were welcomed warmly by Lieutenant-Colonel Harrison who waved away Paul's apologies for not sending warning that he was bringing Anne and arranged for his quartermaster to find them a room close to the magnificent but partly ruined Ducal Palace.

"Don't think of it, General, we're delighted to have a lady guest. I hope you'll both dine with me later. Now, I've arranged the inspection early tomorrow, and I think you'll be pleased with them, sir. We've no time for lengthy training sessions, but we're the closest outpost to the French, so they're not sitting around idly either. I've kept up drills for the entire battalion, and Captain Earle has been given responsibility for training the men in small groups in setting up the new tents and putting up and taking down camp quickly. They're getting much better, sir. Colonel Cadogan has been making a bit of a contest of it, pitting us against the 71st or the 92nd and it concentrates their minds wonderfully if they think they might lose face against another regiment."

Paul was smiling broadly. "I don't think you need me here at all, Colonel. I'm riding up to visit brigade headquarters at Banos when I've finished here, so I'll speak to Colonel Cadogan then, but from what I'm hearing, this will be a very pleasing report to write. As my wife is here, would we be in the way if we took a walk around the town? It's very pretty and I've been telling her about it."

"Not at all, not at all. I'll lend you Lieutenant Delgado, he is from the local area, he can act as guide."

"I didn't know you'd Spanish troops here."

"I don't. I do have Portuguese, though, General Hill recently sent me the 6th caçadores. He was concerned that our position was a bit exposed out here. Some of the local scouts are reporting that the French had been intending to march on the town before we arrived, and that Foy is still keen on the idea, so we keep a careful watch. Lieutenant Delgado is a liaison officer, recently seconded to General Hill's staff. He is anxious to get some real combat experience, and asked if he could spend some time out here with us. So far he has been disappointed."

"Why are we so keen to accommodate this particular junior Spanish officer?" Paul enquired, taking Anne's hand to help her over an area of broken up cobblestones in the square outside the palace.

"Because his father is the Marquess of Acrio, a prominent member of the Spanish Regency who holds a nominal command in the Spanish army. He has been pushing hard for a promotion and a more senior posting for Lieutenant Don Miguel de Delgado, so I expect he'll be moving on soon. Still, he's a nice enough lad and he'll enjoy showing you round. I know you speak excellent Spanish, but let him practice his English, he's desperate to improve."

Don Miguel was eighteen, a slender olive-skinned boy with melting dark eyes and a charming smile, which lit up his face as he was introduced to Anne. Anne gave him her hand and he bowed over it gracefully.

"Señora van Daan, it is an honour. And General van Daan, I am so very proud to meet you."

Paul returned his salute. "I hope you don't mind acting as tour guide, Lieutenant, we're only here for a couple of days and my wife would like to see the town."

"I am very happy. Very happy, sir. I will show you all the best places, then you will tell me if there is anything more you wish to see. And if you become tired, Señora, you must tell me, no?"

"I will. Thank you, Don Miguel."

The boy hesitated and Anne was puzzled, but Paul grinned. "Am I right in thinking you prefer to be called by your army rank, Lieutenant?"

"Yes, sir. Thank you. Will you come this way, Señora? First, I will show the palace. It is old, from the...the sixteenth century. First, before then, the Arabs were here, you can see in the style of some of the buildings."

The palace faced onto the main square, an impressive building with two huge cylindrical fortified towers. It was built on the highest part of the ridge, and the outer walls, and huge staircase with its iron balustrade, were in good condition but the interior, and most of the ornamental stonework, were in ruins, leaving only a shell. Even so, some of the remaining stonework was beautiful and Delgado pointed out the edge of the windows and the parapet of

114

the tower, where the masonry was designed like a chain. Anne wandered through the ruins looking up at blue sky where there had once been ceilings and listening as their guide described the history and varied uses of the palace through the ages.

The old town was a maze of historic buildings, graceful churches and dim little shops, many of them selling locally woven cloth including some beautiful lace and embroidered linen. Textiles were the main industry of the area and many households seemed to be employed in carding and cleaning wool for the cloth factories. Women sat in groups at their doors, picking the wool and preparing it for the loom while gossiping with their neighbours and keeping an eye on their roaming children. Anne stopped to speak to some of them. She had grown up in a cloth manufacturing town in Yorkshire and her father's wealth had come through the excellence of his wools and worsteds. As a child she had learned these techniques from some of the cottagers who provided wool for her father's looms, and the women were visibly surprised both by the fluency of her Spanish and her familiarity with the process. One of them, a pretty girl of no more than fifteen, handed her the carders and watched as Anne wielded them, clumsily at first and then with increasing confidence.

They clapped and cheered as she handed her work back and rejoined Paul, who was laughing. Anne took Paul's arm, smiling back at the group of women, who waved as they followed their bewildered Spanish guide up the street. They visited the Church of Santiago and of Santa Maria la Mayor where they climbed up narrow winding stairs to the top of the square bell tower and gazed out over jumbled roofs and across to the bluish peaks of the mountains rising above the town. Climbing back down, they walked along the riverbank, where locals fished from the shore or pushed flat bottomed punts bearing goods or passengers along the swift current. There were market stalls including several food vendors along the shore, and Paul bought slices of hot tortilla when Anne became hungry, and they sat on the grass watching the boats as Delgado told them stories of the town's history between mouthfuls. A lemonade seller hovered deliberately within view, and Anne looked at Paul, who laughed and reached for his purse.

Refreshed, they walked back up into the town and looked at the bullring then climbed the steps onto the town walls, which originally dated from Moorish times. There were five entrances by arched gateways, but none of the gates were in good condition. The town wall was in a miserable condition, with gaps and piles of rubble all along its length, and Delgado explained that Colonel Harrison had organised working parties of both soldiers and local workmen to try to repair the various breaches. Until this was done, it was necessary to set sentries at every gap in the wall, not just at the gates, and the duty was unpopular.

"The townspeople are very hospitable, Señora, they like to entertain the soldiers, and hold many balls and dances for the officers, but Colonel Harrison is concerned that the French will attack, so each night he sets two or three companies on picket duty not only outside but all around the walls, and they must stay there until dawn." Delgado's eyes danced with amusement.

"They do not like it, the officers, for it is very cold at night at this time of year, and often damp and frosty. They pace up and down and are cross with their men, until dawn is sighted and they are relieved by the day sentries and may go back to their warm beds, or to breakfast where they hear the tale of the night's entertainment from their more fortunate comrades. Always, it seems to me, when they tell of those parties, the music was of the best and the señoritas most beautiful and the dancing most delightful."

Anne gave a peal of laughter. "And do you also take your turn on the walls at night, Lieutenant Delgado?"

"Si, Señora. Sometimes, I offer to take the place of one of the officers, when he especially wishes to attend a dinner or a ball. This makes me many good friends in the 50th, and I do not mind. I did not come here to dance, I could have remained in Cadiz for that."

Something in the boy's voice impressed Anne, and she was not surprised when her husband turned to look at him. "Is that where you're supposed to be, Lieutenant?"

"Yes, General. My father has an ADC post that he wishes me to occupy, and is writing me angry letters saying that I have spent enough time with the English and I should return to take up my duty. And I will sit and write letters and grow fat and smoke cigars - which I detest - and watch other men, not Spanish, fight and die for my country."

Anne saw Paul smile. "Keep dodging the letters, Mr Delgado. If you're that determined to fight, I'm sure something can be done. I will give it my personal consideration, I give you my word."

The dark eyes brightened. "Do you think so, General? I will fight anywhere."

"I'll think about it, I promise you. Thank you for the tour, you've been an excellent guide."

"I enjoyed it very much, General. Do you dine with Colonel Harrison?"

"We do. I hope to see you there," Anne said warmly, and Delgado bowed.

"I shall be there. Afterwards, the officers are invited to attend a ball at the public ballroom. All will attend." Delgado looked at Paul. "I would be honoured if you would consider it, General."

"We'll be there, Lieutenant, I never turn down the opportunity to dance with my lady. Thank you."

"You will excuse me, I have duties."

They watched him walk away and Anne turned to Paul. "Do you think we have time to visit one or two of the shops? I'd like…"

"I've been expecting that, girl of my heart, I saw the acquisitive gleam in those beautiful eyes at the sight of some of that lace. Come on, we'll make time. I'm so glad you decided to come with me."

"So am I," Anne said, slipping her arm through his. She could feel the lightening of her spirits, as though a burden had been lifted. Happily, she put her arm about Paul's waist and hugged him. "I love you."

"I love you too, bonny lass. Come on, let me buy you something extravagant to prove it."

"I was thinking of buying a gift for Keren and Teresa."

"Let me spoil you anyway, it will please me."

They spent a pleasant hour in and out of the small shops. Anne bought a lace collar and cuffs for Teresa and a pretty lace fichu for Keren and then paused beside a display of beautiful lace fans.

"These are lovely."

"They are. Allow me to buy you one, to replace that over-painted object that Don Julian Sanchez sent you last year."

Anne laughed aloud. "I cannot believe you are still going on about that. Actually, I think I've lost it, I've not seen it for ages. But I have that very pretty lace fan you bought me in Salamanca. I was thinking that perhaps I could get one of these for Mrs Mackenzie and Margriete. Do you think they would like it?"

Paul did not speak for a moment, then he said:

"Yes. But you don't have to, Nan, I know you're not all that fond of her."

Anne felt her heart sink. She had tried very hard to conceal her ambivalence about the arrival of Katja Mackenzie. "I don't dislike, her, Paul, and she's done nothing wrong. In fact, I feel as though we ought to get on very well, and she's trying so hard."

"Is that the problem?"

"No, not at all. There is no problem, apart from in my head. She is just so…so competent. And recently I've been feeling so useless. I've never really thought much about my lack of housekeeping skills until Mrs Mackenzie arrived. The reception rooms sparkle. She must think I'm a very poor housewife."

"I think she is more interested in the work you do, than your enthusiasm with a duster, Nan, but if you're looking to build some bridges, I think it's an excellent idea. Let's finish here, there's a shop we passed just by the end of the bridge that I wanted to go back to."

Anne saw it as she entered the shop and stopped, gazing up, entranced. Paul laughed at the expression on her face and smiled at the shopkeeper as he came forward to lift down the shawl. It was made of black silk with a deep fringe and a riot of flowers lovingly embroidered in brilliant colours, forming sprays of roses which hung from Anne's shoulders and down her back as Paul draped it around her shoulders.

"It's exquisite."

"So are you."

Anne met the blue eyes and laughed at the gushing enthusiasm of the shopkeeper, visibly excited at the prospect of selling his expensive showpiece. "You're not going to get much off the price of this through bartering, Paul, you should see the expression on your face."

117

"I do not give a damn, bonny lass, I'm looking forward to you dazzling Colonel Harrison at dinner wearing that. Let's make this gentleman's day and get back, I'm hungry."

Dinner was a convivial affair, with the officers of the 50th scrambling for Anne's attention and paying her extravagant compliments which made her laugh. She felt very relaxed, and her recent troubles seemed trivial and a very long way away. At the end of the meal, they made their way through the narrow streets, with the officers calling cheerful greetings up to some of their disgruntled comrades whose duty it was to supervise the sentries on the walls that night. Anne held Paul's hand in the cold evening air and enjoyed the impromptu party.

The public ballroom was brilliantly lit, although wreathed with cigar smoke which made Anne wrinkle her nose. The officers were clearly very popular, and as the small orchestra struck up a waltz, many of the ladies abandoned their current partner for a red coat. Anne and Paul had learned the waltz the previous year in Madrid, it had not been danced in England at the time of her debut and she wondered if it had reached the fashionable ballrooms of London by now. Anne loved the dance and loved to dance it with Paul, who was a surprisingly graceful dancer. They swirled about the floor, and Anne was pleasantly aware of eyes following them. At the end of the dance, he bowed, raising her gloved hand to his lips.

"They're about to descend upon you like a swarm of locusts, girl of my heart, so I'm handing you over to young Delgado first or he'll never get near you. Behave yourself, I will claim you back in an hour."

Anne danced, forgetting everything in the rhythm of the music and the joy of moving her body. She adored dancing and had recently been learning some of the Spanish dances from the camp women. The dramatic, staccato moves were very different to English country dances, and Anne loved the theatrical aspect of the flamenco and bolero.

Paul reclaimed her for another waltz then took her to find refreshment. They drank lemonade on the balcony overlooking the square, and Anne leaned into him as he put his arms about her. "I'm so happy."

"Good. Let's keep it that way, girl of my heart, it suits you. I'm always happy when you're with me."

"I'm looking forward to seeing the children."

"They might even be there when we get back, they should be at sea right now. I wonder how much Francis will have grown, he was a giant last year. And Will."

"I'm so excited. He won't remember me, though."

"He'll soon get to know you again, look how quickly Rowena got used to us last year."

"It's very pretty night."

"Do you want to go for a walk?"

Anne looked up at him. "Yes. Can we?"

"Yes. I'll say our farewells to Colonel Harrison and we'll walk down to the river and then take the long way round to our billet. I'm looking forward to the inspection tomorrow, I like what I've seen of these lads and Harrison looks as though he's got them very much on their toes. It'll be nice to have something positive to report to Wellington."

"I wonder how Michael and Giles are getting on," Anne said as they walked down the stairs and out into the cold, fresh night.

"I wonder how long it will take them to send that blasted girl back. Hopefully with Johnny's horse."

"I can't believe she did that again. I hope she's all right, Paul."

"I have a lot of faith in Brat, she's like a cat, she always lands on her feet, but she has to stop doing this. Poor Michael."

The streets of the town were dark and quiet with a few lanterns lighting the main streets and they strolled hand in hand down to the banks of the river. It was too dark to see much but it was pleasant to hear the soft rush of the water. There was a breeze, and Anne shivered a little. Paul laughed and put his arms about her.

"We should have brought your cloak. Come on, bonny lass, time to go. In a while they'll douse those lights and I don't fancy making my way back in pitch darkness over these cobbles, they could do with a bit of road maintenance here."

The room was dark and cold and slightly damp and Anne had grown cold on the walk up from the river. She stood shivering as Paul found her cloak in the darkness and draped it about her, then collected a candle and went down to light it from the porch lantern. He lit several others around the room and collected a bottle and two cups from his pack. They huddled under the blankets drinking brandy and Anne giggled.

"This isn't quite as luxurious as the Marina Palace last year, General. Or even Santo Antonio. But I'm very happy."

"So am I. We're together, and you're laughing again. How tired are you, Mrs van Daan?"

Anne set down her cup. "Not tired at all, but I could do with help getting warm."

Paul got up to blow out the candles on the table. "Generally I'd leave them burning, but those windows are letting in a howling gale and if one of these candles goes over, this place will go up like a chimney."

"That's all right, General, you can feel your way."

"I like the sound of that. Come closer, girl of my heart, and let me warm you up a bit."

***

Paul awoke suddenly, his heart racing and all his senses immediately alert. He sat up in bed, one hand on Anne who had moved beside him. There was momentary silence but he was in no doubt about what he had heard.

"Paul, was that gunfire?"

"Yes. It might have been an over-enthusiastic caçadore shooting at wild pigs, but somehow I don't think so. Wait…"

119

There was an immense crash of musket fire which ripped shockingly through the still darkness. Now that his eyes had adjusted, Paul realised that there was a faint lightening of the sky heralding the approach of dawn. He had woken briefly to the sound of troop movements during the night and remembered that young Delgado had told him that Harrison was accustomed to keep several companies under arms through the night, and assumed it was the changeover. Now he was not so sure, and he swung his legs over the side of the narrow bed and reached for his clothing which he had draped over a chair.

As he was dressing, the sounds of firing increased and there was no longer any doubt that the town was under attack. Paul went to the window, pushing open the shutters, and looked out. He could hear shouting, the calling of orders and the sound of marching feet on the cobbles as more men headed for the fray. Flashes of fire could be seen in the distance and Paul guessed that the French had launched an attack on the outlying pickets of the 50th. He was momentarily furious that Harrison had not sent a message but realised immediately that he was being unfair; Harrison's job was to defend the town, not to pay attention to a visiting officer and he wife, and he probably thought Paul and Anne would be better out of the way.

Paul turned to Anne who was pulling on her clothes. She looked concerned, but there was no sign of panic. "What's the best thing for us to do, Paul?"

"I'm not sure. This is Harrison's command, I've no intention of charging in, yelling that I outrank him. On the other hand, I don't know enough about the defences here or the number attacking us, to be confident enough to stay here and assume we'll be safe. Especially if these buildings catch fire, I'd rather be outside. I don't think they're going to break through, but if they do, I want you with me."

"I'm glad you said that."

When she was dressed, Anne pulled on her warm dark cloak. It was impossible to do anything with her hair in the darkness so she tucked it inside the back of the cloak to keep it out of the way, then took Paul's hand and allowed him to lead her down the dark stairway and outside into the street. There were a lot of people about, as householders, woken like Paul by the sound of gunfire, stood on their doorsteps talking quietly and anxiously.

Paul and Anne made their way through the streets, following the sound of battle. At one point, they had to step back into a doorway as a company of Portuguese caçadores ran through, muskets at the ready. It was growing lighter, and Paul studied their grim faces and felt further reassured that they looked like men who knew exactly what they were doing.

The firing was intensifying, and they made their way towards the Salamanca gate. To the left was a church with a solid stone bell tower, and Paul caught Anne's hand and drew her to the big, iron studded door. It gave immediately and they stepped inside to a strong smell of candles and incense and the murmur of prayer as a robed priest led a dozen of his congregation in prayers for the delivery of the town.

A younger cleric, also robed, stepped towards them with a look of enquiry, and Paul shook his head and pointed to the stairwell. The cleric nodded and Paul took the stairs at a brisk pace with Anne coming more slowly behind him, hampered by her skirts. At the top, the wind blew briskly but there was a fine view over the walls and as Paul had the thought, a voice said sharply:

"Who goes there?"

"At ease, Private. General van Daan, 110th light infantry and his wife. We're visiting Colonel Harrison and it's proving more exciting that we expected."

The soldier, a sallow veteran of around fifty, shouldered his musket and saluted. "Begging your pardon, General. Private Dawlish, 50th infantry, and that's Private Eden, who is so wet behind the ears they put him up here to keep him safe."

Paul grinned and acknowledged the salute then went to join Dawlish at the parapet which overlooked the walls. "What's going on?"

"French attack, sir. General Foy, trying his luck. He's going to wish he hadn't, he's not getting past our lads, and the colonel's already sent word back to Colonel Cadogan."

"Yes, I must say I think he's a bit optimistic with your lot, Private. I'm supposed to be doing an inspection this morning, but I reckon this is better. Is that cavalry he's brought with him? What in God's name is he hoping to do with them?"

"Not sure, sir." Dawlish pointed through the musket smoke which already wreathed the walls in the pale morning light. "See those buildings? It's a farm house, we've pickets up there under Captain Rowe."

"Looks like their light troops are attacking. Shame it's so misty, it's hard to see the bastards."

Dawlish blinked in surprise and looked at Anne who had come to join them at the parapet. Paul grinned. "Sorry, love, you know my language goes downhill in a fight."

"You're not in a fight up here, General, but I shall forgive you." Anne had pushed back the hood of her cloak to make it easier to see and Paul managed not to laugh aloud at the expression on young Private Eden's face at the sight of her lovely countenance. Paul took out his telescope and put it to his eye.

"Voltigeurs," he said. "You can see them moving between those rocks. There are a lot of them."

They watched in silence as the battle unfolded beneath them. It was a peculiar feeling to be up here, wholly removed from the action and with no part to play. Part of Paul felt immense frustration but he also felt huge respect for Harrison's calm management of his troops.

The French had the advantage of numerical strength against Rowe's small band of pickets and pushed on steadily, while the voltigeurs, crept cautiously behind rocks and trees. They were mostly concealed from view by the fog, and almost reached the walls of the town, but as they drew close enough, the morning sky had lightened and the breeze began to disperse the drifting mist. The muskets on the town walls were abruptly aware of the danger and Paul heard a shouted order. Fire thundered out, clouds of acrid smoke billowed from the walls, and as it began to clear, Paul could see the voltigeurs running back out of range.

With grim determination, Rowe's picket held to its station long after Paul would have given the order to pull back. He watched anxiously, admiring the young captain's dogged defence as his men fought, disputing every inch of ground. It was a pointless fight, Rowe's men faced hugely superior numbers, and were eventually forced to fall back on the reserve which waited anxiously near the town. As far as Paul could see, none of Rowe's men had fallen, although one was being helped along by two of his comrades.

"Oh God, I hope they make it."

"They'll make it, Nan, they're fast and they're very well organised, they're covering that wounded man very well. I'd be proud to command this battalion."

At the walls, Harrison's men waited at arms, drawn up at every exposed and assailable position. The poor condition of the walls made it a challenging task and the defences were very over-extended, around the crumbling and damaged walls and out into the suburbs. Paul wondered if Foy would make it into the town itself. A lucky rush on a vulnerable stretch of wall might gain him access, but once within the narrow streets, the advantage was with the defenders and Paul did not think much of his chances. He knew an urge to go down, leaving Anne in the care of the two sentries, to see if he could be of use on the walls, but he restrained himself with an effort. He would be able to see if Harrison was struggling and would not hesitate to cry rank and intervene if he felt it necessary, but so far he could find nothing to criticise in the colonel's management of his men.

Below, there was sudden movement among the enemy, and Anne caught her breath in alarm. Paul put his arm about her shoulders as the French charged. On Paul's other side, Dawlish swore softly under his breath.

"If they break through…"

"If they break through, I'm going down," Paul said, his eyes on the sea of blue coats racing towards the gate. "Private Dawlish, Private Eden, I'll consign my lady to your care. Who commands the gate party, Dawlish?"

"Lieutenant Deighton, sir, grenadiers company. That's him, the tall one."

Paul looked through his telescope again and could see Deighton. He had ranged his men across the passage into the main street of the town and stood with his sword in his hand, waiting. The French raced towards him, pursuing Rowe's men who were by now in full flight. Deighton waited. The fleeing pickets scrambled up the slope and took refuge behind his men, none of whom moved or looked around. Paul realised he was holding his breath and let it out slowly as the charge continued. Deighton watched them come, held his nerve and the grenadiers stood.

"Why does he not fire?" Eden whispered.

122

"Because he's a bloody good officer, Private," Paul said softly. He assessed the distance and realised that he was counting backwards in his head. He had reached two when Deighton gave the order in clear tones.

"Fire!"

There was a deafening volley. For a moment the smoke was so thick it was impossible to see anything of the grenadiers, but Paul could still see the French and they appeared to roll back in shock. As the smoke began to clear, several of them were on the ground and their comrades were helping them up or dragging them backwards out of range.

Deighton gave another order and the grenadiers stepped forward. Paul prayed that they were not going to charge, but the officer knew his business, and loosed another enormous volley from his second rank, while his first reloaded. This time, some of the French had got themselves into order, and the British fire was answered by a sharp volley from the French muskets. Paul did not think it had done any damage, they were not within range, but it caused the guards to fall back a little and the French surged forwards until they were within a hundred feet of the town walls.

Muskets fired again, not only from Deighton's men, but from Rowe's pickets, who had managed to reform and were coming to the aid of the guards. Another volley crashed out, this time from a different section of the wall. Paul could hear orders being called out from various officers of the 50th as their men found the range and began to fire onto the advancing French. More blue coats were on the ground and their comrades no longer had time to collect them. For several minutes the French line held, and then they broke and were running, tripping over their wounded as they went. One or two paused to help an injured man to his feet, but most did not stop until they were well down the road.

Paul could hear their officers shouting orders to bring the fleeing men under control. As they formed into column, there were shouted orders from the town, and several companies of the Portuguese caçadores appeared, fully armed and ready to pursue. Paul lifted his glass to his eye and watched the retreating voltigeurs, who were making their way back to the main body of General Foy's force. An order was given, and the Portuguese marched forward, although Paul approved the caution of their pursuit.

Paul and Anne made their way down into the town, where the relieved townspeople were beginning to emerge into the morning sunlight. Paul found Harrison at the gate, in conversation with Lieutenant Deighton. The colonel saluted.

"General van Daan. I'm feeling very guilty about you and your wife, sir, ought to have given you some warning, we were so busy…"

"No apology required, Colonel. We took ourselves to the top of the church tower to see what was going on. Very well done, you should be proud of your men. Lieutenant Deighton?"

"Yes, sir."

"I'm supposed to be writing up an account of this morning's inspection for Lord Wellington, but it'll be a rather different report as it turns out. Your name, along with Captain Rowe's, will feature fairly prominently.

Well done for holding your fire there, you're a credit to your colonel and your regiment."

Deighton flushed scarlet through the powder blackening his face. "Thank you, sir."

"Under the circumstances, Colonel, I think we'll dispense with the parade. Congratulations on a successful and very well conducted action. We'll remain within the town until we're sure that the French have definitely retreated and then we'll ride on to see Colonel Cadogan. Did you lose anybody?"

"No, General," Deighton said. "Two or three of the pickets were wounded, and there are a few minor injuries among my men. Also, Private Jones fell off the gate through cheering too hard when they ran, and has twisted his shoulder."

"Sir. Begging your pardon, Colonel Harrison."

Harrison turned. "What is it, Sergeant Barrett?"

"It's the French dead and wounded, sir."

"Are the Portuguese back, Barrett?"

"Yes, sir. Their officer reports that the French troops are retreating, marching back towards Salamanca, sir. We've set pickets again, just in case they turn back, but I don't suppose they will. The thing is, sir, there's a lady out there."

"Out where?" Harrison demanded, looking bewildered.

"Outside the gate, sir. She's giving instructions to Mr Deighton's guards to bring in the French wounded, and lay out the dead for burial."

"A lady?" Harrison said, sounding appalled. "And are they following these instructions?"

"I think so, sir. Do you want me to…"

"It's all right, Colonel," Paul said. He could hear the quiver of laughter in his own voice. "I think I know the lady in question, and she knows what she's doing. Why don't you see to your men, and I'll make myself useful and see that the wounded get to the surgeon, I'd like to earn my keep, since you may have us with you for another night."

"You're very welcome, General," Harrison said, baffled but making the best of it. "Thank you, sir."

Paul went to the gate and peered over the pile of rubble. Three dead Frenchmen were neatly laid out and covered with sheets in the shade of the wall while half a dozen grenadiers were lifting the French wounded onto a handcart that had been brought out for the purpose. In their midst, a slender figure in a dark cloak with her hair unbound about her shoulders was directing operations. One of the guards spoke to her and Paul saw her smile and reply. The guardsman saluted smartly and turned to do her bidding and the sight made Paul unaccountably happy. He scrambled over the top of the rubble and slid down the other side to join her.

Chapter Nine

It was very late when the horsemen rode in, clanging the bell at the convent gates. Giles was awake immediately, sitting up and reaching for his clothing. It was dark in the guest hall and he could hear his companions moving about.

"It's late for visitors," Michael said softly.

"A lot of visitors," Antonio responded.

Giles pulled on his boots and made his way to the window which looked out over the courtyard. The gate had been opened and the yard was full of men on horseback, around twenty of them. Several of the convent grooms and servants were emerging sleepily to see to the horses, and Giles could see the Abbess and Father Luis, accompanied by a nun holding a lantern. Several lanterns were being lit over by the stables and a cloaked man had dismounted and was speaking to the Abbess while his men led horses over to the big barn beyond the stables; there were too many of them to be accommodated in the stable block itself.

"What is happening?"

Giles turned. Brat had appeared, holding a candle, ghost-like in a long white shift with her cloak thrown on for warmth. She was shivering violently, which was making the candle shake in her hand. Giles went forward quickly.

"Give me that, you're going to set fire to yourself in a minute. Jesus, you're freezing."

"There is ice inside my windows."

Giles used the candle to light several lanterns in the room. "I think it's colder at that end of the building. Look, get into my bed for a minute and get warm, I'm going to find out what's going on downstairs. I'll come back and tell you."

"Do you need me to come?" Michael asked.

"I'll call if you're needed. Look after Brat, she's turning blue. Antonio, why don't you grab a lantern and get some firewood up here? If this cold continues, she'll have to move into this room, survival is more important than modesty."

Giles arrived in the tiled hallway just as the Abbess came in with Father Luis and the newcomer. The hall was dimly lit by two lanterns, but as the man turned, Giles recognised him immediately. It had been a year since he had last seen General Juan Diaz Porlier and the Spaniard looked cold and exhausted, but he managed a smile.

"Captain Fenwick. It is very good to see you again."

Giles saluted. Porlier was in his mid-twenties, a slight, dark man with a ready smile. Giles had met several of the great guerrilla leaders during the past two years, but Porlier was his favourite.

"It's good to see you too, sir. What on earth are you doing here? I wrote to you..."

"I have received no letter, Captain, I had no idea you were here. We are seeking shelter, my men were attacked by a strong French force three days ago and had to disperse into the hills very quickly. I was cut off with these few and they chose to pursue, even up into the mountains."

"They knew it was you?"

"They knew a great deal, or we would not have been so surprised."

"An informer?"

"It must have been. When I return, we will find out who, and he will regret his treachery. For now, I thought it best to leave them well behind. The snow helped, they do not know the paths and were quickly floundering in snow drifts. Several of my men were injured - one died yesterday - and we had no food, so I thought it best to ride on and take refuge here with my cousin. A few days rest and we will make our way back to join up with the rest of our forces."

"Do you know where they are?"

"Always, we have a prearranged rendezvous in case we are separated. I know where to find them. But Captain, I wish to know what brings you here, in such poor weather."

"It is a long story, cousin, and you should know it, but not tonight," Father Luis said firmly. "You need rest."

"Do you need the guest hall?" Giles asked. "We can..."

"No, it is not necessary," the Abbess said. "The men prefer to sleep in the barn with their horses, there is plenty of hay and the sisters are taking food and blankets to them now. The wounded are being taken to the infirmary, and General Porlier will take the small guest room next to Father Luis, we keep it for visiting priests. Tonight, you shall rest, General. There will be time enough to talk tomorrow."

Giles heard his dismissal and agreed with her. Three days of riding for his life with the French at his heels was written in exhausted lines on the Spaniard's young face. Giles saluted.

"You're right, ma'am. General, I'm so glad you made it."

"So am I, my friend. This one was too close, I think, the shadow of the gallows felt very dark."

Giles bowed to the Abbess. "Reverend Mother, we're going to move Brat into one of the beds in the guest hall. There's ice inside her chamber and

126

she's blue with cold. I've asked Antonio to get a fire going, I hope you don't mind."

"Captain, our hall is your hall, you are our guest. Take some brandy from the pantry and get the child warm, if you are to leave soon she must not become ill."

Giles thanked her and left, hiding a smile at Porlier's obvious curiosity at the mention of a woman with his party. Giles hoped the Abbess would explain so that he did not have to.

***

Michael was surprised when Brat initially declined the invitation to join General Porlier at the Abbess' dinner table the following day.

"I will eat with the nuns," she said, when the message came. "I do not wish there to be awkwardness."

"There won't be," Michael said. "Look, Brat…"

"Ariana, are you intending to stay with the nuns or are you travelling on with us?" Giles interrupted. Brat stared at him, round-eyed with surprise at his use of her name.

"I wish to come with you," she said finally. "Am I permitted to do so?"

"As if you'd take any notice," Michael said, torn between amusement and exasperation. "Giles…"

"It's a serious question, Michael and I need to know her answer. I'm not going to try to stop you, Brat, partly because you've proved your usefulness as well as your hardiness and partly because as Michael says, I don't trust you not to follow. But you can't do that here. We travel together or you remain here. You won't last three days out there on your own, if the French don't get you, the wolves or the bears will and if you get picked up by a local band of irregulars, I couldn't honestly answer for what they might do to you either, there are men in every army who will take advantage of an unprotected woman. I don't want Michael distracted worrying about you. And actually I'd worry about you as well. You've earned your battle honours, little one, but if you come on with us from here, you're under my command, you do as you're told and you don't put any of us at risk. Or you wait here with the nuns and when this is over, we'll find a way to get you an escort back to the army. What is it to be? Can you take an order?"

Michael saw her square her shoulders a little and he silently blessed Giles for finding the way to get her to listen. "Yes, sir."

"You promise?"

"I give you my word. And I will never break my word."

"Good girl. Then head back to your ice cavern and get changed into your boy's clothing and come and be introduced to General Porlier, he should meet the whole party and I don't want any of us dressed as clerics."

Brat scrambled to her feet and disappeared at speed and Michael gave Giles a faint smile.

127

"I take my hat off to you, Captain Fenwick, they put the right man in charge of this expedition, I shall be following your orders myself."

Antonio snorted. "Me, I only follow his orders when they are sensible. He has given some very silly orders in the past, he might have got me killed."

"The only reason you're not dead already is because I can still find a use for you, you cheeky Spanish bastard. Best hope that continues."

"You would get lost before you reached the coast," Antonio said scornfully and Giles laughed and threw a boot at him.

Porlier looked better for some sleep. He was accompanied by his lieutenant, an older man with thinning hair who was introduced simply as Carlos. The Abbess made the introductions and Michael guessed by the two men's placid acceptance of Brat that they had been told how to behave.

As they ate, Porlier told of his frantic flight into the mountains, pursued for many miles by French cavalry. He was clearly anxious about the rest of his forces but had no way of knowing how many of them had escaped.

"They have called off the chase by now, if they have not died in the mountains," Carlos said. "We rest for two days then ride back to the rendezvous. Then we will know."

"Do you think that they knew they were chasing you, General?" Michael asked.

"Assuredly, Captain, or they would not have risked their lives."

"I suppose it was worth the risk to capture General Juan Diaz Porlier."

"I doubt that they would have troubled to take capture me, Captain. Usually they slaughter our men where they stand, and I do not see why they would make an exception for me." Porlier surveyed Giles in some curiosity. "You know everything now, of why I am here. What of you, Captain Fenwick?"

"As a matter of fact, General, I was on my way to find you. We've been tasked with a problem and I was hoping you might know something about it. An English diplomat has gone missing along with his French escort somewhere on the high road and we have no idea what has happened to him. My government would like to know."

There was a long silence. Michael looked at Giles. The younger man had the reputation of being one of the best card players in Wellington's army, and it was rumoured that his skill was the only thing that had kept him from having to sell out to pay his debts. Watching his face, Michael could read absolutely nothing which must be a big advantage at the card table. He could see Porlier studying Giles as well.

"A diplomat? Travelling with the French?"

"His mission was completed, they were escorting him under a flag of truce to join a Royal Navy ship back to England. He never arrived."

"And what does your government fear has happened to this 'diplomat' Captain Fenwick?"

"My government doesn't confide in me, General. What I personally think, is that the French should know better than to travel that road and expect the Spanish to respect a flag of truce, and that Sir Horace Grainger might have

128

died mistakenly in the ensuing skirmish. Nobody would put blame on Spanish irregulars for such a tragedy, but it would be good to be sure."

Michael realised that Giles believed Porlier knew something. He looked from one man to the other, waiting for one to speak. After a long wait, Giles shrugged and began to eat again. "If you know nothing, we'll have to try to make contact with General Longa or…"

"He did not die," Porlier said. "But he was very badly wounded. Longa's men picked him up and fortunately he was able to tell them who he was, so they did not kill him with the rest of the escort. Unfortunately, I believe his servant was killed in the fighting."

Michael had begun to think that they were never going to find out what had happened to Sir Horace Grainger, and he was a little shocked.

"Do you know where he is, General?"

"They took him to Castro Urdiales. The man who led the attack was from the town, and Longa writes that Grainger is being nursed by his family."

"Why didn't they tell anybody?" Michael asked.

"I imagine they were afraid when they discovered that they almost killed an English diplomat. They seem to have taken their time reporting it to Longa. Perhaps they were waiting to see if he lives or dies."

"We can't wait for that."

"Why not, Captain?"

"Because we can't allow him to fall into the hands of the French," Giles said bluntly. "Sir Horace is rather more than a diplomat, General, as you've probably guessed, and I'm told he left France with valuable intelligence. He may have found a way to destroy any letters or documents and the French may still have no idea what he really is. Or they may have worked it out by now, and Grainger might be unconscious or dying with his baggage stuffed full of documents that we don't want to fall into their hands. What we do know, is that it's Bonaparte's stated intention to take back every one of those coastal towns. I need to get to Castro Urdiales before the French find him, if he's still alive."

"It will be dangerous, Captain. Up in these mountains, the French will only follow so far but closer to the coast, you are more likely to run into French patrols. And if you reach him, and he is unable to travel, what then?"

"All we need to do is get him to a boat. There's a Royal Navy squadron patrolling these waters, still throwing in aid and guns where they can. I don't know who commands it, now that Popham has gone home, but we should be able to make contact. Once we reach Castro, as long as it isn't already in French hands, it should be relatively easy."

"As you wish," Porlier said. "You may travel with us to the rendezvous, and I will give you a letter to take to General Mendizabal and Longa. My men will also be able to advise you which is the safest route to take."

"My thanks, General. I'm hoping we find him alive and able to travel, he's a brave man. If not, at least we will know for sure and can tell his family what became of him."

"He is married?"

"A wife and a daughter, I am told."

"A dangerous life for a man with such responsibilities, Captain.

"When do you leave?" Michael asked.

"We will rest for another day. Reverend Mother has agreed to take care of my wounded men."

"They'll be well looked after here, as we have been," Giles said, with a faint smile at the Abbess. "We'll be ready to leave with you, General Porlier. And thank you."

***

The visit to Bejar lifted Anne's spirits, and with Paul away for a series of inspections and parades with the fifth division at Lamego, she turned her attention to her medical duties. The new surgeons and their assistants had arrived, and Anne hosted a private dinner for the entire medical staff of the brigade, including those from the Portuguese and King's German Legion battalions. She invited Dr Oliver Daniels of the 110th to act as host and made an effort to charm the new men, while making her own role in assisting the surgeons and helping to organise the care of the sick and wounded very obvious. While she could not return to the wards until after the children's visit, Anne had no intention of giving up her hospital work, and was hoping that the new men would get used to the idea more quickly if she remained involved, even at a distance.

The dinner was a great success, helped to a large extent by the presence of Dr James McGrigor, Wellington's surgeon-general. McGrigor had been appointed the previous year to replace Dr Franck, and Anne had been worried that he would take exception to her presence in the surgeons' tents, but after his initial surprise, McGrigor had proved very supportive. He shared some of Anne's ideas, particularly with regard to advantages of cleanliness on the wards and when treating wounds, and had been quick to dismiss any complaints from some of the more traditional surgeons. Anne was delighted when he accepted her invitation, and even more so at his willingness to completely ignore both her lack of formal training and the fact that she was female, and to discuss professional matters openly with her at table. Anne hid her amusement at the slightly nauseated expression of one or two of the young hospital mates at the tone of the dinner table conversation and thanked McGrigor warmly at the end of the evening.

Paul was away for almost a week, and Anne kept herself determinedly busy with her daughter and with administrative work. When that ran out, she took up the big volume of surgical notes that she had begun writing earlier in the war, and had added to ever since. Anne was a compulsive note taker, and even in the aftermath of battle, she tried to make notes on some of the cases she treated. She found the notes and diagrams an invaluable reference tool and occasionally wondered if one day she might turn them into a book, although

130

she could not imagine who would publish a treatise on wound management written by an unqualified woman.

Anne was seated at her desk working when Paul arrived home. She was alone in the study, as Ross had ridden to Ciudad Rodrigo with Lieutenant Sinclair to visit the district stores and discuss uniform orders. Anne's notes lay open on the desk and she had been staring for some time at a paragraph about the relationship between the death of patients from gangrene and the cleanliness of the wards. The paragraph was nonsense. Anne had rewritten it three times and could not bear to write it again. She had no explanation for her theory and she knew that most surgeons laughed at her idea. Her only evidence, which was no evidence at all, were the numbers of men who survived, and it was easy to come up with a dozen alternative explanations for that. It did not change Anne's belief that keeping patients and wards clean was healthy, and she knew that a number of other surgeons, including Dr McGrigor himself agreed with her, but the sight of the words written down in what was intended to be a scholarly volume was vaguely depressing. Anne sighed, put down her pen and unnecessarily blotted the ink which had already dried.

Outside the window she heard the sounds of arrival and then her husband's voice. Anne got up and went to the window, her mood immediately lifting. She was missing Paul, on these frequent trips, and found herself silently cursing Lord Wellington for giving him this job. Anne had been looking forward to some time together during winter quarters and it seemed to her that she saw him less than during the campaigning season.

From the window, Anne could see that Paul had dismounted on the driveway and Charlie Bannan came to help Jenson to take the horses to the stables. Paul turned towards the house and Anne saw him stop and wait and then a woman joined him from the direction of the farm cottages. Katja Mackenzie was dressed in blue with a dainty straw hat perched on her fair hair. Sunlight caught golden lights off the blonde coils and lit up the attractive face with a warm light. She smiled up at Paul with open friendliness and spoke, probably an enquiry about his journey. Paul replied, and stood talking for a few minutes.

Anne could not hear their words and had no idea what their conversation was about. She thought, watching them, that they might almost have been related. Katja appeared to be telling a story, and Paul was listening, and then laughing with her. Anne had been about to run to greet him on the driveway, but something stopped her, and she stood immobile, her hand on the window frame, unable to tear her gaze away from them. There was nothing remotely wrong, no reason for unhappiness, but Anne felt something twist like a knife in her heart. The pain was so sharp and so shocking that it took her breath away for a moment and she pressed her hand tightly against the worn wood until she realised that a splinter was digging into her wrist.

The real pain took her mind off the emotional one and Anne stepped back from the window and turned away. She was appalled at herself but could not forget the flash of sheer jealous rage she had felt at the sight of Paul laughing with the other woman. It was utterly ridiculous, and Anne knew it.

She had complete trust in Paul's feelings for her, they had stood the test of both time and terrible adversity and he had never faltered. She had also spent enough time around Katja and Ross Mackenzie to sense the depth of their affection. Her jealousy was stupid and unworthy and had nothing to do with them and everything to do with her own confused state of mind. Anne realised she was crying, tears running unchecked down her face.

"Nan, are you in here? Katja just told me the funniest story, it'll make you..."

Paul's voice faltered and Anne turned away quickly although there was no way she was going to be able to hide her tears.

"Nan, are you all right? What on earth is wrong?"

For a moment, Anne could not thing of anything to say. She realised that her wrist was hurting and looked down. To her astonishment, it was bleeding copiously, several splashes of blood staining the skirt of her muslin gown. It was almost a relief. She turned to face him.

"My wrist. I was at the window, I heard you come in. I'm sorry."

Anne saw his eyes widen in horror and he came forward quickly, taking her hand in his. "Jesus, love, how did you manage that? Oh Christ, it's a splinter, isn't it, I can see the damned thing. Hold on a minute. Here, sit down, you're very pale."

Anne did not think that had anything to do with the splinter or the blood, given the amount of time she had spent digging musket shot out of wounded men, but she was happy to sit. At this particular moment, the look of concern in Paul's blue eyes was exactly the balm she needed, so she sat, cradling her hand, and he went to the door.

"Jenson! Oh - I'm sorry, Katja, I didn't intend to make you jump, I didn't see you there."

"Is something wrong, General?"

"My wife has had an accident, I wanted some water and..."

"May I see?"

It was the last thing Anne wanted, but she could not protest. Katja came into the room, crossed to where Anne sat and knelt to examine the wrist. It was bleeding a lot more than Anne would have expected. She could hear Paul giving instructions to Jenson in the hallway. Katja looked up and gave Anne a reassuring smile.

"That must hurt very much, it looks deep. Would you like me to remove it or would you prefer that your husband do it? Do you have some tweezers?"

Anne studied the older woman's attractive face and decided not to behave like a child. "There are some in my medical bag," she said. "I feel so stupid, I was leaning on the window frame, watching Paul come in. I must have leaned too hard somehow, I didn't see the splinter."

Paul came forward with the bag. He set it on the desk and rummaged through, then brought the tweezers. "Are you sure, Katja?"

"If your wife is, General."

Anne held out her arm. "Please."

Katja examined the injury as Jenson came into the room with a bowl of water and some cloth and bandages. "Thank you, Sergeant Jenson. Are you ready, Mevrou?"

Paul pulled over another chair and sat beside her. "This feels the wrong way round," he said teasingly. "Take my hand, girl of my heart, and look at me."

Anne obeyed. She felt a prickling as the tweezers took hold of the splinter and then a surprisingly sharp pain. Katja dropped the tweezers onto the table and held a dressing over the wound, which was bleeding more heavily, the blood soaking through. Anne turned to watch as Katja reached for a bandage.

"No, wait a moment. I just want to be sure."

The Dutchwoman paused, looking at her in surprise. Anne reached for a cloth and bathed the wound carefully. She could feel something catching. "Pass me the tweezers."

Katja did so. Anne rested her hand on the desk where the light was better and bent over it.

"Mevrou, you cannot, let me…"

"No, let her do it herself, she'll be all right," Paul said.

Anne swabbed away some of the blood and probed gently, wincing at the pain. She saw it immediately, just a dark speck, but easy enough to grasp with the tweezers. Anne withdrew it with great satisfaction and set the tweezers down, then bathed the wound again and looked up at Katja with a smile.

"Would you mind? It's difficult to do one-handed, and Paul ties a bandage like a three-legged donkey."

The Dutchwoman smiled broadly and picked up the bandage again, while Paul gave an indignant snort. Anne surveyed her handiwork with approval.

"Thank you. I'm sorry to have been so much trouble, I'm not generally this clumsy."

Katja got to her feet. "It is very usual to be so, this soon after having a baby. I tripped over my own feet for three months, I am sure. You should take care with that window, though, the frame must be damaged."

"I'll get one of the lads to have a look at it," Paul said. "Thank you, ma'am, I'm very grateful."

"So am I," Anne said, and was pleased to find that it was true.

"You are a very good patient, Mevrou, but I think an even better doctor. If my boys get a splinter, I will bring them to you."

"I hope you will," Anne said. She realised she was feeling shaky, but she suspected that it had nothing to do with her injury. The confused jumble of emotions had left her feeling exhausted, but she also felt better. Katja was looking at the bowl and the bloody rags on the desk and Anne read her thoughts without any effort whatsoever and realised that her resentment must have been horribly obvious to this very nice woman. She felt ashamed.

"I think I might lie down for a short time before dinner," she said. "I'm feeling stupidly shaky, which is not at all like me."

133

"That's an excellent idea," Paul said, getting up. Anne smiled at Katja.

"Mrs Mackenzie, would you mind awfully getting somebody to clear this up for me, I've made such a mess. And I'll need to wash the tweezers and..."

"I will do it, Mevrou. I am very happy to help. And I will bring up some wine."

"Thank you. And please - I am not generally a formal person. Will you call me Nan? All my friends do."

Anne could see the brightening in Katja's expression and she was suddenly furious with her own stupidity. "I would like that very much, Nan. Please, call me Katja."

***

Paul had intended to spend some time after dinner with Carl and Gervase, discussing the ongoing problem of Major Vane, but after the odd incident with the splinter, he was concerned about Anne. She was quieter than usual during dinner, leaving it to Paul to explain the bandage on her wrist, but she seemed thoughtful rather than upset. When the meal ended, she went to collect her daughter and Paul joined her in the nursery where Georgiana had just finished feeding.

"Do you fancy a walk with her, bonny lass? It's a pretty evening, we could go down to the river."

The warmth of Anne's smile reassured him. "I'd love to. Let me change my shoes and find another shawl for her. Why don't we take Craufurd?"

They walked through shady orchards, vineyards and olive groves, dappled with late evening sunlight, and Paul enjoyed the feeling of his tiny daughter curled in the crook of his arm, and Anne's hand in his. Agriculture was cautiously beginning to return to the war-ravaged borders of Portugal and Spain. Many of the village smallholdings remained deserted and overgrown, their walls smashed by artillery fire and their cottages empty and crumbling into ruin, but some of the more substantial farms and the large estates were regaining at least a portion of their prosperity. The army was a good customer, making it worthwhile to grow wheat and plant corn, and some of the more enterprising farmers were building mills and bread ovens to fill the apparently insatiable need for bread and tack biscuits from Wellington's army. George Kelly, who had developed a good working relationship with Señora Mata, the sharp tongued widow who owned the Santo Antonio estate, had supervised a working party of Paul's own men to build a bakery with brick ovens, which was run by her daughter and several of the estate children, bringing in a steady income while making it unnecessary for Paul's brigade to pay the extortionate prices charged by the village bakers to any man in a red coat.

Emerging from the trees, Paul and Anne crossed the small stone bridge which led out towards Castelo Mendo, where the 115th were billeted,

134

then turned left and took the leafy track beside the river. During the day, it was often lined with officers with fishing rods, dozing through sunny afternoons in the shade of the willow trees, but it was deserted now. Paul handed Georgiana over to Anne and found a stick for Craufurd to chase, and Anne sat down on a fallen tree trunk and held the baby up so that she could watch the big, shaggy grey dog splashing in and out of the water. At almost three months, Georgiana was becoming very alert and interested in the world around her, far more so, Paul thought, than her brother William had been at the same age. Every time Craufurd surged out of the river with the stick, Georgiana waved her arms and kicked her legs, with excitement, making Paul laugh.

"She wants to join in," he said.

"What a good idea." Anne got up and kicked her feet out of her sturdy walking shoes, then handed the baby to Paul who watched with interest as his wife hoisted her skirts and removed her stockings. Neatly she kilted the skirts up to her knees, scooped up her daughter and waded into the cold water. Georgiana seemed frozen with either excitement or fear, and Paul was poised to intervene, as Anne bent and allowed her daughter's toes to touch the water. Initially, the baby pulled her legs up away from the cold. Anne did not move, and after a moment, Georgiana stretched out her legs and touched the water. The expression on her face made Paul laugh aloud. He took the stick from Craufurd, who was waiting patiently, and threw it, so that the dog had to run past Anne to retrieve it. Water splashed up over both her and the baby, and Georgiana screeched with glee, and almost overset Anne with her kicking.

Laughing at her excitement, Paul took his daughter, wading into the shallows in his boots and lowered her a little further, so that she could dandle her feet fully in the river. Georgiana looked thoughtful for a moment, then surprised him by smacking both fists into the river repeatedly, crowing with delight as water splashed up.

"She's a fish in the making," Anne said. She had taken over Paul's duty with Craufurd, and the big dog gambolled around her waiting for the throw, visibly delighted that both his favourite humans were in the river with him. Anne's serious demeanour had cleared and she looked relaxed and happy. Paul swished his daughter through the water, ignoring the fact that her garments were getting soaked along with his boots and trousers, and gave himself up to a moment of pure happiness.

They remained until the sun began to sink faster and the evening air was getting chilly. Anne sat watching, waiting for her feet to dry while Paul removed Georgiana's drenched gown and wrapped her securely in the woollen shawl. Both he and Anne were wet from the waist down, both from the river and from Craufurd's enthusiastic shaking, and Georgiana was showing signs of restlessness, but once she was wrapped up and settled against Paul's body for the walk back, she fell asleep immediately, exhausted by the adventure.

"Sally will go mad, she's convinced the sight of water will give a child a fatal chill," Anne remarked as they crossed the bridge.

"My daughter is tougher than that. She's going to be hungry though."

They left the baby feeding hungrily with her disapproving wet nurse and retired to strip off their wet clothing. A full moon spilled silvery light over the gardens and fields of Santo Antonio and Paul stood at the window for a long moment before picking up the brush to attend to his wife's long black hair. Neither of them spoke for a long time and Paul wondered if she was falling asleep, but her eyes remained open in the candle light, steady on his in the mirror. Paul kissed the top of her head and went to set his boots outside the door for Jenson to clean then took off his coat. Anne still had not moved. Paul hung up the coat and began to untie his neckcloth, his eyes on the back of his wife's shining head. He saw the moment her shoulders shook a little and he dropped the neckcloth on the bed, took her arm and drew her gently but firmly to her feet and into his arms. Anne's face was wet with tears. She buried her face into his shoulder and Paul held her, stroking the long hair as she cried.

Eventually she was still in his arms. Paul eased himself away from her and placed a finger under her chin, tilting her face up to his. "Better?"

"Yes. I'm sorry, Paul. What a watering pot."

"It's a relief, to be honest, Nan, it's been coming for weeks. You're cold in that shift. Get yourself into bed while I finish undressing, I can't talk to a lass when her teeth are chattering."

As Paul joined her in the bed, Anne blew out the last candle. Paul drew her into his arms and kissed her for a long time. "I don't need to be able to see your face to know that you're upset, girl of my heart, but if you want darkness, you shall have it. Now talk to me."

"I'm not upset. Not with you. I'm sorry I've been so irritable, Paul, I've not been myself. But I've decided it needs to stop."

Paul shifted to allow her head to settle onto his shoulder. "Do you feel unwell?"

"No. I'm tired, but that was just the birth and those weeks of feeding Georgiana. Getting a wet nurse has helped, but I'm still not sleeping well. I wake up early and I lie there, thinking nonsense."

"What kind of nonsense?"

"Nonsense that I don't want to tell you."

"That's not part of our marriage agreement, Mrs van Daan, and you know it. If something is upsetting you this much, I want to know about it, however nonsensical. Are you having bad dreams again?"

Anne did not reply immediately and Paul forced himself to wait. After a long time, she said:

"Not in the way that I was. Sometimes I still dream about it, but that awful terror seems to have faded. But I dream about other things. A few days ago I dreamed that Georgiana had died, that she was stillborn after the retreat. When I woke up, I'd been crying in my sleep. It took me a while to stop."

"Why in God's name didn't you wake me up?"

"You weren't here," Anne said in a small voice and Paul tightened his arms about her.

"I should have been. I will be. I'll speak to Wellington, he doesn't need me..."

136

"Yes, he does, Paul. He's given you a job and you need to do it. It's not as though I'm on my own, I've all my friends around me, and the children will be arriving any day. I'm all right, really I am, but I do have a confession to make. If I tell you something, will you promise not to be angry?"

"Yes."

His wife laughed, sounding more like her normal self. "Liar. You can't help yourself."

"I don't think I could be angry with you just now, girl of my heart. Tell me."

Anne did not speak immediately, and Paul knew that she was thinking about what she wanted to say. "When I hurt my hand on the window earlier, I think I was clumsy because I was upset."

"What about?"

"I was in the study when I heard you ride in. I got up to go to the window, and I could hear you talking and laughing. I couldn't hear what you were saying, but you were with Katja."

"She was telling me about the escaped pig."

"I know that now, but I didn't then. She was wearing that blue gown and she was telling you something and you were listening and smiling at her and you looked so happy and she is so beautiful. And I don't feel beautiful at all just now."

Paul pushed himself up onto one elbow to look down at her, studying the beloved face through the darkness. "Are you telling me that you were jealous?"

"I've been feeling it for a few weeks, and it's so stupid, I'm furious with myself. She's nice. She's lovely. And I think we could be friends, if I didn't feel so awkward around her."

"Nan, this is crazy. There is literally nothing between…"

"I know, Paul. This is not about you. It's about me."

Paul could hear tears in her voice and he made himself stop speaking. Instead he drew her close and lay holding her. Any irritation was washed away in a rush of love and compassion that he could find no words to express and he thought about his response carefully, because he knew that no easy declaration of love would satisfy Anne at this moment.

"What did you mean when you said you don't feel beautiful, girl of my heart?"

"I'm embarrassed to even say it, Paul. I'm so conscious of how I look to you. Of how much my body has changed. When I undress for bed, I try not to look at myself, and I'm scrabbling to blow out the lamp before we make love, because I don't want you to look at me."

Paul did not speak. After a moment, she said:

"I'm sorry. I told you it was stupid."

Paul kissed her very gently on the tip of her nose. "I didn't expect it to be quite that silly, I'm shocked."

Anne swiped at him, caught between laughter and tears and he caught her flailing hand, kissed it, then eased himself from the bed, picked up a candle

137

and went to the door. There was a lamp kept burning on the landing and he lit the candle and came back, locking the door. Anne sat up in the bed, watching him wide-eyed as he moved about the room lighting lamps and candles until the room was brightly lit. Then he turned to her, stripped off his underclothing and slid into the bed.

"Give me your hand."

Anne obeyed, looking puzzled and a little nervous. Paul pushed back the covers and put her hand on his leg. "Tell me what you feel."

Anne ran her fingers over the skin, puckered and smooth now after so many years. "A scar. This one was from India, at Assaye."

"That's right. Adam Norris dug the ball out and stitched me up. He told me later I was lucky not to have been left with a permanent limp. Now this one."

"Also Assaye?"

"No, that's higher up, on my neck. This one was from the skirmish just before Assaye."

Paul led her through them, scars collected over eleven years in the army and two and a half in the navy as a boy. He could feel Anne relaxing as they talked, laughing over his stories, even though she had heard them all before.

"Now your turn, bonny lass."

Paul felt her hesitate, then she pulled the linen nightgown over her head. Paul reached out and touched her left shoulder, where a thin white line barely showed against the creamy perfection of her skin.

"This one?"

"That was my first husband. He beat me with a riding crop after I came back from Talavera because he thought that I was having an affair with you."

"He wasn't entirely wrong." Paul's hand slid very gently down her spine where another, more obvious scar crossed her lower back. "And this?"

"Colonel Dupres. Another beating, just before he raped me."

Anne's voice was determinedly steady. Paul leaned over and kissed her for a very long time, then moved his hand down to her belly. He stroked it, feeling the tiny running scars under his fingers then he eased her gently back onto the pillows and slid down to kiss the marks.

"And these?"

"Childbirth."

"That's cheating."

He felt her body quiver with laughter under him. "The pale ones are from William's birth. The darker ones are from Georgiana."

"I can't see the pale ones in this light, Nan, I need daylight for that."

"I know. And it didn't bother me at all after William. I wasn't like this, then."

"Have I ever confessed to you that I am a little proud of my scars? Even though some of them were caused by me being an idiot on the battlefield, they're a symbol of survival."

"It's different, Paul."

"No it's not. You and I sat beside Rowena as she died giving birth, these are battle scars make no mistake. They'll fade, bonny lass, until we barely notice them, but with or without them, you're beautiful, every man thinks so. But that's not why I love you. There are so many things that you can do and so many things I admire about you, but I don't make lists of your talents and weigh them up against other women. Give me your hand."

Anne did so and Paul placed it on a broad white scar on his chest. "This one?"

"Talavera. You almost died."

"That ball was so close to my heart, Norris said he couldn't see how you'd managed to dig it out without killing me. My heart beats because of you and it beats for you, Anne van Daan, every day that I live. Nothing will ever change that."

"Oh Paul." Anne was crying again, but there was laughter through the tears. "I'm such a fool."

"Not usually. Are you getting cold? Where's your nightgown?"

"I don't need it."

Paul reached for her, wiping the tears away with his hand. "Do you need me to blow out a few candles?"

"No. I want to look at you. And I want you to see me."

They lay afterwards tangled together, and he could hear her breathing, matching his own. "Paul?"

"Yes, love?"

"Thank you."

"I didn't do anything."

"Yes, you did. Tomorrow, I'm going to start again with Katja Mackenzie."

"I'm glad. I think you have a lot in common."

Anne gave a soft laugh. "I know you do, Paul. I rather think that has been the problem. But it's all right, don't change anything. I'm the one who needs to fix this. I love you. Goodnight."

She fell asleep quickly, and Paul lay listening to her breathing and letting it soothe him until he too slept.

Chapter Ten

Giles and his companions set out from the convent in crisp, dry weather, and Porlier led his men north through the mountains, rising steeply to icy passes where even the agile little ponies slipped and slithered along some of the tracks, then down into valleys where the snow had begun to melt, causing streams and rivers to overflow their banks, and turning rocky surfaces into temporary waterfalls. The weather was becoming milder, and on the lower slopes and in the valleys, spring flowers peeped out between rocks, or occasionally splashed riotous colour over an entire meadow.

The Spanish irregulars set a fast pace, and Giles kept an anxious eye on Brat in case she was struggling. He was not surprised that she had decided not to remain at the convent, and he was confident by now that she would not slow them down, but Porlier's speed was punishing. Giles thanked God that he had decided not to bring his own horse. The Cantabrian ponies had extraordinary endurance.

They spent most nights in the open, huddled in cloaks and greatcoats around the fire, and Giles took the opportunity to question Porlier about recent French activity in the region.

"Father Luis told me that Clausel is taking over."

"Clausel is already in command. The French are attacking all along the northern coast, they are under orders to suppress all resistance and re-establish French control through the region. They have also been ordered to keep the high road open and make sure that supply columns and mail is able to get through."

Giles studied the other man thoughtfully. "And how is that going?"

Porlier gave a wolfish grin. "Not well," he said. "They do not have enough men. They have some successes, but while they drive us back in one area, our countrymen attack in another. Meanwhile the French will not follow us up into the mountains. Those who do, do not return."

The words were chilling and Giles understood. The mountains in winter were no place for bodies of regular troops. They could not live off the land and there was nowhere to hide and the guerrillas picked them off ruthlessly, taking no prisoners.

"Clausel is a better soldier than Caffarelli," Michael said.

"Even the best soldier cannot do the impossible. It is true that he hunts us throughout the region, and sometimes he has success. He has constructed blockhouses between Irun and Burgos, but while his men are tied down manning them, they cannot be chasing General Mina or putting a garrison into Santander or laying siege to Castro Urdiales."

"It's to be hoped your men are keeping them too busy to do that until we manage to get Sir Horace out."

"Or attend his grave," Porlier said unemotionally. "Either way, we have an early start, we should rest."

They encountered Porlier's forces one misty afternoon, sentries materialising from behind rocks and bushes quickly and silently, guns steady in the hands of men who looked more like bandits than soldiers. Giles held up his hand to his party and remained very still as Porlier rode forward. After a brief exchange there were smiles and then laughter and back slapping, and Porlier waved them forward.

"They are here. Half a league to the west. Come, join us for a meal and we shall celebrate our survival."

The camp was set up around a small village with a neat little church and narrow lanes of red tiled houses tumbling down a hillside to the banks of a river. Porlier received a hero's welcome, with women and children running to cheer him and lay bright scarves and shawls for he and his men to ride over as they entered the village. Giles glanced at Michael and could see that the Irishman was amused.

"Reminds me of entering Madrid. We were popular for months there. Happy times."

"I'll bet you were less popular when you marched out," Giles said.

"Jesus, yes, it was like a funeral. Where were you?"

"Up here, and then at Burgos. I still think you had a better time than I did."

"I'm not arguing with it. How long do we stay here?"

"A day or two, no more, I want to be on our way. I'll see what news we can pick up about the position of Clausel's troops, they'll have more up to date intelligence here, and I'd like to get a letter back to Wellington, he's waiting for news. If Porlier can't spare a rider to the coast, I could send Antonio but I'd rather keep him with us. I know the country fairly well, but not like he does."

They ate supper in the village that evening, and drank Cantabrian wine, watching Porlier's men dancing with the village women. One of them approached Brat, beckoning her to join the dance, and she shook her head firmly. The man held out his hand, laughing, insisting, and Michael unfolded his long length and got to his feet.

"It might be a while before we've the opportunity to dance again, Brat. Up with you."

Brat stared at him in wide-eyed astonishment, but let him pull her to her feet and lead her into the circle. Antonio was already dancing, combining bear-like clumsiness with joyous enthusiasm. It always made Giles smile to watch him, and he smiled again, as Michael spun Brat around so fast that she almost lost her balance. The women and girls were dressed in traditional white shirts with brilliantly coloured skirts in bright orange, green or yellow, decorated with bands of black velvet. Married women covered their heads with brightly patterned headscarves but the young and unmarried girls wore their hair loose.

One of them approached Giles, a pretty girl with black hair held back at the sides with two combs and big hooped earrings that brushed her cheeks. Giles shook his head, and she bent and took both his hands, pulling on them. Giles resisted for a moment longer and then got up. The dance was unfamiliar to him, a country dance where each couple faced each other in a circle and mirrored steps, then spun around before changing partners. It was not difficult to follow her lead, and after a while, Giles found himself caught up in the fast rhythm of the guitars.

The music changed and another woman took his hand, showing him the steps to the new dance. Giles had intended to spend the evening talking to Porlier's men to garner as much intelligence as possible about French dispositions, but he realised that with the wine flowing this freely, he was unlikely to get much sense out of any of them until morning. Instead he danced, relaxing into the evening as stars appeared in the velvet sky and men hung lanterns outside the church and the houses. More than one couple had slipped away from the square into the darkness of the village and Giles found himself searching for Michael and Brat. He was relieved to see that they were still there, sitting on the low church wall sharing a cup of wine, watching the dancing.

The music ended, and in the brief pause for the guitarists to refresh themselves, Giles bowed to his partner and moved away. His path was blocked and he looked down into the dark eyes of the young woman who had first asked him to dance. She was holding out a full wine cup and Giles took it and drank. He handed it back and she drank as well, her eyes still on his. Giles felt her hand in his and he allowed her to lead him out of the lamplight and into the shadows of the churchyard.

"Señorita, this is not a good idea."

"Yes, it is." She handed him the cup again, and Giles drank, watching her as she walked on into the darkness beyond faded gravestones to a small, grassy garden. He could not see her clearly, but her movement was unmistakable, as she removed the bright, fringed shawl and dropped it to the ground, then turned and waited. As he approached, she was unlacing the front of the white linen shirt.

Giles handed her the cup and she drained it and tossed it to one side. Reaching up, she buried her hand in his fair hair, then took his hand and guided it to her breast. Giles bent to kiss her neck, sliding the shirt down bare shoulders, feeling her tugging at his jacket to remove it.

"We shouldn't be doing this," he said, against her skin.

142

"Tonight, I will be doing this with somebody," the girl said, and Giles flinched internally at the casual bitterness in her voice. "They are heroes, they will expect it."

Giles pulled back with an enormous effort. "I don't expect it," he said.

She smiled, and there was sadness but also genuine warmth. "I can tell that. You speak my language very well, Señor. This night, I would like to choose for myself, and I choose you. If you want me."

Giles studied the pretty features through the darkness, then reached up and very gently removed first one then the other comb, dropping them on top of her shawl. He stripped off his jacket, folded it and laid it down as a pillow for her head. "I want you," he said. "And I am honoured. May I know your name?"

She laughed, a rich warm sound in his ear. "My name is Rosita."

"Rosita. Such a pretty name. My name is Giles."

"Giles. Are you also a hero?"

Giles lowered her gently to the cool springy grass. There was a sweet perfume, coming from some kind of climbing flower over the church wall and he could still hear the guitars playing in the square, the intensity of the music mirroring the sudden intensity of his desire as his body touched hers. "No," he said, tracing a line of very gentle kisses across her shoulder and up to her ear. "But I think you may be, *querida.*"

They left in a cold, misty dawn two days later. Giles' letter was written and coded and dispatched with a fast rider from Porlier's men, and Porlier slapped him on the back as Giles gave the messenger instructions and watched him leave.

"He is a good man, Captain, he will reach Corunna safely. And now you have another night, with no responsibilities. We shall dine on roasted sheep and drink more wine, and this time you shall take your pretty friend into a warm bedroom, and put a smile on her face before…"

"My private life is my own, General," Giles said shortly. Porlier looked at him and laughed aloud.

"It is wartime, my friend. Such encounters happen all the time. She had her eye on you from the moment you sat down. Suppress that English conscience and enjoy her, next week you might be dead. And so might she."

The thought bothered Giles, but when she came to sit beside him at the meal, there was something hesitant about her, almost shy, and Giles could not reject her. Instead he took her hand and smiled at her and when they had eaten and drunk she led him silently into one of the cottages and put her arms about him, and Giles pushed his conscience to one side and kissed her very tenderly. There was a bed, and privacy, and despite the impermanence of their connection, there was kindness and warmth alongside desire, and he lay afterwards holding her as she slept and wished that he had a gift that he could give her, since she had given him so much and he would not insult her by giving her money like a prostitute.

Outside in the chilly dawn, he found himself beside Brat, checking his saddle and girth and making sure his pack and saddlebags were securely strapped on.

"Captain."

Giles glanced at her. She was holding something out and he took it and felt softness under his fingers. He shook it out and saw that it was a scarf, some soft silky material, in a vivid emerald green.

"It was a gift from Mrs van Daan, when I helped her at the quinta. I do not wear it, it is not a scarf for a boy."

Giles understood and was startled and moved. "Brat, I can't take this."

"I want you to have it."

"How did you know?" Giles said softly.

"It is the kind of man you are."

Giles watched her turn away then went in search of Rosita. She took the scarf, wide-eyed, and looked up at him. Giles kissed her very gently.

"To remember me by. I wish I had something better. Goodbye, Rosita, I will not forget you."

She looked down at the scarf and then raised it to her cheek, feeling its softness. "I have nothing to give you."

"You gave me friendship, *querida*, and that's no small gift."

She looked up at him for a long moment, then said:

"Wait. Just one moment."

She was gone, and he waited, hoping she was not going to give him something of value. She reappeared quickly and pushed a folded piece of cloth into his hand.

"Do not open it now, you will laugh at me. Later, when you have gone."

Giles kissed her again and went to his horse. A number of villagers had come out to see the Englishmen off. Michael was already mounted, wrapped in his greatcoat against the cold morning air. Giles patted his pony's neck, waiting for Antonio to mount up. Surreptitiously, he slipped the cloth from his pocket and opened it. There was a long coiled strand of dark hair, and beneath it, a white bloom, a little crumpled from being wrapped, but still sweet smelling in his hand. Giles raised it to his nose and inhaled the perfume, then dismounted and handed the reins to a surprised Antonio. He crossed the square, took her face in his hands and kissed her long and hard.

They clattered across the old stone bridge and Giles looked back. She was the last person standing there, waving the bright green scarf. Giles waved back, as the others rode on ahead of him. The mist was coming down thicker and after a moment, it swirled about her, and he could no longer see her. Turning his mount, he nudged him into a trot to catch up with his companions.

***

As the party rode north west towards the coast, the weather began to improve dramatically. It was fully spring, and the countryside was green, with

144

new growth on trees and shrubs and crops, where any had been planted, beginning to sprout above dark red earth. Growing closer to French held territory, they rode more cautiously, keeping away from the main roads and travelling cross country. Once or twice there were signs of occupation, with tracks churned up by cavalry and gun carriages.

It was new to Michael and he found it unnerving. He was accustomed to marching with an army, or at least moving with his fellow skirmishers, and although he had known a number of unexpected encounters with the enemy, they had all been part of a bigger campaign, with the lines of the army close by. Out here, they rode in isolation, knowing the French to be near. Michael watched both Giles and Antonio, seeing them differently in this hostile setting. They were alert, constantly scanning the horizon, pausing before cresting every hill or crossing every bridge or ford.

At night, with the weather improved, they bivouacked in the open, and Antonio went to get supplies from local villages while Michael and Giles hunted rabbits and pigeons, which Brat cooked expertly over the fire. One evening they made camp in a small wooded area not far from the river. Brat disappeared with a murmured excuse, which Michael took to be a need to relieve herself. She was gone so long that he became worried enough to go in search of her. He met her coming back up from the river looking immensely proud of herself, with three large fish hanging from a branch over her shoulder.

"How the devil did you manage that?" Michael asked, astonished.

"I speared them with my knife. My father taught me to wait patiently in the shallows, so that they do not realise you are there. It takes much practice, but I have not forgotten how to do it. See?"

The fish were delicious, and they burned their fingers in their eagerness to eat them, with some dark bread that Antonio had managed to buy from a farmer's wife. Brat sat cross-legged, licking her fingers, and Antonio laughed and threw her another piece of bread.

"Finish it, little fox, it will not keep."

Brat smiled at him and used the bread to scrape the last vestige of fish from her mess tin, tossing the bones into the fire, which spat indignantly. Giles sat with his back against a tree, long legs stretched out before him, looking more relaxed than he had for days.

"If the French are within three miles of us, Brat, they'll smell that fish cooking. It was worth it though, you wouldn't believe what Antonio and I usually subsist on. We'll see them coming anyway, and there's plenty of cover. Where did you learn all this?"

"My father," Brat said composedly. "My mother died and there were just we two for many years. He did not have a son and felt the lack, I think. So I became both son and daughter to him. I cooked and tended the house, and he taught me about horses and how to ride."

"How big was your farm?" Michael asked. He had never really asked Brat about her younger life. Their roles as master and servant had precluded this kind of conversation, but over these past weeks, barriers had come down between all of them.

"It was the biggest in the village. We had a proper house, and a horse, and two mules who pulled the cart when we went to market to sell our produce. I tended the gardens and the orchard, and my father hired men to help in the fields and with the sheep. At harvest time, many of the villagers came to help and afterwards there was a feast and a dance."

"I saw you reading at the convent," Giles said. "Did your father teach you?"

"Of course. He learned with the priest in the village school when he was a boy and he taught me well. We had books in our house. He liked me to read to him in the evenings."

"How old were you when he died?" Antonio asked. Michael flinched. He had not wanted to refer to the horrors Brat had faced after the French came and he wished Antonio had not asked. He saw Brat's face go very still but then she looked up.

"I was fifteen. Afterwards, there was a long time, when I could not think of him at all. I could not think of all that I had lost, because I would have gone mad with grief. But now I can see his face again, and I think he smiles at me."

Michael felt his heart break. He tried to speak but no words would come. Across the fire, Giles said:

"I think he smiles at you too, little one. He would have reason to be proud."

"What about you, Captain Fenwick? Did you go into the army to become a famous general?"

Giles laughed aloud at her impudence. "I did not, urchin. I went into the army, because I came from a very proud, very ancient, very noble family, which means that there is almost nothing one can do to earn a living which would not earn you the contempt of your social equals. My father was the younger brother of an Earl, and as poor as a church mouse, although far less well behaved. I was raised in luxury, but without a feather to fly with, and as my father and his brother did not get on, I was grateful when my uncle at least agreed to finance my first two commissions. My parents are dead, and I've not seen my cousin for years, although I suppose we get on well enough - better than our fathers did."

"You were with the second battalion for a while," Michael said.

"No, I bloody wasn't. I was with the only company of the first battalion to miss out on General van Daan's rise to glory, owing to the fact that I was stuck under the worst captain in the army and Van Daan loathed him. I was sent to Alexandria and to Walcheren, both of them foul campaigns, until they finally sent us to join the rest of you in Portugal and I managed to get rid of bloody Longford and get promoted. It's not made me rich, in fact my pockets are permanently to let. But it has definitely been interesting."

Michael was smiling, remembering how defensive Giles had been when he first arrived in Portugal. He looked over at Antonio and the Spaniard looked back with calm eyes.

"I don't need to ask why you're here, do I, Antonio?"

146

"I am here to fight for my people. Before, I fought with the partisans, but then we were attacked and most were killed. I was asked to act as guide to Captain Fenwick for a time." Antonio regarded Giles loftily. "At first, I thought he was just another English lord who would get me killed. But he is not so bad."

Giles had taken out his flask and was drinking. He choked with laughter. "You arrogant Spanish bastard, you'd have been long dead if it hadn't been for me. But it's mutual. Here, have a drink and stop talking before you convince yourself your stories are true."

Antonio took the flask with a grin. "The best thing about you is your brandy," he said, taking a swig. "When you get yourself killed, I will steal it before I run away."

Michael was shaking with laughter. "They should put you two on the stage, you'd be a lot funnier than the light division amateur dramatics company. Although most things are, to be fair."

Giles turned to look at him. "And what story do you have to make us laugh, Michael?"

Michael felt a slight knot in his stomach. He studied the younger man in the firelight. "I joined the army to see the world," he said cheerfully. "Like many another young Irishman."

"And made the step up to the officers mess as if you were born to it," Giles said lightly. "A man listening to you talk, Michael, would think you an educated man, not a starving Paddy with an empty belly ready to sign his life away for regular rations and a red coat. What year did you join?"

Michael did not speak for a long time. Finally he took a deep breath. "At the beginning of 1799," he said quietly.

"And what were you doing before that? Skip the bit about taking part in Wolf Tone's rebellion, I've already worked that out."

"I was studying classics at Trinity in Dublin," Michael said.

Giles gave a splutter of laughter. "Jesus Christ, look at us. The nephew of an Earl and a classical scholar sitting eating fish out of a tin can with a Spanish farmer and the daughter of another, who's dressed up as a boy. My esteemed parents would turn in their graves. What about yours?"

"I don't know," Michael said. He had never admitted this to anybody, and it felt very strange. "I don't even know if they're dead or alive. I joined under a new name, I was a wanted man, and even writing to them was too dangerous. For them and for me. I always thought that a few years down the line, I'd find a way to get a message to them. But a few years down the line, I was in India, playing death or glory with the maddest young officer I'd ever met in my life, and the moment passed. And now I go for whole months without thinking of them, and when I do, I feel a weight of guilt. But I don't know what I'd say to them now, since I can't tell them where I am or what I've been doing or even what I'm called. Perhaps they're dead. If not, perhaps they're better not knowing."

There was a long silence. Into it, Giles said:

"I'm sorry, Michael. I shouldn't have asked."

147

"Jesus, no, it's all right. And it's a relief to say it. We're all getting maudlin with the fire and the brandy, we should get some sleep."

"We should. Brat…"

"I will wash the things at the river, I need to be private anyway." Brat got up and began collecting the mess tins and cups. She paused in front of Michael. "I think, when this is over, you should write to them. General van Daan would help you do it, in a way that nobody would know. So long after, nobody will look at their letters."

It was true and it was obvious. "I know, Brat. It's rather gone beyond that. They may be dead."

"Then you may find out. Or not. But you should try. Then you too will be able to see their faces smiling at you. It is a good feeling, Captain."

Michael watched as she walked into the trees and could think of nothing more to say.

***

By the end of Major Vane's first two months in command of the 115th there had been six regimental courts martial, one flogging, and a furious complaint against Paul's new brigade major, with a request that he be immediately arrested. Paul read the angry letter twice, trying to work out exactly what charge Major Vane wanted to bring against Captain Manson. There were so many ink blots and exclamation marks, that it could have been almost anything. Paul put the letter down with a sigh, went to the door and yelled for Jenson.

"Jenson, do you have any idea where Captain Manson might be?"

"Yes, sir. You sent him over to help out with the new recruits for the 112th. By now, he's probably making the poor buggers wish they'd never taken that shilling."

"They'll have been wishing that long before they encountered Captain Manson, Jenson, but I admit he probably won't have helped. Will you send Charlie over with a message that I'd like to see him please."

"Yes, sir."

"And get Charlie to take Craufurd with him for a run, will you? I need to finish this report for Lord Wellington and he keeps trying to climb onto my lap, the damned thing is going to be illegible."

"That won't have anything to do with the dog, sir. I'll tell Charlie."

Manson arrived without a trace of the defensive belligerence that Paul would have expected from another young officer. He knew that was not a good sign. Manson saluted and stood to attention before Paul's desk and Paul studied him. With another officer, he might have prolonged the silence to make a point, but he knew it was pointless with Manson, who would stand there all day.

"Is it going to surprise you to hear that I've had a complaint about you, Captain Manson?"

"Not really, sir."

148

"Any guesses?"

"Major Vane, sir?"

"The doubt in your voice alarms me, Captain. Any others likely to complain?"

"Possibly Dr Fielding, sir."

"Dr Fielding? What in God's name have you done to him, he's only been here five minutes? Oh sit down for God's sake, Leo, and have a drink, you can pour one for me as well. What the hell happened? I spent a long time lecturing the junior officers of the 115th about this. I didn't expect to have to do the same to my Brigade Major."

"You probably should have, sir."

Paul studied his junior and realised that under Manson's calm exterior, he was furious. He reached for the brandy that Manson had poured and waited until Manson had taken a drink, then said:

"What happened?"

"I hadn't received the monthly return for the 115th. It was only a few days late, but I knew you wanted to keep an eye on it, so I made an excuse to go over there. I arrived in the middle of a flogging. It felt very poetic."

"Oh." Paul studied Manson with genuine concern. "Oh shit, I'm sorry, Leo. Why the bloody hell didn't you come and talk to me?"

"I needed some time," Manson said. "Would you believe, it's the first flogging I've witnessed since that day more than two years ago? I can't believe I've avoided it, but I have."

"You're in the 110th, lad, it's not that hard. I can't remember the last time we ordered a flogging. Although I've definitely administered the odd punch along the way. But I can see why you got upset."

Manson sipped the brandy and did not speak for a minute and Paul gave him time. Manson had arrived in Portugal at the end of 1810 as a nineteen year old lieutenant with no experience, and his early weeks with the 112th had been coloured by the death of a man he had ordered to be flogged. Paul had arrived part way through the flogging and he could imagine how Manson must have felt, finding himself in the same position.

"Did you stop it?" Paul asked eventually.

"I ordered the surgeon to stop it. It needed to be stopped, and I was watching Captain Carlyon and Captain Witham, who were clearly about to explode. Rather me than them, they've got to serve under the bastard."

"What happened with the surgeon?"

"Nothing much. He's new to the job and I don't think he was sure if he was allowed to override Vane."

"What was it about?"

"It's in the return, sir, I'm guessing you've not looked yet."

"Tell me anyway. What was the charge?"

Manson took another sip of brandy. "Drunk on duty. Which, according to Witham, he probably was. Witham hauled him up about a month ago for the same thing and he spent a week emptying the latrines without a bottle for comfort. He settled down for a bit after that, but apparently he went

149

on a spree with his Spanish girlfriend and hadn't sobered up in time for morning drill and training. There have been a few of them up on charges for various different things, but no floggings ordered. I think Carlyon and Witham have been talking to the other officers, trying to persuade them that if they want to stay on the right side of their brigade commander, they should vote for a different punishment."

"The trouble is, once you get as far as an RCM, there aren't many options, which is why I try not to use them." Paul eyed Manson sympathetically. "Look, Leo, we get away with it in the 110th and 112th because most of the officers came up under me or under Johnny and they don't need to resort to court martial for minor offences, but I don't blame the officers of the 115th. It takes time."

"Sir, he was trying to give more than the regulation number of lashes."

Paul froze. "He can't."

"He was. Witham told me. This man - O'Connell - was up in front of a court previously and Major Vane was furious when the court failed to order a flogging, merely stopped his pay and confined him for a week. This time around it was different officers on the court. Not our men, sir. They ordered three hundred, given that it was a repeat offence. It seems that Vane had a quiet word with the drummers. Sergeant Barforth told Witham that Vane also spoke to O'Connell and assured him that he'd get an extra hundred to make up for the previous time he should have been flogged. He also ordered Dr Fielding not to stop the punishment - he said that the doctor hadn't the experience to know when a man was malingering or not, and…"

Paul got up. "I am going to flay him alive and nail his hide to the door as a warning to others," he said furiously. "How dare he try to flout army regulations and think he's going to get away with it? By the time I've finished with him, he'd going to wish he'd gone back to England and got a post at Horse Guards along with the rest of the fucking idiots who haven't a clue how to run an army. Jenson!"

His orderly limped into the room so quickly that Paul knew he had been standing outside the door. "Did you miss any of that, Jenson?"

"Not a word, sir."

"Good. Get Rufus saddled up, I'm riding over to see Major Vane."

"I'm not sure if that's a good idea right now, sir."

"Your privileged position, Sergeant Jenson, doesn't give you the right to question my orders. Get Rufus saddled and do it now."

"Don't, Sergeant."

Paul turned on Manson. "Did you just countermand my order, Captain Manson, or am I hearing things?"

"You shouldn't go over there, sir, until you've heard the full story."

There was a long moment of silence during which Paul fought the urge to swear at both Manson and Jenson and storm across to the stables, but he knew that Manson probably had a point. Eventually, he said:

"Sergeant Jenson. Saddle my horse. I am going over there, but I will hear Captain Manson out first."

"Yes, sir."

"And if I come out of this room and you're still standing there, I am going to hit you, Jenson."

"Yes, sir."

Paul closed the door on his orderly and stalked back to his chair. "Get on with it."

Manson picked up the brandy bottle and topped up both glasses. "I didn't know all this when I intervened, sir," he said quietly. "I rode in. I knew what was happening of course. It was the oddest feeling. As if I'd gone back in time to that day in Lisbon, but I was where you were then. I need to tell you, I was going to stop that flogging regardless of how many he'd been given, sir."

"I understand that, Leo. How many did he have, in the end?"

"A hundred and eighty two, according to Barforth, although Vane swore it was less. Carlyon and Witham said it was definitely well over a hundred. The drummer who was administering the punishment didn't want to say anything at all. You can't blame him, poor bastard."

"No, he knows he'll be next. That's how officers like Vane work. What did Fielding say?"

"He wasn't happy, sir, but he was in an impossible position. Vane was yelling at him to authorise the continuation of the punishment, I was telling him I'd have him cashiered if he let it go on. I did lose my temper a bit, sir. Eventually, he checked O'Connell over and said he was recommending that it be stopped, to be completed on medical advice, but that he would be writing to Dr McGrigor about it."

"That's not a problem. Actually, it was an excellent way of handling it, I take my hat off to him. Either Nan or I will speak to McGrigor and explain." Paul studied his junior and grinned. "All right, you can stop panicking. I've calmed down a bit. I'll see that O'Connell's sentence is commuted, a hundred and eighty is more than enough for being drunk. I will also speak to O'Connell to explain how much worse his life could get if I take a personal interest in his drinking habits. And then there is Major Vane."

"If he wants me charged, sir, I don't expect you to intervene. I was bloody rude to him, I don't deny it. Happy to stand my trial."

"I've always known that the next officer of the 110th to get hauled up before a general court martial was likely to be you, Captain Manson. Wipe that expression off your face, or it'll be me bringing you up on a charge."

"You wouldn't do that, sir. You might punch me..."

"It is looking increasingly likely. Of all the bloody days. Wellington wants to see me, I'm supposed to be travelling to visit the cavalry tomorrow, and Sir Stapleton Cotton is not one of my admirers, and I'm weeks behind with these bloody reports for his Lordship."

"I'm really sorry, sir."

"Don't be, you did the right thing. I'll speak to McGrigor tomorrow about Dr Fielding, and I'll see Vane on my way back from headquarters. It'll

151

give me a chance to speak to Wellington about it, so I can tell Vane with confidence that if he goes after you, Wellington will chew him up and spit him out in a heartbeat. Depending on how rude you were, may I suggest a letter of apology? You can make it as offensively civil as you like, providing there's an apology in there somewhere."

"If you'd like me to, sir."

"I would, Leo. You don't have to mean it. This was going to happen at some point, don't worry about it. How is everything else going?"

"I think it's going well, sir."

"So do I. I never had any doubt about my choice of brigade major, and I don't now. But try to stay out of his way for a bit, I'll put somebody else onto watching him."

"I will. Thank you, sir."

Paul studied him, and thought how attached he had become to Manson over the past few years. "How close are we to having the new men allocated and settled?"

"Pretty much there, sir. Captain Mackenzie is bringing all the records up to date, to reflect their new battalions and companies, but we should have those by the end of this week."

"Excellent. When it's done, take some leave."

Manson's hazel eyes widened in surprise. "Sir?"

"Don't look so shocked. It's something you're supposed to be allowed to do in winter quarters. Even I'm taking some time off when my children arrive. Take a few weeks and take yourself off to Elvas. Write to her today to tell her you'll be coming."

Manson's eyes lit up. "You don't object?"

"It's an order, Captain. You'll come back all the better for it, I've seen how good she is for you. Go and waste some of your prize money on her."

"Thank you, sir. I'll make sure everything's up to date before I go. It means a lot."

"Enjoy it. Now get out of here. Oh - is Jenson lurking outside that door?"

Manson opened the door and peered. "Not Jenson, sir. I think you can come in, ma'am."

Anne came into the room and studied him. "I don't think I'm needed after all," she concluded. "Leo, would you tell Jenson to unsaddle Rufus, if he saddled him up."

Paul got up. "Did Jenson tell you that I was about to kill somebody?"

"Yes."

My orderly is an interfering bastard."

"Paul."

"Sorry. Don't bother, Captain, I'm done for the day, I need fresh air. Come riding with me, girl of my heart, and I will tell you the full story of Major Vane. You'll be swearing yourself by the end of it."

**

152

Lord Wellington received Paul's report on the matter of Captain Manson and Major Vane with a blank expression. At the end of it, the commander gave a deep sigh and motioned for Paul to sit.

"I am disappointed, General. I had high hopes for Captain Manson."

"I wouldn't write him off just yet, sir, he didn't hit anybody."

"Have you spoken to Major Vane?"

"Not yet, sir. I'm riding over there after this."

"Try to resolve this in a civilised manner, General, I do not have time for your antics at present. Have you the reports I requested?"

"One of them, sir. I'm still working on the others."

"Work faster, General. I need information."

"Yes, sir."

Wellington took the report, glanced at it and nodded. "I have received a report from Captain Fenwick. They were snowbound at the Santa Ana convent for almost a week, so he took the opportunity to bring me up to date with what has been going on in the district. He is a very useful officer."

"He is, sir." Paul wondered if Giles had mentioned the unexpected inclusion of Brat in the party. He suspected not. Michael had also written from the convent, a brief scrawl to inform Paul of Brat's presence and to express hope that the horses had arrived back safely. Paul wished he could write to reassure Michael that they had, so that Johnny's horse would be safely in the stable when he returned from England.

"Very well," Wellington said. "Speak to Major Vane and you may tell him that Captain Manson has my support."

"Thank you, sir."

"There is something else, and I wanted to tell you about it in person. It concerns Sir William Erskine."

"Erskine?" Paul could feel his hackles rising immediately. "I thought he was in Lisbon on sick leave? Is he back? I'm going to visit Sir Stapleton Cotton later this week, it'll be a much easier meeting if I don't have to deal with..."

"He is dead, General."

Paul froze, staring at his chief in astonishment. "Dead? How? Was he ill? I'd assumed that his absence was..."

"He killed himself, Paul."

"Oh. Oh God, no."

Wellington was watching him with unusual sympathy. "Your assumption was correct, he was removed from his command because it was clear to all of us that his mental instability was becoming worse and worse. There were several incidents during the retreat when he put lives at risk. For the sake of his family I have disguised the worst of his mistakes, but I could no longer allow him command of my men."

"Is that why...?"

"I don't know, General. We will never know. Witnesses say that he threw himself from an upper window in the house where he was staying in Lisbon. He died almost immediately of his injuries."

"Poor bastard."

"He was a very troubled man, I hope that he is finally at peace."

Paul sat quietly, thinking about it. He had an appalling relationship with Sir William Erskine, and could remember a number of occasions when he had quite publicly wished that a stray shot would remove him and put the army out of its misery, but he was unexpectedly upset to hear that the man had been desperate enough to take his own life.

"Thank you for telling me like this, sir," he said finally. "I don't really know how I feel about it. I couldn't stand Erskine and I hold him largely responsible for the death of a lot of men, including young Will Grey, who meant a lot to me. But to die that way…"

Wellington gave a wry smile. "I recollect that you became very angry with me when I failed to inform you of poor Bevan's suicide, Paul. I realise the circumstances are very different, but I thought I should tell you myself."

Paul was touched, but he knew better than to say so to his reserved commander. Reverting to practical issues, he said:

"I suppose this makes your reorganisation of the cavalry easier, sir."

"Indeed. I could not say this to anybody else, but it has solved a difficult problem for me. With Erskine dead, and Charles Stewart going back to England, I can reorganise my cavalry as I wish, and Cotton will give me no trouble."

Paul rose to leave. "I should be going. In a peculiar way, I'll miss Charles Stewart. He was a pain in the arse, but he was entertaining."

"After trying to manage him on my staff, General, I assure you the entertainment wears very thin. My regards to your wife. Are you attending this theatrical performance on Tuesday?"

"The light division amateur dramatic society? Apparently so, sir, my wife accepted on my behalf. Personally, I would rather have a tooth drawn than watch Ensign Granville dressed up as a sweet young debutante about to elope with Captain Martin, but it appears I have no choice."

"Excellent. I will make sure that seats are reserved beside me."

"Is that because you want to hold my wife's hand through the dramatic moments, sir?"

"Mostly it is because I will enjoy watching you hate every moment, General, but your wife's company is always a delight. I will see you there. During your conversation with Major Vane, feel free to mention that if I see Captain Manson's name coming up for a general court martial on some spurious charge which will waste my time, I am going to be extremely displeased. If the boy is willing to apologise for his hasty tongue, I consider the matter at an end. Make sure he knows that, will you?"

"I will definitely mention it, sir," Paul said seriously, and left, closing the door quietly behind him.

The 115th was quartered two miles from Santo Antonio, close to the attractive medieval village of Castelo Mendo. Anne had negotiated with the owners of the Casa de Insua, a beautiful eighteenth century mansion with spreading grounds and a flourishing estate, for the use of two partly ruined barns which had originally been part of the winery. Paul's men had worked to repair the structures to be used as barracks, along with a four roomed cottage which could be occupied by the duty officers. Major Vane and his officers occupied billets in the village. The arrangement had worked reasonably well the previous year for the short time that Patrick Corrigan had commanded the battalion.

Major Vane was billeted on the top floor of the substantial house of a prosperous cloth merchant and his wife. Señor Rivero's two sons and son-in-law were all with the Portuguese army and his daughter and grandson lived with him. Paul had met the Riveros socially on a number of occasions, and Tasia was very popular with his officers. She opened the door to him with a ready smile, an attractive young woman in her twenties with her small son peering out from behind her skirts. Paul knew what was expected of him and he scooped the boy up, swinging him around several times to shrieks of laughter. Tasia was laughing too as Paul lowered the boy gently back to the ground beside her.

"Good afternoon, Señora Ronaldo. Is Major Vane around?"

"He is upstairs, General. Would you like refreshment? I shall see if he is..."

"Don't trouble yourself, ma'am, I'm his commanding officer, he doesn't get a choice about seeing me." Paul watched as little Felipe scampered through into the kitchen area and lowered his voice. "How are you finding him as a guest, Señora?"

"He is very well. Always, we are happy to have an officer staying with us. I was so sad to hear about Major Corrigan."

"He's much missed." Paul studied her thoughtfully. He detected something in her tone that suggested she was not enthusiastic about Major Vane, but he was not sure and decided not to push her further. Instead, he made his way to the polished staircase and climbed two floors to the rooms that Corrigan had briefly occupied the previous year. He knocked, and a voice said:

"Who is it?"

"General van Daan. I need a word with you, Major."

After a long moment, the door opened. Paul stepped into the room and wrinkled his nose. The air was thick with cigar smoke which masked another unpleasant odour. Vane was in shirt sleeves, a glass in his hand. He stared at Paul and then put the glass on the table and gave a half-hearted salute. Paul did not bother to return it. He walked across the room and threw open both windows.

"What in God's name is that smell?"

Vane looked at him in some surprise then shrugged. "Chamber pot. I've asked a dozen times for it to be emptied, these people live like pigs, they..."

155

Paul slapped his hand onto the table so hard that Vane jumped violently. Glass and bottle rattled, and two playing cards slid onto the floor.

"They aren't living like pigs, Major, you are, it isn't their job to wait on you. Don't you have a valet or an orderly with you?"

"My valet died last year. Fever. Had to get rid of the orderly, he was a drunkard. I'll get one of those idle buggers from the regiment up here to clean up."

"Well, be sure you find yourself a permanent servant soon, Major, Lord Wellington is very strict about his officers taking men away from their duties to use as personal servants."

"You do it."

"Actually, I don't. Sergeant Jenson isn't on strength, he lost half a leg at Assaye, I pay his wages myself. I'm sure if you ask Señor Rivero he'll be able to find you a servant, although it isn't his job to sort out your domestic arrangements. I received your letter about my brigade major."

"Hah! Manson, eh? Arrogant young bastard, ain't he?"

"I don't find I have much trouble with him myself, but it's clear you two aren't going to be friends."

"I want him on a charge. Speaking disrespectfully to a senior officer. Bloody disgrace, how he spoke to me, and in front of the men, too."

Paul realised that Vane was slightly drunk. He wondered if it would be more sensible to postpone this conversation and then decided not to.

"I can't have a conversation with you in here, I can't bloody breathe. Get yourself cleaned up and I'll meet you in the garden in ten minutes. And get a move on, I've other things to do."

When Vane joined Paul, he was at least properly dressed and looked slightly more sober. It was a grey afternoon with the threat of rain in a heavy looking sky. Paul seated himself on a wooden bench.

"I've been informed that you tried to administer more that the regulation number of lashes to Private O'Connell, Major."

"Is that what Manson told you? He's a bloody liar, he's trying to get himself out of trouble. Ask any of the men present, ask the drummer who was giving the flogging, they'll all tell you."

"I've heard the same story from four people so far. I expect I can get more, but I don't need it."

"Who? Which of them bloody dared…"

"Don't bother, Major, you're in enough trouble and I'm tired of you already."

"You've no proof."

"I don't need proof, this isn't a court of law, and it isn't going to be. You've been here just over a month, and you've already held more RCMs that my entire battalion does in a year. Your returns aren't properly made up…"

"Those returns are only supposed to be inspected every six months."

"If I've got reason to be concerned, Major, I can require a return once a week, if I like, I'm your brigade commander. I've attempted several civilised conversations with you already, it isn't working and I'm bored with it."

"Flogging is in the army regulations, General, and Lord Wellington…"

"I've just come from Lord Wellington, Major, with orders to put a stop to this nonsense before it irritates him. Leo Manson is not on a charge. He accepts that he spoke too freely and you will receive a written apology. You are ordered to accept it. Discipline within your battalion is naturally your business, but if you're having this many problems, you're not working them hard enough. I'm concerned to find you drunk in your rooms at this hour of the day when you should be out working your men. I'll put together a training programme and will send the memorandum out to all your company officers to make sure they know what they're doing. There will be a full battalion inspection next week."

"How dare you…?"

"You use that phrase a lot, Major, so I'm guessing it's worked for you before but it's wasted on me. You're in my brigade now, get off your lazy arse and do some work, or you'll be the one up on a charge. Any questions?"

Vane did not speak. Paul stood up. "Excellent. I will assume that we're in agreement, then. I look forward to a much improved relationship in the future, Major Vane. Good day."

Paul watched as Vane turned on his heel and went back into the house. The conversation made him feel considerably better. He had no illusions that anything he had said would have any impact on Vane, but at least now he had stated his position clearly. He intended to write a very straightforward letter to Lieutenant-Colonel Norton, urging his swift return and planned frequent, unannounced visits to the 115th which he hoped would annoy Vane so much that the man would seek a transfer to a more peaceful brigade.

"General van Daan."

Paul turned with a smile. "Señor Rivero. How are you, sir, it's good to see you?"

"You also, General. I was at the warehouse, we have just had a delivery from Oporto."

"How is business?"

"It is good. One day, when trade opens up again, it will be better. General, I do not wish to trespass on your time, but if you could join me in the parlour for a glass of port, there is something I wish to speak of."

Paul felt a twist of concern in his gut. He studied Rivero and thought that the man looked nervous. "Of course, Señor. How are your boys, have you heard from them?"

"Better than that, they have visited, all three of them. It is good that they are so much closer. Only for a few days, but their mother and Tasia were so happy. Here, come in. Sit down. It is very good port."

Paul accepted a drink, and talked easily about the war, his recent encounter with the French at Bejar and the perfections of Rivero's grandson. He was sure now that the Portuguese was trying to bring himself to raise a difficult subject. Eventually, Paul set down his glass.

"Forgive me, Señor, but I think something is troubling you. Please speak freely, you won't offend me."

Rivero stared into his wine glass. "I am reluctant to speak of this, General. My daughter indeed, has forbidden me to speak of it at all, but I cannot...it is not right."

"What is not right, Señor?" Paul asked gently.

"Major Vane. General, you know that we have always willingly given rooms to English officers. Major Corrigan and before him Colonel Grant. Him, we treated like a family member. He attended Tasia's wedding."

"I know, sir, he spoke very highly of all of you. I can see this is difficult, can I make it easier? Is Major Vane annoying your daughter?"

"Yes," Rivero said bluntly. "Sir, you know my daughter. Always she is friendly, she talks easily to all men. But she is a good girl and a good wife and mother. It is hard for her, with Alfredo away but she minds her son and helps her mother and would not think of another man."

"I know, Señor."

"This man - this officer - is not respectful. He is not a gentleman. Always he is demanding this, demanding that. He speaks to us like servants, not equals. But this, I have ignored. Until last week, I had my servants clean his room and do his laundry, though he pays us no extra for it. But then late one night, my man heard screams from his room. He ran there quickly and found Maria, our maid, crying with her dress torn and..."

Rivero broke off at the expression on Paul's face. "Did he rape her?"

"No, General, he did not have time. I spoke to him, told him that in my house he must behave like a gentleman or I would speak to Lord Wellington. He laughed at me and told me that she had said she would lie with him, but that they quarrelled over payment, that she was a prostitute. I do not believe that, General. So I told him that none of my maids would clean his room again and that he must find a servant to take care of him now."

"He has no right to expect anything from you other than a room, Señor. What of your daughter?"

"When I told my wife and daughter what had happened to Maria, and why the servants would no longer wait on Major Vane, Tasia began to cry and asked if we could not make him leave. I was surprised, but then she told me that ever since he came, he has been pressing unwanted attentions upon her. Whenever he finds her alone, he takes hold of her and kisses her, and he has begun to touch her in a way only her husband has a right to. He asks her to go to his room or threatens to come to hers in the night. She has begun to take little Felipe into her bed, so that she is not alone, because she is afraid."

"Why did she not tell anybody?"

"She is afraid, General. Alfredo, her husband, is an officer of our army and a man of honour. If he found out what Major Vane is doing, he would challenge him. Possibly he might kill him. She fears that her word would not be believed over an English major, and that Alfredo or even her brothers would get into very great trouble."

"I believe her," Paul said flatly. "Implicitly."

Rivero let out a huge sigh. "Thank you. I told her you were a good man, that you would not turn away from this. But General, she will not make a complaint against this man. She is embarrassed and ashamed and she does not want others to know, especially her husband and her brothers. And people are not kind. They would say she encouraged him, or that it was her fault for being too free in her speech and manner."

"She's done nothing wrong, Señor. Is she here now?"

"Yes, General."

"Will you do something for me? Go and tell your wife and daughter that you are all invited to dine with us today, at Santo Antonio. Get them to put on their fine gowns and have the carriage hitched up. Bring little Felipe, my daughter's nurse will take care of him. Come to dinner and by the time you are home, he will be gone, I give you my word."

Rivero looked as though he might cry. "You can do this?"

"Yes. Go on, go and get ready, I'll meet you outside, I can ride back with you."

Paul watched as the older man left, then walked back into the house and up the stairs. Sometimes, when he was really angry, he had the strange sense of being detached, as though he was standing outside his own body, watching. He had that feeling now, and he knew that it was dangerous, that in this frame of mind he could do anything. In the past, he had done things he did not care to remember.

Paul did not knock. Vane was seated at the table drinking brandy. He had closed the window and the room still reeked. Paul closed the door. He thought briefly about the stinking chamber pot and pushed the thought aside: one of the maids would have to clean it up and it would not be fair.

"You're in need of a new billet, Major Vane. Luckily, I know that there's space in the farm cottage up by the barracks. It's not quite as comfortable as this, but I'm sure you'll find a way to make it homely, in time. Get packing. Jenson will be over with a cart to move your bags in an hour or two, and if you come within a mile of this house or any of the women living in it again, I will fucking castrate you."

Vane stood up. "You've got no right..."

Paul took two steps forward and punched once, low and hard, into the major's midriff. Vane doubled up with a strange whooshing sound and remained so, clutching at his gut.

"Don't make me tell you again, Major. The next time, I'll be going to Lord Wellington and informing him that I'm putting you on a charge for conduct unbecoming an officer and a gentleman. Señora Ronaldo and her maid are understandably reluctant to press a charge, but I'll bet I could persuade them, given time. Let me know if you want me to make the effort. Or you can fuck off out of here and leave them alone, and you might manage to keep your commission for a short while longer. Although if I were you, I'd sell out now, because I am after you, and sooner or later I'll find a way to take you down that doesn't hurt anybody else."

"I'll report this," Vane wheezed.

159

"Do so. Let's go to headquarters right now, and we'll find out if your friends in London are worth more than Lord Wellington's word and my past service. Get your boots on."

Vane looked as though he was about to vomit. Paul waited. After a long silence, he said:

"I thought not. The Rivero family are dining with us today. You will be gone by the time they get home, I'll accompany them to make sure. And if you go near Señora Ronaldo or her maidservant again, I'll kill you, I swear to God. Now get packing."

He had reached the door when Vane said:

"I'd probably get the pox from her anyway, she's bedded half your officers, I've seen what she's like."

Paul turned and walked back into the room. He grasped Vane's collar and spun him around, taking hold of the back of his trousers. Vane struggled briefly but was too surprised to put up much resistance. Paul marched him across the room to the tall window and shoved. There was an enormous crash of breaking glass and splintering wood as Vane disappeared, arms and legs flailing, a scream floating in the air. The tin roof of the kitchen annex was just below his window and Paul heard a crash as he landed. After a moment he looked out. Beyond the kitchen was the midden heap, where food scraps and other refuse were piled up and Paul was both surprised and impressed at his accurate memory of the layout of the house. Vane had rolled down the sloping tin roof into the midden and was scrabbling out of the foul smelling rubbish, yelling in rage. He did not appear to have broken any bones, so Paul left the room and went to find Jenson and his horse.

***

With Paul away visiting Sir Stapleton Cotton and the cavalry, Anne set about organising rooms for the children, who were expected any day. Señora Mata employed few servants, but while the 110th were billeted at the quinta, Anne arranged for a number of local women to come in daily to help with cleaning and kitchen work. She kept several rooms free as guest rooms because Lord Wellington had very little accommodation available at headquarters and frequently billeted his guests with the 110th.

Given her sister-in-law's pregnancy, Anne was sure that only Paul's father, and probably the children's tutor would accompany the children. She had been hoping for a letter confirming this, but she had heard nothing since the letter confirming the date they were expecting to sail. Even given delays due to weather, or poor roads from Oporto, the party should be arriving any day, so Anne summoned her assistants and set to work with a will. The logistics of juggling rooms and organising cleaning and bed-making occupied a long morning and by the end of it, Anne was hot and tired and very dusty, but satisfied with her achievement. She dismissed her assistants with thanks and went back to her room, laughing silently at herself. There was nothing particularly difficult about cleaning and preparing a few rooms for guests, but

160

Anne loathed housekeeping and usually avoided it at all costs. She had often wondered if her well-known adaptability to life on campaign was greatly helped by the fact that there was very little housekeeping to be done in a tent.

The success of her morning inspired Anne, and after some time with Georgiana, she returned to the bedroom and surveyed the neat pile of very battered luggage stacked in one corner. When they had arrived back at the quinta in November, Teresa had unpacked, but there were one or two boxes stuffed full of odds and ends that had never been properly emptied, simply because nothing in them had been required. The bags and boxes could all do with being properly cleaned and aired, and Anne decided that she would also take the opportunity to check both hers and Paul's clothing to see what needed mending or cleaning.

Anne's clothing chests were not too bad, since she had had the opportunity to replenish them in Madrid. There were one or two older gowns that she used for working at the hospital, and after considering them for a moment, she decided she would pass them over to Teresa, who would know which of the wives or camp followers was most in need. Paul's boxes were another matter, because he never threw anything away. Anne began to unload shirts and underclothing, wedged into unlikely places and the boredom of the task gave way to bubbling amusement at some of the unlikely objects she found. There was a pile of her letters wrapped up in two shirts and a pair of stockings with holes in, and at the bottom of one chest she found Paul's portable writing case which he had sworn that Jenson had left behind in Madrid.

There was soon a substantial pile of laundry and mending, and a bundle of garments to be given away, although Anne wondered if some of them should simply be burned. At the bottom of the final chest, when the clothes had been sorted she removed a bundle of rags which looked as though they had been used to clean a rusty weapon, a broken comb and another pile of letters, this time covered in Paul's scrawling handwriting. Anne threw the rubbish into the fireplace and glanced over the letters with a smile, wondering if Paul had somehow forgotten to send them in the haste of the retreat, and been furious when he had not received a reply. His handwriting was worse than usual here, suggesting either urgency or carelessness, but the name at the top of the first page surprised her.

"Beloved Nan."

Anne stared at the letter, running her eyes over the words, and felt her stomach lurch as she realised what she was holding. During the previous year, after the horror of her ordeal at the hands of Colonel Dupres, Paul had told her that he had written several letters to her during the long nights when he could not sleep, waiting to hear if she was alive or dead. He had promised to let her read them but had not done so and Anne had completely forgotten about them until now.

For a long time, Anne sat on the edge of their bed, in the midst of chaos, holding them, wondering if she should read them or even if she wanted to. Finally, she lifted the first sheet. Paul had given her permission, and the letters were addressed to her. He had laughed at the time, saying that they were probably illegible. His distress was written clearly on the page, but Anne was very accustomed to deciphering her husband's hand, and she was easily able to read the words, even where they were smudged or badly written. Anne wondered about the smudges, there were a lot of them and she suspected that some of them were caused by tears.

Anne was crying herself before she had finished reading. There were three letters, the third unfinished. She and Paul did not often write to each other since they were seldom apart for very long. Anne had never really received a love letter and she had not known Paul capable of writing this way. The outpouring of emotion was painful to read and made Anne smile through her tears. Her recent moments of petty jealousy felt ridiculous in the face of these letters.

When she had finished, Anne sat with the letters in her lap. She wanted Paul here now, not in two days' time, so that she could put her arms about him. She was suddenly angry with herself for letting her own irrational emotions spill over into her time with him. Sitting quietly, with written evidence of his devotion under her hands, Anne made a small, fierce promise to herself, that she would never do so again. Their time was too precious.

"Nan, are you up here?"

Anne jumped in surprise and got up quickly. "I'm here," she said, and then realised she should not have done so, given the state of her. It was too late, the partly open door was pushed fully open and Katja stood open mouthed, staring at her. Anne stood, the letters in her hand, trying to think of a single thing to say. She opened her mouth, but no words came out, so she closed it again. It occurred to her that the room looked as though it had been ransacked by a passing army, her face was streaked with tears and probably red and swollen and her gown was covered in dirt from Paul's appalling boxes. She saw Katja's wide blue eyes move over the wreckage of the room and then return to the wreckage of her hostess.

"Nan, are you all right?"

"Oh yes - yes, I'm perfectly well," Anne said, with false brightness. Her voice sounded, to her own ears, like that of a naughty child, caught in some misdeed. "I just…I was…do you know, in this entire room, I do not think either of us possesses a single handkerchief."

Katja Mackenzie looked at her for a long moment, then unexpectedly she gave a little laugh. It was almost apologetic, but it made Anne smile, because it was obvious that the other woman was trying to control it. That struck Anne as very funny, and she could feel the laughter bubbling up. She met Katja's gaze, and the Dutchwoman began to laugh in earnest. Anne laughed until the tears came again, and she sat down on the bed, still nursing the letters to her breast, crying with mirth. Katja reached into her sleeve and brought out a snowy white square of linen which she passed to Anne, who mopped her eyes gratefully.

"Oh, but I am sorry," Katja gasped. "It is just, it sounded so funny."

"It was funny," Anne assured her. She realised suddenly that Katja was wiping her eyes on her sleeve. "And now you have no handkerchief."

Katja started to laugh again. "I must remember to carry two when I come to visit your chamber," she gasped. "Oh, but I am truly sorry, because I can see that you were weeping in earnest before I came. Are you all right, Nan?"

Anne took several deep breaths, bringing herself under control with difficulty. "Yes," she said firmly. "It was nothing serious. I found some old letters that Paul wrote to me at a difficult time, and they were so sad. And yet, so lovely."

"Oh, but I do understand. Still, I have some letters that my first husband wrote to me so many years ago. He was not romantic, my Cornelius, but there are some passages that bring tears. But what has happened in this room?"

Anne looked around and laughed again. "This? Oh, this is what happens when I turn my hand to housekeeping. You will see the reason why I generally stick to surgery and administration."

Katja was shaking her head, smiling. "It is not so bad. We shall take this to be laundered and this to..."

She broke off suddenly, the smile a little fixed. Anne looked at her, puzzled, and then abruptly understood.

"Oh," she said. "Oh no, have I really been that obvious?"

"It is not your fault," Katja said quickly. "Always, I take too much onto myself, I know this. I am trying to change it, but I am so used to running my household and my business..."

Her apologetic tone horrified Anne. "Katja, no, it is not you. And I truly understand because I am the same. Although not, obviously, when it concerns housekeeping."

Katja looked around the room and started to laugh again. "Would you like me to help?" she asked.

"I made the mess, I should clear it up."

"Is that what your Mama used to tell you?"

"She is my stepmother, and she gave up very early."

"Well, I think we should do this together, because I came to find you for a reason. There is a message to say that a carriage and two baggage wagons are approaching from the west, they will be here within the hour."

Anne's heart leapt. "The children?"

Katja nodded, smiling. Anne looked down at Paul's letters which she was still holding. She walked to her own chest and placed them carefully inside, then turned to Katja. "Will you help?" she asked.

"I will. What is this pile here?"

Anne was downstairs before the carriage made its slow progress up the long driveway and drew up outside the house. The chaos of her room had been cleared very quickly and while she changed, Katja had gone to speak to Sergeant Kelly about dinner. She sounded apologetic as she suggested it, and

163

Anne thanked her as warmly as she could, and made a mental note that she needed to put things right with Katja Mackenzie when she had time.

The carriage door opened, and one of the grooms let down the steps. Anne ran forward just as two children scrambled through the door. Both were fair, a boy and a girl, and Anne was surprised to see that he was now the taller although the younger. She held out her arms and they flung themselves onto her. Anne bent to kiss them more easily. She was crying again and laughing all at the same time.

"Grace, Francis, let me breathe! Your father is away, but he'll be back tomorrow. I'll send a rider out to him just to make sure. Francis, you've grown so much, you're huge! Grace, you are so beautiful. Thank you for all those letters, they've made me so happy."

"Mama, come. Look at how much Rowena and Will have grown!"

Grace, her fair hair escaping from its braids, was tugging at Anne's hand. A young woman whom Anne did not know had stepped down from the coach. She was holding a child in her arms, a chubby boy of seventeen months. Behind her, a man in a dark suit was lifting a small girl from the carriage with one arm and Anne felt a lump in her throat at the sight. At two and a half, Rowena van Daan was the image of her dead mother. She regarded Anne from wide, thoughtful blue eyes.

Anne froze for a moment, then decided to go to Rowena first. She crouched down. "Rowena, I'm so happy to see you," she said, very softly. "You've grown so much."

"Mama?" The child's voice was uncertain. Anne was fairly sure Rowena would not have remembered her from the previous year, but she had clearly been told whom she was going to see. Anne smiled through her tears and reached out to caress the tiny face.

"That's right, Rowena. Will you take me to meet William?"

Rowena put her hand trustingly into Anne's and towed her to where William was wriggling furiously in the arms of the young woman. He was far bigger than Anne had expected, and she felt ridiculously nervous at meeting this, her own son, for the first time in nine months, but her sympathy for the struggling woman overcame her uncertainty.

"Will, hold still, you're going to end up on your head," she said firmly, and reached out, taking the child. For a moment, William stared at her in absolute astonishment. He was clearly about to cry, and Anne steeled herself not to be hurt. She bent forward and very gently kissed his nose.

William paused and looked at her. He reached one chubby finger to rub his nose, looking surprised. Anne laughed at his expression and did it again. William wrinkled his nose. Then he reached out and touched Anne's nose in response and Anne felt her heart melt. She drew William close and kissed the top of his head, inhaling the scent of him, her whole body flooded with emotion.

"Hasn't he grown?" Grace said proudly, as though she was personally responsible.

164

"You all have, you're so tall, Grace. And look at Francis. I'm so happy you're all here, I've missed you every day."

Finally, Anne was able to take notice of the adults. Mr Harcourt, the children's tutor, she remembered from his time as a junior officer of the 110th before he had lost half an arm at Fuentes d'Onoro. She had no idea who the woman was. She was thin and dark, with a determined jaw and a pair of beautiful brown eyes, which were currently fixed on Anne with what appeared to be an expression of sheer terror. What puzzled Anne was that there was no sign of any of Paul's family.

"Mr Harcourt, welcome. Thank you so much for bringing them. I'm sorry the general isn't here to greet you all, but..."

"General?" Francis said instantly, and Anne looked down.

"You didn't get our letter? Yes indeed, Francis van Daan, your father is now a Major-General."

"Oh that's capital!"

"Isn't it? Look, I want to know all about your journey, and every single thing that's happened to you since I last saw you all. But you must be tired and so hungry, and I need to speak to Mr Harcourt. Why don't we..."

"Nan?"

Anne looked up. Katja Mackenzie was standing there, with her three children grouped around her.

"I thought that Hans, Cornelius and Margriete could show the children to their rooms. I can take the little ones. I do not wish to take over, but while you speak to their escort..."

Anne felt a rush of gratitude. "Katja, thank you. Would you? Francis, Grace, this is Mrs Mackenzie, the wife of one of our officers, and her children are visiting this winter, just like you."

Anne saw Francis' eyes brighten at the sight of the other boys and he and Grace went forward readily. Anne handed Will over to Katja with a final kiss and Margriete came to take Rowena's hand. Anne watched the little cavalcade heading into the house and then turned back to Mr Harcourt, a well-built young man in his late twenties with his left arm tucked neatly into the front of his blue coat and a pair of worried hazel eyes.

"Mr Harcourt, it is very good to see you again. You look exhausted, which doesn't surprise me at all. But I am a little surprised..."

"You're wondering why the general's family aren't here, ma'am."

"Yes, I was, really."

Harcourt took a deep breath. "They didn't come, ma'am."

Anne stared at him blankly. "They didn't come?"

"No, ma'am. As a matter of fact, we weren't supposed to come either."

"Mr Harcourt, you were supposed to come. I wrote the letters myself, the arrangements were very clear. I'm sorry, I just don't understand."

"Mrs van Daan changed her mind. Because of the baby. She's with child, ma'am, and it's gone further than it normally...anyway, she didn't want to come, so then Mr Joshua van Daan didn't want to come either. And then Mr Franz van Daan broke his leg in a hunting accident in Lincolnshire."

"Oh my goodness, is he all right?"

"I think so, ma'am, but he can't travel. So he wrote to say that Mr Joshua van Daan should go, and Mr Joshua refused, and Mrs van Daan said that nobody should be going, that it had always been a mad idea to send children into a country at war, and that...anyway, we had all the travel arranged, and Mr Franz was in Lincolnshire, and Mr Joshua and Mrs van Daan were in Leicestershire, and I had all the travel papers and permissions and we were packed to go. I couldn't have done it on my own, but then Miss Webster said that she would accompany me. She is the new governess, you know. We were supposed to bring the nursery maid, but when she heard that Mrs van Daan was not coming, she refused. So we just went. I'm sorry, ma'am. It's a very long story."

"I see that it is," Anne said faintly. "I think you had better come inside, Miles, and have a very large drink."

***

Paul arrived back at the quinta into a warm afternoon, and he knew as he dismounted that the children had arrived. There was a shrieking of laughter coming from the training ground which had been laid out to the west of the house and Paul did not think that his men had suddenly found that much joy in close order drills. He handed his horse to Jenson and set off at a run around the house, then stopped, his heart full.

Nobody saw him immediately. They were playing football, and there was a scrimmage in the centre of the ground. It took Paul a moment to realise that his son was one of the three boys, since he was as tall as Hans, who was two years older than him. The girl was smaller than all of them, but her determination was obvious as she pushed her way in, lifting her skirts out of the way so that they did not hamper her. As Paul watched, she hooked her foot neatly around the ball and kicked it free, passing it across the ground to where Anne stood waiting, holding Rowena in her arms. As Anne ran to kick the ball, Rowena yelled with excitement, and the three boys chased after her. Halfway through his run, Francis caught sight of Paul and stopped so abruptly that Cornelius ran into the back of him.

"Papa!"

Francis reached Paul first and Paul swung him up into his arms. He was still holding him when Grace arrived, flinging her arms about his waist. Anne arrived, and the happiness on her face melted his heart. Paul kissed Grace and Francis, setting him down, and took Rowena into his arms, holding her close. The resemblance to his first wife shook him a little.

"Where's Will?"

"He's taking a nap in the nursery with Georgiana, I think we've worn him out. Sally is with them. Paul..."

"Where are Josh and Patience, have you worn them out already as well, Nan? Mrs Mackenzie, it looks as though your children have been making friends."

"They are very happy, General. Children, shall we go inside and have some lemonade, and the seedcake that I baked this morning? Come, Rowena, we will wash your hands and face and your Papa shall join you very soon."

Paul set his daughter down and Grace took her hand. He was interested to see how quickly the two sets of children had integrated, and even more interested at the quick, relaxed smile his wife gave to Katja at her intervention. He mentioned neither, however, because he could see that Anne had something to tell him that required privacy.

"I need to wash and change, girl of my heart. Come and help me and then I want to see Will."

"You'll be shocked, he's huge."

"We're a tall family."

Anne said nothing until they were in their room with the door closed. Jenson had placed a jug of hot water on the wash stand and Paul began to undress, noticing that the room was very neat and that the pile of luggage had been removed from the corner.

"What is it, Nan?"

"Paul - your family didn't come."

Paul stopped, his shirt halfway over his head, staring at her. "What? What do you mean, they didn't come?"

"They remained in England. Miles Harcourt and the new governess brought the children. How on earth they managed it with only two of them, I cannot imagine, but they did it. It seems that a lot has been going on."

Anne told the story as Paul washed and changed his clothing. Paul listened mostly in silence, interposing an occasional question when he did not understand. He could feel himself becoming angry.

"Have we heard anything from my father?"

"A letter arrived with the post this morning. There's also one from Joshua, but both are addressed to you only, so I haven't opened either of them." Anne hesitated. "Paul, I'm not sure how you feel about this. Mr Harcourt is very worried about whether he did the right thing. You may find out more in those letters, but I have a feeling there is a lot that he has not told me, I think the whole situation was very acrimonious."

Paul put his arms about her. "I should go and read them, if only to find out how my father is doing, he's too old to be throwing himself over the fences on the hunting field like a twenty year old. Not that he'd listen to me if I told him so."

"You'll be just as bad at his age, Paul."

"Probably. Still, I don't understand why they didn't just hire extra help for the journey."

"I don't think that Patience wanted the children to come at all, Paul," Anne said quietly. "She would have been all right with Lisbon, but she thought this was too far and too dangerous."

"Nonsense. She cannot seriously have thought I'd put my children at risk. Did she tell you that?"

"She wrote. If she is genuinely likely to carry this child to term, I understand, she's been disappointed so many times."

"I wouldn't have expected them to come, Nan, under those circumstance. But they didn't even write to me about this, they just made the decision. I'd have told them to arrange for an escort and let the children come anyway." Paul broke off and took a deep breath. "I'm not going to let it spoil my time with my children. And I'm very grateful to Miles and this young woman for doing what they did. But did you say they came out here alone with the children?"

"Yes. The nursery maid refused to go against the orders of her employers. Poor Miss Webster has had to manage Rowena and Will for the whole journey, which is not at all the job of a governess. She must be exhausted, and she's terrified that she will lose her position when she goes back home. And Miles Harcourt is worried about her reputation, given that she effectively travelled alone with him for weeks."

"If either of them could manage to get up to anything with my children wedged in between them, I'd be surprised and impressed," Paul said. "I hope you've reassured her, Nan, that her job is safe, and they are both due a hefty bonus for the trouble they've gone to. We'll manage something better on the way home. Right, I'm going to read those letters and then I'm going to spend the rest of the day with my children, nothing is going to spoil this for me, bonny lass. Although I need to find some time to decipher my notes and write up these reports for Wellington, he's beginning to foam at the mouth."

"Give them to me," Anne said.

Paul looked at her, feeling a mixture of guilt and sheer relief. "Are you sure, Nan? You'll have the children, and…"

"Paul, I do better when I have too much to do than not enough. I thrive when I'm busy. I intend to make the most of the children, but I can find time to help you with your reports. Especially now that I have somebody to help me. Katja has volunteered to help with the housekeeping while she's here, it seems she took over running the barracks at Melton, so she is very used to doing this. That will give me plenty of time to work on your reports, and to help out with one or two other projects. Oliver Daniels has asked me to help him teach the new medical staff what they need to know before the campaigning season starts. All the children seem to be making friends very quickly, so Katja and I can share looking after them. Thank goodness she's here."

Paul remembered to close his mouth, but he knew she had seen his expression, because she began to laugh aloud. "Your face, Paul."

"Sorry, love, but I think I may have missed one or two things in the past couple of days."

"Katja and I needed time. You were right, we're very alike in many ways, and I realise that I've been very accustomed to being in charge. Of course, so has she. We've talked a lot, these past few days. She's an

168

extraordinary woman, Paul, she has been telling me how she ran her first husband's business single-handed after he died, and although she is still a partner at a distance, it was very hard for her when she first went to England and was suddenly just a wife again. So she decided to do very much as I did, and to throw herself into army life and to find ways of helping Ross. She's been telling me about the schools and…" Anne tailed off as she realised how hard Paul was laughing. "I am so glad you find me amusing, General."

"One of the many things I love about you, Anne van Daan, is how thoroughly you run up your colours when you decide you like somebody. Come along, I want to see William, and then I'm going to read those letters. My father is too old to be breaking limbs all over the place."

Chapter Twelve

After days of cautious travel, scouting ahead and watching endlessly for the enemy, Giles and his party were taken by surprise by the French. They were encamped in an orange grove, part of a large estate, and Antonio had gone cautiously to one of the farm cottages to buy bread and cheese and some apples. The story he gave on these occasions was that he was one of a small escort, taking wounded men back to their home villages. Most of the locals supported the guerrillas, whether from patriotism, hatred of the French or fear of reprisals, but there was a small core of afrancesados who supported Bonaparte. Even to these, a lone Spanish peasant buying food for a few wounded men posed no threat and nobody ever questioned Antonio's story.

After eating their simple meal, they slept, taking turns to keep watch. During the early part of the journey, Giles had refused to allow Brat to take sentry duty. She had not argued, she simply chose to remain awake through the night with Michael, and after a few weeks, Giles gritted his teeth and reorganised sentry duty to include Brat, which gave all of them extra rest. It was not yet dawn, although there was a faint lightening in the sky when Giles awoke to find her shaking his shoulder violently. He sat up, looking around, and saw that Michael and Antonio were awake too, getting to their feet. Brat beckoned and Giles followed her to the edge of the trees. He already knew they were in trouble, he could hear sounds of marching feet far too close and the creak of wagons and gun carriages. A dark figure stood in the shadow of an orange tree, wrapped in a dark cloak with a hat pulled low over his eyes.

"English?"

"Yes," Giles said, very softly. The man spoke with the Cantabrian dialect but was easy to understand.

"You need to leave very quietly, Señor. French troops, thousands of them, marching in from the Bilbao direction. They are going to attack Castro Urdiales."

"How close?" Antonio asked, joining them.

"Less than two miles, Señor. Some officers came to my door, demanding food. I gave what I had, and I listened while they ate. General Foy commands, he has French and Italian troops."

"Guns?"

170

"They talk of bringing guns across the land from Bilbao, and also across the bay if they can get past the English ships."

"The English are here?"

"Yes, Señor, three ships."

"You're from the big house?" Giles asked.

"I am. The French have been here before. They will steal anything they can, including oranges."

"Well they're not going to find oranges at this season," Michael said.

"They might still search, Michael. We need to get moving. Señor, my thanks. Best get going. If they do come this way, you can't be found here."

It took minutes only to load their few possessions onto the ponies and mount up. Antonio produced a worn sketch map as they were packing, and he and the Cantabrian pored over it, speaking in low tones. As the man disappeared through the trees, Antonio joined the others.

"We have a choice," he said. "We can ride west and try to join up with Mendizabal, who is supposed to be in the region of Ampuero with some of his partisans. We can go south, back up into the mountains, where we have just come from. Or we can ride north, try to avoid the French, and hope to make it into Castro Urdiales before they close it down."

Giles studied the map pointlessly; he had looked at it so often that he knew it by heart. Riding back up into the mountains would achieve nothing. They could retrace their steps over long and exhausting miles, knowing that this whole journey had achieved nothing apart for some useful intelligence sent to Wellington. Grainger would be taken with the town and whatever information he carried would fall into the hands of the French.

Riding west to join the Spanish irregulars would afford them some immediate protection but would not achieve anything. If Foy were coming in force, Mendizabal would need to pull back fast into the mountains, leaving Giles the choice of remaining with him, waiting to see what happened at Castro Urdiales, or giving up the mission and returning to Corunna. Giles did not want to find himself caught up with Mendizabal's flight into the mountains, his small party would be safer alone, if they had to flee.

"Giles?" Michael said quietly. Giles realised that they were waiting, looking at him, and he felt a sudden weight of responsibility that he did not want. He had grown so used to working just with Antonio, that he could predict what the Spaniard would say. Michael O'Reilly and his servant were an unknown quantity and he wished suddenly that Wellington had not insisted that the Irishman accompany him. Giles knew what he would choose for himself, and he was sure that Antonio would agree, but he took a deep breath and said:

"What would you do, Michael?"

"Castro Urdiales," the Irishman said without hesitation. "It's where Grainger is, it's what we came here to do. We're ten miles away and we can travel a lot faster than a French infantry brigade."

"If we make it without them catching us," Giles said.

"How many times have you outrun a French patrol, Giles?"

"Frequently."

"Exactly. Yes, we're likely to get locked in. I've no idea how long it will take for the French to break through, but…"

"Not very long," Antonio said. "I know the town, the defences are partly ruined. They cannot hold."

"Then we should try to make contact with the lads from the navy and get Grainger out of there, if he's still alive. It's what we came here to do."

Giles felt an enormous sense of relief and wondered why he had doubted it. He looked at Brat, who had not spoken. In the pale, early light her face was very white, framed by chestnut curls and he thought irrelevantly that she was going to need a haircut if she intended to keep even the faintest pretence of being a boy. He wished passionately that she had stayed with the nuns.

"It was my decision, Captain, and I do not regret it," Brat said, as though she could read his mind. "You are thinking that I may not be safe. Me, I know that nowhere is safe. I was not safe in my own home, and I was a child then."

Giles did not reply. She was right, but it did not help. He swung himself into the saddle. "Let's get moving. Quickly, quietly and keep together."

***

There was a side gate into Castro Urdiales, and the sentries took a long time to let them in, arguing among themselves and finally sending for an officer to make the decision for them. It was clear that the garrison knew that the French were very close and there was an air of suppressed urgency about the troops. A young lieutenant arrived to greet them, listened briefly to Giles' explanation, and then guided their weary ponies through narrow cobbled streets to a wide central square.

"The garrison stable is here, you may leave your horses. My men will find a place to store your kit until we find you a billet. First, I must take you to Colonel Alvarez, who commands the garrison. We did not expect to see English officers here, you were lucky to get through alive."

"Just so," Giles said evenly, and Michael wanted to laugh aloud. He was not sure if it was hysteria, he still felt slightly sick after six hours of stopping and starting, of hiding on horseback in wooded copses watching French troops march by and then galloping frantically across rutted roads, recently churned up by enemy troops. Antonio had led them unerringly, playing a deadly game of hide and seek through the countryside, and Michael had barely spoken, but had obeyed every order without question, wondering why the hell he was here. Beside him, Brat had been just as silent, speaking only when spoken to. Their arrival at the town seemed like a miracle and Michael had never before truly understood how Giles and Antonio lived their lives. If he managed to return alive to his company, Michael promised himself that he would never again agree to such a mission. He had always considered himself a brave man, but he did not have the stomach for this.

172

The castle looked impressive on the walk up from the town, towering on a promontory over the coastline, with the graceful lines of the Church of Santa María de la Asunción beside it, outlined against a brilliant blue sky. It was warm, and people sat outside their houses, women weaving or knitting on their doorsteps, gossiping with their neighbours, and watching the little procession curiously.

Colonel Pedro Alvarez met them in the wide courtyard inside the castle keep. He was a tall spare man, dark hair peppered with grey and deep frown lines etched into a striking face. Giles introduced the party and Alvarez ran his eyes over them.

"I do not understand why English officers should be here at this time, Captain. And you have brought a woman? Dressed like that?"

His voice was outraged, and Brat's face flooded with colour. Michael wanted to punch the Spaniard, but Giles was quicker.

"Señorita Ibanez found herself alone and in difficult circumstances, and she is dressed as she is for her own safety. Would you have us leave one of your countrywomen unprotected with the French on the loose, Colonel?"

Alvarez flushed at his tone. "No. My apologies, Señorita, I misunderstood. We will find you proper clothing. Captain Fenwick…"

"We are searching for a missing English diplomat, Colonel. Sir Horace Grainger. I have letters from Colonel Porlier and General Longa."

Alvarez took the letters and scanned them briefly then looked up. "The Englishman is here," he said briefly. "But he is sick. Very sick. He was injured by accident, in a skirmish with the French. No doubt you will wish to see him."

"I will, sir. I would also like to make contact with the Royal Navy squadron currently offshore. I don't know what the situation is, but…"

"The situation is that the French are surrounding our town. I do not understand why you are here, it is madness, but you will not be able to leave now. There are ships, English, and some Spanish, keeping an escape route open seawards. Boats row out regularly, if you write a letter, we will convey it. My men will find accommodation in the town for you, perhaps in the house where Sir Horace is lodged. I will speak with you when I have time, forgive me, I have much to do."

Giles saluted very correctly, which told Michael everything he needed to know about his opinion of the Spanish commander. "Thank you, Colonel. We will keep out of your way, if you will provide us with a guide."

"Of course. Lieutenant Nadal will give you all the assistance you require."

The house was just off the plaza, an elegant stone building with a coat of arms above the doorway. Nadal, a slim dark young man, left them kicking their heels in the square while he went to speak to the householder, but he returned within fifteen minutes.

"Señora Palomo can provide you with two rooms, Captain, and will take care of the young lady."

Michael carefully did not look at Brat. He had a suspicion that taking care of her would involve getting her into a gown as quickly as possible, and he could imagine her expression. Nadal led the way to the stables to collect their kit and then took them to be introduced to Señora Palomo.

Their hostess was a handsome woman, probably in her forties, a widow with two grown sons serving with Mendizabal and a daughter of thirteen who lowered her eyes modestly when spoken to and eyed Brat's scandalous attire with unconcealed horror. Michael saw the gleam of mischief in Brat's eyes and resolved to speak firmly to her as soon as they were alone. The situation was difficult enough, without Brat turning the entire household upside down.

Señora Palomo showed them to a big room on the second floor with one enormous bed and a wooden pallet which she had arranged to be brought in from another room. Brat was escorted to a little box of a room further along the corridor, which contained a bed, a wooden chest and a wash stand. Their hostess and her daughter remained firmly by the door as Brat entered, preventing Michael from speaking to her alone. Michael took the hint and joined his companions in their shared room, reflecting that it was unlikely that Brat would have taken any notice of him anyway.

"Any news of Grainger?" he asked Giles, who was unpacking his dusty saddlebags.

"He's upstairs. Apparently he's sleeping, I've asked to see him when he wakes, but I doubt that she'll let me near him until tomorrow morning now. It hardly matters, we're here."

"And we're not going anywhere," Michael said. The sounds of military activity were clear through the open window. "Alvarez wasn't best pleased to see us."

"I noticed that. Probably not at his best today, though. You've more experience of siege warfare than I have, Michael, what's your opinion?"

"I've not seen enough of the town, yet, but from the little I've seen, they'll storm it in a week if they've got proper siege equipment."

"Porlier said they've made several attempts at this place and come off worse, but they're throwing in a lot of troops this time."

"Yes, they look determined to me."

"Have we made a mistake?"

"I don't know, Giles. If we have, we all made it, and it's too late to worry about it now. I'll be happier when we've heard from the lads from the Royal Navy. The big disadvantage that the French have, is that they can't close this place off by sea, and if there's a navy squadron out there, Alvarez possibly has a way out for the garrison. And so do we, with Grainger, if he can be moved. But we'll have to wait it out; if they've orders to assist the garrison in defending the town, they're not going to detach a brig to take us to safety until they're ready."

"I agree. You were at Ciudad Rodrigo and Badajoz, weren't you?"

"I wasn't at the storming of Badajoz, I was badly wounded in the trenches, during a French sortie. But I've been through a few sieges here and there. In fact my first experience of battle with the 110th was at Seringapatam in '99."

"Was the general there?"

Michael stripped off his filthy coat and dumped it over a wooden chair. "No, he joined in 1802. My first experience of siege warfare with him was at Ahmednagar the following year when some of the troops ran wild after the town was taken. I learned a lot about Lieutenant van Daan that day, and so did the light company."

"What would you do? If you were Alvarez?"

Michael shook out a spare shirt and studied it, trying to decide if it was any cleaner than the one he was wearing. "Me? I'd surrender."

"They don't always give quarter to the Spanish."

"They will if they make it easy for them. Everything I've learned since I've been in this part of Spain tells me that Bonaparte is furious that he can't get the locals under control and is expecting Clausel to perform the miracle that Caffarelli couldn't. By now poor Clausel has probably worked out that it's an impossible task and that his glorious emperor hasn't a clue. If Alvarez offers him a nice easy victory without any bloodshed, he'll throw a party for him in the plaza, so he will."

Giles studied him for a long moment and gave a crooked smile. "I think you're right. Whether we can get Alvarez to see that is another matter."

"Is it our job to try?"

"I never know what my job is, Michael, until I'm in the middle of doing it."

Michael grinned. "That's for sure. Antonio, are you…?"

There was a tap on the door. Michael opened it and stared for a long moment.

"Brat."

"When you forget to close your mouth in that way, Captain, you look like a wild pig," Brat said conversationally. "I have come to tell you that if you will leave your laundry in this basket, I shall do it tomorrow. Also mending, Señora Palomo will lend me needle and thread."

"I see that's not all the good señora has lent you," Giles said gravely, coming to the door.

Brat stalked past them into the room, dumped the large wicker basket on the floor and began to pick up scattered clothing viciously. "If you laugh at me, I will get my knife and stab you," she said, without looking around. "I am to tell you that dinner will be served in one hour in the dining room, and that if you wish to sit in the courtyard, the servants will bring wine."

Giles opened his mouth to speak and Michael silenced him with a look. "Do I need to explain to Señora Palomo that you'll be dining with us rather than the servants, Brat?"

Brat turned, her arms full of filthy clothing. "Señora Palomo says I may dine with you now that I am dressed like a respectable woman and not a prostitute. This gown belonged to her in her younger days, she is waiting for Gabriella to grow tall enough to wear it."

175

"Did she say that to you?" Antonio asked mildly.

"She did."

"I will speak to her."

"I'll do it," Michael said.

"No, Captain. She is my countrywoman, if anybody complains of her manners, it will be me." Antonio came forward and placed a hand firmly under Brat's chin, lifting her head. "The gown becomes you well, little fox. You are a beautiful girl. Better when your head is high, like this. Now, put those rags in the basket and I shall carry it to the scullery for you."

For a moment, Brat glared at him. Then suddenly she gave one of her unexpected smiles and dumped the dirty shirts into the basket. Michael watched as she went through the room like a whirlwind, scooping up anything that could be washed. Antonio picked up the basket and followed her down the stairs to the service area.

"I have to say, Captain O'Reilly, you have the most remarkable taste in servants," Giles said seriously.

"I'm glad you find it funny, Fenwick."

"No, really. If we weren't in danger of our lives, I'd be inclined to see if I could tempt her away. She combines the roles of groom, valet, laundry-maid and cook with equal facility and she looks damned good in both skirts and breeches. How much do you pay her?"

"Giles, I don't have a sense of humour about this right now," Michael said, running his fingers through his hair. "This is bloody ridiculous, I thought she was a child when I took her on, and it was never meant to be for more than a couple of months. What in God's name am I going to do with her when we get back to the lines, she can't come with me on campaign. Especially looking like that."

"Michael, your reputation suggests that you know perfectly well what to do with her."

"That's not how I see her, Giles."

Giles did not reply for a long time. Eventually, he said:

"Well it's how every other man in the army is going to see her, Michael. But now isn't really the time. Put your boots on and let's go and find that drink, for God's sake."

***

Giles slept deeply, the sleep of sheer exhaustion, and woke late. A maid served breakfast on a sunny terrace, and informed Giles that Sir Horace Grainger was awake and could see him. As Giles followed her up to the top floor, the sound of singing floated through an open window, and he paused to look out. Brat was hanging laundry on a long washing line at the back of the house, singing part of a litany that Giles thought he recognised from the convent. She had a clear, true soprano and the sound made him smile. Brat's ability to bounce back from adversity was remarkable.

176

Grainger was propped up against pillows and Giles' heart sank at the sight of his white, drawn face and shadowed eyes. Grainger was only in his fifties but he was clearly a very sick man. He managed a smile as Giles saluted.

"Captain Fenwick, is it not? Come in. Pull up that stool and sit down. It is a pleasure - and a surprise - to see a fellow countryman."

"I'm here in search of you, sir," Giles said, sitting down. "London had no word and had no idea what had become of you, so they sent out a small party to search."

"I'm sure they did," Grainger said with pleasant irony.

"We met with Porlier at the Santa Maria convent and travelled part of the way with him. He told us you were here, and injured, but I didn't know how badly. How are you, sir?"

"I am unwell, Captain, as you can probably see."

"Can you tell me what happened?"

"We were attacked on the high road. I was unhappy about my French escort and I made it very clear to them. Close to the garrisons, it is relatively safe, but I knew that whole sections of that road have been effectively impassable to French convoys for a year or more. I begged them to allow me to travel on alone, but they were insistent. Mendizabal had issued travel papers for my escort and advised them to travel under a flag of truce."

"They must have known that they were still at risk. Not all the irregulars would have got that message, and even some who had might not hold to it if they saw the opportunity to take down half a French cavalry troop. Why didn't they listen to you?"

"I think because they did not trust me, Captain," Grainger said tranquilly. "With some cause. I would imagine they had been given orders to watch me very carefully and to search my baggage thoroughly. Extraordinary, when I consider how often my baggage had already been searched during my time in France."

"Did they find anything?" Giles asked.

"If they had, I would be dead. The French shoot spies, which is why you ride these hills wearing that uniform. I have no such protection. Ironic, that it seems that instead, I will die at the hands of my allies."

"I'm guessing they had no idea who you were."

"No, it was a lightning strike and they took no prisoners. My valet and my Spanish guide were both cut down in the first rush, and I took a shot in the leg and then a sword cut across my shoulder. I thought I would die there and then, but one of the troop spoke good English and had heard me cry out. He protected me as I lay on the ground. When they realised who I was, I think they were afraid. Their leader, a man by the name of Palomo, is from Castro Urdiales and arranged for me to be brought here and delivered into the care of his mother and sister. They have nursed me very well, but both wounds became infected. The shoulder wound seems to be healing, although slowly. The leg is not."

Giles did not reply. He had noticed the smell as he came into the room. He looked at the older man's shrewd dark eyes, bloodshot and slightly yellow, and knew that no hollow reassurance would work with this man.

"Have you seen a surgeon?"

"There is an apothecary and a barber surgeon in the town. They have bled me dry and given me more potions and poultices than I can remember. At one point, it was suggested that the leg could be amputated, but I do not think I would have survived it. Probably I have only delayed the inevitable. But now that you are here, I am optimistic that it will not have been for nothing."

Giles studied him silently for a moment. "Can you tell me?"

"My notes are encoded, but you should know at least what they contain. You are aware that ostensibly, my mission was to inspect the conditions of our prisoners of war, and possibly to negotiate for the exchange of a number of high level prisoners. What I have actually been doing, is collecting information about individuals and groups opposed to Bonaparte, who might be instrumental in bringing about a coup, with support from his European enemies."

"Jesus Christ, no wonder they wanted to find you. Had the French no idea?"

"I believe not, at first. I have served his Majesty in a diplomatic capacity all my life and have been to France many times. My credentials are impeccable."

"And for how much of that time have you also spied for his Majesty?" Giles asked, and Grainger gave a sardonic smile.

"Most of it," he admitted. "But very successfully, as you may imagine, or they would never have accepted me for this mission."

"So what makes you think they suspected you by the end, sir? And if they did, why are you still here?"

"In Toulouse, I was visited by a certain Major Sevigny, whose interest in my work was very flattering. He was undoubtedly an intelligence officer. I don't know what made them suddenly suspicious, but since this Russian disaster, the whole of France is looking over its shoulder."

"Is it as bad as they say it is?" Giles asked.

"Worse, I think. The army is destroyed and he is going to find it hard to get enough men to build it up again. Arrogant little man."

Giles could not help smiling. "That is a very damning statement about the master of Europe, Sir Horace. Have you met him?"

"Several times. The emperor likes me, which is probably another reason why my activities have passed unnoticed for so long. He is not particularly scrupulous about his treatment of diplomats, a number have been imprisoned simply because he did not like what they had to tell him. But it was clear to me that when I left France this time, I should not be returning while he still reigns. Sevigny tried hard to find evidence, but he could not, so he insisted that I accept a French escort all the way to the ship. I wonder if he regrets that now, given that he sent those men to their deaths."

Grainger fell silent and closed his eyes. Giles watched him for a moment, feeling a growing sadness. He suspected that Grainger was right, and that the infection had taken too strong a hold of his body, and it bothered Giles because he felt an instinctive liking for the older man. He got up.

"I'll leave you to rest, sir, you look exhausted. We're going up to the castle to talk to Colonel Alvarez and to send a message out to the navy, but with your permission, I'd like to visit you again."

Grainger opened his eyes. "Come later, after I've slept. There are things I need to tell you, Captain, in case I die suddenly. They won't wait. There's another officer with you?"

"Yes, sir. Captain O'Reilly of the 112th, and also my Spanish guide, Antonio."

"And who is the songbird hanging laundry on the terrace?"

Giles smiled. "Her name is Ariana Ibanez, but we call her Brat. She's been acting as servant to Captain O'Reilly and she followed him. I wish she hadn't, she's the worst kind of responsibility in this situation. Do you know Colonel Alvarez?"

"We have met. He is not a bad soldier, but he is not the man I would choose to have in command in this situation."

"I believe you, sir. He's behaving as though this place can hold out, but even the little I've seen of the defences tells me he's wrong. He should have surrendered."

"He may live to regret his decision, but my worry is that the rest of the garrison and the townspeople will regret it more. Am I to assume that it is your intention to try to get me to a Royal Navy ship?"

"If I can, sir."

"Do not make the attempt, Captain, I would never survive it. Concentrate on ensuring that when the time comes, there is a place aboard that ship for you and your companions. Later, we will talk about the information I carry."

Giles saluted. "I'm hoping to change your mind about that, sir."

"I would die before I reached Corunna."

"Perhaps. Or perhaps we'll be able to get you to a surgeon who could do you some good, but we'll have that argument another time. I'll report back on my conversation with Colonel Alvarez. Sleep well."

***

Major Vane's spectacular quarrel with his brigade commander caused a strained awkwardness which was new to the officers of Van Daan's brigade. English, Portuguese and German battalions were used to a good deal of social interaction during winter quarters. Anne van Daan organised dinners and dances, and there were endless invitations to balls and parties thrown by other regiments and by the local population on both sides of the border. While Keren's difficult social position prevented her from being invited to formal social events, she loved the regular informal hops where the officers were

179

happy to invite local girls from a variety of social classes which enabled Keren to blend in. In particular, while in Madrid, she had formed a friendship with Juana Smith, the very young wife of the capable Captain Harry Smith of the 95th, and found herself a regular and popular guest at all the dances and was never without a partner. It was a relief to Keren that Vane never attended these events, but she knew that Paul's battalion commanders were concerned about the rift that had opened up between the 115th and the rest of the brigade.

Individual friendships were not affected. Captain Simon Carlyon and Captain Nicholas Witham dined frequently with the 110th and there were one or two other officers who were regular visitors but some of the newer men, who had transferred over from the 117th with Vane, clearly felt that they owed some loyalty to their commander. A friendly challenge to a cricket match was abruptly declined, and at one or two local balls and receptions, the 115th kept to themselves.

"This can't go on," Carl said gloomily, the morning after a particularly strained evening at a ball in Castelo Bom. "The rest of the army is beginning to snigger about it behind their hands, it's so obvious."

"I know. Lord Wellington isn't amused," Paul said. "He has informed me that I need to find a way to make this work before we march in the spring. He's right as well, I can't command men who can barely speak to me. I'm furious with myself."

"What else could you have done, Paul?"

"Not thrown him out of a window, perhaps? I lost my temper, Carl. To be honest, just looking at Vane makes me want to punch him, but I should…"

"He tried to rape a Spanish maidservant and would quite possibly have done the same to Rivero's daughter. He shouldn't still hold a commission, let alone command a battalion."

"He wouldn't, if I'd been able to persuade either woman to give evidence. But they won't." Paul stood up and walked to the window. Keren had the impression of anger, barely contained. "Do you know how many rape or attempted rape trials we manage to prosecute in this army, Carl? Virtually none. The last successful prosecution that I actually know about was in Lisbon, when I sent those three bastards from the 112th to trial. I wanted them hanged, but we don't have the death penalty for rape, so they were flogged and they were supposed to be sent back to me, except that I refused to have them and told the assistant provost that if he sent them back, I'd shoot them in the head."

"I always wondered what happened about that," Carl said. "I wasn't there, but I remember Manson telling me the story, he said you scared the shit out of the whole of the 112th that day."

"And have never regretted it. In the end, Sym Armstrong intervened and offered to take them into the commissary depot on detached duties. Funnily enough, two of them died very soon afterwards in an outbreak of camp fever. For all I know, the other one is still there. But the point is, that poor woman had to stand up before a court and describe in detail what those bastards did to her in order to get a conviction. She was a brave woman, and

180

she had an unusually supportive husband, but most women are too embarrassed or ashamed to come forward. Or their male relatives don't want them to for the same reasons."

"You cannot blame them, General," Keren said. Both man turned to look at her in surprise. Keren folded the shirt she had been mending and put it neatly into her work basket. "I attended that court martial. Mrs van Daan went, to support the victim, so I accompanied her. I found it intimidating enough, and I was just watching. They asked her all sorts of embarrassing questions, and one of them even suggested that she might have been paid to lie with them. As if it was her fault."

Paul's brows drew together in a formidable scowl. "It's probably a good thing I didn't attend," he said. "I know you're right, Keren, and I don't blame the women. I just wish we could find a way to convict some of these bastards, it happens far too often. Badajoz still haunts me."

Keren went to the door. "At least your men know that you wouldn't tolerate it, sir," she said. "Will you excuse me, I promised Mrs van Daan I'd go with her today, she's taking the children to the market."

"Rather you than me, it's too close to headquarters and I'm avoiding Lord Wellington at the moment. Thank you, Keren, it was a useful insight. We should probably talk to women about this rather more."

Keren was glad to escape. The conversation was uncomfortable, not just because of the unpleasant memories it had stirred up, but because of her present difficulties with Major Vane. Keren had not spoken to anybody about Vane. After that first encounter on the road back to Santo Antonio, she had adjusted her behaviour, and had begun to ride, if she wanted to go beyond the estate. Keren had assumed that it would be easy to avoid Vane, especially now that he was no longer likely to visit Santo Antonio, but she quickly realised that it was impossible to avoid a man who was so determined to seek her out.

It had grown worse since Vane had moved his billet out to the farm cottage near the winery. He was now closer to the quinta, and it was easy for him to waylay Keren as she went about her business. She had gone to a neighbouring farm to buy milk one morning, and found him waiting for her at the roadside on the way back. It was no longer safe to visit the village, unless she was accompanied, and on the rare occasions she still went out alone, Keren found herself jumpy and nervous.

Most of Vane's tormenting was verbal, although on the morning he had waited for her on her way back with the milk pails, he had badly frightened Keren by taking hold of her and forcibly kissing her. It was revolting and it brought back painful memories of the months she had endured Simpson's groping hands and drunken assaults. When Vane released her Keren scrubbed fiercely at her face with her sleeve, making him laugh.

"You'll get to like it in time. They all do."

"If you touch me again, I'll speak to General van Daan."

"If General van Daan lays another hand on me, I'll report him. Even a Major-General isn't allowed to assault a fellow officer and the rest of the army will be sniggering because the officers of the 110th are more concerned with the feelings of a camp follower than the honour of their regiment."

"Stay away from me." Keren tried to sound forceful but she was close to tears and she knew that Vane could see it.

"I can afford to be generous, Keren, and you're a pretty little thing. You should think of your future."

Keren lay awake at nights, trying to think of a solution. She knew that Carl was beginning to realise that something was wrong. He had begun to ask her repeatedly if she was all right, and Keren forced a smile and assured him that she was. She longed to be able to tell him, but she was under no illusions that both he and the general would be furious and would try to deal with Vane. There were enough problems within the brigade over Vane's behaviour towards the two Portuguese women and it would be worse if Paul knew that Keren was also a victim.

Keren had no idea how Carl would react. Her lover was generally very placid, renowned for keeping his temper, but Keren could still remember how protective he had been when some of his own officers had behaved disrespectfully in the early days of their relationship. She was terrified that Vane might manage to provoke Carl to a duel, and she was determined not to be the cause of it. Keren had survived both hardship and brutality during her first year with the army, and a fair number of casual insults since, and she knew she could survive this. She had immense faith in Paul van Daan's ability to find a way to get rid of Vane eventually. Until then, she tried to remain close to home and avoided going out alone if at all possible. In the quinta, wrapped in Carl's arms each night, she felt safe and loved and she told herself it was enough.

The market in Freineda was in full swing and within minutes of being released from the carriage, the older children were gone, racing among the stalls. Keren watched them, smiling. She could remember the weekly market in Truro which was twice or possibly three times as big as this. It amused her that these children of privilege, who came from big towns with shops that the villagers of Freineda could not even imagine, should find an outing like this so exciting. Keren supposed it was the novelty of the dusty village square, the strangeness of hearing other languages spoken around them, of seeing Portuguese women in local costume, and everywhere the ubiquitous red coats of Wellington's army.

"It is surprisingly easy to entertain them," Anne said beside her, and Keren laughed.

"They amuse themselves, ma'am."

"They do. Well, I have an appointment with Señor Rivero, who has had a delivery of luxury fabric. What is ridiculous is that in a few months' time, I will be up to my ankles in mud, and these gowns will barely see the light of day, but the general is determined that I buy myself a gift. Keren, if I find anything that I like, do you think you would have time to make something up? I know I've a nerve asking, and I promise I'll pay you for your time, it's just that you're better than any dressmaker in the area. I'd like to get something for Grace and Margriete as well, they're being so good at helping with the little ones."

"I'd be happy to, ma'am, you know how I love to sew."

"I know how you never say no to me, I take shameless advantage of you."

"You can't take advantage of your friends, ma'am. And you wouldn't anyway."

Anne put her arm around Keren's shoulders and gave her a brief affectionate hug. "I don't know what I'd do without you," she said. "Katja and I are going to inspect material, would you do me a favour and drop these reports into headquarters before you join us? If I do it, somebody will see me and I won't get out of there for an hour."

"Gladly, ma'am. I'll come and find you."

Keren took the bundle of papers and weaved her way through the crowded square to the long low house opposite the church. She was briefly challenged by a sentry, who inspected the reports then led her through to where Lord Fitzroy Somerset was working at a small table by one of the windows. He rose, looking surprised, and Keren curtseyed.

"Mrs van Daan asked me to deliver these, sir, as I was passing. They're for his lordship, with General van Daan's compliments."

Somerset came forward and took the papers. He glanced down at them and then up at Keren and gave her a singularly charming smile.

"Capital, he's been waiting for these. Thank you so much, ma'am. I wish all our messengers were so pretty."

Keren blushed but returned his smile. Some of Lord Wellington's ADCs and staff members were visibly awkward in her presence, unable to decide how to treat a young woman who dressed and behaved like a lady, but was reputedly of humble origins and was very openly living in an irregular relationship with another officer. One or two, notably Charles Stewart, before he left, had been inclined towards over-familiarity until Anne had noticed it and given Wellington's flamboyant adjutant-general a frosty set-down. Lord Fitzroy Somerset had never shown anything other than impeccable manners and Keren appreciated it.

Señor Rivero had a small warehouse on the edge of the village, past the church. Keren could see the older children, clustered around a food stall, trying to decide between a selection of sticky looking honey treats. When Keren had first come to Freineda last year, it would have been difficult to imagine a market stall given over to anything other than basic survival needs, but since the border fortresses had fallen into Allied hands, some cautious normality had begun to return to the towns and villages. There was little prosperity yet. Portugal had been ravaged by the war, and many villages would never be re-occupied. Agriculture would take years to recover but this year had seen some planting, and farmers and estate owners were beginning to sow crops again and tend vines and olive groves with more confidence.

As she passed the children, Keren noticed that Margriete and Grace were holding little Rowena and Catriona's hands between them and the sight

183

made her smile. Growing up in an overcrowded miner's cottage in Cornwall, it was the job of the eldest daughter to look after the younger children. As she had expanded her horizons and taken work occasionally in the houses of the gentry for the annual spring cleaning, Keren had always been astonished at the number of nursemaids and servants employed on such a simple matter as childcare and even more surprised at how many families still sent their young babies away to live with a wet nurse. Both Katja Mackenzie and Anne van Daan seemed to take a relaxed approach to motherhood, and Grace and Margriete seemed to enjoy looking after their small sisters.

Keren was thinking about the children as she rounded the church, when a hand on her arm made her jump. She gave a little squeak of alarm, turned, and pulled her arm away at the sight of Vane

"You startled me."

"You're very nervous, Keren."

Keren took two steps back. "If you touch me, I'll scream," she said, as forcefully as she could. "There are a lot of people about here, someone will hear me."

Vane held up his hands in mock surrender. "I'm not going to hurt you. Where are you going?"

"I'm meeting Mrs van Daan, and she'll be looking for me if I don't hurry."

"Well I wouldn't want to upset the lovely Mrs van Daan, I'm told she can be a bitch when she's roused. I often wonder how a woman like that came to be married to a boor like him, she could be the toast of London."

"Let me pass."

"In a moment. I have something for you."

"I don't want anything from you."

Keren stepped forward and Vane caught her and pushed her back against the cold stone of the church wall. He took something from his pocket. Keren closed her eyes and turned her face away and she heard him laugh again, then felt something cool brush down her cheek and caress her neck before sliding down the front of her simple muslin gown.

"A gift."

Keren opened her eyes. His face was inches from hers and she could see that he intended to kiss her. She placed both hands on his chest and shoved hard, then reached into the front of her gown and withdrew a gold pendant, three pearls in a delicate setting on a gold chain. Vane was laughing.

"I think it suits you, sweetheart. Why don't you put it on?"

Keren whirled around. At the end of the church was a railing where a number of horses and mules were secured, while their owners visited the market. Keren marched towards it and dropped the necklace into a pile of dung, then ground it in with her shoe. She heard Vane's furious protest and turned back to look at him.

"You little bitch, that cost me good money."

"I hope they'll let you return it once you've cleaned it up then, Major. Leave me alone."

Keren turned and walked away, her head held high. She always felt faintly unclean after an encounter with Vane, but this time, she also felt a sense of satisfaction. She could hear him swearing, and glancing back, she saw him trying to retrieve the pendant from the dung using a twig broken from the hedge. He was too busy to attempt to pursue her, and Keren went to find Anne and Katja. She knew she had enraged him and it made her feel a lot better.

Chapter Thirteen

With the reports for Wellington up to date, Paul had time for his children and Anne found herself with little occupation for the first time in three weeks. Paul had arranged an inspection visit to part of the sixth division who were in cantonments around the mountainous country of the Serra da Estrela, and he approached Anne so warily that it made her want to laugh.

"I was wondering if I could take the boys with me, bonny lass? I've spoken to Mackenzie and he's keen to show his boys something more of the country while they're out here so he could come with me and we can take Harcourt. It's around fifty miles, but on good roads, and we'll take a wagon and a decent escort. I thought they might enjoy camping, and..."

"What about the girls?" Anne asked, keeping a straight face with an effort.

Paul eyed her warily. "Do you want to come?"

Anne gave up and laughed aloud. "No. Not that I wouldn't enjoy it, but I'd actually quite like to spend some time with Rowena and Will. But Grace will be bitterly disappointed if you leave her behind, and I think Margriete might like the adventure."

"I'd be happy to take them, girl of my heart, but we'd need a woman with us in that case, and I can hardly ask that poor governess, she's been through enough."

"I'm not sure, she's surprisingly intrepid," Anne said. "It will be up to Katja of course, but I don't think you need her, Margriete is fourteen, she's almost a young woman and she'll take care of Grace. I could ask Señora Mata if you could borrow one of the maids to sleep in their tent with them, if you're worried, though."

Paul laughed and kissed her. "Leaving you to have a very peaceful week spoiling your youngest children and gossiping with Katja Mackenzie. I see through you, Anne van Daan. Very well, let me know what Katja says and I'll make the arrangements."

Anne waved off the extended party then collected her three youngest charges along with Katja and her daughter and set off through the gardens. Anne loved the old ornamental gardens at Santo Antonio, a maze of low walls, hidden niches with stone benches, orange and lemon trees and a neglected pond with trailing willows sweeping the dark water. At the back of the formal gardens was a wide meadow which the officers had arranged to be scythed short for cricket matches, and games of battledore and shuttlecock. It was empty at present, and Anne and Katja spread two blankets on the grass below a tree and settled Georgiana on them. Anne's youngest daughter was growing fast. She had begun to smile at the sight of Anne, and two days earlier, had surprised Anne by giggling as Anne tickled her. Anne had missed so much of Will's babyhood, that she was completely enchanted, and had spent two days finding ways to make the baby laugh again.

Anne had discovered, quite by accident, that her daughter loved to lie under trees, watching the branches wave over her head. She lay back happily, cooing at the leaves rustling in the breeze while Katja took out a soft ball and showed Will how to kick it to Rowena and Catriona. After a few minutes, the children were absorbed in the game and Katja joined Anne on the blankets beside Georgiana and watched. Rowena was older than both Will and Catriona and far more co-ordinated, but she was patient with them in a way that reminded Anne of her mother. When Will fell, Rowena was quick to help him up, and their obvious closeness touched Anne's heart. She thought of Paul's gentle first wife and hoped that somehow she could see them.

"You look sad."

"Do I? I'm not really, I was just thinking about Rowena, Paul's first wife, and hoping she can see how very well her children are doing."

"Did you know her?"

"Yes, we were close friends."

"That is very good for the older children, that you have memories of their mother to share.

Anne lay back on the blanket beside Georgiana, watching small white clouds drifting lazily across the blue sky.

"I feel very happy."

"That is why days like this are so good. Often we are happy, but only when we have time to be still, do we really know it."

Anne turned her head to look at her. "That is very true. You are very wise, Katja. I am not sure I have had such a wise friend before."

Katja laughed. "I am sure you have."

"To be honest, I have not had many close women friends at all. I have Keren and Teresa, and I am probably not supposed to think of them as my friends, although I do. Mary Scovell is a good friend, and I am becoming very fond of Juana Smith, although she is much younger than I am. But it has been very good having you here, I'm going to miss you a great deal when you leave."

"It makes me happy to hear you say that."

"I was horrible when you first arrived. I am sorry."

"You were never horrible. You were unhappy, and I wanted so much to help, but I did not know how."

Anne sat up and inspected the basket that Katja had set down. "You've been raiding that overgrown mess of a herb garden again. What have you found?"

"This is thyme, and here we have ivy leaves. I have a recipe for an excellent cough remedy which uses both, I shall copy it out for you."

"Where did you learn about herbal medicine?"

"My mother and also my grandmother. I have a stillroom at home, and there is a book of recipes which must be almost a hundred years old. I add to it when I find new remedies that work."

Anne was studying the bundles of leaves. "What are all these?"

"This is comfrey, this is garlic and we have sage, betony, rosemary, hyssop, rue and chamomile. That is cumin, it is good to spice food and also for soothing ointments. I am so envious of this, it grows best in warm climates and I have had to build a glass house to grow with success at home, but it is so useful."

Anne picked up a stalk of lavender. She inhaled deeply. "Lavender. I love this, my stepmother had a lot of it planted at home. She used to put little bags into our clothing and under our pillows to help us sleep. This smells like home."

"Do you miss it? Your home?"

Anne looked round in surprise. "No, not really. I married very young and came out here with my first husband, and I've never been back, I wanted to stay with Paul. It means I don't see the children very often, this is only the second time I've met my older step-children. I know that some people think that's very wrong of me."

"Your children are being raised in comfort and safety, Nan. I think nobody would say that General van Daan is wrong to do his duty with the army.

"He's a man, Katja. The rules are not the same."

"That does not mean the rules are correct. When my first husband died, and left the business to me, everybody was very shocked. I wanted to make him proud, so I worked all the time to keep it running, but it meant I had less time for my children. I hired a governess and a tutor and hoped they would understand. I think they forgive me. And in truth, I like to be very busy. I am lucky that Ross understands that. I am still a partner in the business in Vlissingen and Middelburg, so I spend much time on correspondence and accounting. Now we have a warehouse in Scotland for the wool also. I am never idle. That is why…"

Katja stopped and Anne picked up her thought. "That's why you've spent the entire time here looking for things to do. You were bored."

"I was. I am grateful that you understand so well and have allowed me to become involved. I feel very at home here, I shall be sad to leave."

"We'll write," Anne said. "And now that the children have become friends, I'm hoping you'll rescue them occasionally from Patience. Grace can talk to you."

"It will be a joy." Katja shaded her eyes against the sun and indicated to a red coated figure approaching from the house. "It looks like Lieutenant-Colonel Swanson."

"So it is. How exasperating, he is going to want something and I feel very lazy."

Katja laughed. "You love your responsibilities, Nan. I will go and play with the children in case he wishes to speak with you privately."

Anne watched Carl approach and considered getting up, then decided against it. He bowed and Anne smiled and indicated the blanket that Katja had just vacated.

"I am too idle to rise, Carl, so if you want to talk to me you'll have to come down to my level."

Carl sat down. "This looks idyllic," he said, his eyes on Katja, who was over by a flowering shrub pointing out the bees, busy about their work. "I wonder if the general is having such a relaxing time?"

"With five children in tents? I imagine he's exhausted already. Can I help you, Carl, or is this a social visit? If it is, you're very welcome."

"I shouldn't be socialising, I've paperwork to attend to. I don't know how the general managed to leave me without himself, Mackenzie and Manson all at the same time, it's torture."

"I'll give you a hand tomorrow if Keren will help Katja with the children. And we can co-opt Sergeant Hammond, he's my favourite assistant. Anne studied him and realised there was something wrong. The green eyes looked tired, and unusually, there was no trace of a smile. "What's wrong, Colonel?"

Carl hesitated. "I'm worried about Keren," he said abruptly. "There's something the matter, and I can't find out what. I've asked her. In fact, I've asked her so often, I'm trying to bite my tongue, she must be sick of it, but she assures me there's nothing. You spend a lot of time with her, ma'am. I wondered if you'd noticed anything."

Anne thought about it. "I don't know," she said. "With Mrs Mackenzie about, we probably don't talk as freely as we usually would. I did think she looked tired this past week, though. Has she been ill?"

"I don't think so, but she's not sleeping." Carl realised what he had said, and flushed. "I'm sorry. I shouldn't have said that, it's just I'm so worried."

Anne stared at him blankly and then understood. "Oh for God's sake, Carl, don't treat me like a child. Keren has been your mistress for two years or more, you cannot think I am about to swoon because you refer to the fact that you are sleeping in the same bed."

"Sorry," Carl said. "I'm not at my best. I'm really worried."

"Since we are being very frank, is there any possibility that she might be with child?"

"This is proving to be a very unsuitable conversation with my commanding officer's wife."

"Given that you're openly living with my former maidservant outside of marriage your scruples sound very silly," Anne said irritably. "Stop being so missish, I'm trying to help."

"There's always a possibility that she might be with child, ma'am. I don't think you're aware of the fact that she lost a child last year, are you?"

"I had no idea," Anne said. "When? Why on earth did nobody tell me?"

"It was just before Badajoz and it was very early, we think. She wasn't really unwell with it and refused to see a doctor. I thought she should tell you, but you'd only just suffered your own miscarriage, and you'd been through so much. She didn't want to worry you."

"Well she should have," Anne snapped. "She's my friend, don't ever let her do that again."

"I won't. But the thing is, she was very open with me about it. She didn't seem to find it difficult to tell me, or to talk about it. It was very strange, finding out that I might have become a father. We talked a lot, and I said…I promised her that if we had a child in the future, we'd find a way to take care of it together. She trusts me, ma'am. I think if it was that, she'd just tell me about it."

Anne said nothing. There were a number of things she wanted to say to Carl but she bit her tongue, knowing that none of them would be useful. He was clearly very worried, and Anne approved his concern but longed to slap him. It had mystified her from the beginning that Carl Swanson, who was a kind, considerate and very honourable man, had managed to create a situation so appallingly difficult in his relationship with Keren.

Anne would have understood, although not approved, if Keren's liaison with Paul's oldest friend had followed the path they had all expected. It was not at all unusual for officers to take a mistress, often local women, but such relationships seldom lasted beyond winter quarters. An honourable man would give a generous parting gift, if he could afford to, and take some responsibility for paying for the upkeep of any child that might result. Not all men were honourable, and there were women in the army's tail and in many local brothels who had ended there when their families had refused to have them back after their disgrace.

Anne knew that Carl would be good to Keren, but what had developed over the past few years looked more like a marriage than a casual relationship and the couple were inseparable. Carl had proved an affectionate, generous and faithful lover, but seemed genuinely oblivious to the awkwardness of Keren's situation and the number of times she was subject to unwelcome advances and unpleasant remarks from men who saw her as nothing more than a privileged camp follower. It infuriated Anne, and she was finding it increasingly hard to bite her tongue on the subject.

"I don't know, Carl," she said eventually. "I'm glad you've told me, I'll find an excuse to spend some time alone with her, and see if I can get out of her what's wrong."

"Thank you," Carl said, with real gratitude. "It's worrying the life out of me, I can't think what it can be that she won't tell me."

"I'll see if I can find out," Anne said, more sympathetically. "I know how much you care, Carl."

Steady green eyes looked back at her. "I hope so, ma'am. I know how much you worry about her, but you don't need to. Whatever happens in the future, I'll always take care of her."

"You'd better, Colonel." Anne kept her tone determinedly light. "Because if I have to do it for you, you will be very, very sorry. I'll let you know if I find anything out."

***

With the weather improving daily, Carl began to step up training for the 110th. He had kept a steady routine through the winter weeks, knowing that his men needed rest, recovery and proper food after the misery of the retreat. In the meantime, he spent extra time working with his new recruits and the men who had transferred in from the disbanded 117th. Paul was scathing about the new men, but Carl was very patient and had been through this process many times during his eleven years in the army. He knew that it was easier to train new recruits than men who had learned bad habits, so he separated the two groups and worked harder and longer with the remnants of the 117th. By the time Paul set off on his family trip, Carl was ready to incorporate both groups into his existing companies and to increase the length and difficulty of training for them all.

Gervase Clevedon had been going through the same, exacting process with the 112th. They had received word that Johnny Wheeler was on his way back and could be with them any day and Carl was impatient for his return, he had missed Johnny badly. When he was not away touring other divisions, Paul organised regular parades and inspections for all three of his English battalions as well as his Portuguese and German troops, but otherwise left the management of the 110th entirely to Carl. It was hard work, but Carl loved it.

The battalion was still not fully up to strength, but it was better than most in Wellington's army, and there was no danger that it would either be sent home or broken up into one of Wellington's controversial provisional battalions. A lot of men had developed camp fever or dysentery and spent weeks in hospital. Some died but many of them were beginning to return to duty now and numbers were looking much better in all Paul's battalions. New uniform and kit had begun to arrive, and watching his men lining up after a long morning of drill and bayonet training, Carl felt a lift of pride at the sight of them.

"They're looking good, sir."

Carl called the order to stand the men down and turned. "Captain Manson, welcome back. When did you arrive, I didn't think we'd see you until Christmas?"

Manson saluted, laughing. "I might have missed the campaign at that point, sir. I arrived last night, although I wish I'd known the general was away, I'd have stayed another week."

"You look very well, so I'm guessing you had a good time."

"I did, sir. There'll be a mountain of paperwork awaiting me, but it was worth it, I think I needed it."

"If you can take some of that paperwork off my hands, I'll be eternally grateful, I'm sick of it. How's Diana, Leo?"

"Very well, sir. Very happy to see me and it was entirely mutual."

"Excellent. I'll let you catch up with the post, but we'll talk properly at dinner."

Carl went into the office on his way back to his room to collect his mail and found Anne at her desk with Sergeant Hammond in attendance, checking off a list of equipment which had just been delivered. Anne wore a ferocious scowl which suggested that somebody had made a mistake, and Carl took his letters and retreated, before his general's wife began to express her dissatisfaction. It was very satisfying to be able to hand over his administrative tasks to somebody else.

Up in his room, he found Keren putting away his laundry. Carl dropped the letters onto the bed and caught her about the waist from behind, nuzzling her neck which he knew was very ticklish until she was giggling helplessly.

"It's a beautiful afternoon, and I've worked very hard today. Shall we go for a ride? We could raid the kitchen and picnic by the river."

Keren turned into his arms. "I'd love to."

"Just let me read these letters while you get changed, there's one from my father."

Keren retrieved her riding dress and Carl picked up the letters. Four were addressed to him, one from his father, two from army friends stationed in England and the fourth from his banker. The fifth was a slim package, addressed to Keren. Carl stared at it in surprise. Keren had never received a letter. Carl did not think her family knew where she was or anything about her current situation. When she had first been employed by Anne, Keren had been unable to read and write, and Anne had taught her. She had proved an apt and enthusiastic pupil and probably read for enjoyment more than Carl did, but he was not aware that she had started a correspondence with anybody.

"What's that, Carl?"

"It's for you," Carl said, trying to sound casual. He handed her the package and Keren stared at it blankly.

"For me?"

"It has your name on it, Keren."

Keren looked up at him and there was something in her expression that chilled Carl. He studied her and realised that she was afraid, although he could not imagine of what. For weeks, he had been watching her and wondering and worrying, and he was suddenly afraid as well, with a knot in his stomach.

192

"Why don't you open it, lass?"

Keren looked down at the package again, and then broke the seal and untied the ribbons. She was very pale and Carl thought that she looked as though she was going to cry. He did not take his eyes from her as she unfolded the letter. Something slid out and onto the floor, and Keren looked down at it. Carl followed her gaze. She did not move, so he bent and picked it up. Keren was staring at it as though it were a scorpion about to attack. Carl placed it on the palm of his hand, a pretty pearl pendant on a gold chain. It was delicate and beautifully made and Carl thought how well it would look against Keren's honey coloured skin. He looked up into her eyes and clenched his fist around the necklace. Reaching out, he took the letter from her lifeless fingers. It was written in a bold hand.

"For you, sweet Keren, until next time. You were unforgettable. When can we be together again?"

The signature was an indecipherable scrawl. Carl looked up and saw that Keren was crying.

"Carl..."

"Don't." Carl could barely speak and the raw anger in his own voice shocked him. "Don't speak. Don't tell me anything. I don't want to know."

"Carl, I'm sorry. I should have..."

Keren was sobbing, her voice so choked that Carl could hardly understand her. He put his hands over his ears. There was a roaring in them and he recognised, in complete horror, that it was rage, a blind fury that he had never experienced in his life before. He wanted to strike out, to find whatever man had touched her and to kill him. He also wanted to hit Keren, and he knew that he needed to get out of the room fast.

"Stop talking," he said, and his voice sounded harsh and strained and completely unlike himself. "You need to stop, Keren, I can't hear it. I don't want to know who he is or why you did it or why the hell you didn't tell me it was over. I've been a bloody idiot, lying awake worrying about what was the matter with you, whether you were ill or unhappy or whether I'd done something wrong. And all the time, you've been...I don't want to know. Get out. Pack your things and get yourself out of here. If he's got the money to buy you expensive trinkets like that, he can bloody well find you house room as well, I'm sure he'd be glad to. Just make sure you get as much as you can out of him before we march out of here, I'd hate to think of you back in the army's tail selling yourself for pennies. I'm going for a ride, I want you gone before I get back."

***

The slamming of the door was so violent, that the room seemed to shake, and a few plaster flakes fell from the ceiling above the frame. Keren did not move for a long time but eventually, her need for a handkerchief overcame her paralysis and she went to find one, then sat on the edge of the bed, mopping her streaming eyes and trying to bring herself under control. She was shivering badly, despite the warmth of the afternoon so she got into the bed fully dressed and pulled the blankets up around her, trying to calm herself. Keren had seen Carl angry before, usually about some stupidity that had caused problems for his battalion and his men, and she had heard him occasionally arguing with his fellow officers about the right course of action, but he was known in the army for his calm good sense and the force of his rage broke her heart.

The necklace lay on the floor where Carl had flung it as he left the room. Eventually, Keren got up and picked it up, putting it beside the note on the table. The sight of both must have been a shock to Carl, but Keren knew that it was her own stupid response that had caused him to think the worst. She had recognised the necklace and had been frozen with horror, realising suddenly all the reasons why she should have told him and trusted him, but she could see how easily he might have misinterpreted her response as guilt. Miserably, she wished that she had talked to him sooner, but it had not occurred to Keren that Vane would be this vicious over her rejection.

Keren had spent weeks agonising over what to do about Vane's unpleasant behaviour, but she had not been afraid that he would try to force her. Men like Vane relied on a woman's fear and shame to keep them silent, and he must know that Keren was far from friendless and that any violence would bring the Van Daans into the picture. What she had not expected was that his spite would be so inventive. Adding the note with the necklace to the regimental mail made it almost certain that Carl would see it, and whatever his response, it was bound to cause trouble.

Keren's shivering had stopped. Reluctantly she slid from the bed and stood looking around her, fighting back the tears again. This room was the same one they had occupied last year and it was as familiar to her as the small cottage on the cliffs above Mousehole where she had grown up. Her things were scattered around the room along with Carl's, looking as though they belonged there. It was a shared room, a couple's room, and Keren had grown used to feeling safe and cared for. She knew that she had friends and would never again be obliged to sell herself to survive, but the world without Carl Swanson beside her felt cold and bleak and unwelcoming.

Carl had asked her to pack and leave, and Keren decided that she would do so. At some point, he would return and Keren hoped that when he was calmer she would be able to talk to him. He had every right to be angry with her, for not telling him the truth and for allowing Vane to work his mischief unchecked, and Keren had no idea what would happen now to their relationship. They had never before had a serious quarrel. The occasional irritations and bad tempered moments of a life together had never disturbed her, never caused her to doubt their affection for each other and never made her feel insecure, despite the genuine uncertainty of her position. Keren could not help hoping that when he was calmer, she could make him see the truth and he would ask her to unpack her boxes and come back to him, but she could not rely upon that. The world had shifted beneath her and she was unwilling to expect too much.

194

Keren remembered clearly the day she had returned to the barracks to pack up her meagre belongings when Anne van Daan had taken her into her employment and she had been able to leave Charlie Simpson. It had been a tiny bundle, wrapped in her only shawl. It brought tears to Keren's eyes as she pulled out several bags and her small trunk and began to fold her clothing, one or two simple items that Anne had given her at the start and far more that Carl had bought for her as their relationship progressed. Keren was suddenly unsure what she should take and what she should leave. She packed the clothes, crying into their folds, because he would have no use for them. There were a few items of jewellery, a gold cross and an exquisite little gold locket that he had bought her in Madrid for her birthday, with five semi-precious stones set around an engraved heart. There were heart shaped earrings to go with it and Keren cried again as she laid them on the table, remembering how she had scolded him for spending so much on her.

Suddenly Keren could not bear it. Going to the wash stand she splashed cold water onto her face then combed her hair and twisted it up into something resembling a respectable knot. Outside the room she hesitated, looking around, not wanting to run into any of the other officers in her current state. The house was quiet, most officers were either still at training, or had taken themselves off on their own pursuits. Keren slipped silently along the corridor to Anne's room and knocked. There was no reply, and after a moment, Keren went along to the children's nursery and peeped around the door. Sergeant-Major Stewart's wife was seated comfortably in a chair feeding Georgiana, while Will, Rowena and little Catriona were on the floor playing with wooden blocks.

"Sally, is Mrs van Daan at home?"

"No, ma'am, she's dining out with Mrs Mackenzie at Mrs Scovell's. She'll be back this evening."

"Oh. I'll speak to her later, then."

Sally shifted the baby more securely on her arm. "Are you all right, ma'am?"

"Yes. Yes, I'm perfectly well, thank you."

Keren withdrew quickly, not wanting Sally to ask any more questions. She returned to the room and continued to pack with a heavy heart. Anne would support her unquestioningly and welcome her back into her household, but the thought did not comfort Keren. She wanted Carl, ached to see him and to assure him that she had not betrayed him and would never do so.

With most of the bags packed, Keren was exhausted. Until Anne returned, there was nowhere she could go and she did not want anybody to see her like this. The sun was sinking lower in the sky and there was no sign of Carl. Keren wondered if he had stopped at some tavern or was visiting friends in one of the other brigades to avoid coming back. For a long time, she sat on the edge of the bed and tried not to think. Eventually, she kicked off her shoes and lay down to rest until she heard Anne returning. It did not look as though Carl was coming back for dinner.

The opening of the door woke her. For a moment, Keren's heart leapt, hoping that Carl had returned, but there was still enough light in the room to see clearly, and it was not Carl who stood leaning against the closed door, smiling.

"You've been crying, Keren. Have you had a lovers' quarrel, by any chance? And you're packing, I see, what excellent timing. Leave the bags here, you can ride back with me and I'll send a cart over to collect them. You can stay with me for a while at least and we'll see how it goes. Not had a regular woman in keeping for a long time, but…"

"Get out!" Keren said. Unexpectedly, her exhausted misery flared into white hot fury. "How dare you walk into this room and assume I'd let you touch me, you're not fit to breathe the same air as me. You're a horrible person who takes pleasure in insulting and hurting people, but you've done your worst with me. If you come anywhere near me, I'll have you arrested for assaulting me."

Vane did not move, but his smile broadened. "Keren, Keren, how charmingly naive. I'm not going to rape you. I don't need to. You can sell those pretty little trinkets he's given you. You can even sell the horse, if he'll let you keep it. Sooner or later the money will run out and you'll be hungry enough. I can wait."

"The fact that you think so little of the care my friends have for me, Major Vane, tells me a good deal about you."

"When they find out Swanson is done with you, the officers will be queuing up, sweet Keren, but they're going to expect a lot more than laundry and mending. Come on, I don't have all evening. I saw him riding out towards the river earlier, and by the expression on his face, he'll want you out of here before he gets back. Stop making such a fuss about it, it's a business transaction, not a love story. He'll find himself a pretty little local within a week, and she'll be cheaper than you. He couldn't really afford you, Keren, but I can. Come back to my billet and prove you're worth it and I might even take you with me on campaign, I like to have something to warm me up when it's cold at night."

Keren wondered if she could manage to be sick on his boots. "I'd rather starve. Get out of my way, I'm going to find Mrs van Daan."

Vane laughed aloud and folded his arms. "Make me," he said, mockingly.

There was a sound on the other side of the door. Vane had heard it too, and began to straighten, but he moved too slowly. With an enormous crash, as if it had been kicked, the door flew open, precipitating Vane across the room. Keren's trunk lay, still open on the floor, and Vane stumbled into it and sprawled headlong onto the wooden boards. Keren backed up quickly against the opposite wall, her hands over her mouth to prevent her screaming. After a moment, Vane pushed himself up onto his knees, shaking his head as if to clear it after the shock.

"What the bloody hell…"

A booted foot landed hard on the back of Vane's neck, sending him flat to the ground again. The boot remained there, pinning Vane to the floor. "Stay there. As you're in my room, threatening my girl, I'd like a word before I let you up again, you nasty-minded, underhanded piece of shit."

***

Carl had no idea where he was going when he rode out of Santo Antonio. He allowed his horse to take the lead, needing to put as much distance as possible between him and Keren. All he could think about for a while was his anger. It filled him up, making him incapable of thought or reason, and until it eased, he could not consider what to do next.

He reined in finally, beside a bubbling stream and led Carrick, his black gelding, down to drink. It was quiet and still, the sky streaked with the gold and orange of a spectacular sunset. Carl listened to the gurgling sound of the water and felt, finally, the rage beginning to subside. There were birds singing in the warm evening air, and Carl roped Carrick to a branch to let him graze, and knelt, splashing icy water over his face. The anger had gone, and instead he was filled with melancholy and an intense longing for Keren. They often rode out after dinner, loving the quiet of evening, and he could see her smiling up at him, the warm tones of her skin lit up by the dying sunlight and her hair, burnished mahogany, curling from under her hat. It was impossible not to think about her. He had tried to leave her behind but she had travelled with him.

Remounting, Carl set Carrick on the narrow path back towards Freineda and let his mind wander over the two and a half years with Keren. She had become part of his life, slipping easily into the role of mistress, confidante and friend. Carl had seldom stopped to examine exactly what she meant to him and he had deliberately closed his mind to the future but he realised it had never once occurred to him that the ending of their liaison would come from her. There had always been officers who could have offered her more money but Keren had never seemed to care about that and never seemed to yearn after the respectability of marriage with one of the enlisted men or NCOs. She had devoted herself to Carl's interests from the beginning and he rode along rutted paths and thought about how much he had taken that for granted.

They had never really quarrelled before and Carl was bitterly ashamed of every angry accusation he had flung at her. Keren owed him nothing, and he had no right to blame her if she had found somebody else. Carl wondered who he was, and if he would be good to her and realised that he was crying. He rode with tears streaming down his cheeks until he was within sight of the gates of the quinta and then he reined in and waited, trying to get himself under control.

Carl had never believed that marriage to Keren was a possibility. Raised in genteel poverty in the rambling vicarage in Ingleby, he was a gentleman's son, for all his father's unworldly disinterest in money. Carl had not been wealthy enough to afford a wife, and then as his prospects improved a

197

little with promotion and prize money, he had no time to court a respectable girl. His native caution had made him avoid situations where he might grow attached to a girl to whom he could never afford to propose so he had taken the soldier's usual bought pleasures until Keren Trenlow had walked into his life. Carl had thought himself safe, knowing the impossibility of falling in love with a miner's daughter. He recognised, with furious regret, that he had been an idiot and had been in love with her from the start.

The house was ablaze with lights and Carl stabled his horse and then walked around to the back door, hoping to avoid having to speak to anybody. His misery was tinged with anxiety now. He hoped that Keren had ignored his order to get out, but if she had gone, he had no idea where and he needed to know that she was safe. He approached his room cautiously, almost afraid to open the door and find her gone, her few possessions missing and the ache of loneliness real. Instead, to his immense relief, he heard her voice.

"I'd rather starve. Get out of my way, I'm going to find Mrs van Daan."

The rage was back, but with a purpose, this time. Carl raised his foot and kicked the door hard. He heard a satisfying crash and a yell, and he stepped into the room. Vane was sprawled on the floor and Keren was standing on the far side of the room. As Vane struggled to rise, Carl moved forward fast and forced him back down with his boot on the back of his neck, his eyes on Keren. She stared back at him.

"What do you want me to do with him, Keren?" Carl asked quietly. "I couldn't help overhearing, and it didn't seem that you wanted him here."

There was a flash of anger in her eyes. "Did you honestly think I would?"

Carl shook his head. "Oh love, I was so angry I didn't think at all or I wouldn't have behaved like an arsehole. Let me kick him out and we can talk. Not through the window, I think, we'd have to get it repaired. Hold on."

He bent and dragged Vane to his feet. Vane was coughing, as though the boot had cut off his air for a time. The thought pleased Carl. He went to the door and opened it.

"Out. You can go on your own or I'll kick you down the stairs, it's up to you."

Even in the half light, Carl could see that Vane's face was scarlet with rage. "You'll meet me for this."

"At any time or place of your choosing. Send me a note. Now get out."

"Wait," Keren said. Her voice was strong and angry. "You're not leaving this behind."

Carl watched as she picked up the necklace and the note. She crumpled up the paper, walked up to Vane and thrust both into his unresisting hand.

"The next time I see that worthless piece of junk, I am going to throw it into the barracks latrine," she said. "Get out."

198

Vane went to the door, and Carl stood looking at Keren and let understanding wash over him. He could make no sense of the tumult of emotions; relief and anger and guilt and shame and above it all a soaring hope that he had not, after all, lost everything.

"You little bitch," Vane said. "Stay with him if you like, you won't have long, I'll make sure of it. Cashiered or dead, it makes no difference to me."

"If I'm cashiered it'll be because you're dead," Carl said. Common sense had gone, and he did not care what happened. "If I'd known that gift was from you, I wouldn't have been worried, she's got better taste. Now get out, and if you go near her again, I'll kill you."

"Are you challenging me, Swanson? You'll be the laughing stock of the army, fighting a duel over a camp follower."

Carl took two steps forward and hit him hard, in the midriff and Vane doubled over, gasping in pain. Carl punched again, full in the face and Vane fell back with a muffled cry, blood spurting from his nose. He was backing up fast as Carl moved forward.

"Carl, no, stop. It's not worth it. He's not worth it."

Carl could hear real fear in Keren's voice and he turned to look at her. "You're worth it," he said. "But I'll defer to you, Keren, in this, as in everything from now on."

He reached for Vane, who was trying to stem the flow of blood, grasped him by the collar and propelled him out into the corridor and almost into the arms of an astonished Leo Manson who had apparently come to find out what the noise was about.

"Piss off. She's not interested and she isn't going to be."

Vane was holding his sleeve to his nose. "You'll meet me for this," he said thickly.

"No, he won't," Manson said hastily. "You look as though you need some help, Major Vane. Let me get you to the kitchen and..."

"Get off me, you interfering bastard. Name your friends, Swanson."

"Willingly."

"He has no friends," Manson said quickly. "Look at him, sir, does he look like a man with friends? Let's not be hasty, think about it overnight and I think you'll find..."

"Captain Manson, will you act for me?"

"Captain Wynne-Smythe will second me," Vane said.

"No, I bloody won't act for you, sir. There's friendship and then there's sheer idiocy," Manson said. "When General van Daan gets back to find you standing your trial for killing this arsehole, he'll be looking for people to kick, and it isn't going to be me."

"Then I'll ask Captain Carlyon."

"Oh no you won't," Manson said. "You're not pulling him into this, Mrs van Daan will kill you. All right, I'll second you, but only with the hope of talking you out of it."

199

"Thank you," Carl said. He felt suddenly very calm. "If you'll excuse me, I need some time with my lady. Tell me the details later."

Carl closed the door firmly and latched it then turned to Keren. She stood, rooted to the spot on the far side of the room and the sight of her white, anxious face broke his heart. He wanted to walk forward and take her into his arms but he stopped himself. This was not like any of their other minor squabbles, which could be mended with a kiss and an apology.

"It's too dark in here to talk properly, I can barely see you," he said quietly. "Wait a moment."

Outside in the corridor there was an oil lamp on a table to light the stairs. There was no sign of either Vane or Manson apart from some splashes of blood on the wooden floor. Carl lit a candle from the lamp and went back into the room, lighting candles until he could see her properly. She was dressed in elegant sprigged muslin and he thought that she would not have looked out of place in any drawing room in England.

"I doubted you," he said. "There's no apology I can give that would make up for that. I was terrified that you'd be gone when I got back and I wouldn't be able to tell you."

"What do you want to tell me, Colonel Swanson?" Stress highlighted the rounded vowels of Keren's Cornish accent and the sound of it pierced his heart anew.

"I love you. I've loved you for so long that I cannot remember when it started and I can't believe I've waited until now to say it. It would serve me right if you had found another man who would treat you better than I have, but you're still here."

"I was packing…"

"It doesn't take you this long to pack a bag, Keren Trenlow, I've seen you pack for both of us in ten minutes in an emergency. You must have known I'd come back."

Keren's eyes had filled with tears. "I wanted a chance to explain," she said. "I should have told you before, Carl, but I was afraid you'd be angry."

"I should have known better. It's just that there's been something wrong for weeks, and you wouldn't tell me what it was. I've been worrying that you were ill. I even wondered if you were pregnant. And then I saw that jewellery and I thought I'd found the reason. I was an imbecile. What's been going on, Keren?"

"He's been following me," Keren blurted out. "Every time I go out alone. I've been afraid to step outside the gates, but then he began hanging about the grounds, always with some pretext of brigade affairs."

"Has he touched you?" Carl asked and read the answer in her unhappy expression. "What did he do?"

"Nothing that bad. Touching. Twice he grabbed hold of me and kissed me. It made me feel sick."

"It's making me feel sick," Carl said truthfully. "Keren, why didn't you tell me?"

"Because I was afraid you'd do what you've just done," Keren said. "I knew how angry you would be. And I thought if I kept telling him no, he would get bored and give up. They always do."

"What do you mean they always do? Has this happened to you before?" Carl's head felt fuzzy and too full, and his heart was hammering. He dreaded her reply but he needed to know.

"A few times. But Major Vane was by far the worst."

" A few times? You're telling me that other men have been annoying you and insulting you as you go about your business, and you didn't think I needed to know that?"

"What could you have done, Carl? This?" Keren sounded suddenly angry. "You can't fight him, a gentleman does not fight a duel over a girl like me. You'll be laughed out of the army and I don't want that. This is your life. You should apologise for hitting him and forget about it."

Carl felt as though she had slapped him. "Apologise? After what he's done to you? Is that what you think you mean to me?"

"I don't know what I mean to you."

There was a stark, painful silence, and into it, his world fell apart and lay broken at his feet. He stood staring at her, understanding suddenly everything she had been through for him, and he was not sure whether he wanted to kiss her, shout at her or be sick.

"How would you have known?" Carl said, when the silence became too much to bear. "I've never told you. I've used words like 'caring' and I've told you that you 'mattered'. I've practically swallowed my own tongue trying not to tell you how much I love you, because I didn't have any idea what to do after I'd said it."

"You don't have to do anything, Carl. Just knowing that you feel it is enough for me. More than enough." Suddenly she moved, and her arms were about him. "You came back, that's all I care about. Let him go. Write a letter, apologise and let it go. I have you, and we can go on as we were and that's all that matters to me. I love you."

Carl kissed the dark curls, then tilted her head back and kissed her very gently on the lips. "Stop trying to protect me. Stop trying to take care of me. I don't need it, Keren."

"Carl..."

"We're not going back to that. Even if I manage to get rid of Vane, there is always going to be some arsehole who thinks he can treat you however he likes because we're not married. I've been so bloody stupid, I'm surprised Nan hasn't stabbed me, but I'm going to put it right now."

"Carl, you can't marry me."

"Yes, I can."

"I'm not a lady."

"You're enough of a lady for me."

Keren was laughing through her tears, reaching up to run her fingers through his disordered hair. "You're crying."

"Only if you refuse my offer."

"Carl, I'm a miner's daughter."

"So you tell me. Who cares? When I'm with you, I'm happier and more complete than I've ever been in my life before. Yes, there'll be gossip and some of the officers and their ladies will hold up their noses. Let them. Marry me, Keren, and make me happy, and I swear I'll try to make you happy too."

"You make it sound so easy."

"It is easy." Carl kissed her again, very tenderly. "It's easier than what we have been doing, that's for sure."

"If you decide in a few years' time that you want something else, a wife of your own station, and you've married me…"

"Then what? Do you think I would leave you, after all you've done for me and all we've shared together, just because of who your father was? That would make me a thoroughgoing bastard, and I'm not. If we're unhappy in a few years and we're married, then we'll stay married and work out how to be happy again. I'm optimistic, we've proved very good at it so far. That's what people are supposed to do, Keren. That's what marriage is. That's what I want, with you. How to address the squire's wife when she comes to tea at the Rectory, you can learn in five minutes. You've learned so much already, I am in awe of you. This is just the next step. Please take it. Please hold my hand and we'll take it together."

Keren was laughing and crying at the same time. "What will the general say?"

"You can't look to him for advice, he has no standards at all and she's worse. They'll be overjoyed."

"Carl, you know I'm going to say yes. I've never been more happy in my life. But I don't want you to fight that horrible man."

Carl sighed. "I very much doubt he'll accept an apology, Keren, but I'll speak to Leo. If he will, I'll make it."

"He could kill you."

"He's not going to kill me. It was his challenge, which means I choose the weapons, and I'll choose swords. I've no idea if he can shoot, but I've seen him fence and he's not that good. I won't kill him, I promise you. Honour will be satisfied and he'll leave you alone."

"I don't believe it will be that simple."

"It is that simple. Have you eaten anything at all today?"

Keren shook her head and Carl kissed her again. "Stay here. I'm going to speak to George and get him to send something up, along with a bottle of wine. No more talk about Vane tonight, I'll deal with him tomorrow. I thought I'd lost you, and it turns out I'm going to marry you. Let's celebrate, shall we?"

Chapter Fourteen

During two frustrating days of trying to prevent the duel, Manson was torn between desperate sympathy and the desire to punch the commanding officer of the 110th. Manson had always liked Carl Swanson, and despite the difference in age and rank, had come to think of him as a friend during the two years he had served under him, but he was rapidly losing patience with his senior officer. Carl's reputation as an even-tempered, intelligent officer was well known throughout the army, and Manson knew that people would have been genuinely shocked had they know what was going on. He was careful to make sure that no gossip spread about either the duel or the surprising betrothal. It would be much easier for one of the two principals to withdraw from the affair of honour if nobody knew about it.

Manson hardly knew Captain Wynne-Smythe, an older officer, formerly of the 117th, but he suspected the man was as reluctant as he was to see the duel go ahead. For two long days he met with his fellow second, trying to find a way to reconcile the principals. Carl had grudgingly agreed to apologise to Vane, but insisted in return, that Vane apologise in writing to Keren. He had not been specific to Manson about Vane's offence, but Manson remembered meeting Vane on the road with Keren and could imagine the kind of behaviour that had enraged the usually placid Carl.

Vane had initially agreed to withdraw his challenge on receipt of Carl's apology, but then insisted that it be made publicly, in front of other officers, and had further refused any kind of apology to Keren. Manson knew that Keren was pushing Carl to accept the terms, but was met with a curt refusal. After two more visits, backwards and forwards, Wynne-Smythe said abruptly:

"He wants to fight, Manson. We're wasting our time here. Might as well concentrate on getting sensible terms for the duel."

"He's a bloody idiot," Manson said, in exasperation. "Colonel Swanson is a far better swordsman than he is, and he's also a very popular and well-thought of officer. If he ends up in front of a court-martial for duelling, they're going to be looking for ways to let him off, but I don't think you could say the same of Major Vane. What is he hoping to get out of this?"

"Saving face, I'd guess," Wynne-Smythe said gloomily. "He was furious with General van Daan over those Spanish women and everybody knows Colonel Swanson is the general's oldest friend. Also, I should tell you that he's claiming that Colonel Swanson challenged him, not the other way around, so it should be his choice of weapons."

"Well he can piss off," Manson said flatly. "I was right there and I heard the challenge issued, and I'm prepared to swear to it in front of the entire army. It's his challenge, Colonel Swanson chooses swords, he will not fight to the death, but he'll fight to first blood, and at that point they will shake hands like gentlemen and we can all pretend this never happened. And if we really can't reconcile them, I would very much like to get this over with before General van Daan gets back, because I am rather enjoying my new role as Brigade Major and I'd rather not find myself demoted to ensign and on picket duty for the rest of my life."

Wynne-Smythe gave a bark of laughter. "He's difficult, I've heard."

"I'm not sure difficult is the right word. Have you found a surgeon?"

"I thought we could use your man, Daniels."

"Think again. Oliver Daniels is very close to Mrs van Daan, and she can't get a whiff of what's going on, I'm more scared of her than of the general. We need a surgeon from outside the brigade."

"I'll ask my brother, he's in the cavalry. He might be able to come up with a man."

"I'd be grateful." Manson ran his hand through his short dark hair. "I wish this was over, I can't believe I'm doing this. Especially for Colonel Swanson, I thought he had more sense."

"Matter of a woman, ain't it? Some pretty little…"

"Colonel Swanson's fiancée, and a friend of mine," Manson cut in coldly, and the other man coloured to the roots of his hair.

"Oh. Oh. Sorry, old man, must have been misinformed. Bad form. Won't mention it again."

It was still dark when Manson tapped softly on Carl's door on the morning of the duel. It was opened immediately, and Keren motioned for him to come inside. Carl was buckling on his sword. He looked very composed in the dim light of a branch of candles. Keren looked less so. She was dressed in a loose morning gown and her hair was unbound. Manson realised he had almost never seen Keren with her hair down and he was surprised at how different she looked. Despite his preoccupation with the coming duel, he found his eyes following her about the room, and he dragged them away with an effort. He had always thought her a pretty girl, but like this she was beautiful and Manson felt a sudden sympathy for his commanding officer and also a burst of sheer exasperation.

"I need to go," Carl said. "I'll be back soon, Keren."

Keren turned from straightening the bed. "What if you're not?"

"I will be."

"What if he kills you? Or if you're arrested?"

"Keren, it's a symbolic fight. One of us will end up with a bloody arm and we can all go home."

"Then it is ridiculous, and you are both very foolish."

"I think you're right. But I still have to do it."

Carl picked up his hat, and abruptly, Keren reached out and snatched it from his hands, putting it back on the table.

"Don't go."

"I have to."

"No, you don't. You are choosing to, because of some stupid male sense of honour. You are fighting because of me, and if you die or are disgraced, I will have to live with that. It isn't fair."

"I'll wait outside," Manson said.

"No, Leo. We have to go." Carl stepped forward and put his hands on her shoulders. "I'm not asking you to understand, Keren. I'm asking you to accept it and carry on loving me, no matter what. Can you do that?"

"Oh for goodness sake." She sounded exasperated and also close to tears. "As if anything you do is going to change that. Kiss me and go, or we'll argue about this all morning and you'll miss your chance at playing the hero."

Carl laughed aloud and bent to kiss her. "I love you. And I will be back, hopefully for breakfast. I'll see you soon, sweetheart."

The duel was to take place in one of the orange groves at the far north of the estate. Visibility was better by the time Carl and Manson arrived and dismounted. Manson shivered in his great coat in the pale light of early dawn. There was a sense of unreality, as though he could not really be here, helping with this madness. Duelling was not uncommon in the army, although Wellington loathed the practice and had forbidden it. Manson knew that General van Daan felt the same way and would be furious when he found out.

On the opposite side of the clearing in the orange grove, Captain Wynne-Smythe was inspecting both weapons. Manson supposed that he should do the same and he went to join him. He felt completely ridiculous studying two regulation issue officers' swords.

"What am I looking for?" he asked.

"Any irregularities, I suppose," the other man said. "Have you done this before?"

"No, it's not likely, serving under General van Daan, he won't accept a challenge, he just tells them to fuck off. I admire his approach, to be honest. I don't think there's been a duel in the history of the 110th since he took over. I'm shivering in my boots imagining his reaction when he finds out about this, we're all going to wish we were a long way away. I think I'm prepared to pass these, if you are."

"Is your man any good?"

"Yes, he is. He practices a lot, we all do. Yours?"

"Bit showy. Fast, mind you, but he blows up quickly. Doesn't like getting off his arse much."

Manson turned his head very slowly to look at Wynne-Smythe and knew that he had not misunderstood. "He won't kill him," he said.

"I wouldn't give a damn if he he did, old boy. The man shouldn't hold a gentleman's commission in my view."

"And yet here you are, acting as his second."

"He's my senior officer, Captain, what else could I do? Isn't that why you're doing this?"

Manson looked over at Carl. He had removed his coat and stood in shirt sleeves, shivering a little in the cold dawn air. "No," he said. "He's a friend. Come on, let's get this over with. Oh wait, where's the surgeon?"

"No idea, he should have been here."

Michael looked around. "I can hear a carriage," he said. "It must be him."

He recognised the surgeon as Dr Harrison, an assistant surgeon from the 43rd and was relieved that Wynne-Smythe had managed to find somebody from outside the brigade. Manson went to shake his hand and exchanged a few meaningless words. Carl had collected his sword and was making passes, loosening up his arm, the blade swishing through the air. Manson watched him with a critical eye. Along with Paul, he knew he was by far the best swordsman in the battalion, but Carl was very good and Manson did not think he needed to be worried, although he could not help it.

"Is he really going to marry that woman?" Harrison asked.

Manson turned and looked at Harrison until the surgeon wilted. "Are you referring to Miss Trenlow, Doctor? Then yes, and I think he's a very lucky man."

"What in God's name is Wellington going to say to that? She was a camp follower, wasn't she?"

"I don't believe Colonel Swanson requires Lord Wellington to give permission, but he has General van Daan's full support which is all that matters. I think they're ready."

Manson walked to where Carl waited. He seemed completely calm but he looked tired and Manson wondered how well he had slept.

"Honour will be satisfied at first blood or if you disarm your opponent, sir," he said. "Wynne-Smythe tells me he's fast and showy but tires quickly, so all you have to do is keep him at arm's length until you can pink him and we can all go home."

Carl gave a weary smile. "Thank you, Leo. I'm sorry to have dragged you into this, I know you don't approve."

"If it was a matter of personal preference, sir, I'd tell you to cut his bloody throat, he has it coming. I just don't want you to get hurt or to get into trouble, you know how angry the general will be if he finds out about this."

"You mean when he finds out. Leo, this isn't about my honour, I don't give a damn about that. Vane both insulted and assaulted the girl I intend to marry. The rest of the army believes that a gentleman doesn't fight a duel over a miner's daughter. I'm telling them that this gentleman does. It isn't about Vane or anything he did, it's to make damned sure that every one of them knows that I'll defend my wife to the death."

Manson studied him. "I'm proud to serve under you, sir."

"Thank you, Captain. Now let's get on with it, before I freeze to death out here."

The two swordsmen met, and saluted. Carl did not speak, merely stepped back into his stance, but Manson heard Vane laugh. "Very pretty, Colonel. I hope you're as good as you think you are, because I'm intending to kill you."

The words chilled Manson. He watched as the fencers circled each other, wondering if Vane had been serious or if he was just trying to rattle his opponent. It did not seem to have worked. Carl seemed very calm, the green eyes watchful as Vane made a preliminary lunge or two, testing his opponent.

When he attacked, it was swift and savage and Manson felt his heart leap in fear. Steel clashed on steel as Vane advanced, the blade flashing so fast that Manson could not make out exactly what was happening. Carl parried quickly, backing up and for a horrible moment, Manson thought Vane had broken through his guard, but then Carl moved smoothly aside, and counter-attacked, with Vane on the back foot and Manson breathed again.

Once more the two men circled each other. Manson thought that Carl looked more wary, as if something in Vane's attack had confirmed that he intended this duel to end in death. It worried Manson, who knew that Carl intended nothing of the kind. Manson could see beads of sweat on his forehead in the cold morning air.

Steel clashed on steel again and the swordsmen came together. This time it was Carl's attack and he did not withdraw, continuing to press. In skill, they were more evenly matched than Manson liked, but he realised that Wynne-Smythe had been right about Vane. He was a showy fighter, with very dramatic movements and covered a lot of ground. Carl's style was more economical and looked less impressive, but he was not even breathing harder, whereas his opponent was already red in the face and puffing. This time it was Vane who withdrew and he clearly needed to catch his breath.

Carl gave him no time. He advanced again almost immediately and Vane was struggling, scrambling backwards with a decided loss of dignity. Manson realised he was holding his breath as the swords clashed. He thought that Carl was trying to disarm the other man and applauded the intention, but Vane's defence was too solid. He was trying desperately to push back but Carl did not give. Vane had backed up almost to the path through the trees where the surgeon waited beside his gig. Carl paused for a moment and Manson wondered if he too had run out of breath. Vane saw his opportunity and lunged forward and Manson caught his breath as he saw what Carl had done. In his desperation to turn the attack, Vane had let his guard drop badly and Carl took a step, lunged and neatly pinked Vane's left arm.

A red stain spread on the sleeve of Vane's white shirt. The major looked down at it in apparent astonishment and then up at Carl and his expression changed. Carl stepped back and dipped his sword in a salute.

"Honour is satisfied, Major Vane."

"Not yet," Vane said, and lunged. Manson gave a yell of furious protest and saw Carl fall back. Vane's blade had gone deep into his right shoulder and as Vane withdrew it, blood spurted.

"For shame, sir, the fight was over," Dr Harrison shouted. He was running forward and Manson reached him and dragged him back, because it was clear that Vane had not finished and in his rage, Manson was not sure what he might do.

Carl had not fallen although his sword arm had dropped. Manson had left his own sword lying beside Wynne-Smythe's on the far side of the clearing and he began to run towards it. Vane was moving towards Carl slowly and Carl lifted his sword and parried as Vane attacked.

It was a wholly unequal contest. Twice more Vane lunged, and Manson could see the agony on Carl's face as he hoisted the sword, blood pouring from his shoulder, his movements clumsy. Manson reached his sword and drew it, dropping the scabbard to the grass and turning towards Vane. He had no doubt of his ability to disarm the major, he was better than both the duellists, but he was terrified that Vane would strike before he could reach him.

The pistol report echoed through the trees making Manson physically jump. Vane gave a scream of pain, dropped his sword and fell to his knee, both hands clutching at his foot. Manson dropped his own sword and ran to Carl, catching him as he collapsed and lowering him to the damp grass.

"Harrison, over here."

"My foot," Vane roared. "I'm shot in the foot."

"If you continue to make that noise, Major Vane, you'll be shot in the head," the newcomer said, and Manson looked up, unbelieving, and met the cool grey eyes of Colonel Johnny Wheeler. Wheeler was reloading his pistol in a leisurely manner. "Captain Wynne-Smythe, you may assist Major Vane, if you please. Dr Harrison, attend to Colonel Swanson, I think his need is the greater."

Harrison dropped to his knees, opening his bag and Manson made way for him, getting to his feet and saluting. "Colonel Wheeler. I'd no idea you were back. Thank God you're here."

Wheeler's eyes rested briefly on the sword Manson had dropped and then moved back to his face. "It was certainly very fortunate for Major Vane, Leo, I've seen you with a blade. I arrived in Freineda very late last night, my horse threw a shoe. Lord Wellington very kindly offered me a bed and supper at headquarters. I arrived at the house fifteen minutes ago to find Keren about to mount up and come in search of you all, she was frantic. I told her to stay there, as I wasn't sure what I'd find."

"I'm sorry," Carl said weakly. "Christ, I'm sorry. It wasn't supposed to go this far."

"It shouldn't have happened at all, Carl, but unless you have gone completely insane during my absence, I am guessing there's a really good reason for this. The matter is now closed. Doctor, what is Colonel Swanson's condition?"

"It's deep, but a clean wound. I can bind it up, but he should see your surgeon, he'll probably want to bleed him."

"Thank you. Major Vane, as you seem able to stand, I believe it is usual to salute a senior officer."

Vane did so. Johnny looked him over with an expression which made Manson flinch. "This is an illegal duel," he said. "Was it agreed that you would fight to the death?"

"It was not," Harrison said. "Colonel Swanson achieved first blood and honour was satisfied. Major Vane attacked a defenceless man."

"Clearly not that defenceless, thank God, or he'd be dead," Johnny said. "You're a disgrace to that uniform, Vane, and I'd dearly like you to get all that you deserve. If I report this to Lord Wellington, you'll both be sent for court martial and possibly cashiered. If I report to General van Daan, that you just tried to murder Colonel Swanson in cold blood, you won't reach a court martial because he'll beat you to death. Of the two, I am rather in favour of the latter. There is a third option, however, which I suggest we adopt for the sake of Colonel Swanson and his fiancée. This was a friendly challenge to a bout of swordplay and an accident occurred. You are very upset about it and I shall write a stern reprimand about your carelessness."

"My foot…"

"I barely nicked it. You'll come up with a story. Are we all agreed?"

"You're not lying for me, Johnny," Carl said. Johnny went to kneel beside him. Harrison was winding a bandage around his shoulder. Manson watched as the colonel inspected the work and touched Carl's blood soaked shirt.

"I thought you had more sense, Carl."

"I'm sorry, Johnny. I did it for Keren."

"I understand your need to make a declaration, Carl, but you could have found a less dramatic way of doing it. Still, that's why we're going to do it my way. Sometimes, standing up for your principles is the right thing to do. At other times, you need to put the people you care about first."

"He shouldn't get away with this."

"You shouldn't lose your commission because of a piece of shit like Leonard Vane. We'll find another way of dealing with him, Carl. Not at the expense of your career."

Carl was silent for a long time. Finally he nodded and Johnny rose.

"Captain Wynne-Smythe, will you take Major Vane back to his billet and see that a surgeon attends to his injuries?"

"Yes, sir."

"When General van Daan returns, Major, I am sure he will wish to speak to you further about this. In the meantime, please be assured that the future Mrs Swanson is to be considered under my personal protection, and if I hear that you've so much as spoken to her in passing, the next ball will be going through what passes for your brain. Now get out of here."

Manson watched as Vane limped towards his horse. He watched Vane mount up with difficulty and then went to collect his sword and to help lift Carl into the carriage to take him home.

**

Paul thoroughly enjoyed his trip to the Serra da Estrela. The weather remained fine and the children were enthusiastic about camping. Paul had spent a lot of time with Grace and Francis when they were younger, but he had seen little of them in the past few years. They were growing up fast, and their excitement turned a routine journey into an adventure. They travelled at a leisurely pace, with the children mounted on the sturdy little Spanish pack ponies, hunted and fished for their supper and sat wrapped in blankets around the camp fire late into the evening telling stories and catching up on too many years apart.

General Pakenham was visibly astonished at Paul's arrival with a convoy of children, but immediately entered into the spirit of the adventure and co-opted some of his officers to take them shooting and even to teach them some rudimentary drills with the men. Margriete was content to remain with the Portuguese maid, watching the parades and enjoying the admiring glances of some of the younger officers but Grace insisted on marching beside the boys and even trying her hand with a musket, although she could barely hold it.

"I'm not sure that your daughter wants to be a girl," Ross remarked. He and Paul were sitting on a blanket drinking wine in the sunlight, watching the children receiving instruction from three young officers of the 32nd in how to shoot a pistol.

"I think yours has definitely got more of an idea," Paul said, and Ross looked over at Margriete and laughed aloud. She was seated gracefully on a fallen tree trunk making a flower chain, a dazzled ensign and a lieutenant who was old enough to know better sprawled at her feet.

"She has, hasn't she? Until last year, she was still very much a little girl, and now suddenly she has learned how to flirt and I've no idea who taught her, I've watched her like a hawk."

"It comes naturally. Although just at the moment, I think that Grace is more interested in beating the boys at marksmanship."

"She looks as though she might. Sir - thank you, for this. It's been so good to have this extra time with them."

"I should be thanking you. Having Katja and the children out here this winter has been good for all of us. At moments like this, I find myself wondering what the hell I'm doing out here. Why don't I just sell out and go home with them?"

"Why don't you?" Ross asked.

Paul sipped the wine and shot his quartermaster a sideways look. "And that, coming for a man who has just agreed to join me in this madness."

"I suppose we're both crazy, sir."

"We are. Although this feels like a brief interval of sanity. I'd have a word with Lieutenant Beauchamp though, I'm not sure he knows that the lady he just slipped a clandestine note to, is only fourteen."

Ross choked on his wine. "He did what? Are you joking, sir?"

"No, I'm not, the cheeky young bastard. I admire his taste, mind, she's lovely. But she's a bit young for trysts in the moonlight. Would you rather I spoke to him?"

"No, I'll catch him later, I've no wish to embarrass Margriete, although I will definitely have a word with her. She's lucky it's me, her mother wouldn't let her out again for a month."

Arriving back at the Quinta de Santo Antonio, Paul was delighted when a familiar figure with a very slight limp emerged from the house to greet him. He dismounted, handing his horse to Corporal Browning who had come forward to take him, and went forward to embrace his friend.

"Welcome back, Colonel Wheeler, you have been very much missed. I can see that your furlough has done you good, what on earth have you been eating? You look ten pounds heavier and five years younger."

"Steak and kidney pudding and some very good local cheese. You're looking very well yourself, sir. I gather from your wife that the new quartermaster is working out very well."

"Yes. I'm dying to hear Flanagan's version of that story over a bottle of wine one evening, since what he told me about Ross Mackenzie was complete and utter bollocks, but it can wait. Where is my wife, by the way? Normally she'd be out to welcome me home."

"She's with Carl."

Something in Johnny's tone made Paul pause. He studied his friend and realised that something had happened, and that Johnny was not willing to talk about it in public. The sheer pleasure of having Johnny back, and being able to pick up his thoughts so easily again made Paul happy, even as he wondered what was going on.

"Right, I'll just get the troops organised and I'll join you." Paul turned to the excited children, who were milling about and raised his voice. "Company, halt. Officer on the parade ground. Get your ponies to the stables, and your bags up to your rooms and get yourselves washed and changed and fit for dinner, or you won't get any. Before you go, I'd like to compliment all of you on your behaviour on campaign these two weeks, I'm very impressed, it's been an honour to command you. Margriete, Grace, get young Bannan to help you take your bags up. Mr Harcourt, Ines, thank you so much for your assistance, you are both treasures. I'm going to find my wife."

Inside the house, Johnny beckoned him into the office and closed the door. Paul went to collect a bottle of wine and two glasses. "This is not really the reunion I'd hoped for, Colonel Wheeler, since it's clear something has happened, and the air of mystery worries me. Is Carl all right?"

"He will be, sir, but he's been injured."

"Injured? How, for God's sake?"

Johnny took a deep breath. "In a duel," he said, with the air of a man expecting the worst. "With Major Vane."

Paul set his glass down on the table. "I cannot have heard that correctly."

"I'm afraid you did, sir. Lieutenant-Colonel Swanson was stabbed through the shoulder in a duel with Major Vane over an insult to Miss Trenlow. I'm sorry."

Paul lost his temper. "That fucking arsehole," he roared. "Where's Jenson, I want one of my spare horses saddled up. I am going to ride over there, rip his fucking head off and mount it over the gateway to remind people what a bad idea it is to piss me off!"

"Yes, sir," Johnny said patiently. "Only..."

"Don't give me 'yes, sir'. You haven't been here, you've no idea what I've had to put up with this winter from that pointless sack of horse dung. His only purpose in life is to go around upsetting people, terrorising the local females and stirring up bad feeling in my brigade. He can't be trusted to sit on a chamber pot without knocking it over, he's got the manners of an oaf and the understanding of a garden slug and if I have to go into battle next month with him commanding one of my battalions, I'm going to shoot him in the head before he has the chance to get his men slaughtered by being a fucking idiot. Do you know...?"

"Sir, will you just listen for a moment?"

"No, I bloody won't listen for a moment. I've been listening to people advising restraint with that indescribable gobshite for weeks now and all it's done is to give him the impression that he can get away with whatever the hell he likes in my brigade. If he..."

"Paul, if I've been correctly informed, you threw him through a window without bothering to open it. What else are you planning to do to the man?"

"I thought I'd start by nailing his balls to the doorframe while he's still wearing them, which might remind him how to behave with a woman, since it's clear nothing else has worked. And if you don't think I mean it..."

"I know bloody well you mean it, which is why you're not getting out of this room until you've calmed down a bit. Drink some wine, take some deep breaths and let me tell you exactly what's been going on. If you're going to kill one of your battalion commanders, you should at least know why."

Paul was silent for a long moment, breathing deeply. He picked up the glass and sipped the wine, then put it down again very carefully. Johnny did not speak either. The silence lengthened, and Paul felt his pulse begin to slow. He looked up. Johnny sat opposite, one booted foot crossed over the other, drinking his wine as if he were at a gentleman's club, awaiting a dinner reservation. Paul began to laugh.

"I have missed you so bloody much, Colonel Wheeler."

"I've missed you too, sir."

"Pass me that bottle and get on with it. I will try to restrain myself until you've told me everything."

212

"I will try not to leave anything out."

When Johnny finally fell silent, Paul did not respond immediately. They sat quietly together, drinking wine, and Paul felt calmer. There was always something soothing about Johnny's presence and Paul was very glad he was back.

"I'm sorry you had to walk back into this, Johnny."

"It's my job, sir."

"I wish I'd seen it, though. He was lucky it was you and not me, I'd have shot him through the head."

"That did occur to me."

Paul set down his glass. "All right, Colonel, you've achieved your aim. I am going to postpone my visit to Major Vane until tomorrow. I'm going to see Carl and then I'd quite like to spend some time with my wife."

"That's an excellent idea, sir."

Paul rose. "It doesn't matter when I see him, the result is going to be the same, Johnny. I want him out of my brigade and I'm going to tell him so. How we achieve it depends on how cooperative he is."

"And what about Carl?" Johnny said soberly.

"Don't be an ass, I'm not going to throw Carl to the wolves, which means I can't charge Vane over the duel. But I am going to get rid of him, Johnny, one way or another."

Paul met his wife at the top of the stairs. He stopped and waited and Anne walked into his arms, smiling broadly. "Welcome home, General. I've just been hearing of your adventures from two very excited children. I take it they had a good time?"

"They did. Ned Pakenham is working out how soon he'll be able to offer Francis a commission. What worries me is that I think if he could, he'd also offer one to Grace. How are you, girl of my heart, you're looking very beautiful?"

"I'm well, I had a lovely time with Katja and the little ones until Major Vane disturbed the peace. Have you heard?"

"Yes, Johnny just told me the whole story. How is Carl?"

"Very happy," Anne said. "Very determined. And very angry. He wants to be married as soon as I let him out of his bed, which isn't going to be for a week or so, because it was a very deep wound and he's got a slight fever."

"It's not infected?"

"No, I don't think so, but I want to keep an eye on him. He's also worrying about having let you down."

"Idiot," Paul said amiably. "Well a wedding is easy to arrange, and it will make all our lives easier to be honest, because if she's his wife, we can stop this nonsense about her not being part of the mess."

Anne gave a gurgle of laughter. "You do know that there are still going to be a number of people who will refuse to acknowledge her because of her origins and their past relations, don't you, Paul?"

"I do. And every single one of them will be people I don't want at my dinner table anyway. Is he awake, can I see him?"

"Yes, go in. He's asked me to approach Lord Wellington's chaplain about the wedding."

"Good. Let's get it done as soon as possible, bonny lass. I've really missed you."

Paul found Carl sitting up in bed, a book propped open beside him. Paul walked over and picked it up. He studied the title then looked at Carl.

"Am I imagining things or are you reading a book of sermons, Swanson?"

Carl reached out and took the book with his good hand. "My father sent it to me," he said. "Hugh Blair was professor of divinity at Edinburgh, I read some of his work at Oxford."

"I don't remember seeing you pick up a book at Oxford."

"Unjust and untrue, Van Daan, I took my studies very seriously, which is more than I can say for you. How are the children, did you lose any of them?"

"I thought about trying to get them to enlist Francis and lying about his age, but it came to nothing. As a matter of fact, we left a little earlier than I intended, there's been some camp fever in the 42nd and I wasn't going to tour the lines with five children if there's sickness about. They all had a very good time, though. Francis wants to join the army and Margriete received a proposal of marriage."

"What? Are you making that up?"

"No. To be fair, she'd told the besotted youth that she was seventeen, and she easily could be. Mackenzie is handing her over to her mother for that conversation and I don't blame him. How are you?"

"Well. Sore. Feeling stupid. And very happy."

Paul pulled up a stool and sat down. "Congratulations, Carl. I know you've been struggling with this for a long time, but I'm bloody glad you've seen sense. She is the perfect wife for you, and I'm delighted."

Carl smiled tiredly. "I've been such a bloody idiot, Paul. Thank God I realised before she really did get tired of it and find somebody else. I just wish I'd not made such a mess of this. Look, I know Johnny has concocted this story of a fencing accident but nobody in their right mind is going to believe that I'd voluntarily spend time fencing with Leonard Vane. If this gets awkward for you, I'll resign my commission, I'm not going to…"

"You are leaving this brigade before Vane does over my dead body," Paul said. "Stop talking fustian, it must be the fever. I'm going to ride over and speak to Vane tomorrow and then I'm going to talk to Wellington. Between us, we'll come up with a transfer for him, and I'm going to force him to accept it. I'd like him out of the army, but I'll settle for out of the brigade. Wellington will support me if I dig my heels in, he always does. Stop worrying about it and concentrate on getting well enough to get married. And get some rest, you'll addle your brains reading bloody sermons, no matter how erudite they may be. Where is the love of your life, I want to offer my congratulations and kiss the bride."

214

"She's with Sally Stewart. Which is another problem, I'm afraid, sir, Stewart has been hitting her again. I've ordered them to put him in lockup for a few days, but we're going to have to…"

"I'll deal with him," Paul said, getting up. "Stand down, Colonel Swanson, I'm back and Johnny is back and you're on sick leave until further notice."

***

Paul found Sally Stewart in the kitchen with Keren and George Kelly and the sight of her drove Vane temporarily from his mind. She was seated in a wooden armchair beside the big range while Keren bathed her face. One eye was so swollen it was almost shut and there was a cut on her forehead. She was sitting awkwardly, cradling her right wrist in her left hand.

Kelly was making tea. He saw Paul first and straightened, saluting smartly. "General van Daan. Welcome back, sir, very glad to see you."

"Thank you, Sergeant. Given what I've walked back into, I don't think I'll dare leave again for a while. Although it's not all bad news. Miss Trenlow, congratulations. I cannot believe he's taken this long over it, but I am very pleased. He's given me permission to kiss the bride."

Keren came forward, blushing, and Paul embraced her and kissed her on both cheeks. "Go and see him, and if he's reading that dreadful book, take it away from him, it'll give him brain fever. I want to talk to Sally alone, give me ten minutes, would you George?"

Alone with the woman, Paul pulled up a stool and sat down. Very gently he reached out and touched her face, turning her head to one side to inspect the bruises.

"Where else are you hurt?"

"Nothing too bad, sir, I'll be…"

"Stop it," Paul said sharply. "For Christ's sake, stop it, Sally. I've seen it before and I know bloody well that for every bruise I can see, you'll have had five that I never knew about. What happened to your wrist?"

"I fell on it. When he…"

"Have you seen the doctor?"

"No, sir, there's no need. It's not broken."

"I'll get my wife down to look at you in a minute, she'll be able to tell. Where are the children?"

"Maggie Bennett is looking after them for a bit, sir. I'm very grateful, and Miss Trenlow has been very kind, but this isn't right, you're a general, you're not supposed to be taking care of the men's wives."

How long have you known me, Sally Crane?"

Paul saw a flush rise to her bruised cheek. "I've not been Sally Crane for a long time, sir."

"Well maybe it's time you thought about that, Sal, because the girl I met in a bar eleven years ago wouldn't have put up with this, no matter what."

Sally looked down at her injured wrist. "Things change. I've two children, sir, and lost another three. Back then, I thought I could do anything I wanted. Now…now I'm Mrs Stewart."

"What's wrong with him, Sally? Is it the drink?"

"The drink. The life." There were tears in the blue eyes, but she blinked them back. "He gets angry, sir. There's not much money, we're always behind with getting paid, and I nag him, I suppose about the children and the money and…"

"Nobody should be going hungry in winter quarters, Sal, and you bloody know it. If you're short of money, you speak to the officers and we'll see you're fed. But I don't understand, rations are plentiful at the moment. What else?"

"He gets jealous, sir."

"Is that what this was about?"

Sally nodded. Paul hesitated and then placed a finger under her chin and lifted her head so that her face was on a level with his. "Sally, I'm going to have to follow this up. We've been making allowances for him for a while, but this is too much. I'm bringing him up before a regimental court martial, and it's likely he'll be demoted."

"I know, sir. I understand."

"I'll give him a night to stew and then I'll talk to him. I wish Michael was here, he might be able to talk some sense into him."

"Until the next time," Sally said, and Paul knew that she was right.

He found Anne in their room. "Did you talk to Sally?"

"Yes. She's a mess, bonny lass. I think you should have a look at her, she's not keen to see the surgeon."

"I'll go down in a moment as long as you promise not to go to sleep while I'm down there."

Paul grinned. "I'll keep myself awake."

Anne stood up. "I'm going to put her and the children in one of the empty guest rooms for now, Paul, I want to keep an eye on her for a few days."

"That's a good idea."

"She can't go back to him."

Paul had known something was coming. He studied his wife. Anne was dressed in a particularly charming yellow gown that Keren had made for her the previous year and it suited her dark colouring. Occasionally, even after three years of marriage, he was struck anew at how beautiful his wife was.

"Are you listening to me?"

"Sorry, girl of my heart. I suddenly thought about how much I love you and it distracted me."

"Try to concentrate," Anne said, and Paul caught her tone and decided that compliments were not appropriate at this moment.

"Go on."

"Paul, I've had an idea, and I think you'll approve. Sally shouldn't go back to Sergeant Stewart, especially if the court martial demotes him, that will only make him more angry and he'll take it out on her and the children."

216

"He's hitting the children?"

"According to Sally, he hit Callum quite hard this time, when he tried to defend her. And Callum's going to keep doing that now, he's ten and he sees it as his job to take care of his mother. I've no idea if Sergeant Stewart can sort out his problems, but in the meantime, I've decided to ask if she will take employment as my maid."

Paul felt a jolt of pure discomfort. "Your maid?"

"Yes. You've been nagging me to find one for a year. Both Teresa and Keren have been very good at helping out, but I cannot ask the wife of Colonel Swanson to do my hair for me, and Teresa has her own family. I really like Sally, and she's been so good with Georgiana. The children are ten and eight, and I thought we could find them jobs helping Charlie with the horses, or doing laundry, which will bring in some extra money. Keren can teach Sally what she needs to know about doing my hair and taking care of my clothes. She's very bright, she'll quickly learn. And it will give her some time away from the sergeant. Perhaps when they are apart for a while, he will realise what he is doing and…"

"Nan, wait a moment." Paul paused. His discomfort had been increasing with every word, and he could see the surprise in his wife's eyes at his tone.

"What on earth is the matter?"

"I just want you to think about this. Are you sure that Sally is the right person for this? I know you like her, and she has been a good wet nurse…but what about Georgiana?"

Anne was very still. "Georgiana is going back to England with the other children. She is weaning very well, in fact she eats like a small horse. I've written to my stepmother and she is sending out two nursery maids to help Miss Webster on the journey this time, but she won't need a wet nurse. Paul, I thought you liked Sally."

"I do. I've known her for years."

"Then what is the problem?"

Paul realised that he was going to have to explain. He knew, from talking to friends who were married, that some men expected their wives to accept their decisions without question. That had never applied to Anne, and he did not want it to. On this occasion, however, he was briefly envious.

"Sit down, bonny lass. We need to talk."

"Why?" Anne said frostily.

"Because there is something that you don't know. And you should know it before you make this decision."

Anne seated herself on the edge of the bed, arranging her skirts with a precision which terrified Paul. "Speak," she said.

Paul perched on a wooden chair and studied her. "I'm sorry," he said abruptly. "I probably should have told you about this before, but it all happened a long time before I knew you, when I was very young and very stupid."

"Go on."

"When I first joined the regiment, I was twenty-one, with a lot of money and not that much sense. I always had an eye for a pretty girl, that's not news to you. I was at the *Boat Inn* one evening with Carl, and Sally worked there as a barmaid. She was a couple of years older than me, very attractive, and Michael O'Reilly rather dared me to...anyway. What I'm trying to tell you is that I...that we..."

Anne stood up. "Are you telling me that you shared a bed with the wife of Sergeant-Major Stewart?" she demanded.

"Not exactly. I mean I did. We did. But he wasn't a sergeant-major then, and I didn't know. That she was his girl. They weren't married. And it wasn't that important, just a couple of nights."

"Stop talking!"

Paul obeyed. He seldom saw Anne very angry, and almost never with him, but he could see that his anxiety had not been misplaced. She was visibly furious, the dark eyes flashing with anger and her face flushed. She looked very beautiful and Paul knew that if he were to tell her so at this moment, she might kill him.

"We've been married for three years, and I've been in love with you for five. And in all that time, with Mrs Stewart in and out of the house, and flirting with you around the camp, it did not once occur to you that I should know that you were lovers?"

"It honestly didn't," Paul admitted. "It meant so little. I was an irresponsible young idiot back then, Nan, you've always known that about me. Stewart found out about it some days later. I don't know how, but I think she intended him to know, she wanted marriage and he was holding off. I made the point for her nicely. He got drunk and tried to gut me on the parade ground at Melton. I let him off with a warning, and they married. Over the years...Nan, I swear, I've barely thought about it. It was before you, it was even before Rowena."

"Did Rowena know?"

"No. We never discussed such matters, she wasn't like you."

Anne did not speak and Paul closed his mouth and forced himself to stop talking. He badly wanted to continue to explain and apologise, but he knew that there was nothing else useful he could say, and he would only irritate her if he continued to babble excuses. Instead, he sat quietly, watching her expressive face as she thought over his words and tried to assimilate what he had told her.

Finally, Anne got up. "I'm going to see to Sally," she said unemotionally. "We'll talk about this later."

Paul rose. "Whenever you're ready, girl of my heart. I think I can promise you that I'm unlikely to fall asleep until you're back."

"Are you worried, Paul?"

"Yes."

"Good."

Paul did not reply. Anne collected her black medical bag and went to the door. As she opened it, Paul said:

218

"Nan, you can't mention this to Sally. She's been through enough this week, she'd die of embarrassment…"

Anne turned on him. "Don't you dare tell me what I can and cannot say, and to whom I can say it. You've said your piece. What I choose to do about it is my decision, not yours. Don't wait up for me."

The door closed behind her very quietly and Paul sat down on the bed and buried his face in his hands. He felt completely drained and very miserable, but he knew that going after Anne would be a mistake. She was upset and hurt, and he suspected that she felt humiliated by the fact that she had not known. Paul thought about all the times when he could have told her about it, and it would not have mattered at all, and he was furious with himself. Anne was a very practical girl, and would not have been shocked to hear of his youthful indiscretion, but keeping silent about it for so long had turned it into something it was not.

Paul went to bed eventually, but did not sleep. He lay listening to every sound in the house, every opening and closed door as officers came and went. When she arrived, he did not hear her until she entered the room, closing the door quietly behind her and locking it. Paul sat up.

"Nan?"

She was holding a lighted candle and set it down on the table, putting her medical bag back in its usual place. Paul got out of bed and went to collect the brandy bottle and two glasses. He poured for both of them then retreated to the bed again. Anne sat to remove her shoes and stockings, then took the pins from her long dark hair. Paul watched as she reached to unbutton her gown.

"Do you want me to help with that?"

"Yes, please."

Paul got up and went to unbutton the gown. He was longing to touch her, to sweep aside the black hair and kiss her neck, to take her into his arms, but he had no idea where he stood.

"Usually at this point, you would tell me that I needed to find myself a maid."

Paul mentally saluted her; it was a perfectly timed volley. "I thought I might not mention that this evening."

"Very wise, General." Anne stood up and turned to face him. "You may kiss me," she said regally. "Once."

Paul did so, very gently on the lips, then stepped back, studying her. After a moment, Anne's lips curved in a smile.

"And now I want more," she said.

"So do I, bonny lass, but I'm not coming near you until we've resolved this. I'm feeling a distinct chill and it's putting me off."

"I am beginning to warm to you, General," Anne said, picking up the brandy and sipping it. "This definitely helps."

"How is Sally?"

"Better. I've settled her with the children in the guest room, but George is going to clear one of the store rooms at the back for them tomorrow. I spoke to her about employment and she is very happy to give it a try. Keren and Teresa will teach her how to go on for a week or two. I hope you find that acceptable."

"If you're happy, Nan, then I'm happy."

"Then it will not be awkward for you?"

"The only awkwardness I felt, was that you didn't know, Nan. Sally is one of the army wives, nothing more. If she suits…"

"No she isn't, don't lie to me, Paul van Daan. She's always been more than that, I've been watching you with her for years. I thought it was because of Rory, but it's the other way around, isn't it? You've been patient with him because of her?"

Paul thought about trying to argue and decided against it. "Yes."

"You were wrong not to have told me. It made me feel very stupid and very young and very naive, that I didn't guess."

"Oh Nan, why would you have?"

"Given your reputation with women, it wasn't an unreasonable assumption, Paul, but I didn't make it. I did not raise it with Sally, because I think it would have embarrassed her horribly."

Paul knew that he was gazing at her like a lovestruck boy. "Nan, what I did back then has nothing to do with how I feel about you now, I hope you know that."

Suddenly she smiled, and Paul's heart melted. "Of course I know it, fool. But it was such a stupid thing not to have told me."

"I know. I'm so sorry, love."

"I'm very tired, but I think you may take me to bed and convince me that you love me."

Paul set down the brandy glass. "I will do my best," he said gravely.

"Before you do, is there anything else I should know? Any other female of my acquaintance…?"

Paul stepped forward and scooped her up into his arms. "No, little witch, there is not."

Lying beneath him on the bed, Anne reached up and ran her fingers through his hair lovingly. "It's been a very odd winter," she said. "I've never experienced jealousy before and now I seem to be suffering on a weekly basis."

"You've no need, love."

"I know. But keep telling me anyway, it's very soothing," Anne said, and Paul bent to kiss her.

Chapter Fifteen

Castro Urdiales was an attractive little fishing town which lay at the foot of the mountains approximately halfway between Bilbao and Santona on the northern coast. Many of the buildings were medieval in origin, with narrow winding streets running down to the harbour, and the Castle of Santa Ana and the beautiful church of Santa Maria de la Asuncion dominating the town from the seafront. Within the fragile walls of the town, life continued. The townspeople went to church and to market, ran out their fishing boats, smoked pipes in the plaza and scolded their children when they followed the soldiers of the garrison about. Outside, the French army of General Foy settled in and began to dig the first trenches. Michael watched from the walls and the castle and could see that they were making very good progress.

According to local intelligence, Foy had left the initial siege works in the hands of General Palombini and his Italian division, while he led his own men to disperse the Spanish bands under Mendizabal at Ampuero. The Spanish had taken up what looked like a strong position on the river, but Foy drove them back into the mountains without difficulty, clearing the way for siege supplies to be brought in by ox-wagon from Santona. He then returned to the siege lines and established his headquarters at Campijo, and with the arrival of more guns over the difficult roads from Bilbao, Castro Urdiales was entirely closed in by land.

The sea was another matter. After an exchange of letters, Giles and Michael were rowed out to meet Commander Bloye, who commanded the small British squadron of three brigs, the *Lyra*, the *Royalist* and the *Sparrow*, currently operating off the coast of Castro Urdiales. Bloye was an energetic man in his forties who greeted them pleasantly, served wine and regarded them with a bewildered expression.

"What in God's name is the army doing here, Captain?"

Michael sipped his wine and listened as Giles explained. Bloye heard him out, asking one or two questions. Eventually, he said:

"You've chosen a hell of a time to visit, Captain. I'd no idea there was an English diplomat in the town, I'm surprised I've not been notified."

221

"Nobody knew where he was, which is why we were sent out," Giles said. "Although, I'm surprised General Alvarez didn't tell you, or ask about arrangements for transporting him home."

"Is that what you're hoping to do?"

"It's what I'd like to do, Commander, but I'm not sure how we'll manage it. He's a very sick man, the leg wound became infected and he's bedridden."

Bloye studied Giles. "Is he dying, Captain?"

"I think he might be," Michael said. Giles gave him a look but he ignored it. Giles had taken a liking to Sir Horace Grainger, and Michael was sympathetic, but he agreed with Grainger's own assessment. The diplomat was very weak, with a high fever and Michael thought that carrying him to a boat, rowing him out to the *Lyra* and getting him aboard, might well kill him.

"Could it be contagious?" Bloye asked, and Giles set his glass down with a clunk.

"Oh for God's sake, of course it's not bloody contagious, it's a wound gone bad, not camp fever."

"Has he seen a surgeon?"

Giles got up. "Why don't you send yours over to look at him, Commander? Grainger has a long and distinguished career, he's very well-connected and his Majesty values him both professionally and personally. That's why we were sent to find him. I've yet to persuade him to make the attempt to come aboard, but I haven't given up, and when I do so, I'll expect you to be ready to receive him."

Bloye stood up as well. "I would be delighted to offer Sir Horace every available courtesy, Captain, including a passage home, once I am certain he's not going to introduce some Spanish fever to every man of my crew. I'll find an opportunity to get my surgeon over to see him as soon as possible, and I'll be guided by him."

Giles was looking furious, and Michael moved forward and touched his arm. "That's a very good idea, Commander," he said mildly. "Given the speed that the French are digging those trenches, mind, I'd make it sooner rather than later, if I were you. As Captain Fenwick says, Sir Horace is an important man, you'll want to be able to report that you did all you could to get him out of here before the French break in. We'll be off now, it's clear you're a busy man."

"It won't be for a few days," Bloye said. "You may have heard from Colonel Alvarez that we're intending to land extra artillery to help with the defences, I'll need all hands."

"That's bloody ridiculous," Giles said flatly. "A glance at those town walls should tell you that they can't hold. Alvarez should surrender. If the town is taken by storm, they'll slaughter the garrison and the townspeople."

"Not while we're offshore," Bloye said, belligerently. "We've some smaller Spanish vessels standing by and some of the civilians have boats. We can get the garrison off if it goes wrong."

"When it goes wrong. Do you guarantee you can get every man, woman and child out of this town?"

"Don't be stupid, that's an emotional response, not a military one. I'll send Dr Mackay over after we've landed the guns. Look, Captain, we'll take him if we can. But you should think about your own safety. If the town falls, we'll be standing by to get the garrison away, and any civilians we can manage. You need to be ready to come with them. I'd never willingly abandon English officers, but I can't send out a search party. And if you can't bring Grainger, you'll have to leave him. I'm sorry."

Neither Giles nor Michael spoke until they were back in the boat, being rowed across choppy dark blue waves towards the shore of Castro Urdiales.

"I wonder where they're going to place more guns," Michael said. "I would think…"

"They can insert them up Colonel Alvarez's arse for all the good they're going to do," Giles snapped. "They've as much hope of defending this place as a house of cards, and when the pack comes tumbling down, as it will, it'll be the townspeople who have to suffer the consequences. Bloody Bloye ought to be telling Alvarez that, not encouraging him with extra artillery. He should surrender."

Michael watched his friend's face with compassion. "He's not going to, Giles. Bloye is right, we need to have a plan."

"I'll talk to Grainger again," Giles said. "I'll make him see sense."

***

As Sir Horace Grainger continued to drift in and out of fevered consciousness and Giles continued to urge him to allow them to make the attempt to get him aboard one of the Royal Navy brigs, Michael spent his time with the Spanish troops, attempting to strengthen the defences and prepare for a French assault. He had the frustrating sense that for some of the townspeople of Castro Urdiales, the danger was not real. Alvarez had a garrison of thirteen hundred men, and there were just under three thousand civilians. Supervising a work party to try to shore up part of the damaged town wall, Michael paused to drink from his water bottle and watched as three young women who had brought food up to the labouring men, stood laughing down at the French who were sweating in the trenches. One of the girls, a pert redhead, turned her back to the French and lifted her skirts high, displaying a shapely bottom. There were shrieks of laughter from her friends, and the Spanish soldiers cheered loudly, shouting encouragement. Emboldened, all three of the girls climbed higher and repeated the performance, wriggling their behinds. Michael swore softly under his breath and scrambled up behind them.

"Down," he said in Spanish, pointing to the steps. "Those muskets aren't accurate, but sooner or later one of them will make a lucky shot and the surgeon will end up digging a ball out of your nether regions."

The girls slid down the loose stonework, still giggling. The last of them threw a saucy smile at Michael over her shoulder and lifted her skirt again for his benefit. Below in the trenches, the French were yelling insults, and a few shots flew harmlessly past. The Spanish sentries on the wall returned fire with enthusiasm, and Michael retreated to well below the parapet until the flurry was past.

Colonel Alvarez, watching the swift advance of the French earthworks, attempted several sorties. They were poorly organised and badly outnumbered, and after a number of losses, Alvarez decided against any further attempts. He had received several demands from the French to surrender, and rejected them, running up a black flag in defiance. Giles tried desperately to persuade him to reconsider, and eventually Michael removed his friend from the castle, before Giles lost his temper completely and kicked the commander of the Spanish garrison off his chair. Michael had been impressed through these past weeks, at Giles Fenwick's calm temperament, but Colonel Alvarez seemed to bring out the worst in him.

Michael understood why Giles was so worried. The French were having a difficult time in the siege works, but they were making very good progress. There were no supplies immediately available, and those troops not on guard duty or digging trenches, could be seen setting off into the mountains in search of food. The weather had turned very warm and the French sweated over their spades, listening to insults shouted down from the walls of Castro Urdiales. As an enlisted man, Michael had laboured in similarly unpleasant conditions and he knew that when the French and Italian soldiers came over the walls, as they were certainly going to, they would remember.

The walls of Castro Urdiales were around twenty feet high at their tallest point and six feet wide and the castle was balanced on a rock jutting out into the sea above the harbour, which was narrow and almost dry at low tide. After surveying the ground, General Foy had established a battery opposite the curtain wall which faced the mountain, consisting of two twelve pounders. Two more batteries were being built on a rise overlooking the Santa Catalina gate, armed with two howitzers, a mortar and three field guns. Foy's engineers were working on sheltering trenches and a wide communication road, and seemed to be building another battery close to the convent of Saint Francois.

During daylight hours, the French came under regular artillery fire from the walls. Commander Bloye and the marines from his small squadron managed to land several guns, including one on the little islet of Santa Ana, close to the castle. These guns were effective in silencing some of the early fire from the French batteries, which were too far away to do much damage. The citizens came out to watch the exchange of fire, cheering every time a French target was hit, and yelling enthusiastically when the gunners manning one of the batteries were scattered by firing from Santa Ana and ran headlong back to the shelter of the trenches. Michael watched from the roof of Señora Palomo's house with Giles, Antonio and Brat.

"They've plenty of artillery and they've got the range," Giles said. "Another couple of days, I'd say."

"And Colonel Alvarez will not surrender?" Antonio asked.

"No. He doesn't need to, of course, the navy has promised to get the garrison off once the French break in. Alvarez made a very fine speech yesterday, promising to defend the town street by street if necessary. What he doesn't say is that he'll be conducting a running retreat through the town, which will end on the beach at the back of the castle, where the Royal Navy will have boats waiting."

"Will they take the townspeople?" Antonio asked.

"According to Bloye, they'll take any that can get to the brigs, but that won't be many. Some of the wealthier citizens are keeping their sailing boats at the ready, and others will row for their lives with their families. Some won't have anywhere to go."

"I thought the lads from the navy were supposed to stop them from landing these guns," Michael said.

"They did their best, but they had to watch from two directions and they don't have enough ships. They stopped the landings from Bilbao, but the French managed to get these in from Santona instead. Alvarez can blow the hell out of those batteries as much as he wants, once the French have finished building the one over to the south-east and west, they're going to open a hole as wide as the mouth of hell in this wall and they'll be in."

Michael was studying his friend. "Giles, we need to talk to Grainger again. We're going to have to make a decision soon, if we're going to try to get him aboard."

"I know. I'll see if he's awake now."

Giles found Señora Palomo's young daughter, Gabriella, in Sir Horace's room, feeding him broth. Giles waited until she had collected the tray and gone, then went forward to take her place on the stool beside her bed. Sir Horace gave a faint smile.

"You again, Captain. What new arguments do you have now, I wonder?"

"None, sir," Giles said. "I've run out of arguments and we've almost run out of time. They're going to breach tomorrow or the next day, no question. They'll try to get the garrison off by sea, but the townspeople are going to be left to the mercy of the French and Italian troops, and it's not going to be pretty."

"You need to leave, Captain, and make sure you take that engaging young woman with you. I could not bear it, should anything happen to her."

"Listen to me," Giles said harshly. "I'm going to tell you what's happening out there. And then I'm going to tell you what's going to happen."

Giles spoke for ten minutes, and Grainger listened in silence as he outlined the progress of the siege works and the condition of the defences. The older man was so quiet that Giles wondered at the end if he had fallen asleep again, but as he finally fell silent, Grainger stirred.

"Damn," he said softly.

"Sir?"

"I had hoped to be gone before this moment. It was only a matter of time, after all, I can feel myself growing weaker every day. But it appears that fate has not been kind."

Giles stared at him for a long time. "You've been waiting to die."

"I am dying, Captain. It is just a matter of time. Sadly, my time has run out."

"Sir Horace…"

"No, please. It is exhausting to talk, I cannot argue. We must plan."

Giles studied him. "What do you want to do, sir?"

"There are documents that I need to give you. Once you have them, your responsibility changes. It is no longer your job to take care of others, it is your job to get yourself and these letters on a ship and away from here. I know that you understand that."

"Yes, sir."

"I was hoping to be dead before the French came, but I have not been so fortunate. Probably, they would kill me in my bed, but I cannot rely upon that. So I must rely on you instead."

"Sir?"

"Make the arrangements," Grainger said wearily. "I consent to your absurd attempt to get me aboard a ship. My only stipulation is that if I expire en route, as I suspect I will, you leave me and get yourself away. Promise me, Fenwick."

Giles did not speak. After a long silence, Grainger said:

"I am sorry. This is not fair on you, but I cannot be taken alive. They probably have no idea who I am, but we cannot assume that. In the letters I shall give you, are lists of names. That is all they are, to my employers in London. That is all they will ever be. But to me, they are men and women, with families. People willing to risk their lives to oppose Bonaparte. Even to dispose of him, if the opportunity presents itself. These are brave French patriots and I have met them personally. I will willingly die to protect them."

Giles got up. "I need to speak to Bloye, he wants his surgeon to see you," he said. "We'll find a handcart if we can, to get you down to the beach, but they'll have to find a way to get you up onto the brig. I'll be back as soon as I can."

Grainger gave a faint smile. "I will try to get some sleep then. Before I do, pass me that pack. I will give you the documents. I am trusting you, Captain Fenwick."

"I'll get them away, sir, and if I can't, I'll destroy them."

"I know you will. But you may also need to do the same for me."

Giles felt his stomach lurch. He stood looking down at the older man. Grainger looked back steadily.

"I will probably die in the attempt," he said gently. "But there might come a point where you have to abandon me and run. If that is the case, I need to have your word that you will not allow them to take me alive, Fenwick. I know those names. Your word."

Giles felt very sick. "My word, sir."

"Thank you. Take these documents. Then I will sleep a little, I believe. It seems that I may have an exhausting time ahead of me."

Dr Mackay arrived with the early tide the following day, and Giles met him at the boat. The sound of the guns was deafening, both Spanish and French, and they spoke little on the climb up to the town. There were fewer people out in the streets today, as though the reality of their danger had finally reached the townspeople of Castro Urdiales.

Giles left the doctor with Grainger and climbed the stairs to the roof again. He found Brat up there, seated precariously on the edge with her feet dangling over the street below, watching the French guns battering the town walls. She looked around at him as he lowered himself to sit beside her.

"I take it you're not afraid of heights, Brat."

"There are worse things to be afraid of."

Giles did not answer, since there was nothing he could say to a girl who had been through what she had been through, that would not sound trite or patronising. After a moment, Brat said:

"I have been trying to decide which part of the wall is going to break down first. Me, I think it is that section over there."

Giles followed her pointing finger. "I think you might be right. Although if they get that other battery up and running today, that lower section there might go first, it'll be under fire from two directions."

"I think that the French think that too, because they have begun to clear a wider path through that vineyard, and I think that is so that the troops can reach the wall more quickly when they have blown a hole in it. It will not take them long to get up into the town, but it will be more difficult to get into the castle. I suppose that is where the troops will flee to, so that they can escape from the beach below."

Giles studied the attractive face. Wearing Señora Palomo's spare gown, with the chestnut curls reaching past her shoulders, Brat no longer looked even slightly like a boy, and Giles had noticed the soldiers of the garrison turning their heads to follow her progress when she walked through the town.

"Brat, let me ask Dr Mackay if he'll take you back with him today," he said abruptly. "You'll be safe aboard ship and we'll join you as soon as I can get Sir Horace moved."

"Captain O'Reilly will not join me," Brat said in conversational tones. "Once I am away safely, he will see the French coming, and what is happening in the town, and he will stay to try to help. I have seen this before, during the retreat, he almost died in the river, trying to save the women and children. He is a soldier, he cannot help himself. If I go, he will remain until it is too late and he will get himself killed."

"Look, Brat, I don't know Michael that well, but from what I know of him, you might be right. But if you stay, and something goes wrong, we might not be able to get you away in time, and I can't stand the thought of you being here when they come over that wall. We might die, it's true. You might not, or not straight away."

"I know, Captain. Thank you, truly. But I cannot leave him, because I may be the only thing that will get him to leave when he should. I am very afraid for myself. But I am more afraid for him."

Giles could not speak for a while; emotion closed his throat and he wondered if he was going to embarrass himself in front of this odd, endearing girl by bursting into tears. She did not seem to find his silence uncomfortable, and they sat, listening to the boom of the guns and the crackle of musket fire, smelling acrid smoke on the breeze. Eventually Giles thought he could probably speak again.

"Does he know how you feel about him?"

Brat shot him a sideways look. "Of course he does not, and you must never tell him. If he knew, he would try to send me away because he would think that it was wrong. While he sees me as his funny little servant, who is more boy than girl, he will let me stay. He thinks he needs to take care of me."

"I think it might be you that's taking care of him," Giles said.

There was a sound behind him, and Giles turned to see the maid. "Captain Fenwick, the doctor wishes to speak to you."

Giles found Mackay awaiting him in the parlour. "Dr Mackay, thank you. What's your assessment?"

"Well, I'm happy to tell Commander Bloye that he'll not be bringing fever aboard the Lyra if he offers Sir Horace passage, Captain. But that's not really the problem."

"What is the problem?"

"Gangrene," Mackay said bluntly. "Have you looked at that leg?"

"No."

"It should have come off, and it's too late now. I could do it, but the shock would kill him. It's spread the full length of the leg. The fever has gone, he's cold and shivering now, and there's some mental confusion. He couldn't remember why I was there for a bit. He's dying, Captain."

"If we can get him to the ship, could you perform the operation there? Even if there's the slightest chance...please, Doctor."

"I could, but not for a while. Commander Bloye thinks they're about to breach, he wants to get back the guns that we landed, we can't have them falling into the hands of the French. We'll need all the boats for that. I'll get back to the ship and speak to him, and we'll send a message to tell you when we can send a boat for you. How many in your party?"

"Five, including Sir Horace."

"I'll be honest with you, Captain. I think just moving him might kill him."

"Better that than leaving him to the mercies of the French."

"Perhaps you're right. Very well, find a way to get him down to the beach and I'll send word as soon as I can."

***

Paul found Sally in the kitchen the following morning, feeding oatcakes to her children. She gave a reserved smile but said nothing. Her wrist was neatly strapped and some of the swelling had gone down over her eye. Paul accepted tea from Kelly and waited until Callum and Sarah had finished eating and left.

"How are you feeling?"

"Much better, thank you, sir."

"I'm just going over to tell Sergeant Stewart that I'm making a formal charge this time."

"Yes, sir." Sally's eyes followed George Kelly out of the room. "Sir, did Mrs van Daan speak to you...?"

"She did. I think it's an excellent idea, you'll get on well with her and she's easy to work for."

"She's lovely, sir, we all think so. It's just that..."

"She knows," Paul said quietly. "I thought it best."

"Oh, no."

"She doesn't care what I did six years before I met her, Sally, and she likes you. Don't let it trouble you, and I hope it works out."

Paul's meeting with Stewart was brief and unsatisfactory. The Scot was sullen, nursing a sore head and bubbling resentment about his wife, although Paul could not get a clear picture of what he thought Sally might have done. He gave up and handed the matter over to Lieutenant Williamson, who commanded the first company in Michael O'Reilly's absence. Riding over to the farm cottage where Vane was now billeted, Paul thought about Michael and wondered where he was. He had heard nothing from him since the letter from the Santa Ana covent and as far as he knew, neither had Wellington. Paul was worried and was trying not to think about it, since he could do nothing about it.

The cottage looked deserted, although there were signs of life over at the old winery and big barn which housed the 115th so Paul rode on and found the battalion in a field at the back, moving from line to square under the supervision of their officers. Paul reined in and sat watching for a while.

"Captain Witham, who's in command here?"

"Captain Tyler, sir, senior officer here."

Tyler approached and saluted.

"Captain, well done. They've come a very long way since the last time I saw them do this. Now concentrate on speeding them up a bit. I suggest you use a pocket watch to start with, and when you're ready, we'll get them out at the same time as the 110th. There's nothing better than a little competition."

Tyler looked pleased. Paul thought that he looked considerably better than he had when he had first arrived; he had put on some weight, and lost some of the sallow, unhealthy colour.

"Thank you, sir."

"I'm looking for Major Vane, is he about?"

There was a perceptible hesitation, then Tyler said:

"Is he not in his billet, sir? He's not been at training, he hurt his foot. Some kind of hunting accident, I believe."

Paul met Tyler's limpid gaze. "Do not try my patience, Captain, you're in my good books at the moment. I know bloody well what happened to Major Vane's foot and I imagine you do too. Where is he?"

"I think he's away, sir."

"What do you mean, he's away?" Paul demanded. "This isn't spring in Brighton, it's the bloody army, if he wants to go anywhere, he needs his commanding officer's permission. Which given the absence of Lieutenant-Colonel Norton, would be Colonel Swanson, Colonel Wheeler or me. Where is he?"

"I've no idea, sir," Tyler said woodenly, and Paul gave up and looked over at Simon Carlyon.

"I'm getting irritated," he said.

"I can see that, sir." Carlyon saluted and gave Tyler an apologetic glance. "Major Vane has done this before, sir. Taken off for a few days. I think he goes to Ciudad Rodrigo. To the brothel, sir."

"I'm a little out of touch these days, Captain, but isn't there a perfectly good brothel less than five miles from here in Castelo Bom?"

"Yes, sir, but the Abbess won't let him through the door," Witham said helpfully. "There was some kind of upset. So you see…"

"What I see, is that the commander of the 115th is absent without leave and you're all standing around trying to pretend to me that there is absolutely nothing wrong with it. Captain Tyler, I understand that you're the most senior captain in the battalion currently, is that correct?"

"Yes, sir."

"Excellent. From the little I've just seen, you seem to be doing a very good job. I'm formally handing command of the battalion to you."

Tyler looked completely astonished. "Yes, sir. Until Major Vane returns…"

"When Major Vane returns, I will want a full account of his actions before he resumes command, but you don't have to deal with that, I'll write the orders myself. Does the major have a personal servant?"

"Not really, sir. Private Collins was acting as his orderly."

"I'll have a word with him to see if he knows any more. In the meantime, Captain Carlyon and Captain Witham, please give Captain Tyler your full support and as much help as he needs in his new role, since he may be occupying it for some time."

"Yes, sir."

Paul could see that Simon Carlyon was bursting with questions, and approved his junior's restraint in not asking them in front of the battalion. He walked his horse over to the barracks, and dismounted, looping the reins around a fence pole, while Carlyon went to summon Private Collins.

Collins was tall and skinny, with lank dark hair tied back with a leather strip, and a pair of nervous brown eyes that reminded Paul unaccountably of his wife's enormous dog.

"At ease, Collins. I just want to ask a few questions about Major Vane. I understand that you've been acting as his orderly?"

"Yes, sir."

"Did you know he'd gone to Ciudad Rodrigo?"

"N...n...n...n...no, sir. Not t...t... t... t... to start with."

"When did you last see him?"

Collins took a deep, agonised breath. "W...w...w..."

Paul heard a murmur of laughter from the assembled battalion, quickly silenced by a command from an NCO and understood. He put his hand on Collins' shoulder.

"Come with me. It's not going to help you to have the rest of these nosey bastards waiting to see if you can get to the end of a sentence."

He led Collins round to the far side of the barracks. There was a wide cleared dirt space which had been laid out as an informal recreation yard, with several felled trees lying at right angles which could be used as seats, and a few crates and boxes scattered about. Paul sat down on one of the tree trunks and indicated that Collins should do the same. "You can just nod," he said. "Is it only when you get nervous?"

Collins nodded.

"I understand. When I was a boy, we'd a groom with the same problem. Once he started stuttering, it was hard to stop. Look, Collins, you're not in any trouble, I just want to know where to find Major Vane. Did you see him on Wednesday? Was that when he came back with his foot hurt?"

Collins nodded.

"Did the surgeon look at it?"

"Yes, sir."

"Were you there?"

Gradually, Collins began to relax, and was able, in short sentences, to tell his story. Vane had returned to his billet after the duel in a foul temper, and had sent Collins for Dr Murray. Collins had returned the following morning to prepare Vane's breakfast and found that he had already taken his horse and left. He had not been seen since.

"Doesn't he have a groom?" Paul asked.

"N...no, sir. Not now. Portuguese lad, he ran away."

"Jesus, it must be hard work being as popular as Major Vane. How long does he usually stay when he goes on one of these little jaunts of his?"

"Three days. Maybe four. But I expected him back sooner this time, sir."

"Why's that?"

"He took no baggage, sir. All his kit is still in his billet."

Paul was startled. "Nothing at all?"

"No, sir."

Paul studied him, frowning. "That's odd, isn't it, Collins?"

"Yes, sir."

"Did you think that at the time?"

Collins looked back, and spoke fluently for the first time.

"Just glad he wasn't there, sir. That's all."

Paul understood. "Does he hit you, Collins?"

231

"Yes, sir."

Paul sighed. "Major Vane is very predictable. All right, Collins, thank you, you can go back to your company. I'm going to give orders that he isn't to use any man of this battalion as a personal servant again, and if he tries to bully you, speak to Captain Carlyon or Captain Witham and they'll send a message to me. I might come back to you and ask for more information later on. I'm beginning to hope that Major Vane has finally broken enough army regulations for me to send him for court martial, and we can get rid of him once and for all. Do not repeat that."

Unexpectedly, Collins' thin face broke into a broad grin, showing broken teeth. "Hope so, sir," he said cheerfully, and saluted. Paul sat thinking for a while, then went to find Rufus, and rode back to the quinta to write his orders regarding his absent battalion commander.

***

Paul found a message from Lord Wellington awaiting him when he returned from bathing in the river with Anne and the children. Jenson met him in the hall with an apologetic expression.

"Sorry, sir. Lord Wellington wants to see you. Apparently it's urgent."

Paul opened his mouth to swear and stopped himself just in time. Anne was laughing. "Well done, General. We shouldn't really complain, he's left you alone for a long time."

"Yes, he's been very good," Paul admitted. "It's probably about Vane, I wrote him a long report about it. Where's Sally…ah, there you are, lass. Take Rowena from me, will you? I need to change and make myself respectable, before his Lordship gives himself a seizure."

Paul found Wellington in his sitting room, which doubled as his study, and he was not alone. The other man was probably in his twenties, of medium height with short dark hair and was dressed in the blue braided jacket of the 14th light dragoons, with a red scarf tied around the right arm. Paul saluted and Wellington acknowledged it and turned to the younger man.

"General, this is Captain Zachariah White of the newly formed Cavalry Staff Corps. Captain White, Major-General Paul van Daan of the 110th light infantry."

White saluted and Paul surveyed him with interest. "I've been talking about this with Colonel Scovell but I didn't know you'd started recruiting yet."

"Captain White is one of the first officers to be selected," Wellington said. "One troop is being raised in Ireland, one in England, and two troops will be formed from volunteers out here. As you know, I have been asking for a more effective military police force for some time, and I hope that Captain White and his men will enable us to cut down on some of the appalling lapses of discipline…but I digress. Sit down, General. You too, Captain. This concerns Major Vane."

"He isn't back yet, sir" Paul said. "It's been three days without a word. To be honest, I was about to send one of my junior officers over to Ciudad Rodrigo to order him back, but I probably need to have a conversation with you about..."

"Major Vane is dead, General. His body was found early this morning."

Paul froze and stared at Wellington in complete astonishment. "Dead? What the hell happened? As far as I knew, he'd gone for a few days entertainment with the ladies of Ciudad Rodrigo. Where was he found?"

"The body was found three miles to the north of here in a deep gully beside the river. We were alerted when one of the officers of the guards brought in his horse. His own horse threw a shoe and he stopped in the nearest village that had a blacksmith, and noticed a very conspicuous animal in the barn while he was waiting for the shoe to be completed. I will allow Captain White to tell you the story."

White cleared his throat. "Mr Vennor asked the blacksmith about the horse. At first, the man lied, and tried to claim it as his, but eventually he admitted that he had found the horse running loose near the river. He still had the saddle and tack and it was clear to Mr Vennor that the horse belonged to an officer, so he brought it to headquarters yesterday, where it was recognised as belonging to Major Vane. This morning, I took six of my new troopers out to search the area and we found Major Vane's body."

"He must have been thrown," Paul said. "Poor bastard, I hope he wasn't lying out there injured. When..."

"He was not thrown, General," White said. "At least, if he was, it did not kill him."

Paul felt a slight chill. "What killed him?"

"Major Vane was stabbed, sir. Twice, in the chest and once through the throat."

Paul stared blankly at them. "You mean he was murdered?" he said finally.

"I'm afraid so, General," Wellington said. "I viewed the body earlier. It is impossible that such wounds could have been caused accidentally."

"Oh bloody hell."

Nobody spoke for a moment. Then Wellington said:

"Who is currently in command of the 115th?"

"Captain Tyler, he's the most senior captain, but I've just received a letter from Lieutenant-Colonel Norton announcing his imminent return. He should have sailed by now, I'm expecting him within the next couple of weeks."

"That is good to hear. What's your opinion of Tyler?"

"It's improved a lot since Dublin," Paul said. "He's working hard with those men, and I've spoken to one or two of his juniors and they really like him. It'll be up to the regimental colonel, and I'll talk to Norton when he gets here, but I'm hoping they'll give Tyler his majority. I don't know if he can afford to purchase, but with Vane dead he shouldn't need to." Paul paused. "I can't believe he's gone. I've stayed awake at night trying to work out how to get rid of Major Vane. But God, I didn't expect this."

Wellington sighed. "I know," he said. "But it places us all in a very difficult position. General, I have to ask you if you have any idea who might have killed him."

Paul stared at him blankly. "Brigands?" he said. "I know the roads are usually very safe, but what else could it have been."

"He was not robbed," White said flatly. "Once the blacksmith realised that the horse belonged to a murdered English officer, he produced Major Vane's effects very quickly, and nothing was missing. Even his purse was intact."

Wellington picked up a paper from his desk and Paul realised it was his own letter about Vane. "You had a very long list of complaints about Major Vane, General, which suggests to me that a number of people might have reason to want him removed from his command."

"I'd be at the top of that list, sir, but that doesn't mean I killed him," Paul said. He was suddenly on his guard. "Am I under suspicion?"

"There was a report of a fight, General, some weeks ago, at Major Vane's billet in Castelo Mendo," White said. "I believe some damage was caused."

"I wouldn't call it a fight," Paul said. "I was told that Major Vane had attacked two women in the household of Señor Rivero, one of them Rivero's daughter. The Riveros are friends of ours and my wife is very attached to Tasia. I lost my temper and threw Vane through a window. Naturally, I paid for a carpenter to replace it."

"Naturally," Wellington murmured. He was looking at White's shocked expression with barely concealed amusement. "General van Daan is fortunate to have private means, Captain White, which means he can afford to compensate his victims. I presume that is why the major changed billets?"

"Yes, I wasn't having him annoying respectable females. You haven't answered my question, sir. Am I being investigated for the murder of Major Vane?"

"No, sir," White said calmly. "I have already made enquiries about your whereabouts, and it is clear that you had not returned from your journey when the major was killed."

Paul stared at him in complete astonishment. "Did you volunteer for this job, Captain White, or did they pick you because of an impressive record for insolence towards a senior officer?"

"I volunteered, sir. But it seems to me that if I am to perform my duties conscientiously, I need to be able to do so without fear or prejudice regardless of the rank or social standing of my…of the…"

White broke off suddenly and despite the gravity of the situation, Paul wanted to laugh aloud at the stricken expression on his face. He did not know what White had been about to say, but he guessed that it must have been highly inappropriate when addressing a major-general. Paul relented.

"I hope all George's officers take the job as seriously as you do, although I imagine you won't spend that much of your time investigating murder, I think looting, desertion and being drunk on duty are a bit more common. Don't look so worried, I like an officer who isn't afraid to speak his mind. You're right, I couldn't possibly have killed Vane, I was miles away. But I'm not sorry he's gone. Still, I'm guessing you have a list of people you'd like to interview."

"Yes, sir. I will need to speak to the men of his battalion, to ask for information. Lord Wellington is of the opinion that such a crime was probably committed by one of the enlisted men, rather than a fellow officer. Or possibly a local. Señor Rivero…"

"I doubt it," Paul said. "Vane had already been dealt with, and Rivero is a sensible man. If he'd been going to kill Vane for assaulting his daughter, he'd have done it at the time."

"And what of Lieutenant-Colonel Swanson?" Wellington said smoothly. "My sources inform me that he holds a significant grudge against Major Vane. A matter of a duel over a young person….?"

"A matter of Colonel Swanson's betrothed, sir, who is also my wife's good friend. And you may not have heard that the duel left Carl injured. He's not been out of his bed yet, and my wife is personally supervising his care."

"I have no reason to doubt your word, General, but in the interests of justice, I will need to interview the Colonel. Obviously, I cannot ask to speak to your wife, but…"

"Why not? Speak to who you like, Captain, none of my officers or men have anything to hide. I don't know who killed Vane, but I will be frank with you in saying that whoever it was, probably had very good reason. However, if you're going to be talking to any man in my brigade, you'll be doing it under supervision."

"That is not acceptable, General."

"I'm not having you intimidating my men or bullying my junior officers into…"

"I resent any implication that my enquiries would take the form of intimidation or bullying. I…"

"Enough of this," Wellington snapped. "This is no time for my officers to be squabbling among themselves. I am possibly weeks away from a new campaign and I need my army to be ready. General, you will cooperate with Captain White's enquiries. Captain White, you will cooperate with General van Daan in…"

"Leo Manson," Paul said, and Wellington stopped.

"General?"

"You're right, I shouldn't be involved. I didn't kill him and I couldn't have, but I hated the man. At the same time, I want somebody to represent the interests of my brigade to act as a witness in any interviews. Will you accept my Brigade Major, Captain Manson?"

White looked uncertain. He glanced at Wellington and the commander in chief nodded. "Do so. I have immense faith in Captain Manson's intelligence and integrity."

White studied Paul for a moment. "Thank you, General. I will be happy to meet Captain Manson. I assure you that I have no intention of intimidating anybody. I simply want to find the truth."

Wellington rose. "Very well. Captain White, I need to speak to General van Daan alone for a moment."

When White had gone, Wellington sat down and motioned for Paul to sit. "How is Lieutenant-Colonel Swanson?"

"Recovering well, sir. I believe my wife is organising his wedding."

"So I understand. Are you supporting this madness?"

"Yes, sir. I like Keren and I think she's good for him."

"Socially, she is not a suitable wife for him."

"If they don't care, why should I?"

"The right wife can make a good deal of difference to an officer's future career, General. You should know that."

Paul grinned. "My wife is exceptional, sir, we both know that, but you're underestimating Keren Trenlow. She's come a long way in the past few years, and if you were introduced to her without knowing, you wouldn't take her for a miner's daughter. I've always believed, people aren't constrained by where they were born, they're constrained by how they're obliged to live."

Wellington gave a scornful snort. "By those lights, General, you would be recommending your sergeant-major for promotion to captain."

"I did recommend my sergeant-major for promotion to captain, sir, but you would only give him a lieutenancy at the time."

"Oh for God's sake, O'Reilly was different."

"Well so is Keren Trenlow."

"When is the wedding?"

"Tomorrow morning, in the church here. The priest has been very good about allowing us to use it, although your chaplain will conduct the service. It will be very quiet, just a few friends." Paul was silent for a moment. "I wish Michael could be here. I don't suppose…"

"As a matter of fact, I do have some information, although I am not sure it is what you wanted to hear. I have received letters from General Mendizabal, bringing me up to date with events in the region. It appears that the French are laying siege to Castro Urdiales, and it seems likely that Captain Fenwick and Captain O'Reilly are in the town, along with Sir Horace Grainger, who was wounded in a skirmish between the Spanish and his French escort."

"Oh no."

"I have written to General Clausel informing him that an English diplomat is trapped inside the town and should be immediately allowed to leave, but I am afraid my letter is unlikely to reach him in time to be of any use. I believe the Spanish garrison have the support of several Royal Navy brigs in the bay, though, so I am hopeful that your officers will get off safely."

"I hope so. Thank you, sir. It's not good news, but it could have been worse." Paul sighed. "I'll be glad when we finally march, Bloody Vane. It's typical that he's managing to cause trouble even through his death."

"I do not think he can help that, General." Wellington sat back in his chair. "Who do you think killed him?"

"Oh God, sir, I don't know. Where would I start, he made so many enemies?" Paul considered. "It wasn't Carl, it wasn't me and I very much doubt it was any of my officers. None of us could stand him, but if Carl had wanted him dead, he could have killed him during that duel, Manson was there and he said that Carl withdrew at first blood and it was Vane who tried to kill him."

"What about Rivero?"

"Once again, it doesn't make sense. When Rivero found out what Vane had been up to, he didn't go after him personally, he came to me, and I got rid of him. Why would he seek him out after that?"

"One of his men?"

"That's what I'm afraid of," Paul admitted gloomily. "His record of flogging isn't that bad, mainly because I've been standing over him so that he's barely been able to breathe. But I couldn't be behind him all the time. I know for a fact that his Portuguese groom ran away because Vane was too free with his riding crop and he also used to hit the poor lad he'd got acting as his personal servant."

"Could it have been him?"

"I doubt it, but presumably Captain White will speak to him along with the rest of Vane's men. What a bloody mess."

"It is. General, I know this is difficult for you, but I need you to give White your fullest cooperation. I hope to march out in a matter of weeks, you should not have to do so with this shadow hanging over your brigade."

"Yes, sir." Paul rose. "I presume White will keep you informed. I'd appreciate it if you'd let me know if you have any news from Castro Urdiales."

"I will."

"I'll write up the final reports for you over the next few days. I hope they're what you wanted."

"They were exactly what I wanted, General. I have recently written to the Duke of York regarding those battalions I feel able to send home and those I insist on keeping. Thanks to your hard work, I am considerably better informed about which battles I should choose to fight."

"I'm glad to hear it, sir. I was charged with an invitation to dinner for Monday, but I'll understand if you prefer to keep your distance while this matter of Vane is unresolved."

"Don't be ridiculous, General, I dine where I please. Tell your wife I should be delighted."

Chapter Sixteen

From the moment that the breach batteries opened at daybreak, Michael knew that Castro Urdiales had run out of time. From his vantage point on the flat roof, he saw the flashes of light before the boom of the guns and the subsequent crashing of masonry as the town walls were hit. There had never been any question that the town would fall, and Michael stood feeling sick, watching hours of wasted work on the defences blown apart in seconds. The French would be inside the town that day; the only question was when.

Beyond the guns, as the sky gradually lightened, he could see the Italian sappers, clearing the last of a wide swathe of ground in the vineyards, ready for the assault columns to line up. Michael had been on the other side of a siege many times, and knew the routine, the last minute orders, checking weapons and equipment, speeches of encouragement by many officers to their troops. At Ciudad Rodrigo, he remembered the men cheering Black Bob Craufurd's speech, the last he ever made before falling in the breach. He also remembered Colonel Paul van Daan stepping forward afterwards to speak to his own men, threatening dire consequences should they harm the townspeople. Michael wondered if any of the French or Italian commanders were issuing such orders but he doubted it.

All batteries were firing now, and the damage to the walls was already visible. Michael watched for another few minutes then turned to see Brat emerging from the wooden hatch.

"Did you get any sleep, Brat?"

"No, Captain. And I think you did not either, it must have been dark when you came up here. Captain Fenwick has sent a message to the ships, and Antonio has gone to bring the handcart."

"I can't believe he still thinks it's worth trying to get Grainger out of here, the man's not been conscious for eight hours. What's the point of putting him through it?"

"I think that Sir Horace has asked the captain to make sure he does not fall into the hands of the French alive," Brat said soberly. Michael stared at her, suddenly understanding.

"Did he tell you that?"

"No, sir. But I have helped with the nursing these two days, and Sir Horace talked in his fever sometimes."

"Christ, poor Giles. All right, little one." Michael surveyed her, suddenly noticing that she was no longer wearing the gown. "The good señora is going to have a fit seeing you dressed as a boy again."

"She has other things to worry about. She is trying to persuade me to take refuge in the church, she is packing now to go there with Gabriella. Antonio has told her she would do better to go down to the beach and try to get onto a boat, but he cannot make her understand. She does not know what it will be like. He is very angry with her. I think Antonio likes the señora and is afraid for her."

Michael ruffled the auburn curls. "They might be all right. Sometimes the French have been known to respect religious buildings, Brat. Come on, let's find some food, we might not get a chance to eat later on."

They were eating in the kitchen when a boy brought the reply from Commander Bloye. Giles read it quickly and Michael could see by his expression that he was not happy with the news.

"There isn't a boat available immediately, it's as the surgeon said, they're arranging to retrieve the guns they landed. Bloye suggests we get ourselves down to the jetty at the back of the castle to wait."

"We're not going to get him down there in a handcart, Giles," Michael said. "I've been thinking, we might do better to rig up some kind of stretcher. It's not far, and it would make it easier to get him onto the boat."

Giles thought for a moment. "Good idea, but from what? We can't carry him in a blanket, it won't be strong enough."

"I'll see what there is around the house, I've done this before, for Mrs van Daan when we've needed to move the wounded. Brat can give me a hand."

"I will do so. First, though, I must see to the ponies."

"The ponies?" Michael said, bewildered.

"Sometimes they set fire to buildings. I am taking all the horses over to the public gardens. They will be safer in the open, and horses are valuable. They will steal them, not kill them."

Giles gave a twisted smile. "You're a very good campaigner, Brat. Get on with it. I'll walk down and find Antonio, tell him that the handcart won't be needed."

Michael went out to the stables and stood for a moment watching Brat give her orders to the terrified groom then went in search of materials. He had half-expected to meet with resistance from Señora Palomo, but his hostess was wholly focussed on her own departure for the church with her daughter and servants, clutching a variety of bags, boxes and bundles between them. Michael watched them leave with a heavy heart. The girl looked back once, from the end of the street, and the strained terror in her dark eyes broke his heart. He went back to his task, praying silently that the French and Italian troops would stick to robbing the empty house and leave the townspeople in the convent and churches alone.

Brat returned to find him working on the makeshift stretcher in the tack room. She studied it critically as Michael hammered in nails.

"It is very good," she said, sounding surprised. "What is that canvas?"

"An old sail, I think, I found it in the woodshed, there are piles of junk in there. If they set fire to that, it's going to go up like a beacon. Perhaps Señor Palomo had a boat. I found these poles in the stables, I think they're spare fence posts. They're a bit bulky, but we'll manage, it's a short trip."

"You should put one at each end also, to stop him sliding if the stretcher tips."

Michael studied his creation and decided she was right. The posts were too long, but he found a rusty saw in the woodpile and managed to cut them down. Brat disappeared and returned some time later with two small knapsacks.

"I had to leave some of the clothing," she said apologetically. "But..."

"It's all right, Brat. We don't..."

The crash startled both of them. It was followed by a scream and then a babble of voices. Muskets crackled from the walls and there was another huge thunder of cannon.

"Was that the wall?" Brat asked fearfully.

"I don't know. Come on." Michael caught her hand and they ran back into the house and up the stairs, scrambling up the wooden slatted ladder at the top to the roof. They stood, still hand in hand, looking out towards the town wall.

"Oh shit," Michael breathed. Brat said nothing, but Michael felt her hand tighten in his, as if to ensure that he was really there. The medieval curtain wall was in ruins, a breach of some thirty feet had opened up, and as they watched, another volley tore through the ancient walls of the convent beyond it, smashing into the walls and bringing down the bell tower with a roar of falling masonry, leaving a heap of smoking rubble.

"They're coming in," Michael said. "We need to find Giles and Antonio. Brat, go to Sir Horace, get him ready to be moved. As ready as he can be. Wrap him in some blankets, it might be warm here, but it'll be cold on the boat, if we get him that far. Stay with him, I'll come and find you."

Brat nodded and scrambled down the ladder behind him. On the landing outside Grainger's room she released her hand, and then as she turned away, Michael caught her arm and pulled her into a quick, hard embrace. "I'll be back."

"I know."

Michael ran down two flights of stairs and out into the narrow street. It was filled with people, pouring out of their houses. Some, like Señora Palomo, carried bags and bundles. Others seemed shocked, as if they had still not realised that this was bound to happen. Men, women and children stood bewildered, while the incessant crackle of musket fire told Michael that the garrison was keeping up a steady fire from the walls.

The sound of running feet made him turn, and he saw soldiers, Alvarez' men, racing up the street towards the breach. Michael felt a ridiculous

240

urge to join them. He had been a soldier since he was twenty, and it felt wrong to be watching other men run towards a battle while he made plans to escape. It was clear that Alvarez intended to try to hold the breach for as long as possible and Michael felt both respect and exasperation. Now, if ever, was the time to raise a flag of surrender. The customs of war traditionally allowed a besieging army to sack a town if it failed to surrender once its walls were deemed to have a practicable breach, and there could be no question about this breach.

"Michael."

Michael turned. Giles and Antonio were running towards him looking hot and breathless. "Where's Brat?"

"I sent her to Sir Horace, to prepare him as well as we can. What of the boats?"

"None as yet. We can't get near the jetty, they're guarding the steps and holding people back, I think they're afraid of a stampede. I spoke to one of the officers of marines, they're going to launch the boats to bring off the guns they landed, it will take a while. After that, they'll allow the townspeople who have their own boats down to the quay to make their escape and they'll start taking off some of the civilian population on the ship's boats. We need to be ready."

They found Sir Horace unconscious, wrapped like an infant in several blankets. While Giles and Antonio went to collect their small knapsacks, Michael brought the makeshift stretcher up to the room. Brat spoke little, concerning herself with purely practical matters and Michael watched her, remembering the fierce courage and loyalty she had displayed the previous year, during the misery of the retreat from Madrid. In nine months she had become part of his daily life, but he had never feared for her as he feared now. Of all the women in Castro Urdiales, she knew what might happen when the French and Italians broke through and Michael thought that another girl would have been sobbing in a corner.

Giles and Antonio appeared. The house was empty, and it felt odd without Señora Palomo's vaguely judgemental presence. Sir Horace moaned softly as they lifted him from the bed onto the stretcher, and Michael was angry at the need to drag a dying man from his rest. He looked at Giles and saw that the younger man's face was taut with distress. Giles had liked Sir Horace Grainger enormously and Michael wondered what Grainger had said to him to make him so determined to go through with this madness. He supposed that if Brat was right and Giles had been faced with a stark choice of taking Grainger with them or killing him, Giles had no option.

The stretcher was heavy, and it was difficult to get it down the narrow stairway. Giles and Antonio did the lifting, carefully manoeuvring Grainger around corners and Michael was glad that Brat had insisted on the extra poles to hold the sick man in place. They arrived on the ground floor sweating with their exertions, and lifted the stretcher up and out into the street and into panic.

It was only a short distance down to the beach, but as Giles had said, a dozen of Alvarez' men guarded the access, holding back a mass of terrified people, bearing bundles and baggage and clutching children in their arms. A

241

cacophony of sounds filled the air; men and women shouting, begging the soldiers to let them through, children crying, and over it all the sharp crackling of musket fire and the booming of the French guns as they relentlessly blew away the fragile stonework of Castro Urdiales to widen the breach. The air was becoming thick with smoke drifting from the guns and the acrid smell, familiar from many battlefields, caught at the back of Michael's throat and made him cough a little.

"This is bloody hopeless," Giles said. Michael could hear the anxiety in his voice, and knew it was not for himself. "Stay with Sir Horace, I'm going up to the convent to see if I can get a view of the ships. I want to know if they've got those guns off yet."

They laid the stretcher down on a grassy area away from the crowd, and Brat seated herself beside Sir Horace and took his hand in hers. Michael found a precarious vantage point on a garden wall close by, which gave him a view of the beach, where some of the citizens of Castro Urdiales were launching their own small boats. The afternoon was growing hotter and the air seemed to shimmer above the blue waters of the Bay of Biscay. Around him, Michael realised that the crowd was thinning slightly, as some people despaired of being evacuated and went instead to seek refuge in churches or convents or in their own homes.

Giles appeared after thirty minutes. "They've got the guns into the boats. If we get the stretcher down onto the beach, they'll take him aboard as soon as possible. Brat, you need to go with him."

Brat got up, her eyes moving from one face to another. "I need to go? What of you, Captain? What of all of you?"

Giles looked at Michael and then at Antonio, saying nothing. Antonio gave a little smile. "Captain Fenwick already knows my mind, little fox. I will remain to fight with the garrison until they are evacuated, then I will leave with them. I am a soldier, I do not flee with the civilians. Do not fear for me, go aboard with the others and I will join you."

"I'm staying with Antonio," Giles said. "Michael, I don't ask you to do the same. I think you should go with Brat, get her to safety. This is not a suicide pact, I've every intention of getting onto those ships, but like Antonio, I'll stay to help with the final evacuation. Alvarez agrees, he's in need of officers."

"Then he'll have them," Michael said. He felt a rush of relief at being allowed to do, at last, what he was trained to do and what he knew he was good at. He had fought more than one desperate running retreat and he felt secure in his own abilities. He also felt a sense of dread that had nothing to do with fear of the French, and as he thought it, Brat exploded.

"No! You shall not send me away while you remain to play at being a hero. Always, you must be the one who runs into danger, who stays to the last, who takes the most risks. I have seen it before. You have done your duty here and this is not your fight. You shall not stay."

"I'm staying, Brat," Michael said steadily. "I'm sorry, I know this is hard for you. But this is our fight, it's just a different part of it, and like Giles,

242

I'm an officer, my place is up there with the garrison. I swear to you that I won't do anything stupid and I'll join you on the ship."

"How can you possibly say that, when you do not know what will happen and you are already doing something stupid?" Brat demanded. She spoke in English, and Michael thought inconsequentially that her English had improved as much as his Spanish during these three months and they could converse as easily together in either language now. He also thought how lovely she looked when she was angry, and wondered in passing if she was going to hit him in full view of the interested bystanders.

"You should have chosen an employer with a better brain, lass," he said, trying to smile.

"You shall not try to make me laugh. Not now."

"I know, it's not at all funny. I don't know what to say to you, Brat."

Giles put his hand on Michael's shoulder. "Why don't you walk down to the old bridge and say it privately, Michael? Antonio can help me get Sir Horace to the jetty, you can join us there."

Michael watched them go, then turned and held out his hand. Brat took it. She was crying, and raised her other hand to her cheeks to scrub the tears away angrily.

"I'm sorry, Brat."

"No, you are not. And you should not be. No other officer would think that his servant should tell him what to do."

"You're not my servant."

"Yes, I am."

"I've not paid you for months."

"You have not been paid for months either."

It was quieter by the old medieval bridge which led over to the small islet of Santa Ana. Earlier in the day British guns had still been firing from this place, but they were gone now, on their way back to the ships, and only a few Spanish troops occupied the little isle with its crumbling church. Michael paused by the stone wall and turned to her.

"You're not my servant, Brat. God knows what you are, but let's not pretend just at this moment, since I've no idea what's going to happen next. I don't know what to say to you, *leannán*, because I'm so confused. I picked up what I thought was a frightened child that night in Madrid, and since then you've been everything from a boy to a lioness and I never know what I'll find when I turn to look at you. But it's a very long time since I thought of you as my servant."

Brat did not move. The blue-green eyes were huge in her pale face, fixed on him with an expression which brought tears to Michael's eyes, although he blinked them back. "If you come back to me, Captain, I would like to be your servant again, since it is the only way I can remain with you, and that is what I wish. That is the only thing I wish. For that, I will be a boy, a girl, whatever I need to be."

Michael reached out and brushed a lock of hair back from her face with immense tenderness. He had intended a gesture of comfort and then

243

realised it was a mistake as she reached up and held his hand against her cheek. Her skin was very soft, still damp from her tears, and Michael felt his whole body go weak with longing.

"Oh Christ, Brat, don't. I can't. Look at the age of you, it would be so wrong."

"I am nineteen years old, Michael, and if my father had lived, I would have given him grandchildren by now. I do not expect anything from you, but do not pretend I am a little girl, that insults me."

Michael took her face between his hands. "Yes, it does. Which doesn't mean you're my servant, either. You're my friend and my companion, and the person I look for first at the start of every day and last at the end of every evening. I don't have the words to tell you what you are to me, Ariana Ibanez, and I know how much I'm hurting you right now. I'm sorry."

Brat leaned towards him and kissed him, very gently, on the lips. "Please come back," she whispered. "Please do not die."

Michael kissed her, brushing his mouth against hers, and then suddenly harder as the dam of his self-control broke. They remained locked together for a long time, and the sound of the guns, the muted roar of the waves crashing on the rocks and the babble of distressed voices from the town faded. Eventually, reluctantly, Michael released her and stood holding her hands, looking down at her.

"I'll come back, Brat. But you will make my life easier by getting on that boat and letting the navy take care of you. I can't concentrate if I'm terrified about you. Can you do that for me?"

"Yes," Brat said.

"Thank you. Come on, let's go and find the others."

They found Giles and Antonio at the jetty, and Michael was relieved to see several boats bobbing about on the water. One was already full of townspeople and the seamen were pulling strongly on the oars, heading out to the three Royal Navy brigs. There were several other small sails out there, which Michael guessed were Spanish vessels standing by to help with the evacuation.

The boat currently resting at the small jetty was manned by British marines, and two of them scrambled out to help Giles and Antonio lift Sir Horace into the boat. Michael saw Giles take the unconscious man's wrist and discreetly take his pulse. Michael met his eyes and Giles nodded, his mouth twisting in a lopsided smile. Michael returned it. None of them had really expected Sir Horace to survive for this long and Michael thought that the man must have a constitution of iron.

"Which ship?" Giles asked.

"We're from the *Lyra*, sir, but there's a man o'war approaching from Corunna, Commander Bloye may transfer this gentleman over to her for the surgery, she's a third rater, she'll have better facilities for it."

"Very well. One moment."

Giles turned to Brat and reached into his coat, pulling out a slim package. "I need you to take these," he said. "Sir Horace gave them to me and asked me to get them to safety. I'm expecting to see you again very soon, but if I don't, it's your responsibility. There's a letter there for General van Daan, it explains everything, give the package to him. There's another letter here for the captain of whichever ship you end up on. It will ensure that you're safely returned to the 110th where you belong. I'm hoping we see you very soon and you never need those letters. God go with you, Brat."

Giles turned to the marine. "This is Señorita Ibanez. She is in charge of Sir Horace and should remain with him, wherever he goes. She has given great service and should be treated as an honoured guest. Make sure your captain knows that."

"Yes, sir."

"Good luck, Brat."

Antonio moved forward and gave her a quick embrace, then moved back up the jetty with Giles. Michael took both her hands in his and found them cold despite the warm early evening air.

"I can't say any of it here and now, Brat…"

"Do not try. Tell me you will come back."

"I will come back."

Brat threw her arms about him and hugged him fiercely, then turned and scrambled into the boat beside the stretcher. Michael watched as the boat slipped away from the jetty, the oarsmen pulling strongly, then turned and joined Giles and Antonio as they made their way back up into the town.

***

By early evening, the breach formed during the morning had been widened to sixty feet and the San Francisco Convent behind it was all but destroyed. From their position in the church of Santa Maria, in command of forty men, Giles and Michael stood waiting. The church had a wooden gallery around the inside, with small windows looking out over the town, and the men had broken the glass in order to fire their muskets towards the advancing French and Italian troops. Giles had wondered if Foy would wait until the morning, but watching the troops form up, it was clear that the French general had decided on an evening attack. Columns were mustering in both the first and second parallels within reach of the breach, with other troops placed behind in reserve to support them.

A third column could be seen massing behind a small, rounded hill close to the Bilbao Gate with ladders, evidently with the intention of attempting the wall by escalade. Assessing the height of the defences, Giles thought it was very likely that they would succeed. He stood at one of the windows with Michael and Antonio, and there was a hushed silence now that the breaching guns had stopped firing.

"They're coming," Michael said, and turned, calling out orders in Spanish to the three NCOs. Giles watched him, amused in spite of their grave situation. He had found, throughout their travels through occupied territory, that Michael had been an excellent subordinate, prepared to obey orders and accepting his lack of experience in the murky world of intelligence. As Giles was formally in command of their small party, Colonel Alvarez had placed him in charge of the small garrison in the church, but Michael had quickly taken over. He had a far better eye for placing his muskets than Giles, and his previous experience of siege warfare made him quick and flexible in the positioning of his troops. Giles had not formally ceded command, he had simply stepped back and allowed the Irishman to do what he clearly did best.

Michael spun around. "We need to get them out of here," he said. "We're retreating to the castle. From there, Colonel Alvarez will arrange to destroy the guns and stores in the castle and evacuate the garrison. At least, I hope he bloody will, or we are all fucked."

"Yes, sir," Giles said, and laughed at Michael's sudden realisation. "Get them moving, you're in charge for this part. I hope to God Alvarez is capable of managing this. Don't you wish you'd said no, now, Michael?"

Michael shifted his borrowed musket to his shoulder. "If I'd a wish right now, apart from a lightning strike on the French command post, it would be for Paul van Daan to appear in front of me in the foulest mood of his career. He'd find a way to make Foy regret his decisions, he's a bloody genius at this. But I'm not, so let's get them moving."

By the time Giles and Michael arrived outside, there were sounds of fighting in the southern part of the town, and it was clear that the French were coming through the breach. Michael hesitated and Giles could see that he was thinking quickly.

"We'll head over towards the Bilbao Gate, there are fewer troops there, they might need support as they pull back. This way."

The street leading up to the gate was narrow, with tall houses on both sides. The sound of conflict reached them as they ran up the street, and Michael surged ahead, with Giles at his heels, and came to a halt at the sight of the Spanish troops, already fighting up on the low rampart as the ladder parties fought to gain a foothold. There was a cry, as an Italian infantry man tumbled backwards off the parapet, but almost immediately two others scrambled over, bayoneting the defender who had pushed him back. The man fell, another ran to take his place but by then there were four, and six, and eight and Michael raised his voice into a bellow.

"Retreat, they're coming over. To the castle. We'll cover you. Giles, take the left, two men, skirmish formation. Fall back the minute they're past, running retreat."

Giles obeyed, organising his men on the left hand side of the street, using what cover was available. He could hear sounds of furious combat from the breach, and realised that the defenders had barely managed to get off two volleys before the enemy was in. There were too many of them and there was no time to reload and use firepower. The retreat would be fought with cold steel.

The Spanish were scrambling down from the ramparts, racing along the street in the direction of the castle. Giles shouted a warning to his men not to fire too soon, or they risked cutting down their own troops. It was nerve-wracking, waiting for the men to pass, seeing the French troops swarming over the top of the ramparts in pursuit, but in this moment the Irishman had nerves of pure steel and he neither moved nor spoke, merely waited, sword at the ready until the last of the Spanish passed him.

"Fire!"

The crash of muskets reverberated around the narrow street, seeming to bounce off the stone walls and echoing into courtyards and alleyways. The volley was lethal in such an enclosed area, stopping the French dead, with every one of the front two ranks falling. They were still coming over the walls and the speed of their advance was limited by the number of men who could climb the ladders, which made them temporarily vulnerable to Michael's muskets.

As Michael's men fell back, Giles stepped forward. The Spanish defenders were behind him now, and he judged the range and yelled the order. More of the French fell, but they had managed to open the gate now, and the trickle of invaders was becoming a flood.

"Fall back!"

Giles watched his men run, then fell in behind them. He felt agonisingly vulnerable, knowing the danger of a bayonet in the back, and he glanced behind him every few steps. He was catching up with the rear of the Spanish troops, and there was a sudden confusion as Michael's men clashed and became entangled with the troops retreating from the breach, also making for the castle. For a moment, Giles was trapped in a crush of men, carried along against his will in a headlong flight towards the narrow steps up to the castle. It was tempting to give in and go with the tide, but Giles knew that he risked being knocked off his feet, or being stuck, unable to turn and fight, when the French attacked. Ruthlessly, he fought his way free using elbows, and found himself at the rear of the stampede, facing the hill, where French and Italian troops were racing to attack the fleeing garrison.

"I thought I'd find you two here," Michael said, and Giles glanced left and saw that Antonio was also there, along with around twenty Spanish fighters, hastily organised to protect the men trying to make their way up the steps of the castle.

"I'd rather be here than up there right now," Giles said, lifting his sword. There was no time for further speech as the first wave of French infantry drew closer. One or two muskets fired random shots from the castle and Giles swore, but immediately heard a yelled order to cease fire. A moment later, the French reached the thin line and Giles swung his sword, cutting down a green clad Italian, followed by a French infantryman with bright red hair. Beside him, a Spanish soldier bayonetted two Frenchmen in quick succession and then fell to a third with a scream of pain. Antonio swung around, slashing at the attacker and two men dragged the wounded man back to the steps, a third taking his place in the defensive line.

Shouted orders from above, confirmed that Alvarez had organised the terrified flight into a more structured retreat, and Giles realise that the steps were behind him. There was no space to fight in an extended line any more, and no time either. Giles was exhausted, his sword slippery in his hand with both blood and sweat, and the muscles of his arm and shoulder burning with pain. He knew from experience that this was the most dangerous moment when it would be too easy to drop his guard and allow a bayonet to reach him. The only thing that kept Giles fighting was the fear of turning his back on the enemy to run up the steps to the gate, but he needed to do it soon, or Alvarez would need to close the gate and he would be trapped.

"Giles, run. Now."

Giles risked a look and saw that on each rocky step, a man had been stationed with a musket. Michael was at the top with a Spanish officer beside him, and Giles saw Antonio swing around and begin to run, scrambling up the steps. Some of the Spanish garrison followed, and Giles turned and slashed savagely at a tall Italian who had been about to thrust a bayonet into his unprotected side. The bayonet glanced off, ripping through his jacket and grazing the skin and the Italian fell back with a cry of pain, which turned into a scream as he lost his balance and tumbled down three steps onto his comrades. All four went down in a tangle of arms, legs and bayonets and Giles seized his chance and took the steps at a run. A volley of musket fire right beside him startled him into stumbling, and two of the fleeing Spaniards clambered over him to reach the door. Hands grasped him, pulling him up and then he was inside and the muskets thundered out again.

Giles turned to look back down the steps. Half a dozen Spaniards were sprawled dead or wounded, and as he wondered which, an Italian infantryman paused above one of them and drove his bayonet savagely into the man's unprotected throat. Giles tasted bile in his mouth and thought about reaching for his pistol but it would be a pointless gesture of rage, the man was too far away. There were French and Italian dead as well, but now that the steps were held by muskets, the attackers were pulling back out of range, awaiting orders.

"You're a useful man in a fight, Captain Fenwick, you just need to get better at knowing when it's time to run."

Giles turned at the Irish accent. Michael's face was smudged with powder and he had lost his hat but he looked unhurt. Giles sought the crowd for Antonio and found him giving water to an injured man. Colonel Alvarez stood in the centre of the small enclosure in conference with several of his officers, and Giles found a clump of grass on which to clean his bloody sword and went to join him.

He returned several minutes later. "Colonel Alvarez is going to start evacuating as soon as the boats are available. We're packed into here like rats in a trap, and it's not going to take long for them to get those gun batteries trained on this castle, we'll be slaughtered. It'll be dark in half an hour, which is going to make the whole thing more difficult, although it's also going to make it harder for them to pick us off on the boats. In the meantime, he's putting two companies out to hold the steps and he's leaving a hundred volunteers to throw the remaining guns into the sea and destroy the magazine."

"I'd rather like to be away before then, if it's all the same to you," Michael said. "I've a situation to resolve, to tell you the truth."

He was holding out a silver flask and Giles took it, managing to smile properly for the first time in a while. He took a long pull of the brandy and handed the flask back. "You really bloody have, Captain O'Reilly. As a matter of interest, how do you think your very proper regimental colonel is going to take it when it becomes obvious that the leggy brat you took on as a groom and valet has grown into a very attractive young woman with a huge tendre for you?"

Michael drank some brandy and stoppered the flask. "If you're referring to Colonel Wheeler, you'd be surprised, Giles, he's a lot less staid than he makes out. It's not him that terrifies me."

"Mrs van Daan?"

"Well yes, now that you come to mention it. But I was thinking of Brat herself. I've no idea what I'm going to do about her."

Giles studied the other man sympathetically. "Do you know what you want to do, Michael?"

"Christ, no. When she turned up in Oporto, I wanted to drown her for a meddling urchin who didn't know when she should stay put. Three months later, I can't even remember what that felt like. She turned from a child into a woman overnight, and I can't...I don't know, Giles. I know what I ought to do, but I also know that I don't want to do it."

"She wasn't a child, Michael, she was just skinny and underfed and terrified. It's been a long time since Brat was a child."

"Well that's not much help to me, lad, because if she was a child I'd dump her on the back of my baggage mule and take her with me. But I can't do that with a girl of her age."

Giles could not stop himself laughing. "I can give you the names of a dozen officers who have done exactly that with a pretty girl they acquired along the way, Michael."

"It's not the same," Michael said.

Giles studied him. "No. I can see that. I can't advise you on this, Michael, I'm not much of an expert on successful love affairs, to be honest."

"Aren't you? I thought you managed the situation with the lovely Rosita very well."

"I spent two nights with her and I'll never see her again. I don't even know if she's alive or dead. Or she me. That's not a love affair, Michael."

"It's all I've allowed myself for fifteen years. That, a broken heart at twenty and a faint yearning after a woman I could never have, has kept me going. Am I even capable of anything more?"

"Do you want something more?"

"One day. I've dreamed of going home one day with enough money to buy a few acres and some horses for breeding, and a wife to help me build a life and a home. But it's a dream."

"Michael, stop worrying so much. You've time...Jesus Christ, what the hell is that?"

249

The screaming tore through the night air, cutting across the babble of voices in the crowded courtyard and the sound of musket fire from the defenders on the steps of the castle. It was a woman's voice and the terror in it froze Giles. He met the Irishman's eyes and saw his own horror reflected back.

Around them, some of the garrison were stirring, reaching for arms that they had temporarily set down. Colonel Alvarez rapped out an order to stand down, and the Spaniards did so, clearly uneasy. The screaming continued and then stopped, cut off abruptly with a horrible choking sound that Giles knew without any doubt, meant death.

Michael moved, scrambling up to one of the window embrasures. Antonio was ahead of him and Giles followed. He had placed himself under the orders of Alvarez for the duration of the siege, but he felt no obligation to obey further orders. They stood, looking out through the narrow window which overlooked the town. Other sounds reached Giles, and he thought that probably they had begun some time earlier, but had been lost in the gunfire and the babble of voices inside the castle. Now that he was listening, he could hear them, sounds of distress, screaming and crying and horribly, the high pitched wail of a child, quickly silenced. There was also the smell of smoke, and as they stood watching, a flicker of flames showed against the night sky, followed by another, on the opposite side of the town.

"Oh God," Michael said, and his voice was hoarse with distress. "That's why there was so little pursuit. That's why we were able to fight our way out of there so easily. There was barely a battalion chasing us. The rest of them are down there. They're sacking the town."

***

It was cold on the boat, and the sea, which had been fairly calm earlier in the day, had become restless under the sharp breeze. Brat huddled in her cloak shivering, listening to the swish of the oars through the water and peering through the darkness towards Castro Urdiales, which appeared to be in flames. She was too far out to be able to make out the details, but fires burned fiercely in half a dozen locations and the castle stood out sharply, illuminated by the red glow against the night sky. Brat stared at the shore and prayed.

Her first sea trip, earlier in the day had been warmer as the marines rowed her out to the *Lyra*, a compact ten gun brig-sloop, already crowded with refugees from the town. Brat had arrived in a daze of misery, presented her letter to Commander Bloye and waited beside Sir Horace on the deck as Bloye read it, casting occasional pained glances at her clothing. Brat suspected that under normal circumstances, Bloye would have ordered such a shockingly attired female off his ship, but he could clearly do nothing of the kind at present.

The surgeon came to examine Sir Horace, made puffing noises between his lips, and shook his head. "The man is dying. I am astonished he has made it this far, it smacks of cruelty, sir, to drag such a sick man on such a journey."

"It is not cruel, we had no choice," Brat said angrily, before Bloye could respond. "Sir Horace was determined not to be taken by the French and said he would rather die in the attempt. He made Captain Fenwick promise."

"I daresay he had his reasons," Bloye said dryly. "Can you do anything for him, Mackay?"

"The leg must be amputated, if he is to have any chance of survival, but it will be impossible here, Captain, look at it. Every space on the lower deck is filling up fast, and when the garrison are evacuated, there will barely be room to lie him down. Utter folly."

Brat stood up. "Then do not do it," she said, contemptuously. "If this is your attitude to surgery during battle, I wonder that any of your men survive."

"Young woman, that will do," Bloye said sternly. "Dr Mackay is a well-qualified and highly competent surgeon, and this man's condition is not his fault."

"I will do it if you order me to, sir."

Bloye was silent for a moment, thinking. "I have a better idea. We'll transfer him to the *Iris*. It's a much bigger ship, with better facilities. Let their surgeon deal with it."

"The *Iris*, sir? I didn't know there were any other ships in these waters."

"Nor did I," Bloye said, and Brat thought she heard irritation in his voice. "They're at anchor to the west, they sent a boat just before these people arrived to inform me of their presence and offer assistance if required. It appears Captain Kelly was in Corunna for some essential repairs and received news of the situation here, so came to see if we needed assistance. Mighty kind of him."

Mackay studied the captain and Brat thought she detected a smirk. "Does that mean he's in charge of the squadron, sir. He's a post-captain, isn't he?"

"The *Iris* is not part of this squadron," Bloye snapped. "Kelly probably shouldn't even be here, but since he is, and he's bound to have a surgeon, we'll send Sir Horace off in one of the boats, along with…with…this young woman. Let him deal with the consequences of a dead diplomat and a woman who looks like…"

Bloye broke off, clamping his jaw in an effort to stop himself saying more. Brat did not move or speak. After a moment, she realised that her hand was hurting, where she had curled her fingers into a fist hard, and her nails were digging in. She uncurled them, stretching her fingers and said nothing.

It took some time for a boat to be available, and for Bloye to scribble a hasty note to the unwelcome Captain Kelly. Brat stood miserably, watching sailors and marines lowering Sir Horace Grainger into the boat and was furious with the commander. She thought that if Giles or Michael had been present, they would have unequivocally refused this further journey, but she had not the authority to insist and Sir Horace had barely been conscious. She managed to spoon some water between his cracked dry lips, and even a little gruel, during the wait, and she thought that he recognised her, but he had lapsed into unconsciousness quickly again and Brat was glad. He seemed beyond suffering now.

The wind had picked up as Brat settled into the boat in the inky darkness and began the cold, wet journey out into the night towards the *Iris*. Brat knew nothing about ships or boats, and had no particular desire to learn, but she had felt safe enough on the ship. This tiny rowing boat terrified her, and it seemed madness to head off into the darkness when the *Iris* did not even seem to be within sight. Anxiety about Michael and the others gnawed at her, and she was cold and hungry and thirsty. She was also soaked through within minutes as the wind picked up the spray from the oars and blew it directly into her face. Sir Horace moaned slightly as a bigger wave splashed up over the bow, drenching the blankets that Brat had tucked around him. Brat took his hand because she could think of nothing more to do.

"It's not bloody right this," one of the seamen said. "Poor bastard shouldn't be out here in this weather in his state. Why didn't the captain keep him there and send some of the townspeople out to the *Iris* instead?"

"Doesn't want to be held to account if he dies, I reckon," another man said. "He wants to look good out of this action, can't have that spoiled by the wrong man dying aboard the *Lyra*."

"That will do, Jenkins." The midshipman commanding the boat spoke sharply, but Brat could hear the uncertainty in his voice. Mr Buckland seemed very young, probably no more than sixteen or seventeen, and she thought it unkind to leave such a miserable mission to such a young boy.

"Sorry, sir. But there's no doubt the captain wasn't happy to hear that the *Iris* was in these waters, and you'd think..."

"I said that's enough." Buckland put his glass to his eye. "Ship sighted. It's the *Iris*."

Brat felt a wave of relief. She could see it herself now, the ship's lanterns glimmering through the darkness, making patterns on the black water. As the oarsmen pulled harder, she shifted to look back at the town and felt her already churning stomach lurch again at the sight of still more fires. Somewhere back there, were Michael, Giles and Antonio and Brat was terrified that they were already dead or injured, lying in one of the burning buildings, and that she would never know what had happened.

"Here you go, miss, let's get you up first and then we'll arrange to get some ropes down for the gentleman."

Brat climbed the ladder carefully, her hands numb with cold, and stood shivering on the deck while Buckland addressed himself to a very tall figure in an oilskin cape. The officer asked two or three questions, then turned to survey Brat. Brat could see nothing of his face through the darkness and had no idea what she should say or do, but she squared her shoulders and tried to speak without her teeth chattering too much.

"I have a letter for the captain, sir, if you are he. And Sir Horace..."

"First Lieutenant Durrell, ma'am, at your service. Please do not trouble yourself with explanations just now, you are very wet and very cold and your patient must be more so. Mr Clarke, arrange to have this gentleman conveyed to a cabin and get the surgeon to attend him. Inform Dr Cavendish that when he has made his patient comfortable and performed a full examination, he is to report to Captain Kelly's cabin. Mr Fellowes, ensure that these men get something to eat and a tot of rum before they have to row back. In the meantime, I will escort Mr Buckland and the young lady below. This way, ma'am."

Brat stared at him in surprise as the men around him melted away to follow his orders. Durrell was offering his arm and she took it hesitantly and allowed him to help her down the ladder and into a spacious cabin where a dark haired man in his thirties was writing at a small desk. He rose and acknowledged the salutes of the two officers, but his eyes were on Brat. Brat felt herself colour, but there was no sign of disapproval in the intelligent grey eyes.

"Captain, this is Midshipman Buckland of the *Lyra*. I believe he has a letter from Commander Bloye. He has also brought a very sick man, whom I have sent to Dr Cavendish, and this young lady, whom I am guessing is from Castro Urdiales. More than that, I cannot tell you."

Kelly grinned at his first lieutenant's tone. "Most irregular," he said gravely. "Did you make a speech when they arrived, Mr Durrell?"

"A short one," Durrell said. "I have sent the oarsmen to the galley for food and warmth. Do you wish me to go..."

"No, stay." Kelly held out his hand, and Buckland scrabbled to find the letter. "Will you call Brian while I read this, ask him to bring towels and blankets for our guest, she's shivering. I'm sorry, lass, I don't know your name. Do you speak English?"

"Very well," Brat said.

"Good, because my Spanish is abysmal. Please sit down, my servant will take care of you."

Brat sat, and was immediately engulfed in a small wave of comforts, in the form of blankets, towels, a glass of wine and a cup of hot broth which served to warm her frozen hands as well as to still the growling of her tummy. Kelly read Bloye's letter through and asked the midshipman a series of questions while Brat sat quietly and wondered if Michael had made it into a boat or if he was still trapped in the blazing walls of Castro Urdiales. Lost in imagined horrors, she did not notice that Buckland had been escorted away until the door closed and Kelly said:

"Mr Durrell, have you spoken to the surgeon?"

"Yes, sir. I am afraid to say he is not optimistic. I understand that Commander Bloye was hoping that he would operate to remove the leg, but Dr Cavendish believes that Sir Horace Grainger is too weak to survive the operation."

"If he's had gangrene for a week or more, it would be pointless anyway, it spreads. We'll keep him comfortable and see if he regains consciousness. Sit down, Mr Durrell, and read Commander Bloye's letter. You'll enjoy it, it's a masterpiece of saying nothing useful. In particular, it fails to explain the presence of this lady, other than to say that he didn't want her aboard the *Lyra*. I'm sorry, ma'am, I was hoping to avoid too many questions, but..."

"There is another letter, sir, from Captain Fenwick. It explains...I have it here."

Kelly took the letter, and carefully unwrapped the waxed paper. "Fenwick, you say? Army?"

"Yes, Captain."

Kelly read quickly and Brat finished the wine. It was making her sleepy and she wondered what time it was. Kelly looked up at his first lieutenant and his expression made Brat wake up a little. "It's from Giles Fenwick. He's over there somewhere - or he was."

Durrell took the letter and read, then looked at Brat. "Miss Ibanez, it is good to meet you," he said gravely. "Do you know where Captain Fenwick and the others are now?"

"No," Brat said, and was surprised when her voice broke on a sob. "I hope they got on a boat with the garrison. I hope they have evacuated by now, but there were so many of them, and I am so afraid. Do you know him? Captain Fenwick?"

"Yes," Durrell said. Something about his tone told Brat that she was no longer alone in her anxiety, and the relief was huge. "We met some years ago in Walcheren and became friends. Sir..."

"I agree, Mr Durrell. I'm tired of sitting around being tactful. I've not the least intention of trying to take over command of Commander Bloye's squadron, but I'm not risking the lives of men who could have been evacuated safely because of navy protocol, and if I need to pull rank to do that, I bloody will. We'll take her in to join the flotilla and I'd like you to take direct command of the boats, let's get them out of there and I'll have the argument with Commander Bloye afterwards. Miss Ibanez..."

Kelly broke off as the crash of gunfire sounded loudly. Durrell whirled and ran to the door, and Kelly followed without apology. Brat joined them, since nobody told her she could not do so, leaving the wet blankets and towels on the floor. On deck, the flames of Castro Urdiales could be seen clearly in the distance, but there were other lights, flashes of gunfire coming from both the town and from what Brat realised must be the flotilla.

"Report, Mr Clarke?"

"The squadron has opened fire, sir. I think they're trying to cover the returning boats."

"They're going to hit the returning boats in the darkness if they're not careful, the bloody idiots," Kelly said furiously. "Bring her about, Mr Durrell and let's get moving, I want those boats out as soon as possible. I'm going below to write an order to Commander Bloye. Christ, it looks as if half the town is on fire. I wonder how many people were left in there."

"There were many, Captain," Brat said. She was crying, suddenly unable to stop herself, and Kelly turned to her quickly.

"You shouldn't be up here, lass. Come on, down below, you need to rest."

"I need to know. I need to know that they are safe. I cannot..."

Kelly put his arm firmly about her shoulders. "I will tell you as soon as I've news," he said.

Durrell had gone, shouting orders in clear, precise tones, and the ship came suddenly to life, with men swarming over the rigging, adjusting sail and stowing hammocks. It was bewildering and Brat realised she was completely exhausted and still could not stop crying. Back in the cabin, Kelly poured more wine, settled her down and went to his desk.

"Let me get the boat off with these orders, and then you can tell me everything I need to know that's not in these letters," he said.

The wine helped. Brian had doused the small stove in case of action, but it was still warm in the room. Brat sat quietly, listening to gunfire, and officers and men came for orders and left. Kelly's decisiveness was reassuring and the *Iris* was picking up speed. Kelly finished his final order and handed it to a young midshipman, then as the cabin door closed, he turned to Brat.

"I've asked Brian to find you some dry clothing, you can use my cabin to change, and to rest a little as well, if you can. But since we've a few minutes quiet, are you able to talk now?"

"Yes."

"Good girl. What in God's name has been happening over there?"

Chapter Seventeen

"I cannot help them," Colonel Alvarez said. He had listened to Giles impassioned plea which had been made against the rising sounds of terror from the town. Outside, the two companies holding the steps up to the castle were engaged in a spirited fire fight with a French battalion, but there had been no attempt yet to storm the walls. Michael was not surprised as it was clear that the French and Italian troops had found the wine shops and cellars of Castro Urdiales, and were spending the night ransacking the town, and brutalising the inhabitants.

"We can't just leave them," Giles said. "Let me take a company. Half a company. We'll go over the bridge to the jetty with the men you're evacuating and cut up via the beach, see how many we can help. At least we can tell them there are still boats coming in to get them off, if they can make their way to the jetty. They're hiding in their houses, or in the churches, but this lot aren't going to respect that, they're going to be blind drunk by now. Let me…"

"No, Captain. The garrison must be evacuated now, and the castle and bridge will then be blown up. Commander Bloye took many, many people aboard earlier in the day, but we must get the troops away now, so that they may fight again. What is happening is terrible, but if the people do not resist, if they give them what they want, perhaps…"

"Does that include the women?" Michael said. He had thought that he was doing well at remaining detached from the argument, but he could feel rage building. "What are they supposed to do, lie back and pretend it's not happening to them? Have you ever seen a woman who has been raped by a dozen French infantrymen, or more? It kills them, often enough, or it maims them. And that's just the physical injuries. Mary, mother of God, you can't be suggesting that they…"

"There is nothing I can do!" Alvarez yelled suddenly. A scream, closer than any of the others, ripped through the courtyard, drowning out even the gunfire. Giles swung around and ran up the steps to the parapet with Michael on his heels. They paused by one of the narrow embrasures, peering out into the darkness, and Michael's heart stopped at the sight. The woman was naked, her pale body easily visible. She was running frantically over the rough ground between the castle and the huge bulk of the convent church of St Mary of the Assumption. Two men were chasing her, their drunken laughter interspersed with cursing as they stumbled over rocks on the uneven ground. Both held bayonets, and Michael thought they were Italian although it was hard to pick out the colour of their uniforms in the darkness.

There was a sharp drop down onto the rocks below, not a huge cliff, but high enough to kill or badly injure anyone foolish enough to fall, especially with the sea this rough. Michael found himself clutching the edge of the stone window ledge so hard that his hands hurt, and beside him he heard Giles make a small sound of horror. The woman paused and turned, like a wild animal at bay, and the two men advanced on her slowly. One of them called out something, and then shouldered his bayonet and held out his hand, beckoning, trying to coax the woman back. For a moment she hesitated, then she turned and stepped out into the air, disappearing from view into the thundering waves below, her faint cry lingering in the night air.

"Oh Christ no," Michael whispered. "The poor lassie."

The two Italians stood staring for a moment as though unable to believe that their prey had escaped them, then they turned, muskets over their shoulders, and made their way back towards the town. They had only taken a few steps when a man stepped out of the shadows. He was quick and silent, and the two drunken soldiers had no hope of defending themselves. The first died with a horrible gurgle as a sword slashed across his throat. His companion fell back in alarm and almost overbalanced but made a spirited attempt to use his bayonet. His attacker parried contemptuously and stabbed viciously, withdrawing the sword, and watching the man fall to the ground.

"Who the hell…?"

"It's Antonio," Giles said, and his voice was raw with horror. "I should have kept an eye on him. I should have known what he would do. While we were standing there yelling at Alvarez… it's bloody Antonio and he's going to get himself killed. I'm going after him."

Giles did not bother to inform Alvarez, and Michael knew there was no point. Alvarez was concentrating his efforts on the evacuation. His men had to make a hazardous run from the castle and across the bridge to the small jetty, under constant attack from the French, who kept up a steady fire on the bridge, the jetty, and on the boats which rowed to and from the ships, ferrying the garrison to safety aboard the Royal Navy vessels. The French had stationed voltigeurs, their light infantry skirmishers, among the rocks on the cliffs and on the roofs of some of the houses close to the beach and were picking off men in the boats and on the bridge, as well as any civilians who attempted to run down to the jetty. Two boats had already been sunk, one by the French guns and the other by one of Bloye's own guns, firing to try to protect the retreat. The noise of the guns was deafening but helped to cover their movements once outside the castle.

There was a quieter path which ran around the edge of the town wall which was shrouded with bushes. Giles had stopped to pull on his dark great coat over his red jacket and insisted that Michael do the same. It made some sense. In the darkness, and the chaos of the rioting soldiers, they might pass as Frenchmen, from a distance. Giles ran fast, making no attempt to disguise his progress. After a few minutes, Michael grabbed his companion's arm and pulled him back.

"Calm down," he hissed "We'll find him, but not by charging in like a mad bull. Don't tell me you've never done skirmish training, Captain, I taught you myself."

Giles did not speak, but after a moment, Michael saw him nod. They set off more slowly, dodging between shrubs and rocks and trees, each man covering the other, swinging around to check in all directions for danger before moving on. There was a crumbling archway hiding a small postern gate, and as they reached it, Michael could see that the wooden gate was hanging off its hinges. Michael motioned to Giles, who flattened himself against the wall, while Michael peered cautiously up the darkened street. He could see far more than he expected and realised with horror that it was because the house at the far end was on fire. There were no sentries. Presumably, somewhere, officers were trying to pull the reserve troops into some kind of order to storm the castle, but it was going to take some time. The men who had stormed the town were drunk, riotous and bestial.

"Where would he go?" Michael asked. He had no idea what had made Antonio do this, but he suspected that Giles might.

"The church. To find the Palomo woman." Giles met his eyes. "You didn't realise, did you? He's been sleeping with her."

Michael was momentarily shocked. "That piece of spite and vinegar? Jesus Christ, he's a braver man than I am."

"He's a bloody idiot," Giles whispered furiously. "Do you know where the church is?"

"Yes, it's at the end of the sailmakers' row. The red church. Giles, this is going to be bad, but if we stop and try to save them, we're dead, and so is he."

"He's probably already dead."

Michael knew that it was true but was not sure that Giles had. He met the other man's blue eyes and the misery in them wrenched at his heart. "We can make sure."

"I have to," Giles whispered. "Christ, I'm sorry, Michael. You should have stayed in the castle."

"Well, I'm here now. We'll move from house to house, and we stop for nothing. We can't save them, we can only die with them. If you get heroic on me, I'm leaving you. We'll head to the church and see if he's there. Once we know, we're getting out of here."

"Yes."

"And Giles - if you make it and I don't, tell her I'm sorry and that I'd a lot I wanted to say to her."

"I will."

258

Michael thought, as they slipped through the gate and made their way cautiously up the street, that Giles had asked no similar promise and wondered if it was because he had nobody to receive his last message. The life of an intelligence officer allowed no time for romance, or even for close friendships save one, and Michael thought that explained Giles' crazy determination to find Antonio.

At the end of the street they paused, careful to stay out of the garish light of the burning building. Another house was on fire on the opposite side of the street, and the flames lit up every corner of the square. The old town hall and several of the other buildings around the square had arched walkways beneath them, where market stalls were set up in happier times. They produced echoes, and Michael had a sharp, painful memory of Brat, on one of their first days in the town, teasing Antonio by singing his name loudly in the empty space. Now, they echoed with screams, with cries of terror and with voices, begging for mercy.

There was no mercy from the drunken soldiers. Bodies lay strewn about the square, and Michael could see men, women, and several children. All had been bayonetted, and there were dark pools of what he knew had to be blood, staining the sandy ground. In the darkness under the arches, a woman was sobbing, amidst the laughter and yells of encouragement of a number of Italians, and Michael knew that he was listening to a rape. He froze, his back against the wall of one of the houses, and he could feel Giles beside him in the darkness, taut with anger and distress.

"We can't, lad."

"We might be able to, it's bloody dark under there. More than three and we don't."

Michael hesitated, but the urge was too strong, and he pushed himself off the wall and slipped silently after Giles, moving like ghosts through the shadows from pillar to pillar until they reached the edge of the group. There were five men, all Italians, all with their attention focused on the sixth man who was on top of the woman. She was making no sound, the sobbing came from another girl, lying close by, her clothing ripped apart. Michael looked at Giles, whose face could just be seen, faintly lit by the flames outside. Giles had drawn his sword, so silently that Michael had not heard him, and Michael knew that he had no choice. Giles was going to kill, and he could help him or abandon him. He held up a silent hand, looked around and moved to where two of the soldiers had leaned bayonets against a pillar. Michael had come late to swordplay but had wielded a bayonet since he was twenty and knew it was the best weapon when secrecy was needed.

None of the men had heard them. Michael was not worried about the noise, any cries would be lost in the terrible sounds of the death throes of Castro Urdiales, but he knew they needed to bring the men down quickly. An extended fight might attract attention from other drunken troops roaming the streets looting, raping, and killing. He surveyed the backs of the men and indicated where Giles should attack first. Giles held up three fingers then folded them closed. Michael took a silent steadying breath, and watched the fingers reappear, one at a time. On the third, he attacked.

Bayonet fighting required aggression, speed, and determination. Any hesitation or attempts to fence could mean death. Michael ran quickly and silently to the first man and drove the blade into the soft area over his kidney then withdrew. The Italian gave a cry of agony and fell forward, effectively immobilising the rapist on the ground.

Michael turned neatly and stabbed the second man in the abdomen so hard that it was momentarily difficult to pull the blade out. He did so by placing the flat of his foot on the man's chest and shoving hard. The third man had some warning, but he was very drunk and lacked coordination, and his weapon was still slung over his back. He launched himself at Michael with his bare hands reaching out, and Michael kicked up hard, into his unprotected groin. The Italian screamed, clutching at himself, and fell backwards, and Michael was onto him, stabbing viciously into his chest three times in quick succession. There were no further attacks and he turned and saw Giles moving away from the final soldier, who was sliding down the wall, lifeless, his throat slashed open.

Giles met Michael's gaze over the heap of bodies. "Fuck me, but you're quick with that thing."

"I've had a lot of practice," Michael said. He turned and began hauling the bodies away from the two women. One still twitched with signs of life, and Michael killed him with a swift blow which was a kindness the man did not deserve. Behind him he heard a gurgling sound as his companion despatched the only other living soldier.

Michael dropped to one knee beside the two women. The girl who had been sobbing had stopped, and managed to push herself up to her knees. She crawled frantically towards the other woman who was slightly older, and stroked her hair and her face.

"Maria. Maria, speak. Please. Please."

Michael felt for a pulse and took his time over it in desperate sadness, but he knew the woman was dead. The girl knew it too, and she dropped her head down to place her cheek against the other woman's, silent tears falling. Michael looked at them, assessed their respective ages and made a guess.

"Your sister?"

"Yes."

"I'm sorry, lass. But we need to get you out of here, can you stand?"

She was shaky on her feet, and clearly in considerable pain. Her clothing was in tatters and there was blood running down her legs which made Michael flinch at the thought of the damage they might have done to her, but she managed a few steps and then nodded with an air of determination which impressed him. Giles was busy over the bodies, and Michael wondered what he was doing, but then he rose and Michael understood.

"And that's why you're an intelligence officer," he whispered, and took the coat that Giles was holding out.

It took several minutes to change their coats and Michael took a moment more to bundle up their red jackets and great coats into a looted knapsack. If capture seemed likely and there was time to assume their red coats again it might mean the difference between captivity and being shot as spies. As he tipped out the Italian's pack onto the ground to make space, there was a significant chinking sound, and Michael bent and picked up the bag. The weight made his eyes widen and he looked quickly inside, then put the purse into his pocket. Giles was bundling the girl into an oversized jacket and trousers, which would convince nobody after more than a cursory glance, but was at least decent and would hide her injuries. Michael selected hats, reflecting that in better times he would have laughed at the sight of his aristocratic companion wearing the tall shako adorned with a green feather. The girl, showing again her presence of mind, took the time to bundle up her long fair hair into the hat. Giles was ready first and moved silently to the end of the covered walkway to peer out into the square, where the sounds of drunken brutality were louder than ever. Michael caught the girl's hand and drew her after him, but as they reached him, Giles ducked back, and the expression on his face chilled Michael.

"What is it?"

"Don't let her look. We'll go this way and approach the church from the back."

Michael put his hand on Giles' shoulder. "What is it, lad?"

"Michael, don't. Look away. We can't stop it."

"Take care of her." Michael pushed the girl gently towards Giles, stepped forward and looked out into the square. More houses were burning, and black smoke was beginning to make it harder to breathe, but the drunken French and Italian soldiers were oblivious. They gathered in groups below the windows of the houses, laughing up, and Michael was momentarily puzzled and then suddenly appalled as he understood. There was a struggle at one of the upper windows and then a scream, and a body fell, thrown out by blue-coated soldiers. Michael could not see who it was, although he thought it was a man, and there was a scramble below, as the soldiers jostled, bayonets raised. The scream intensified and was turned to a bloodcurdling cry of agony, and then silence. Three soldiers hoisted high the body they had caught on their bayonets and stumbled into the middle of the square, the bloody trophy held between them until one of them tripped and fell over and the dead man crashed to the ground. Over at another window a woman was screaming over and over and Michael turned away, staggered to the wall and was sick violently.

After a moment he felt a hand on his arm. "Drink this, and let's get going. And don't do that again. Eyes down, don't look round. We'll search the church, if he's not there we're going to have to give up. We shouldn't have come."

"Yes, we should. If we get out of here, there'll be somebody to tell this story. Somebody should."

Giles clapped him on the shoulder and turned to the girl. She was standing in the darkness wide-eyed and Michael remembered suddenly, with

261

complete clarity, another terrified, brutalised girl, looking up at him through the darkness of a Madrid back street. The memory gave him courage and he drank, handed the flask back to Giles and moved forward. "What's your name, lass?"

"Francesca."

"Keep close and do as you're told, and I'm hoping we can get you to the boats. Come on."

Michael did not realise until they approached the door of the church that he had been holding on to hope, but his heart plunged when he saw the shattered door, with a body lying across the threshold. He glanced at Giles but could read no expression on the younger man's face. They moved cautiously along the wall, listening for sounds within. There was silence, with no sounds of drunken revelry, and no movement. Michael felt very sick again.

The body was that of the priest, his belly ripped open, blood staining the white of his robes. Giles looked down in silence, then up at the girl. "You shouldn't come in," he said. "Wait there, in that archway. I think it's over in here, but if we get into trouble, try to make it down to the jetty, you can take the path by the Santa Teresa convent, it wasn't guarded when we came up. Get to the boats and they'll take you to safety."

She nodded, looking terrified. Giles turned his eyes to Michael. "I have to know," he said, almost apologetically.

"I'm coming in."

Giles did not reply. He stepped over the priest and went into the dim interior of the church. It was not completely dark, the flames from the street behind, which was being wholly consumed by the fires, threw a flickering light over the scene within. Michael stopped just inside, concentrating hard on his unruly stomach. He had seen death and bloodshed since he was a boy of nineteen and had thought himself hardened, but this slaughter of people he had met daily and briefly lived among was heart-breaking.

Around twenty people had sought shelter in this church, and they were all dead, bayonetted by the soldiers. The traditional smell of incense was overlaid with the smell of sweat and fear and the strong metallic odour of blood. It was everywhere, splashed on the pews and the stone floor, pooling under the bodies of men, women and children who could not have been dead more than an hour. The men had died quickly, probably trying to defend their families. The women and girls had been raped before they died, their bodies sprawled with clothes ripped from them. Michael bent repeatedly, closing staring eyes and covering them where he could. It meant nothing, but he needed to make some gesture of sorrow and respect and he could think of nothing better.

"Michael, he's over here."

Giles' voice was quiet, almost gentle. Michael rose and went to join him at the altar, looking down. There were three bodies. The two women lay side by side behind the altar, their hands linked, and they looked curiously peaceful, as though somebody had taken the trouble to lay them out. They might have been sleeping apart from one huge wound in each breast, directly

262

above the heart. Their deaths would have been quick and easy and there was no other sign of injury. Michael stared at them bewildered and then understood.

Antonio lay at their feet, his hand resting on the woman's ankle, and he was covered in blood. Michael could count eight wounds, all made by a bayonet. Further away were three bodies, two Frenchmen and one Italian, also drenched in blood. More blood splashed the wooden altar table. Cloths and church plate were long gone.

Giles knelt down and reached out, gently closing the Spaniard's eyes. Michael could see tears on his cheeks although he made no sound. Michael's own throat was closed with the effort of holding back his own tears. He did not speak, he could think of nothing to say. Giles and Antonio had ridden together and fought together for two years with no other companions and Michael could not imagine the depth of Giles' grief.

Eventually Giles stood up, and Michael was relieved; he did not want to interrupt that long moment of quiet mourning. Giles stood back, looking down at the three bodies, then turned away.

"Let's get out of here."

"Do you want to move him?"

"No. God, no. We can't bury him, and why would I take him away from them? He was a devout Catholic and a man looking for a family. I think he found them. He's where he wanted to be."

"I didn't mean that," Michael said. He took hold of the altar table and dragged it to one side, then bent over Antonio's body. Giles seemed to understand suddenly, and moved to help. They lifted the Spaniard and laid him carefully beside Señora Palomo. The bodies had not yet begun to stiffen and Giles took Antonio's hand and placed it over the woman's. He stepped back and stood looking down at them for a moment, then looked around and found what he was looking for. Picking up the sword, which lay under the body of one of the men Antonio had killed, he took it to his friend and arranged it carefully across his body.

"I think that will do."

"So do I," Michael said. "Look, Giles…"

"I know. I bloody hope they've not finished the evacuation yet. Come on, let's get out of here."

It was slow going, partly because of the need to keep out of sight but mostly because it was clearly difficult for the girl to move quickly. She stopped occasionally, doubled over in pain, and Michael could see blood staining the legs of the white oversized trousers. He passionately hoped that she could recover from what had been done to her. Giles paused when she did, displaying remarkable patience given his own desperate misery, and Michael left her to his care. He suspected that the need to look after Francesca was helping Giles not to dwell on his loss.

They stopped at the base of the rock, concealed behind a stunted tree, and Michael swore at the sight before him. It was becoming easier to see now, as the first faint light of dawn began to brighten the sky, and what it showed him was a battle in progress. The French had found ladders and enough sober

263

troops to storm the castle, and it was clear that the remains of Alvarez' men were about to be overrun.

The explosion was huge, startling Michael, and he felt Giles jump beside him. The girl gave a little shriek and covered her ears.

"They've fired the magazine," Giles said. "They know they've lost. We need to get to those boats, they won't be coming back once the French have taken the castle."

"How?"

"There is a path," the girl said. "Below the cliff. It is very narrow and very dangerous. My brother used to collect bird's eggs there."

Giles turned to stare at her. "Show us."

Michael's stomach lurched at the sight of the path. It was less than two feet wide and very steep, hewn into the side of the cliff probably by natural causes. Michael could not see if it led all the way down to the shore. If it did, it must cut under the old bridge, where the last of the garrison would have to fight their way across under fire from the French, which would be appallingly exposed, but there was no choice. Giles took the lead, hugging the cliffside as much as he could, and Michael followed the girl. He was worried about her on this narrow ledge, but she moved confidently enough.

The path ran out just before the bridge. Giles paused, peering down through the gathering dawn to judge the possibility of climbing, and as he did, a sound from above made them look up. Michael did not see what it was, but reacted instinctively to Giles' yell of warning and flattened himself back against the cliff, one arm holding the girl safely. Splinters of rock flew up as a heavy object hit the section of the path they had just traversed, breaking away the edge. Something struck Michael painfully on the cheek and he lifted his hand and was shocked to find a large sliver of rock sticking out of his face. He withdrew it quickly and felt blood trickling down, leaving a metallic taste in his mouth.

The object struck the cliff once more, further down, before bouncing out and into the sea, and Michael realised what it was. The remaining men of the garrison had fired the magazine and were throwing the guns into the sea before abandoning the castle in a final desperate rush to the boats and safety.

"Move!" Giles yelled. He caught the girl's hand, and bounded forward. For a moment Michael thought he had literally jumped off the path into the sea, but he realised that there was a slope of loose sand and scree, leading down to the rocks below. It was far too steep and slippery to be taken at such a breakneck pace, but there was no more time. The girl slipped and fell almost immediately, and Giles threw both arms about her and went with her, sliding and bouncing down, trying to protect her as much as possible. Michael followed, managing to keep his feet. When he arrived on the rocks at the shoreline, Giles was helping her up. Both were filthy, the green jackets ripped, and Giles had grazes down one side of his face, a cut on his head and skinned knuckles on both hands which were bleeding profusely. His protection had worked well and Francesca seemed to have escaped further injury apart from a cut on her forehead.

"Well it was fast at least," Michael said.

"It had to be. Come on."

They scrambled over rocks slippery with seaweed, bruising knees and shins. At the edge of the cliff Giles stopped so suddenly that Michael ran into him and almost fell over. He surveyed the scene on the beach.

"Oh fuck."

There were four boats, two already packed to capacity with men, the oarsmen pushing off. The remains of the garrison poured down the narrow steps which led from the castle to the shore, under a constant hail of fire from the French. Other French troops were fighting on the beach, chasing down men scrambling for the boats with bayonets. As Michael watched, a volley from one of the boats drove them off, but more voltigeurs were swarming through the castle, chasing the men on the steps. Some were fast enough but those who were not were bayonetted in the back, their bodies thrown off the steps to prevent them hindering progress.

"We need to get over there," Giles said.

"There isn't going to be room in those boats for all these men, Giles, they'll overturn."

"Well they're not coming back for us, that's for bloody sure."

There was another explosion from the castle. Michael knew that Alvarez had given orders that the castle be destroyed, but it was clear that the garrison had run out of time for such a decisive action, although it seemed to have had some success with destroying the guns and stores. The noise was a temporary distraction, and Giles grasped the girl's hand and began to run.

There was no point in racing into the boiling surf after the departing boats. It was in the interests of the navy to preserve as many lives as possible, and Michael knew the midshipman in charge would have been given orders to fight off any panicked attempt to rush the boats which might overturn them. They stood, ankle deep in the water, watching the last of the boats pull away, and Michael turned. The French voltigeurs were still waiting, not hurrying now. Some thirty men, along with Giles, Michael and the girl, stood at bay, their backs to the sea, and the enemy could afford to take their time. Michael did not bother to raise his hands in surrender. No quarter would be given today, and he preferred to die fighting, as Antonio had, taking down as many of the enemy as he could manage.

Michael looked around him. There were some rocks that he might be able to reach, not enough to hold off an attack for long but enough to give some cover. No officer had been left on the beach, and the men seemed paralysed, frozen by the certainty of their death. Michael thought about Brat, then his mind shied away from the thought. He would never have time to say all the things that he wanted to say to her, and the regret was so painful it pierced his heart. He could not think of it while he still had strength to fight, so he raised his voice and yelled a command in Spanish.

The men turned, looking surprised, then confused, then some of them seemed to understand and followed Michael's headlong rush to the rocks. The French began to move, firing at the men running along the shore, and several

265

of them fell, but most made it to their temporary cover. It would not last more than a few minutes, few of the men had enough ammunition for a determined stand, but Michael heard himself issuing orders, even while part of his brain mocked him for this fruitless gesture.

"It's been a pleasure, Captain O'Reilly."

Michael turned. Giles was crouched beside him, and surprisingly he was smiling. Michael smiled back, amazed that he could do so.

"You too, Giles."

"I'm sorry. You should have made it back to her. It was my fault."

"Don't be an idiot, you didn't hold a pistol to my head. I didn't know him as well as you did, but I liked him." Michael paused, and his eyes slid to the girl. She was leaning on one of the rocks, her eyes closed. "Talking of pistols..."

"I've a little ammunition, but I'll save one, Michael. If Antonio could do it, so can I. Good luck."

"Good luck yourself, sir." Michael withdrew his own pistol and began to check his ammunition, thankful that everything had remained dry.

There was a cry from one of the Spanish soldiers, and Michael raised his pistol and leaned forward, his eyes on the advancing French, but then he realised that the cry was being taken up by others, and he risked a look and felt his heart leap in sudden hope. Four boats were coming in fast. The lead one was commanded by a blue coated officer, and as Michael watched, he shouted an order and there was a deafening volley of musket fire. The approaching French had not been looking seawards, and Michael realised that the boats had rowed from the far side of the rocks. He had no idea where they had come from, since the boats of the squadron had not yet reached the navy brigs and were still visible in the distance, but they were undoubtedly Royal Navy boats.

The French were running. Most of the attacking force were in the castle, having already dispatched the remains of the garrison on the steps, and had left the voltigeurs to mop up the survivors on the beach. The navy volleys were very well organised with each boat firing in turn, giving the others time to reload, and the voltigeurs had no cover and no time to get off a shot. They fled in disarray up the beach, and Giles surged to his feet.

"To the boats," he bellowed in Spanish. "Get moving, before they open fire from the castle. Wounded men first. You and you. Come and help the girl, get her to safety, she's hurt."

Michael scrambled to join him, pistol at the ready, his eyes on the French. They were out of range now, and an officer was screaming orders, furiously trying to get them into order, but the remaining Spaniards were climbing into the boats, and as each one filled, the officer in command gave the order to push off. Three boats left, oars cutting cleaning through the choppy sea, and the fourth waited to cover the retreat, a dozen marines lined up with muskets. Michael saw the French officer pause, surveying the boat, and then he called the order to retreat. Michael did not blame him. Four of his men lay dead on the beach and there was no point in losing more.

"Captain Fenwick. I was worried you had not made it out of the castle or the town."

The voice was precise and very English, and Michael turned to see the navy officer walking up the beach. Giles stood very still, watching him come. The officer stopped and studied Giles for a moment.

"You look dreadful, Giles. Get in the boat."

Giles opened his mouth and closed it again, as though he could not find the words. Finally, he said:

"Lieutenant Durrell. Why am I surprised, I wonder? You have a history of well-timed rescues."

Durrell's somewhat serious face softened into a smile. "It's very good to see you, Giles. Shall we depart, before they regain their courage?" Durrell looked around. "I was expecting three of you."

"Antonio," Giles said, and his voice sounded rusty. "My guide. He's dead."

"Oh God, I'm sorry, Giles." Durrell came forward and put a hand on Giles' shoulder, looking over at Michael. "Captain O'Reilly, I should tell you that there is a young lady aboard the *Iris* who will be very glad to find you in one piece."

Michael felt weak with relief, not at his own unexpected survival, but at the knowledge that she was safe. He had thought he would never see her again but she was there waiting for him. He shouldered his stolen bayonet from habit, and moved towards the boat. "Thank God she's safe. My thanks for a timely rescue, Lieutenant."

"Just doing my duty, Captain. Mr Stanney, back to the boat, prepare to depart. Let me help you, Giles, before you fall over."

Michael settled onto the wooden seat, listening to Giles and Durrell conversing in low voices. The sun was fully rising, painting the sky with a rich palette of orange, gold and pink, sending jewelled sparks off white tipped waves and bathing the mountains rising behind Castro Urdiales with a rosy glow. Fires still raged in the town, and the smell of smoke drifted across the waves. The oarsmen bent to their work and the boat skimmed across the water, and Michael closed his eyes and for a time, thought about nothing at all.

***

It was warm in Hugh Kelly's dining cabin, and Brian, Kelly's servant, found blankets and brought wine and food, mutton stew with turnips and dark rye bread which was very hard, but welcome when dipped in the stew. Kelly ate with them, asking no questions, simply making sure they were fed and warm and well supplied with wine. The food along with the sense of comfort and safety made Michael sleepy.

Across the table, Giles ate slightly clumsily with his left hand, having injured his right during his precipitous descent of the cliff. Lieutenant Durrell sat beside him, passing him bread and refilling his glass. It made Michael smile inwardly, there was something touching about Durrell's obvious concern, and

267

Giles, who could be prickly about accepting help, seemed very comfortable with this tall, self-contained young navy officer. Michael wondered how they had met. It seemed a very unlikely friendship.

Durrell found space below decks for the exhausted men of the garrison, gave up his own cabin to Francesca, and set his men to providing food, blankets and medical attention. Michael had enquired about Grainger on the boat, and the lieutenant shook his head.

"I am sorry, Captain, Sir Horace died only an hour after arriving on board. Our surgeon did not operate, the gangrene was too far gone. We will conduct a burial at sea tomorrow if you wish to attend."

"We do," Giles said. "I liked the man, I'm sorry he couldn't be saved, but he knew he was dying.'

Durrell studied him. "Why did you move him, Giles?"

"He didn't want to be taken by the French. Given what happened in the town, I'm glad we did it."

Brat cried when Michael told her about Antonio, and Michael held her for a long time. She had not spoken since they sat down. There were huge dark shadows under the extraordinary blue-green eyes, and her face was white, framed by flattened auburn curls.

"You're all exhausted, and small wonder," Hugh Kelly said. "As soon as you've eaten, you should rest. I've asked Brian to sling hammocks in my day cabin for you gentlemen, and for myself and Mr Durrell. Miss Ibanez can have my cabin."

"No, Captain, you should not give up your room to me."

"It's my ship, lass, I can more or less do what I like. I've spoken to Commander Bloye. He's under orders to take the men of the garrison to Bermeo, where they can re-join Longa's forces. I believe there will be provision there for the townspeople, so tomorrow our boats will transfer the girl you brought with you, along with the remaining soldiers over to the *Lyra* and the *Sparrow*. The commander will be writing to London reporting a successful evacuation, and I don't intend to spoil his enjoyment of that. I would like to write a different letter, about what happened to the townspeople."

Brat shivered violently and Michael ignored good manners and moved his chair closer to put his arm about her. "Don't think about it, Brat."

"How can I help it? All those people that I knew."

"There is no need to add to your distress by talking details here and now, ma'am. Tomorrow, once we have disposed of our guests and buried Sir Horace, I would like an account of what you saw, gentlemen. You will of course make your own reports, but…"

"You shall have it," Giles said, and Michael thought with compassion that he sounded exhausted.

"I am guessing you are here because of your work as an observing officer," Durrell said, studying Giles.

"Yes. Sir Horace Grainger was on a diplomatic mission and had gone missing and Lord Wellington was asked to help trace him. He sent me, because I know the countryside and a lot of the Spanish partisans in the area, and he sent Captain O'Reilly in case I got myself killed. Antonio, my Spanish guide was with us. He was killed trying to defend some of the townspeople in a church. We found his body."

"I'm so sorry, Captain."

"So am I, he was my friend."

Michael saw Brat's eyes fill with tears again and he stood up, drawing her to her feet. "Captain, with your leave, I'd like Brat to get some rest. May I..."

"Take her through," Kelly said without hesitation. "I'll be going to bed myself shortly, it's been a long day. In fact, it's almost morning."

The cabin was warm and comfortable and a linen shirt had been laid out on the bunk for Brat to use as a nightgown. Michael watched as she picked it up, running her fingers over the soft fabric.

"Some people are so kind."

"You deserve it, little one."

"Did he suffer? Antonio?"

"No. It would have been very quick. He died fighting, a soldier's death, as he'd have wanted."

"I will miss him calling me 'little fox' although it made me very cross when he did it."

"That's why he did it."

"I know." Brat looked up and smiled, making one of her disturbing shifts from engaging child to mature young woman. "Go to bed, Michael, before you fall over. I will be quite safe."

"I know. There's something I wanted to do first, though, although now that we're here, I realise I'm too scared to try, in case I've got this wrong."

Brat put down the shirt and walked forward. Standing on tiptoe, she kissed him very gently on the lips. "Was that it?"

Michael put his arms about her and held her close. "It was. I'm glad you did it, I thought I might have imagined the other time."

"So did I."

He laughed and kissed her again. "Well, it's good to have cleared that up. Sleep well, urchin. Call me if you need me, I'm just in the next room."

"With three other men. They would think the worst."

"I don't care." Michael touched her cheek gently. "Goodnight, Ariana Ibanez. Dream only of good things."

Chapter Eighteen

The church in Freineda was cool in the morning, although Manson knew that it would be sweltering by mid-afternoon. There were few guests; neither Carl or Keren had wanted a fuss made about their wedding, although Manson knew that the simple ceremony itself mattered a great deal to both of them. Carl was the son of a parson and Keren's father was a Methodist preacher and Manson thought that they had both always seemed slightly awkward in their irregular relationship. He had attended few weddings, but he found this one very moving. The army chaplain mumbled his way through the ceremony, but the bride and groom spoke their vows with unusual clarity, as though the words and promises had real meaning for them. Keren's face was radiant and Manson thought that his commanding officer looked happier than he had ever seen. It had taken them a long time to reach this decision, but their certainty was visible to everybody.

Paul stood as Carl's groomsman, and there was a brief flurry as Johnny Wheeler led the bride into the church, but then stood aside for the unexpected appearance of Lord Wellington, accompanied by Lord Fitzroy Somerset, who slipped quietly into the pew beside Anne. He said nothing, but Manson, on Anne's other side, saw his lips curve at the sight of the bride, who was unexpectedly dazzling in gold silk and Spanish lace, a gift from her former employer. Wellington had learned the hard way how easily gossip attached itself to the commander in chief, and was circumspect in his relationships with women, at least in public, but he had a very good appreciation of an attractive women. Manson wondered with affectionate cynicism if Wellington would have made the same very public gesture of support of Lieutenant-Colonel Swanson's shocking misalliance, if the bride had not been so lovely.

Outside the sun was already hot, blinding them temporarily after the dimness of the church, and the few guests converged on the newlyweds in a flurry of kisses and embraces and congratulations. Anne held Keren close for a long time, and then took her hand and led her to where Lord Wellington stood.

"My Lord, please allow me to present my very good friend, Mrs Swanson."

Keren dropped a curtsey, her cheeks very pink, and Wellington took her hand and bowed over it formally. "Delighted, ma'am. My congratulations upon your marriage. And to you too, Colonel Swanson."

"Thank you, my Lord."

Carl watched as Wellington walked briskly back to his headquarters. "Did you arrange that, ma'am?"

"I did not," Anne said, looking at Paul. "Paul?"

"Nothing to do with me," Paul said cheerfully. "I'm glad he did though, it's neatly solved a social problem. If Lord Wellington took the trouble to attend your wedding, he's making a point. As far as I'm concerned, the rest of them can..."

"Paul."

"I didn't say it," Paul said, holding up his hands. "I am on my best behaviour today, I have finally got Colonel Swanson off my hands and it's a relief. I doubt I'll manage it with any of the rest of you until the end of this war, unless Captain O'Reilly has managed to find a charming señorita on his travels. Colonel Wheeler let me down badly on his recent journey to England, it was his one chance and he let it slip."

"If I ever do find a woman foolish enough to accept an offer, sir, you will be the last to know, I couldn't stand the endless raillery," Johnny said placidly. "I wouldn't place any reliance on Michael either, I think we need to work on Captain Carlyon. Simon, the general requires you to find a wife, he's a sentimental fellow and likes a wedding; would you..."

Paul released his wife and stepped towards Johnny menacingly, and Johnny retreated neatly, placing Carlyon and Witham between them. The party broke up in laughter, and Manson was still smiling back at the quinta as he took his horse to the stable. There had been little laughter in Manson's childhood, and in his early weeks with the 110th he had found his commanding officer's banter with both officers and men difficult to understand, but he had come to realise how important it was. Morale was made of many strands, each of them seemingly frail; patriotism, loyalty, regimental pride and a sense of brotherhood all played a part. Right across Van Daan's brigade, those strands were woven together by the eccentric personality of their commanding officer, and Manson had learned that every joke or anecdote or small kindness shared between officers or men, helped to twist the strands into an unbreakable bond that would make each man ready to give his life for his comrades.

They were still talking and laughing on the packed earth of the carriage drive outside the main house when a horseman appeared, cantering up the road from Freineda. Manson recognised him immediately, and walked out to meet him. He had spent most of the previous day in the company of Captain Zachariah White, and despite the grim nature of his enquiries, Manson found the patient process of question and answer fascinating. White had a knack for getting his subjects to talk to him, although Manson privately wondered how useful the investigation was. Somebody knew exactly what had happened to Major Leonard Vane, but a man who was bold enough to murder an officer was probably going to be a good enough liar to get away with it. Unless somebody had seen or heard something of the crime, Manson suspected that Vane's death was likely to remain a mystery.

"Captain White, I wasn't expecting you this morning, I've been a guest at a wedding."

White dismounted. He had a naturally serious face, but Manson could see immediately that something had happened, and he felt a little chill. It was one thing to sit listening to White asking endless questions about Vane's disappearance and death but it was another to realise that he might be close to accusing a man Manson knew.

"I am aware of that, Captain Manson and had it not been urgent, I would have waited. Unfortunately, I have received information which made it imperative that I speak to Lieutenant-Colonel Swanson without delay."

There was a stunned silence in the group. Anne was the first to speak. "On his wedding day?"

The frosty tone of her voice made Manson want to smile. It would have daunted another man, but White was made of sterner stuff. Something about his rigid determination reminded Manson of his own bewildered first days in Portugal and he felt, along with his unhappiness about Carl's predicament, an unwilling urge to protect White from his own zeal.

"There's nothing so important that it can't wait a day, Captain," Paul said. His voice was pleasant, but Manson could detect the steel beneath the surface. "Colonel Swanson can enjoy his wedding day and will be available tomorrow to speak to you."

White did not respond and Manson realised he was holding his breath. Into the silence, Carl said easily:

"I don't suppose this is going to take long. Why don't we go into the office, Captain White. My wife will excuse me for a short time, she's got the rest of our lives to put up with me."

There was another murmur of laughter, uneasy this time, although Manson appreciated Carl's attempt to lighten the mood. He was watching Paul's expression and he did not think that Carl was going to succeed in shaking him off. He was proved right.

"What an excellent idea, Colonel Swanson. I've a good Madeira that I've been saving for a special occasion and it is your wedding day. Why don't you take care of the new Mrs Swanson, girl of my heart, this isn't going to take long."

Manson flinched internally at Paul's tone and even the imperturbable White looked nonplussed. Carl looked as though he would have liked to argue, but seemed to change his mind at Keren's worried expression. He saluted, ironically, then took his wife's hand and kissed it.

"I'm sorry, sweetheart, it didn't occur to me I'd need to deal with this today. It won't take long, I'll be with you before we go down to dinner. This way, Captain White."

***

272

There was an awkward silence in the office as Jenson served the wine, and the sound of his wooden leg seemed particularly loud on the boards. Jenson often stomped in order to express irritation or disapproval, and Paul wondered if White realised those ominous thuds were aimed at him. He waited until the door was closed and then turned to White.

"What's this about, Captain? And please make it a good explanation because unless you have information likely to lead to an immediate arrest for the murder of Major Vane, I am making a formal complaint to Colonel Scovell about this, I suspect you are exceeding your authority by about a mile here."

White flushed slightly. "I have not spoken to Colonel Scovell about this, sir, because..."

"I know you bloody haven't, lad, because if you had, he'd have told you to leave it alone today. You're very lucky he's been laid up with a fever otherwise he'd have been a guest at this wedding. As a matter of interest, did you go to Lord Wellington for authorisation?"

"I am not required to do so, sir."

"Well it might have been a good idea."

"General, you don't need to be here," Carl interrupted firmly. "Why don't you go back to the party..."

"The officer investigating Major Vane's murder has just seen fit to ride in here on a day which he knew perfectly well would be inappropriate, Colonel. It's my brigade headquarters, I intend to bloody well know why. Telling me it's none of my business is only going to prolong the agony, and when it comes to being bloody-minded, I can outlast either of you, trust me."

There was a brief, difficult silence, then Carl said:

"It's true, he can."

Paul gave him a look. "Ask your questions, Captain White. I am eager to hear them."

Carl sighed. "Sit down, Captain. There's no need to stand there balancing that wine glass like a juggling act. I certainly intend to, getting married has proved unexpectedly tiring."

White seated himself on an uncomfortable looking wooden chair and Carl chose a padded armchair. He looked at Paul.

"I'll stand," Paul said.

"Oh for God's sake, either sit down or go away," Carl said, sounding exasperated. "You don't need to be here. In fact I'd much prefer it if you weren't. I'll answer the captain's questions and I'll explain to you afterwards. Just go away."

Paul saw the flicker of astonishment on White's face at Carl's tone. Normally it would have amused him, but he did not feel like laughing at present. "What bothers me, Carl, is that you clearly know what this is about, and I don't. And I've got a very strong feeling you should have told me."

"If I didn't tell you something, sir, it's not because my memory is going, it's because I didn't want you to know. Unfortunately, I think you're going to have to, but we don't need to put Captain White through that. Why don't you...?"

273

"Ask your questions, Captain," Paul said, not looking at White.

"Yes, sir." White cleared his throat. "Colonel Swanson, I have been told that it was unnecessary to ask you any questions about the murder of Major Vane, because you were confined to your bed with an injury. I have reason to believe that was a lie."

Paul felt his stomach lurch. He fixed his eye on Carl's face, hoping for a denial, but his friend gave a very slight smile. "It depends on who told you that, Captain."

"I did," Paul said.

"Well that wasn't a lie, because General van Daan was away and had no idea that I had been out of bed. Neither had his wife, who was taking care of me. In fact, as far as I knew, nobody here was aware of it, apart from one of the grooms. Who told you?"

"I received the information from one of the men of Captain..."

"Stop!" Paul said sharply. "You can't tell him that, and he'd no right to ask."

Carl's smile broadened, making Paul long to hit him. "No, of course. I'm sorry, I wasn't intending to go after him, I was just curious. I haven't lied to you either, Captain, and if you'd come to me, I'd have told you the truth."

"Why didn't I know about this, Colonel?"

"I saw no need to tell you."

"Bollocks," Paul said furiously. "When I was at your bedside expressing concern, it would have been the most natural thing in the world to mention that you'd been up and about."

"General, I have questions. It appears that Colonel Swanson's journey took him very close to where Major Vane's body was found."

Paul set down his glass so hard that he was surprised that it did not shatter. "Captain White, are you here to arrest Colonel Swanson?"

"No, sir."

"Do you have grounds to arrest him?"

"No, sir."

"Just some questions?"

"Yes, sir."

"You'll get to ask them, I give you my word. However, I'm asking you if you'll come back tomorrow. It's his wedding day, for one thing. For another..."

"For another, General van Daan wishes to yell at me in a highly disrespectful manner, and he can't have a junior officer present," Carl said affably. "I'm sorry, Captain, you've not walked into a murder, but you have stirred up a rather awkward situation. Would you mind?"

Paul saw White hesitate, and bit back his urge to order the other man out of the room. He was entitled to do so, but he did not want to. Paul was a supporter of the new Staff Cavalry Corps, and had discussed ideas about it with both Colonel Scovell and Lord Wellington, so he did not want to undermine Captain White's attempt to do the right thing. At the same time, he could not speak freely to Carl in front of him.

274

White got up and saluted. "By all means, General. I will return tomorrow morning if that is convenient."

"Perfectly convenient," Carl said. "I am sorry, Captain, this has been very awkward for you."

White closed the door carefully. Paul turned and looked at his oldest friend. "Awkward for him?"

Carl drank wine, and set down the glass. "I'm sorry, Paul. If I'd had any idea that somebody had seen me go out that night, I'd have told you. As it is…"

"As it is, it looks as though you've lied about being out and about when Vane was murdered, which given that he put you in that bed in the first place, is awkward. It also looks as though I've got no control over my brigade officers, who pick and choose what to tell me, leaving me looking like a complete fucking idiot in front of the Staff Corps when they come to call. That's a lot more than awkward. I really hope you've got a damned good explanation for this, Colonel, because right now it looks as though you've got something to hide."

Carl stood up. "Do you think I murdered Vane?"

"Don't stand there and try to turn this into an issue of how much I trust you, Carl, I am not fucking stupid. You might not have told a direct lie but you deceived me and you did it deliberately. We'll talk about murder after you've told me exactly why you got up with a high fever and an injured shoulder, got a groom to saddle your horse in the middle of the night and bribed him to keep quiet about it. And if you want to attend your wedding celebrations without a black eye and a bloody nose, you'll tell me quickly."

Carl did not move or speak for a moment and Paul concentrated on reining in his temper as far as he could. Carl had known him from boyhood and had no fear of his anger; a tongue-lashing was only likely to keep him stubbornly silent and Carl could be remarkably stubborn. Paul could see that Carl was angry as well, so he took several long, deep breaths and tried again.

"All right. I'm going to sit down, drink some wine, and give you the opportunity to do what you ought to have done in the first place, Colonel, which is tell me the truth. I will defend you to the death against literally anything, but it is not fair if I don't know what I'm defending you against."

Paul seated himself in one of the more comfortable chairs, picked up his glass and drank, watching his friend. Finally, Carl moved, and sat opposite, picking up his own glass. They drank in silence then Carl set down his glass.

"That is very good Madeira," he said.

"Thank you. I wanted to celebrate your wedding day."

Carl's tense expression softened into a smile. "I know. I'm so sorry, Paul. Bloody White."

"His timing was shit, Carl, but he's doing his job. Why did you go out?"

"Rory Stewart. Ned Browning came tapping on my door in the middle of the night. Keren was sleeping in with your wife, I was so restless with this shoulder, she was getting no sleep, so Nan suggested it. Browning's close to

Stewart, they served together for years and Browning always said Stewart saved his life at the Coa."

"I know. What was wrong with Stewart?"

"Dead drunk in a ditch, literally. I've no idea why he was out, Browning thought that some of the local taverns were refusing to serve him, so he'd gone further afield. He'd just been demoted, and his wife has effectively left him, taking his children. And before you open your mouth, she was right to do it, he's treated her appallingly. But it was raining that night, and bloody freezing, and Browning was worried. He went out in search of him and found him lying there. He'd hit his head, he was covered in blood and Browning couldn't rouse him and certainly couldn't carry him with one arm."

"I imagine not," Paul said. Browning had lost half an arm at Bussaco and had chosen to remain with the regiment, serving as groom, orderly and general servant. Since Carl's promotion to command the battalion, he had acted as Carl's orderly and it did not surprise Paul that Browning had gone to him for help. Paul tried to picture Browning with one arm and Carl, with his injured arm still in a sling, trying to get Stewart to his feet, and began to laugh.

"Two one-armed men trying to hoist up a drunken former sergeant. I'm trying to picture this, and it has its funny side, you must still have been in a sling at that point. Why on earth didn't he rouse some of the lads to go and help him?"

Carl grinned. He was looking more relaxed now that he had told the truth and Paul was feeling better as well, although he could already feel the stirrings of a different unease, which he was not sure Carl had thought of. "It wasn't easy," he admitted. "But we took the small gig. Ned didn't want to get any of the lads involved, Stewart was already in so much trouble, he didn't want anybody else punished for leaving barracks without permission. And if I'd given them permission to bring him in, I'd have had to put him on another charge. I was hoping to avoid that, I've got some of the men keeping an eye on him and we're hoping we can get him dried out and settled down so that Sally can feel safe to give him another chance. And before you say it, I know you don't think he deserves another chance, but he wasn't always like this, Paul. Rory Stewart was a good man. He taught me how to use a bayonet and shoot a musket straight when I was not much more than a boy in India."

Paul could not help smiling, the memory was so clear. "I know. He taught me how to get a fire lit quickly in difficult conditions. It's not a skill they teach you at Eton or Oxford, or even in the Royal Navy. Carl, don't think I don't feel sentimental about Stewart at times, but I'm not sure I'll ever be happy about Sally going back to him. So what happened?"

"Between us we managed to get him into the gig and back here. Ned settled him in an empty stall in the stables to sleep it off, and said he'd keep an eye on him, we put the horse and gig back and Ned helped me back to bed and took my clothes away to launder and dry. I didn't even tell Keren. And to be honest, I didn't ever think I'd need to mention it. I'm an officer, I'm not supposed to be helping an enlisted man to avoid a charge, but we've all done it, including you, if we think the man is worth it. The following day, I sent for

276

him and gave him a dressing down, told him this was the last time, and that if he didn't pull himself together, he was going to have to take the consequences. He seemed very subdued, more so than I've seen him and promised he'd try. I've been getting daily reports from Sergeant Callow, and apparently he's been doing much better, so I'm not sorry I did it. But I am sorry it's put you in a difficult position. I'll talk to White in the morning and explain. It had nothing to do with Vane, and it's not up to White to deal with my indiscretions, it's up to you. Am I on a charge?"

"Oh fuck off, Carl, you're not funny."

"It was sort of funny."

Paul gave a reluctant smile. "You should probably have told me, but I can see why you didn't. I'm sorry I blew up, you made me feel like an idiot. If White needs confirmation of your story, he can talk to Browning, but I doubt that he will. He's a sensible man, although a bit over-enthusiastic, but that will settle down, he's new to this and he wants to prove himself."

"Thank you, sir."

Paul studied him, frowning. "But Carl, it's not completely simple. We don't know exactly when Vane was killed, but they can narrow it down to within two days, and it's clear that your rescue mission fits within that time. Nobody is going to doubt you or Browning, there'll be too many people here to confirm the rest of your story. But if I were White, the next question I'd ask, is what about Stewart?"

Carl's eyes widened. "Stewart? Why in God's name would Stewart want to kill Vane, I don't know that he'd ever even spoken to the man?"

Paul looked at him, troubled. "Nor do I, Carl. But what we do know is that he was there. He was drunk, which usually turns Stewart into a raving beast who will attack anybody. And you found him covered in blood, which might have come from a head wound. But what if some of it didn't?"

Carl did not speak. Eventually, Paul drained his glass and stood up. "Right, that is enough for now. You're going to have to tell him the truth, lad, and you know it. If White turns his attention onto Stewart, I'll make sure he has all the help he needs to defend himself. But we're not talking about it again today. You're a married man, George Kelly has cooked a feast that you wouldn't believe, and I've given leave for the men to celebrate in the field this evening with a dance, which I am hoping you and your wife will attend. Get yourself back to her and forget about it for now. I'll see Stewart in the morning."

Carl rose. "Thank you, Paul. For everything."

Paul put a hand on his shoulder. "You too, Carl. Now get out of here, before she runs off with Simon Carlyon on your wedding day."

***

Private Rory Stewart was arrested for the murder of Major Vane five days after the wedding. Manson brought the news to Paul, who was writing a lengthy letter to his father, giving details of the children's journey home, along with very specific instructions about their tutor and governess. Joshua, probably encouraged by his wife, had written a furious letter dismissing both Harcourt and Miss Webster. Anne had offered to reply, but Paul preferred to do it himself. His family took a traditional view of the position of females, and he suspected that Joshua would simply override his wife's instructions, which would infuriate her. With the new campaign looming, there were a number of domestic issues that Paul wanted to resolve, and he had decided for once, to do so without consulting Anne. He was overjoyed at his wife's return to full health and did not want to disturb her last week with the children with difficulties.

Paul listened to his brigade major's report gloomily. He was not surprised. Captain White had interviewed Carl briefly on the morning after the wedding and immediately shifted his interest to Private Stewart. He had spoken to Stewart, to his company officers and to a number of the men, and then he had not been seen for two days. Paul had hoped that it would be impossible to press charges due to the lack of either evidence or motive. He wondered what White had discovered.

"Where is he being held?"

"There's a temporary gaol in Castelo Bom where the Judge-Advocate General is billeted, sir. White tells me that Lord Wellington has made it known that he expects the trial to be over before the army marches in a few weeks."

"Lord Wellington can fuck off," Paul said. "I am an expert in the law pertaining to general courts martial, Captain, I was instructed by a very bright young lawyer, who oddly enough was recommended to me by Sir Arthur Wellesley, something that he'll come to regret if he tries to force this through to suit his own convenience. Stewart is entitled to time to collect his witnesses and prepare his case. Have you seen him?"

Manson shook his head. "No. Lieutenant-Colonel Clevedon insisted on going with him to inspect the condition of the gaol though. I thought poor White's eyes were going to pop out of his head."

Despite his gloom, Paul laughed aloud, he could visualise the scene. Clevedon was the younger son of an Earl, one of the few officers in his brigade from an aristocratic family, and was generally a quiet, self-effacing man, but on the rare occasions when he was roused to anger, he had an unexpectedly lordly manner and Paul was not surprised that White had been taken aback.

"I'll ride up and speak to him when I've finished these letters, I need to get them off today. I want to have a chat with Mr Larpent about when they are able to hold the trial. It will take some time, I imagine."

"I don't think so, sir. We're in winter quarters, there are no shortage of officers to sit on the jury, and it's not as though Stewart has a large number of witnesses to call. The prosecution has more, but they're all right here."

"The prosecution has no witnesses at all," Paul said shortly. "Nobody saw Stewart kill Vane and there is no possible motive, he didn't even serve in Vane's battalion. They'll probably try to claim it was a robbery, or that Vane caught Stewart out of barracks without permission and drunk, but…"

"They've found a motive, sir."

278

Paul felt a little frisson of shock. He met Manson's steady gaze and knew immediately that this was bad. "A real motive?"

"I'm afraid so."

"Did he do it, Leo?"

"I think he might have, sir."

"Oh bugger." Paul leaned back in his chair. "Get the brandy, will you, I think I'm going to need it."

Manson poured drinks for both of them and sat down again. Paul picked up his glass and swirled the amber liquid around gently. "I love this brandy. Michael O'Reilly gave it to me at Christmas, I've no idea where he got it from, and I'm always terrified to ask. Every time I drink it, I wonder if I'm ever going to see him again."

"You will, sir."

"There's been no news for a while, Leo." Paul sipped the brandy and set his glass down. He stared at it for a long moment then looked up. "All right, Captain, let's have it. Tell me about Stewart and Vane."

"We should have thought of it straight away, sir, it's bloody obvious. What's the worst thing we all know about Major Vane?"

"He was a complete bastard around women," Paul said, and felt the lurch in his gut as he understood. "Oh God, no. Sally?"

Manson nodded. "White interviewed all Stewart's barrack mates, not just those who helped cover up his absence and his drinking. He's good at asking the right questions and one of the things he asked was if any of them knew why Stewart was drinking so heavily."

"Were you present?"

"Yes, sir. I thought you might like me to be, just to make sure none of the men were being bullied into saying anything. To be honest, I wasn't worried about that, White is a good man. I'd no earthly right to be included, but I think he was happy to have me there, as a witness that he's done this properly. Which he has, sir, no question."

"Yes. If all George Scovell's staff corps officers do their jobs as well, they'll be worth having."

"Anyway, most of them shrugged and said that Stewart had always liked a drink and always had a temper on him when he was jug-bitten. But Private Nolan said that Stewart had it under control but that it got worse since he had a falling out with his wife. White looked at dates, which wasn't easy since Private Nolan doesn't know what day it is let alone what month or year it is."

"Don't sound so bitter, Leo, a lot of them don't."

"I think I envy them that, sir."

"I do too, sometimes. I don't need exact dates to know that Rory's falling out with Sally happened not long after Vane joined the brigade. What happened? Am I going to need more brandy?"

"I'll get the bottle," Manson said, getting up. "White asked to speak to Sally. She didn't want to at first. It was obvious that she had some idea what had happened, she couldn't stop crying. I wanted to wait until your wife got back and could be with her, she's taken the children to Ciudad Rodrigo with Mrs Mackenzie. But Miss Trenlow…I mean, Mrs Swanson was there, and offered to accompany Sally, so she agreed."

"And what did the resourceful Captain White find out?"

"Vane raped her," Manson said. He spoke quietly, and it expressed the depth of his fury more powerfully than if he had yelled. "She'd gone over to the 112th to help one of the women with a difficult birth, apparently she's a capital midwife and she's often asked to help out. The child was successfully delivered, they asked if Sally wanted to stay the night but she wanted to get back because of the children. It's only a couple of miles along a good road, and she'd a covered lantern, she wasn't afraid."

"Why would she be? She was the wife of Sergeant-Major Stewart, none of the men would bloody dare."

"Vane was riding back from town. He saw her, dismounted and started to question her. Sally answered respectfully, he was an officer. He pretended to disbelieve her, accused her of theft and prostitution and a lot of other spurious rubbish, and marched her back to that cottage, it was empty at the time, where he said he'd send for the provost. She went. She thought he was being over-zealous, but she wasn't worried because she'd nothing to hide and she knew we'd speak up for her. Once at the cottage, he raped her. Afterwards, he told her that if she told anybody about it, he'd go after Stewart and make sure he ended up on a charge. He'd heard about Stewart's temper, and he reckoned he could provoke him into striking an officer, which would be a death sentence."

"Oh Christ, why didn't she tell me?" Paul breathed. "She must have known she could trust me, and that I'd deal with the bastard. I am such a bloody idiot. I've been congratulating myself that we'd put a stop to Vane's nasty little habits with the men's wives, but all we did was stopped him doing it openly through the courts. There was nothing to stop him terrorising them secretly."

"I don't think it was that simple, sir," Manson said. "I think she was terrified of Stewart finding out, she knows what he's like. And she was right. Stewart found out, I don't know how, but he seems to have thought she'd gone with him either for money or to keep him out of trouble. We know the rest."

"Poor bastard," Paul said softly. "I need to go over there, Leo, these will have to wait."

"Do you want me to come with you?"

"No, it's all right. I'm guessing that if Keren was there through Sally's interview, she'll tell my wife, but make sure Nan knows, will you, she'll want to keep an eye on Sally."

"Yes, sir."

***

Paul found Francis Larpent, the recently arrived deputy judge-advocate general in a miserable little room in a Portuguese farmhouse hunched over his work. Paul had met Larpent several times socially but had not dealt with him in an official capacity. Paul explained his business and Larpent regarded him with an expression of surprise.

"I suppose you may speak to the man, General, but I do not understand what you hope to achieve."

"Stewart used to serve under me, Mr Larpent, and his wife is employed by Mrs van Daan. I'd like to ask him what happened."

"He is unlikely to tell you anything. That class of person will lie right up to the gallows in my experience. So far, he has said very little, but I have to tell you that the evidence of his guilt is compelling. He was found drunk in a drainage ditch on the night Major Vane went missing, within half a mile of where the body was found. His clothing was drenched in blood..."

"I'm told he had a head wound."

"He had a minor contusion. Captain White's men searched the barracks and found Stewart's clothing. It is clear that some attempt had been made to get the blood out of his coat, but shirt, breeches and stockings were rolled up in a bundle and they reeked. That much blood did not come from a small head injury."

"I understand, sir. I'd still like to speak to him."

"Very well, I will send my servant to show you the way. I am currently drawing up the list of prospective jurors, but I believe that we should be ready to proceed with the trial in approximately three weeks."

"That's hardly long enough for him to prepare a defence, Mr Larpent."

"Private Stewart is offering no defence, General. Wait and I will write the order."

Stewart was alone in his cell, a dusty space in the ruined castle which overlooked the village. Paul's guide closed the rough door behind him, and Stewart rose from his bed roll on the floor and saluted. He looked drawn and pale, and Paul thought he had lost a lot of weight recently.

"How are you, Rory?"

"All right, sir." Stewart waved a hand, indicating the bare cell. "Bit cold at night, but I've slept in worse."

Paul did not speak for a long time. Finally, he said:

"I feel as though I've stepped back eleven years and I'm standing in that cell in the barracks at Melton Mowbray, trying to decide whether to put you on a charge for trying to kill me or to give you another chance."

"Aye, happen you should have done it, sir."

"Don't be bloody stupid. You've had a good career, you've a wife who loves you and two healthy children. Don't tell me I got it wrong back then."

"You just put it off a few years, sir. She'll be better off without me, I've not treated her right."

"You treated her right for nine years, Rory. What I don't understand is how the hell you could blame her for what was done to her by that bastard Vane."

281

Stewart turned away. "You don't understand..."

"Oh, yes, I do. I understand perfectly how it feels to know that the woman you love was abused by some bastard who thought he could do whatever he liked to her because nobody would stop him."

Stewart swung back. "And what did you do to him, sir?"

"I killed him."

"I seem to remember we cheered you for that. I'm going to get hanged."

"Don't say it, Rory."

"What does it matter, it's bloody obvious? They've all the evidence they need, they're going to find me guilty and hang me. They probably should. She can find another man, who'll be good to her and the brats. And she won't be looking over her shoulder to see if that bastard Vane is lurking behind every bush waiting to have another go at her. I killed him, and I know I was drunk, but I'm sober now, and I don't regret a thing."

Paul could think of nothing to say. He stood looking at his former sergeant in silence. Finally, Stewart's mouth twitched into an unexpected grin.

"You've not changed since you were twenty-one, sir. You're standing there and you've not listened to a word I just said, you're just turning over ways you might get me off in your head. You can't get me off, sir, and you shouldn't cause trouble trying. I'm glad you came to see me."

"So am I," Paul said. "Do you want to see Sally and the children?"

"No. It'll upset all of us. I've told the judge that I want the trial to go ahead as soon as he can. I've no witnesses..."

"You've one witness. I intend to stand as character witness, and you can't stop me."

"It won't make any difference, sir."

"Then let me do it."

Stewart did not speak for a moment, then he nodded. "All right, I'll tell the judge."

"You'll have to put it in writing, I'll do it for you, and you can sign it. Is there anybody else you want to see?"

Stewart was silent, staring at the ground. Finally he looked up. "Captain O'Reilly. But he's not back, is he? Do you think he's dead?"

"I don't know, Rory. But if he's not, and he gets back before your trial, I'll get him in here."

"Thank you, sir. That's about all you can do for me."

Paul found Anne waiting for him in their room on his return and he could see by her expression that she knew. She brought wine and knelt herself to help him off with his boots, then sat beside him on the bed as he drank. The wine did not help, and Paul set down the glass.

"How is he?"

"Resigned. Determined. Convinced he did the right thing. Did Sally know?"

"She guessed. Keren is with her at the moment and Teresa is keeping the children busy. Poor Sally. I'm wondering if I can persuade her to go back to England with the children when they leave. Katja says she could help to find her work, and she'd be close to her family."

"You mean after they hang Rory?"

Anne took his hand, leaned over, and kissed him. "They're going to find him guilty, Paul."

"I know. I was hoping he'd deny it, give me something to work with. But he did it, no question. There's no chance of a not-guilty verdict, the best we can hope for is mitigation of sentencing."

"Can they do that?"

"Oh, yes. I'm going to appear as character witness, and it's what I'll ask for. I can tell the story of what Vane did to Sally, and I can tell them it wasn't the first time he'd attacked a woman, but I can't call any witnesses to that, and…"

"What about Sally?"

"Do you think she would?"

"Yes." Anne gave a faint smile at his surprised expression. "Paul, she loves him. He's treated her appallingly, but she blames herself for some of that. She shouldn't, mind, but she does. I think if she's given the chance, she'd speak up and tell the truth."

"I'm not sure that she should, Nan, it could be bloody awful. I've no control over who sits on that jury and I've no control over what they'll ask her. They could question her about the rape and if they choose to be arseholes, they could easily imply that it wasn't rape at all, that she went with Vane for money or gifts and only cried rape when Rory found out. Some men will think that."

"Some men should be castrated at birth," Anne said, and Paul winced at her tone. "It will be up to Sally. I'll explain all that to her, but we cannot make that decision on her behalf, Paul, she is a grown woman."

Paul put his arm about her, drawing her close. "Ask her," he said.

"Can Rory refuse to accept her as a witness?"

"He probably could, but he isn't going to. I told him that I wanted to testify as a character witness and that I thought Carl might as well. He doesn't see the point of it, but he's signed a letter giving me permission to call whatever witnesses I like on his behalf."

Anne drew away from him, her face suddenly intent. "Anybody?"

"I suppose so, bonny lass, although it hardly matters, since there aren't any other witnesses. The prosecution are obliged to provide Rory with a list of their witnesses against him, to give him the chance to prepare any questions in his defence. He has to do the same, but he's authorised me to do that."

Anne's brows had drawn together, and she was clearly lost in thought. Finally, she said:

"I need to be clear on this, Paul. If there are any witnesses for the defence, Rory has to get up and question them?"

"Yes."

"And a witness for the prosecution, is questioned by the judge-advocate general?"

283

"Yes, although Rory can cross question them."

"And how does the judge-advocate find his witnesses?"

"I imagine White will give him a list. Nan, what are you up to?"

His wife leaned forward and kissed him fully on the lips. "What do you think?" she asked provocatively and slid her hand down his body. Paul shivered.

"I think you're trying to distract me from asking you any more questions," he said. "If you think you can seduce me into keeping quiet when I know you're planning something you don't want me to know…"

Anne stood up and swung one leg over so that she was sitting astride his lap. Reaching up, she withdrew the pins from her hair, one at a time, very deliberately. Paul watched her, fiercely aroused, and trying hard to pretend that he was not.

"Nan."

"Do you want to talk, General, or can I interest you in something else?"

"You're not getting away with this."

Anne was laughing. She reached behind her to the buttons of her gown, and Paul pushed her hands away and began to unbutton it. As he did so, she was moving against him, and Paul began to laugh with her. He put his hands on her waist, swung her over onto the bed and pulled the gown down her shoulders.

"Anne van Daan, if you get me cashiered for interfering in the justice system, I am going to murder you."

"No, you're not," Anne said. Her mouth was brushing his, and Paul kissed her for a long time, feeling her hands loosening his clothing. He moved finally so that he could lift her gown over her head, and Anne reached for the laces of her stays. Paul pushed her hands away and untied the laces, his eyes on hers.

"No, I'm not. I am however, about to make you very sorry for your complete lack of respect for my male authority."

Anne gave a peal of laughter and pulled her shift over her head. "I regret nothing" she said sweetly and held out her arms. Paul moved into them, his mouth finding hers again, and Stewart's resigned misery faded along with the rest of the world.

Chapter Nineteen

The journey to Oporto to deliver the children to the ship was a riotous affair and took Paul's mind off Rory Stewart's impending trial. Paul relieved Ross Mackenzie of his duties so that he could accompany his wife and children, and they made it a holiday. The older children rode for as long as they were allowed, before Anne bundled them into the big carriage or the baggage wagon. They camped at night, and sang songs around the fire, frightening night birds into flight with their laughter. This winter was the longest Paul had spent with his children for years, and the longest Anne had ever spent with them. The previous year, Paul had been surprised and touched at how quickly she had formed a bond with Grace, Francis, and Rowena, but during these few short months she had created a family. Paul knew that he was going to miss them desperately and savoured every moment, dreading the moment of parting. He was also painfully aware that there was a conversation he needed to have with Anne before they reached the *Lady Emma*, his father's merchant ship, which waited in Oporto to take them home.

They were two days from their destination, and the children had gone to bed earlier than usual, worn out by a long day in the fresh air. Anne settled Georgiana in her crib and joined Paul on the mattress. They lay together in quiet content for a while, then Anne pushed herself up onto one elbow and leaned over to kiss him gently, her dark hair tickling his face.

"What is it, General?"

Paul smiled. "I've been waiting for the question. I'm sure it's witchcraft, you always know."

"I know you."

Paul sat up. "I can't have this conversation lying down."

"You can't have it at all in this tent, we'll wake Georgy. Come outside, the fire hasn't died yet."

Paul pulled on shirt and trousers and Anne reached for her crimson velvet robe. The fire was low, and Paul added some wood from the pile the boys had collected earlier. Out of the corner of his eye, he saw Jenson duck back into his small tent.

"Paul?"

"Love, it occurs to me that we've not really talked about what you wanted to do this campaigning season."

"We have this conversation every year, Paul. Do we have to? You know that I'm going to stay."

Paul poked the fire into life and turned to study her lovely face in the flickering light. "At the beginning of this year, I thought you might give me a different answer."

Anne was silent for a long time. She was looking into the fire, and Paul watched her, trying hard to read her expression and trying even harder not to push her for an immediate answer. Finally she looked up.

"So did I, for a while. But it was only a few weeks. It took me a while to recover from Georgy's birth, and I did wonder if I might need to go home. But I just needed some time."

"I wondered if meeting Katja might make a difference."

"Well it would, if I'd needed to go. Their house is three miles from the barracks and five miles from Southwinds. If I ever did need to go home, we'd be neighbours, and that would make a big difference to me. I'm going to miss her."

"So am I. Look, Nan, when I was thinking about this a few months ago, when I was so worried about you, I did something. I've been steeling myself ever since to a confession, and I've put it off so long it's stupid."

Anne stared at him, wide-eyed. "Heavens, Paul, what on earth have you done?"

"I feel guilty, because we always take decisions together. I should probably have asked you...no, I should have asked you. But you seemed so fragile, and I've been so worried, and for a while I thought you'd want to leave and go home, but your only immediate choices were to go to my family or yours. And both would be difficult."

"What have you done, Paul?"

"I've bought a house."

Anne stared at him, her mouth hanging slightly open. Paul had seldom seen his self-possessed wife so completely astonished. After a long time, she said:

"You've bought a house?"

"Yes. It's an old house, and it's not in good repair, it's been neglected, although you could live in it and we can restore it. But it's three miles from barracks, and it's beautiful. It's an old Tudor mansion, red brick, with those twisting chimneys, and it has a long gallery and..."

"Paul, breathe, you're babbling. How did you even see this house? When? I don't understand."

"It was Rowena's family home. The Carletons had to sell, they've had financial troubles for years. I used to go there all the time as a boy. Rowena wasn't there then, but her cousins were, and our families were on friendly

286

terms. I always loved it. While we were in Madrid, my father wrote to me to tell me it was up for sale. I was tempted, but then we had the retreat and I did nothing until we were back, and you had Georgiana, and you were so unwell. In one of his letters arranging the children's visit, he told me they'd had no luck selling and had dropped the price. It was stupidly low, and I had this mad dream of living in that house with you one day. I should have asked you, but I was worried it would unsettle you, and I thought you'd say no."

Paul was relieved to see that she was smiling and she reached out to take both his hands in hers. "Paul van Daan, you sentimental fool. I'd no idea you were in love with a house."

"Nor had I, until I realised it could be mine."

Anne did not speak, and Paul realised there were tears in her eyes, but her smile was luminous. "You didn't have to tell me this now, Paul."

"Yes, I did. Because I wanted you to know that you have a choice. If you choose to leave, you don't have to live in somebody else's house. We have a home."

Anne leaned over to kiss him. "I'm longing to see it. I hope your father can find a reliable caretaker for a year or two, and I shall write to tell him that he is to ride over with the children when he can, so that they can choose their rooms. But I can wait. Nothing has changed, Paul, I want to be here, with you."

Paul could feel tears behind his eyes and he stopped trying to hide them. "Thank you. There are so many reasons why you should go, that I can't begin to list them, but you know that having you here…"

"I know where I belong, Paul. But thank you for telling me. Anne stood up and held out her hand. "Bed," she said firmly. "You're worse than the children, keeping me up half the night."

The convoy arrived in Oporto during the afternoon, and Paul was relieved to find that the *Lady Emma,* the Van Daan merchantman, was already in port and ready for passengers to board. It was difficult to say goodbye, but strangely this parting felt less permanent than the previous year. Paul watched Anne and Katja inspecting the tiny cabins that the children would share then went to speak to Captain Burrows, whom he had known since childhood.

There were tears at the end, and the older children lined up at the ship's rail to wave goodbye. Anne gave one last, long embrace to Katja Mackenzie.

"Write to me."

"I will write often, I promise, and we will spend much time with the children, so you will have extra news of them too."

"Thank you, Katja, for everything. I'm going to miss you so much."

"You also. Take care of my husband for me, he is not accustomed to managing without me any more."

Anne laughed. "I will. *Au revoir,* my dear, I hope it won't be too long."

"So do I. *Tot ziens*, my very good friend."

287

Paul stood with Anne and Ross watching the merchantman sail then went back to an elegant little hotel which had rebuilt after the depredations of the French and was much patronised by visiting English diplomats and army families. They stayed for two nights, breakfasting on a wrought iron balcony overlooking the harbour and eating dinner on the terrace in the warm air of early summer.

On the second day, Ross tactfully remained in the hotel to write letters and Paul walked with Anne through the winding streets of the town and visited the sites of the battle. They walked up to the convent of Mosteiro da Nossa Serra do Pilar where Wellington had set up his headquarters and Paul held her hand and described the battle, pointing out where the barges had crossed and where the artillery had been placed. They visited the imposing bulk of the Bishop's Seminary where Sir Edward Paget had lost an arm, leaving Paul briefly in command of the English forces. They went to the convent where Anne had worked alongside Dr Adam Norris tending the wounded, and Anne laughed at Paul as he led her to the exact spot in the garden where he had kissed her that day.

"You were kissing a married woman, General, you should be ashamed of the memory."

"I'm not, though," Paul said, and thought about it. "Perhaps I am, a little. Because of Rowena. Are you tired, bonny lass? We've walked for hours, but I thought we could go down to the river."

"Let's, it's our last day. I'm going to miss the children. Every time I say goodbye to them, my heart aches a little more."

Paul drew her close. "I'm sorry, Nan. Please God, we can see Bonaparte off this year and get home to them. Come on, let's walk back down to the river and then we'll go back and have dinner with Captain Mackenzie. I'd stay longer, but I need to be there for Rory's trial, God help him."

"We can travel faster without the children," Anne said. "Thank you, Paul, this has been lovely."

They walked over to the iron gate and Anne paused and looked back. "I grew up in these places," she said unexpectedly. "I was so young then."

"You're twenty-three, Nan, you're hardly a grandmother."

"No, I know. But this was the first time I'd seen men die."

Paul could not speak for a moment. Anne seemed to sense it and they stood silently hand in hand for a while, remembering some of the dead. Eventually, Anne said:

"I wonder how they'll remember them, in years to come? I wonder how this war will be written? I spent hours in my father's library as a girl, reading volumes of history and I never really thought about all those dead. That they all had wives or sweethearts or parents or children to mourn them. Is that how this will be in a few years' time?"

"Yes," Paul said honestly. "Apart from those of us who knew them."

"I'm never going to forget," Anne said. "There are faces I remember, even though I can't remember their names. Even if I never knew their names."

Paul cleared his throat. "I remember the face of the man who shot me at Talavera," he said.

"Do you?"

"As clearly as I see you. I often wonder if he's still alive."

Anne moved closer and Paul put his arm about her. They stood in the gathering dusk until it was too dark for a river walk, and the dead stood with them. Eventually the cork oak trees in the little garden were only outlines against the sky, and stars peeped between their branches alongside a clear half-moon. Paul bent to kiss his wife and was not surprised to find her cheeks wet with silent tears. She leaned into him and Paul held her for a long time. Finally he took her hand again and they left the garden, carefully latching the iron gate behind them.

Paul and Anne rose later than he had intended, and by the time they walked down to the stables, the sun was already warm. Ross Mackenzie was there with Jenson, giving instructions to the Portuguese grooms who were hitching up the carriage and baggage wagon. There was a tavern opposite, with benches and tables outside, and the smell of food drifted over to them, making Paul's stomach growl hopefully.

"Let's eat first," he said on impulse. "It will mean we can travel further without stopping. Jenson, I'll send somebody over with food for you and the drivers."

"Yes, sir."

They crossed the wide baked earth street. A woman emerged, bustling and smiling, and Paul chose a table and ordered cured ham and spiced sausage and fresh bread. Anne sat opposite Ross, fanning herself as Paul gave instructions for breakfast to be taken to Jenson and the drivers and grooms, and as he finished giving the order, he heard a voice from the dark interior of the tavern, ordering food. The voice spoke easy, fluent Spanish, but Paul would have recognised it anywhere.

Paul froze, halfway through a sentence, staring at the dim doorway then took three long strides towards the door, and stopped dead as Michael emerged, blinking in the sunlight. Michael stopped as well, and they stood staring at each other.

"Michael."

"Paul."

Paul stepped forward and embraced his friend, feeling with some shock how thin he had become. Michael held him close and Paul felt his throat tight with tears. He had been refusing to admit to himself how terrified he had been that he would never see this man again.

"You bloody Irish bastard, don't you ever do this to me again. Where the fuck have you been?"

Michael did not reply and Paul held him at arm's length and studied him. "That bad?"

"A bit worse, to be honest."

"Giles?"

289

"He's here, upstairs in the room. And Brat made it, but we lost Antonio."

"Oh Christ, I'm sorry, Michael. Poor Giles, I know they were close. Come and join us for breakfast, I'm here with Nan and Ross Mackenzie, we've just said goodbye to the children. How long have you been here?"

"Two days. We're struggling to hire horses for the return journey, there are none to be had."

"If there's a spare mount in Spain or Portugal I'll be surprised, the army has bought up the lot, but you're in luck. We brought pack ponies for the children to ride, and Nan's carriage for the children. Let me speak to Jenson, he can tell the hotel we're staying an extra night, it will give you a chance to get organised and you can travel back with us."

"That's a relief, I was getting a bit desperate."

"Is Brat all right? I can't believe she followed you again."

"She's well, but she's exhausted. Giles is...I'm struggling to get much out of him at the moment. I doubt he'll come down, but Brat will eat at any time, I'll call her. Look, sir - a lot has happened these past months, and I can't tell you all of it in ten minutes."

"You don't need to, Michael."

"No, but Brat...you'll notice a difference in the way she is."

Paul looked at him steadily and Michael did not look away. "I'm not sure what you're telling me, Captain, but let's not worry about it just now, we're not going to put the girl to the blush, I'm just thankful you're in one piece. Come and greet my lady, she's over there being tactful."

Brat appeared while Michael was speaking to Anne and Ross, giving a brief explanation of his presence. She looked startled, but joined them without hesitation, giving a little bow. Like Michael, she looked thinner, the dark clothing stained and torn and shabby, her red-gold curls tied back from a pale, memorable face that was all woman and held little of the girl Paul remembered in Madrid.

"I'm glad you're safe, lass," Paul said. "We were worried."

"I am sorry. I should not have left without telling you, General, or without thanking you for your kindness, Señora."

"It doesn't matter, Brat, I'm just glad you're here," Anne said. "Is Giles not coming down?"

"I will take some food up to him," Brat said. "He is not good, just yet, with people."

Ross got up. "I'll do it," he said.

"I don't think he'll..."

"Yes, he will, Captain O'Reilly," Ross said, calmly filling a plate. "I won't be long."

***

Giles watched the group around the table from his bedroom window, smiling a little as Brat sat down beside Anne van Daan without apparent embarrassment and began to eat. He wondered what they would make of this new, confident Brat. He was still getting used to her himself, and he had been there to watch it happen, to see her shake off, finally, the horror of her early experiences and emerge as an intelligent, clear-sighted young woman with a mind of her own. Giles thought that from what he knew of Anne van Daan, she would approve of the changes although he also thought it would not take long for her to also notice the tension between Brat and her erstwhile employer. That situation would have to be resolved at some point and Giles had no idea which way it would go.

There was a knock on the door and Giles turned to find Ross Mackenzie entering with a plate of food and two tankards of ale on a tray. The sight of it made Giles feel slightly nauseous. Ross set the tray on the table and stood looking at him.

"Welcome back, Giles. Come and eat. I'm so sorry about Antonio, Captain O'Reilly just told us. How did he die?"

The straightforward question brought tears again, but it was also a relief. Giles went forward and took Ross's outstretched hand. He had not thought he wanted to see anybody, let alone eat with them, but now that Ross was here, Giles was very glad. He had always liked Ross Mackenzie enormously, and their friendship, begun in the misery of Walcheren, had withstood separation and the long silences that Giles' job made necessary. Giles had steeled himself to face his fellow officers, and the inevitable questions and condolences, but it was never difficult to talk to this reserved Scot who had experienced losses of his own.

"It was during the French storming of the town. We were in the castle, waiting for the navy to bring us off, but we could hear what they were doing to the townspeople. Antonio had developed a bit of a thing with the widow we were billeted on and went back to find her and her daughter. They were all dead when we found them."

"Christ, I'm sorry, Giles, it sounds bloody awful. Thank God you got out."

"We almost didn't," Giles said, sitting down at the table and reaching for the ale. "You wouldn't believe it, Ross, but the last boats that came back for us were from the *Iris*. Durrell picked us up from the beach, as calm as you like."

Ross laughed aloud. "Really. I bet that was an extremely efficient evacuation."

"Perfectly executed," Giles said gravely, and suddenly he was able to laugh. "Jesus, Ross, it's good to see you. What on earth are you doing here?"

Ross seated himself opposite and picked up his tankard. "Saying goodbye to my family," he said. "It was very difficult, you're a useful distraction. Talk to me, Captain Fenwick, we've a lot of catching up to do, but you don't have to do it all in one day, you're travelling back with us. Tell me about Lieutenant Durrell."

291

Giles was unexpectedly hungry. He reached for a piece of bread, laid a slice of sausage on top of it and took a bite. "I might start at the beginning, actually."

"Even better," Ross said, and leaned back as Giles began to talk.

***

The general court martial of Private Rory Stewart was held in the municipal building in Castelo Bom, an echoing stone chamber which had once been part of the castle complex. Most of the castle was in ruins now, its final destruction being completed by the French during their invasion, but there were still some rooms intact. Furniture had been brought in, and a long trestle table stretched the width of the room to accommodate the thirteen officers of the bench, with a smaller table and chair for the deputy judge-advocate, who would prosecute the case. There was no other seating; members of the public who wished to attend the trial would have to provide their own seats or stand.

Paul stood in the doorway beside Johnny and Carl, watching a Portuguese boy sweeping the floor of the empty chamber

"Does this remind you of your court martial in London?"

Paul gave a twisted smile. "This is not exactly the Chelsea Royal Hospital, Johnny, but it does bring back memories. I thought my career was over that week, but at least they were never going to hang me."

"Do you think they'll hang Stewart?" Carl asked.

"I've never known a man to be convicted of murder before a GCM and not be hanged, and they're going to convict him. I'm prepared for the worst, Johnny. The best I can hope for is that they'll take his previous good character into account, and commute the sentence to a flogging or transportation. I'll speak for his character and you can do the same, but it's all we can do."

"How is Michael?" Carl asked.

"God knows. He's been through hell and he comes back to find one of his oldest friends about to face a murder trial. He's been to see Stewart a few times, and he was very upset. Nan's been spending some time with him and I think talking to her helped."

"I'm surprised Michael didn't want to volunteer as a character witness."

"He did, but he was concerned his history in the ranks might have met with some prejudice on the bench."

"Your pardon, gentlemen, but the courtroom must be cleared now, unless you have business with this court."

Paul turned and acknowledged the salute of a very young lieutenant. "We're here as character witnesses for Private Stewart, Lieutenant. Where should we wait?"

"Mr Larpent has arranged a separate room for the officers, with refreshments."

"The day is looking better," Johnny said as they left the courtroom. "Did you get refreshments last time, sir?"

"I don't remember, it's a bit of a blur. You all have a nasty gleam in your eye when you remind me that I was once court-martialled, you know that, don't you?"

"It's because we'd all been predicting it for years," Carl said.

The lieutenant ushered them into a brick built store which had been cleaned, but still smelled strongly of goats. Several rickety wooden tables and chairs were scattered about, and two officers sporting the blue-green facings of the 73rd sat at one, drinking ale. They both rose quickly, saluting, and Paul responded.

"I'm guessing there is more than one trial today, Lieutenant?"

"Three, sir. I'm afraid that Private Stewart's trial will be the last."

"Is there a reason we can't sit in on those trials, as we're not witnesses?" Paul asked.

"I suppose not, sir, as long as you're back here ready to be called when the time comes. I could arrange for some chairs."

"Would you mind, Lieutenant? My wife will be joining us."

The young officer looked appalled. "Yes, sir. Although...might not be suitable for a lady, sir. Some of the matters discussed..."

Johnny made a strangled choking sound and Paul gave him a look. "Thank you, Lieutenant. If necessary, I can always escort her out."

"I'd like to see you try," Johnny said, as four wooden chairs were arranged in the public area.

"She's more likely to escort me out. Ah there you are, girl of my heart. Come and join us, we have privileged seating, which is good, because I predict a long day."

Paul's prediction proved accurate. The first case, involving an officer of the 73rd involved an incident which had happened during the previous year's retreat. Lieutenant McTavish pleaded not guilty to charges involving dereliction of duty and showing disrespect to a senior officer. McTavish was a solid young man with a receding hairline and a bad tempered expression, who watched the lengthy swearing in of the thirteen members of the board as though he wished he had a pistol to hand.

When the charges were read, Larpent called his first witness, and Paul listened with increasing irritation to a lengthy series of complaints about pickets not being sent out, men not being disciplined for minor offences and McTavish speaking disrespectfully to a senior officer.

The charges against McTavish seemed largely based on the evidence of his company captain, a vague-looking gentleman with exquisitely styled hair and a slight lisp. Paul, who was prepared to be bored, found his interest caught, and he leaned forward, studying the expressions of Captain Hall and the other two witnesses, both young ensigns from the same company.

"They're lying," he said very softly.

"I agree," Anne said. "I wonder what poor Mr McTavish did to offend his captain?"

293

With the case for the prosecution completed, McTavish rose and called his own witnesses. They came nervously, uncertain in the formal courtroom, one after the other, three privates, a corporal, a sergeant and two Portuguese muleteers and the story they told was very different to that of Captain Hall. Their descriptions of the misery of the retreat, and of the breakdown in discipline among the troops rang true to Paul, and their responses to McTavish's questions were consistent without sounding overly rehearsed. They told a story of an officer trying desperately to hold his men together, harried by the French with no provisions or shelter, on bad roads in appalling weather conditions. At the end of each man's testimony, McTavish asked the same question.

"Where was Captain Hall when this happened, Private?"

"Don't know, sir."

"Did you see Captain Hall at this time, Corporal?"

"No, sir."

"What about Mr Jordan or Mr Kyle?"

"I don't know, sir."

Larpent rose to cross-question the men but could not shake them, and the solid weight of their combined testimony was impressive. There was a break while the board retired to consider its verdict, and Paul went in search of a clerk who could provide pen and paper. He returned to his seat as the board reappeared after only half an hour.

"What were you doing, sir?" Johnny asked.

"I wanted to write a note to McTavish. I've invited him to dinner, girl of my heart, I hope you don't mind. I'd like a chat with him."

"What if he's convicted, Paul?"

"They're not going to convict him, Sir Lowry Cole is a man with a brain and he's going to see straight through that pile of bullshit as quickly as I did and I hope Captain Hall and his acolytes get the bollocking they richly deserve. We're still a lieutenant short in the third company under Captain Harker and I thought McTavish might be interested in a transfer. Something tells me he'd do well with Harker and Dodd. At least this one's over quickly. They might get to Stewart this afternoon, but I doubt it somehow, I think we'll be back here tomorrow."

The second trial was more complex and before it began, Lieutenant Calloway approached Paul with an expression of agonised embarrassment and asked for a private word. Paul complied, then returned to Anne, Carl and Johnny, fighting to keep his face straight, and beckoned for them to join him.

"We are going to have to miss this one," he said. "It's all right though, Calloway tells me Stewart's case definitely won't come up until tomorrow, so we'll come back then."

"What is it, Paul?"

"Sodomy," Paul said apologetically. "It would appear one of the assistant deputy quartermasters has an extremely close friendship with his Portuguese clerk and somebody has reported it. The officers on the board have observed your presence, bonny lass - in fact, Captain Clarkson couldn't stop

294

staring at you, he can't have heard most of the evidence in that last case - and are concerned that having a lady in the room will make it difficult for all the evidence to be heard."

"What utter nonsense," Anne said irritably. "What difference can it possibly make?"

"They don't know you the way I do, love, they probably think they can shock you. Hold on a moment, there's McTavish. I want to congratulate him on his acquittal."

He returned within a few minute. "He'll be joining us at dinner on Thursday. He's a bit bewildered, poor lad, but he almost took my arm off at the whiff of a transfer, he knows bloody well he's going to be ostracised in the mess after this."

"I'm dying to know what really happened," Johnny said.

"We'll find out on Thursday, but I am willing to make a small wager, Colonel Wheeler, that McTavish was working his arse off to keep his men together and get them back in one piece while Captain Hall and the other officers were nowhere to be seen, having abandoned their company to get themselves to safety. They were trying to hang him out to dry in case he did the same to them. Every one of those witnesses who spoke for him, described a bloody good officer, and if the 73rd doesn't appreciate him, the 110th will. Come on, let's get home. I'm dreading tomorrow, I wish it was over with."

***

At eleven o'clock the following morning, the assistant deputy quartermaster was found not guilty of unnatural practices due to lack of evidence, and Michael O'Reilly seated himself in the courtroom beside his general's wife. There were a few more officers present, either from the 115th or the 110th and a small group of Portuguese officers standing at the back.

Stewart looked better than when Michael had seen him in the gaol. Somebody had provided him with clean clothing, his red jacket had been brushed and his hair was neatly tied. He looked pale and tired and older than his forty years and Michael's heart ached for him.

The door opened to admit Judge-Advocate General Larpent followed by the thirteen members of the court. Larpent bore the warrant for holding the court and as the members of the bench took their seats along the table, he said:

"Private Rory Stewart, step forward to the bar."

Stewart did so, saluting. Michael wondered if he had been told what to do in advance. Even in this dusty castle chamber, the court was intimidating.

"Private Stewart, have you any objection to any of the General Officers now appearing to serve on this court?"

"No, sir."

"Very well, as the members are already sworn in, I shall read the charges against you and when they are read, I shall ask you whether you are guilty or not guilty of the matter of accusation. Do you understand?"

"Yes, sir."

295

"Very good. The charges are as follows."

Cloaked in the formal wording of the court, the charge sounded ominous, and the word 'murder' seemed to hang in the air when it was spoken. Stewart's expression did not change.

"How do you plead, Private Stewart?"

"Not guilty, sir."

With the formalities out of the way, the court was seated. Stewart remained standing at the bar as Larpent moved to his table to collect his notes and began his statement for the prosecution. The deputy judge-advocate had a nasal voice, but it was very clear, as he recounted the events surrounding Vane's death. The prosecution stated that Major Vane had been out riding when he had come across Stewart, vilely drunk after a visit to a tavern, sleeping off his excesses under a tree. Vane had dismounted to speak to Stewart, and recognising him, had told him to get himself back to barracks and threatened him with a flogging. Mention was made of Stewart's known propensity for violence when he was drunk, and Larpent suggested that as Vane had turned his back to return to his horse, Stewart had attacked him while he was defenceless and cut him down.

It was a dramatic story and Larpent told it well. Michael wondered how much of it could be proved. He knew no details of the case and was not aware that Stewart was mounting much of a defence at all, other than his commanding officers' character testimony. Nobody could possibly be sure what had happened on that dark evening between Vane and Stewart, but Michael presumed that the prosecution had some evidence that he was unaware of.

With the prosecution case set out, Larpent called his first witness, one of the officers of the 115th who gave evidence about the day that Vane had gone missing.

"Were you surprised when Major Vane did not return, Lieutenant?"

"Not really, sir. We were under the impression he was away for a few days, probably to Ciudad Rodrigo."

"Thank you, Lieutenant. Do you have any questions, Private Stewart."

Stewart got to his feet. "Yes, sir."

Michael leaned forward in astonishment, he had not expected Stewart to say much at all. Stewart's Scottish accent sounded harsh in the echoing courtroom but his voice was surprisingly steady.

"Had Major Vane leave of absence, sir?"

The lieutenant appeared temporarily bereft of speech and Michael wanted to laugh aloud. The man had probably never been questioned by an enlisted man in his life, but here, in this courtroom, Stewart had the right to mount his own defence, although Michael suspected that nobody had expected him to do so.

"I don't know, Private. He didn't tell me."

"Had Major Vane gone off without telling you before?"

"Now look here, Stewart. You can't..."

"I'm afraid he can, Lieutenant Martin," Larpent said, apologetically.

Martin paused. Eventually, he said shortly:

"A few times."

"Do you know what he did in Ciudad Rodrigo on these visits?"

"How the devil should I know, man? What does a man do?"

"Was he visiting the brothel?"

There was a collective intake of breath around the court. Michael glanced sideways at his general's wife. Anne wore an expression of pure innocence, her eyes modestly lowered and her hands neatly folded in her lap. Michael had never, since his first meeting with her, seen Anne van Daan look so demure, and he felt a leap of immediate suspicion although he had no idea why.

"I could not say, Private Stewart. And I think it a dashed impertinent question."

"Thank you, sir. No more questions."

There were more witnesses, as the story of Vane's movements, and those of Private Stewart unfolded. Eventually, Captain White was called. Michael had heard about White's investigation from Leo Manson, and he listened to White's testimony with growing gloom. White was fluent and precise in his testimony, and his description of the state of Stewart's bloodstained clothing was damning.

"The court calls Lieutenant-Colonel Carl Swanson."

Under Larpent's questioning, Carl gave a straightforward account of his late night rescue of Stewart and of the condition he had been in. Carl answered calmly and did not volunteer any unnecessary information, and Stewart did not ask any questions.

"The court calls Private Rory Stewart."

Michael felt slightly sick. Stewart walked to the stand and took the oath and Larpent began his questioning. Once again, Michael was surprised at Stewart's calm demeanour. For a man on trial for his life, the Scot displayed very little emotion, answering Larpent's questions simply. He admitted to being very drunk, and having been turned away from the local inn, had walked to the next village, to the alehouse, where he had drunk for another hour before being ejected. It was late and he was tired, and eventually he remembered sitting beneath an oak tree to rest and then falling asleep.

"What woke you?"

"Major Vane, sir. He kicked me in the stomach."

"To rouse you?"

"To hurt me, I think, sir. He was like that."

"Did you quarrel?"

"I don't remember much, sir, I was very drunk. I think the major was shouting at me, telling me he was going to put me on a charge, for drinking and for being out of camp. I tried to walk away, but he kept hitting me."

"You are saying that the major struck you?"

"More than once, sir. I fell down again, being not yet sober, and he kicked me in the ribs over and over, I was a mass of bruises the next day."

"Is that why you attacked him?"

297

"No, sir."

"Did you attack him?"

"I think so, sir."

"You think so?"

"I don't fully remember what I did, sir. I'd be lying if I said so, and I won't lie on oath, so close to my end as I might be. But I think I went for him when he spoke of my wife."

"Your wife?"

"Aye, Sally. It's why I'd been drinking so much, sir. We'd quarrelled, and she left me, and she had the right of it, for I hit her more than once. I was wrong and I know it, but I was mad with jealousy. She'd been with him, you see, sir, and I got to know of it. I couldn't stand to think on it. She tried to tell me he gave her no choice, but I didn't listen then. When he started on about her, saying things no man should hear of his wife, I lost my mind, sir. I know I struck out. I don't remember exactly what I did."

"Major Vane was stabbed three times, Stewart. Did you do that?"

"I don't know, sir."

"Did you carry a knife?"

"I'd my bayonet, sir."

"You don't remember stabbing him?"

"No, sir."

"What happened then."

"I must have staggered away, then I passed out again. Next I remember, Colonel Swanson and Ned Browning were hauling me up into a cart."

Afternoon shadows were beginning to stretch across the stone floor, and Michael was growing sleepy with the warmth of the courtroom. Stewart was sent back to his place, and there was a brief consultation among the bench, before Larpent stepped forward.

"That concludes the case for the prosecution. The court will adjourn and hear witnesses for the defence tomorrow."

Michael groaned softly as the bench filed out. "The general will have a seizure, so he will. There's only two character witnesses, surely they could have fit those in?"

"The officers of the bench require their dinner, Captain. As do I, I'm famished," Anne said serenely. "Let's go and find Paul and the others. Poor Rory, it must be far worse for him."

Michael glanced at her. "I'm surprised Sally isn't here," he said quietly. "Whatever he's done to her, they used to be devoted."

Anne turned her head and gave him a long, thoughtful look. "Keep your speculation to yourself for another day, will you, Michael? There isn't the least need for the general to get excited unnecessarily."

"Are you keeping something from your husband, ma'am?"

"If I were, Captain O'Reilly, it would be for a very good reason. Look at me. Do you trust me?"

Michael met steady dark eyes. "Yes."

298

"Good. Then let us go home for dinner. I am glad you're back, Michael, I've been worried about you."

***

Paul was the first witness called the following morning. He gave a brief summary of Rory Stewart's army career, a testimony to his excellent service, and expressed the hope that the bench would take these into account when arriving at their decisions. Paul had asked Michael for an account of the previous day's proceedings and it seemed clear that Stewart was going to be convicted. The best hope was that the bench would commute the death sentence.

Paul had requested and obtained permission to watch the rest of the trial, since he would have no further involvement in it. He listened to Johnny's character testimony, which echoed much of what Paul had said. Johnny joined him at the back of the court and Michael rose to give up his chair. Paul sat beside Anne and took her hand. She had spent a long time with Sally Stewart the previous evening, and had been unusually quiet when she returned, so Paul guessed she was upset.

"Are you ready to call your next witness, Private Stewart?"

Paul glanced over at Johnny, surprised. He had been unaware of any other witnesses for the defence and could not imagine who it might be.

"The court calls Mrs Sarah Stewart."

There was a rustle of interest around the court and Paul sat very still, staring at the bench as a large number of unrelated incidents fell into place in his mind. Sally walked to the bar. She looked the picture of respectability in a gown that he recognised as belonging to Keren, with her hair neatly dressed. Larpent came forward to administer the oath. Paul suddenly very aware of Anne sitting beside him. He turned his head to look at her and was not surprised to find that she was regarding him steadily, her lovely face grave.

"Do I need to worry, girl of my heart?" he asked, very softly.

"No, Paul. Forgive me, but in your position, I couldn't involve you."

Larpent returned to his table and Stewart stepped forward. "Sally."

"Rory."

"Are you all right, lassie?"

"Aye, I'm well enough."

"I need to ask some hard questions, Sal."

"I know. Ask and I'll answer."

"Thank you, lassie. Will you tell them what happened to you with Major Vane, if you can bear it?"

Sally took a deep breath and looked over at Anne. Paul saw his wife nod her head encouragingly. Several members of the bench were leaning forward, suddenly interested in a trial which had looked like a formality moments ago. Paul was beginning to have an inkling of what was happening. He reached out and took Anne's hand and squeezed it slightly. She returned the pressure, her eyes on Sally.

299

"I'd seen Major Vane about, since he took over the 115th, but there was a day when I was called to help one of the women with the 112th with her birthing. It went on late into the night, and I should have stayed, but I wanted to get back and I'd a lantern with me so I walked.

"Major Vane was riding back from the village and he got off his horse when he saw me. He was asking me all these questions, and I answered civil like, he was an officer, so I was polite. Then he asked if I was a whore…begging these gentlemen's pardon for the use of such a word. I told him no. He refused to believe me, and he said the men had been complaining of a lot of thievery from the camp followers, and that I should go with him and he'd call the provost on me.

"I went, husband. The assistant provost knows me and you both, he'd know it was nothing, it was easier than arguing. There's that old cottage that the duty officers sometimes used. Major Vane hadn't changed billets at that point, and I thought it was odd, him taking me there, it was empty. He was acting strange, he offered me wine and I refused. He asked me about you and then he said he'd give me money to go to bed with him. I told him no, that I was a good and faithful wife. He argued for a bit, trying to persuade me. When I tried to leave, he took hold of me and dragged me into the bedroom. I fought him, but he was very strong. He pushed me down and he forced himself on me."

The shocked silence in the courtroom went on for more than a minute. Paul could feel Anne's hand tense in his, and he knew that Sally's story would bring back painful memories of Anne's own ordeal at the hands of a French colonel the previous year. Out of the corner of his eye, Paul saw Lieutenant Calloway moving forward, his eyes on Anne. Paul shook his head firmly, putting his arm around Anne. Calloway hesitated, clearly longing to remove Anne from the court.

"Mr Calloway, what are you doing?" Sir Lowry Cole said sharply, from the bench.

"Forgive me, sir, there is a lady in the courtroom, and this is not suitable…"

"Sally is my maidservant, Sir Lowry, and I have already heard this story. I would like to remain to offer my support."

Cole bowed. "If Mrs van Daan's husband has no objection, Mr Calloway, it is not for me to insist. Please continue, Mrs Stewart. Would you like a chair, this must be very distressing for you?"

There was a pause while a wooden chair was brought from the ante-room. Paul looked at his wife again. Anne's eyes were modestly lowered, but he had seen a flash of triumph. The chair was a step in the right direction and she knew it.

Sally was seated and given a glass of water. Stewart stood watching her, and Paul felt his throat tighten at the expression in the Scotsman's dark eyes. All the emotion he had failed to show during the prosecution case was plain to see now; he looked at Sally as though she was the only person in the room, and Paul was filled with impotent fury at having known nothing about any of this. He prided himself on being accessible to his men, but he felt that his frequent absences and then the presence of his children through the winter had made him unavailable when it mattered.

"Carry on, Sal. In your own time, girl."

"When he'd done with me, I was lying there crying. He put some money down on the bed, next to my face. He told me he'd see me again the following week. I sat up and picked up the money and threw it at him. I said I'd report him and he laughed at me. He said that nobody would care, that he was an officer, with friends in high places, and that if I told anybody about it, he'd go after you and make sure you ended up on a charge. He said he'd been told you'd got a fiery temper, and that he was sure he could provoke you into hitting him, and he reminded me that striking an officer, would be a death sentence."

The silence in the room was absolute. Sally was crying, blotting her tears with a white handkerchief, her voice choked with tears. Her husband had no handkerchief, and was wiping his own tears with his hand.

"Oh, lass…"

"Rory, I'm sorry. I ought to have told you. I was afeared of what you'd do, but it made you think I'd done it willingly, when you found out. I'm so sorry."

"Hush, lassie, it's all right. It was my fault, I should never have doubted you. It's all right, now."

There was a long silence, then Larpent stepped forward. "I have a question or two, Mrs Stewart."

"Yes, sir."

"How did your husband find out?"

"One of the lads told him. Major Vane had boasted about it in his cups and word gets around in camp. Rory thought I'd lain with him willingly. He was furious and we quarrelled. It's when he started drinking, sir, and the drink never sits well with my man. I ought to have told somebody, I know, but I thought I wouldn't be believed."

"Are you telling the truth now, Mrs Stewart? This is a very serious accusation against the reputation of a deceased officer. Major Vane was a gentleman."

"Major Vane wasn't no gentleman," Sally said bitterly. "Major Vane was an animal."

Larpent stepped back. "No further questions, Mrs Stewart. You may withdraw."

As Sally left, her face hidden behind her handkerchief, Paul looked down at Anne. "Do you want to go to her, love?"

"No. It's all right, Teresa is waiting, she'll take care of her. I need to be here."

Paul studied his wife's face, and understood that there was more, although he could not imagine what. "Nan, are there more witnesses?"

"Yes."

"Who…" Paul broke off as Larpent cleared his throat.

301

"The court calls Señora Tasia Ronaldo."

Chapter Twenty

Paul turned to stare in surprise as Señor Rivero's daughter walked into the courtroom. Tasia wore black, her head modestly covered with a lace scarf, and she kept her eyes lowered as she took the oath. When she looked up, she looked directly at Anne, and Paul saw his wife's lips curve into a little smile of reassurance.

"Mrs Ronaldo, I thank you for agreeing to come here today," Stewart said awkwardly. "Will you tell the court about Major Vane?"

Tasia told her story. She was very nervous, stumbling over the words, and her embarrassment as she described Vane's behaviour and the things he had said to her was agonising to watch. Stewart asked no questions, simply allowed her to tell her story. Paul watched with deep appreciation. He had absolutely no doubt as to who had arranged for these women to come forward, and coached Stewart, via his wife, in how to manage the questioning.

At the end of Tasia's story, Stewart said:

"Mrs Ronaldo, thank you for being so brave. I know my wife asked you to do this. Why did you agree?"

"Mrs Stewart said that she feared you had fought with Major Vane because you discovered that he raped her, Private, but she was afraid that she would not be believed, that these officers would think you had murdered a good man. I wanted to say that this was not a good man, he was a wicked man, who liked to hurt and humiliate women. I did not tell anybody what Major Vane had done to me, because I was afraid that my husband or my brothers would challenge him and kill him and then they would be on trial as you are. It is wrong."

"Thank you, ma'am."

Larpent rose, and Paul thought he looked shaken for the first time during the trial. "No questions, Señora. Thank you. The court calls Señorita Maria Callas."

The Rivero's maidservant was a slight fair haired girl of fifteen and she broke down sobbing during her account of Vane's assault. Water was brought and haltingly, Maria got through her story. Stewart asked no questions and Larpent seemed relieved to have the weeping girl escorted from the room.

303

For the first time, Paul was beginning to hope. He glanced again at his wife. The lovely face was serene, but Anne's hands, neatly folded in her lap, were clenched in sheer fury. Paul reached out and put his hand over hers.

"Breathe, girl of my heart. If Rory Stewart survives this, it is going to be down to you," he whispered.

"No, Paul. It's going to be down to them. These women. Their courage humbles me."

"Your courage has always humbled me."

"The court calls Mrs Carl Swanson."

Paul looked up sharply, then turned to search for Carl at the back of the court. He could tell instantly that Carl was as shocked as he was. Paul looked at Anne.

"Nan, you shouldn't have."

Anne's eyes were dark pools of anger raised to his. "I shouldn't have?" she hissed. "Do you think I made any one of them do this, Paul? They are adult women. They made their own choices."

Keren took the oath, the warm rounded tones of her Cornish accent sounding pleasantly mellow after poor Maria's sobbing distress. Stewart stepped forward, looking embarrassed and Keren gave him a warm smile.

"Mrs Swanson, it's good of you to do this, I hope the colonel willna mind."

"My husband fully supports me in everything, Private. Do you want me to tell you about Major Vane?"

"If you would, ma'am."

Paul listened in growing anger, as Keren recounted a dozen incidents of Vane's behaviour. Her voice was clear, and at times angry, and when she told the story of having trodden the unwanted necklace into the dung heap, Paul heard a distinct snigger, hastily suppressed, from somewhere behind him. Sir Lowry glared at the miscreant.

When Keren's tale was done, she stood quietly, hands folded and Stewart gave an awkward bow. "Thank you, ma'am. No questions."

"I have some questions, Mrs Swanson," Larpent said, getting to his feet. "But before I do so, I should ask, since it is not at all clear, if you have your husband's permission to be doing this? The nature of your testimony, forgive me, is such…"

"If the court will give me leave, I'm probably the best person to answer that," Carl said, and heads turned as he walked forward, saluting gravely to the bench. "Forgive my interruption, Mr Larpent, but as a previous witness, I imagine my oath holds until the court is dismissed. My wife has my full approval. Not that she requires it."

There was warmth in his voice, and Keren's answering smile caused several of the bench to smile as well. "I wasn't married when these events occurred, sir, or I would have taken my troubles to Colonel Swanson. As it was, when he discovered, he spoke to Major Vane as did Colonel Wheeler and the matter was resolved. It has been much easier for me, married to an officer. Poor Mrs Stewart has no such protection, and her husband no right to defend her honour. Her suffering made me determined to come forward, whatever the cost."

Larpent had his mouth open to ask a question but he closed it abruptly again. Paul wondered what he had been going to say. The cost to Keren's reputation might still be dear, but it was clear that Larpent had decided against challenging her position. Paul did not blame him. The combination of Carl's protective demeanour and Keren's winsome charm was very obviously causing one or two of the bench to experience an attack of sentimentality and Larpent would not help the prosecution by causing her further distress. Larpent bowed and dismissed the witness and Paul looked at his wife, and once again wondered if it was witchcraft.

"The court calls Captain Zachariah White."

White came into court, saluted smartly, and eyed Stewart with a combination of exasperation and admiration which made Paul want to laugh aloud. He knew that Leo Manson was developing a cautious friendship with the young captain from the Staff Cavalry Corps and Paul had considerable faith in Manson's judgement.

"Captain White, did you receive a report at the beginning of April, about some robberies on the road between Freineda and Castelo Bom?"

White stared blankly at Stewart. "I did, Private, although I don't know how you heard about it. Two local villagers complained that they'd been attacked and robbed by three soldiers. I am still investigating."

"Was anybody hurt, sir?"

"Yes," White said briefly. He clearly understood, and had no intention of trying to avoid the questions. "One of the farmers was stabbed in the chest when he resisted. He survived."

"Thank you, sir, I don't have any more questions."

White left. As he did so, Paul saw him glance over to where Leo Manson was standing with Carlyon and Witham. Manson shot him an apologetic grin and White shook his head and disappeared through the door.

"The court calls Dr Justin Fielding."

Fielding came into court, a willowy young man with a gentle expression and a deep voice which did not match his appearance. Paul was watching Stewart in some concern. He knew exactly how draining this experience was, and six years earlier, Paul had been defending his career and his reputation but not his life. He was astonished at how well Stewart had conducted himself, and it had given him a lot of information about Michael's dour Scottish former sergeant who had capabilities that Paul had not realised,

"Dr Fielding, I only have a couple of questions," Stewart said apologetically. "I was told it was you who looked at Major Vane's body."

"I did, Private."

"I think you wrote a letter to Lieutenant-Colonel Scovell about the wounds, and you also said what you thought to Mrs van Daan. Before I was arrested, forbye."

"That's right."

"What did you think made the wounds?"

"At the time I thought they were made by a knife."

"Did you change your mind?"

"I was asked later on if a bayonet could have made them. I said possibly."

"But you first thought of a knife."

"I did. It looked as though the murderer tried to slash the throat, and that's not usual with a bayonet. But it's impossible to be sure. I'm sorry, Private."

"That's all right, sir. I'm not sure either."

There was a rustle among the bench and Paul leaned forward, his eyes on the Scot. He knew that Anne, probably through Sally, had coached Stewart throughout this trial, but that response had been his own, and it Paul could see its effect on Cole and some of the others.

Fielding was the last witness, and as the afternoon sunlight stretched golden fingers across the stone floor through the old arched windows, the bench retired to consider its verdict, Stewart was taken away and Paul took his wife's hand and led her outside, glad to stretch his legs. They walked in silence away from the little crowd outside the courtroom, and clambered up a broken wall onto the remains of one of the castle watchtowers. There was a spectacular view over the countryside, shimmering in the hot afternoon air. For a long time they stood, not speaking, and Paul watched a flock of birds swooping and diving over a ploughed field in the distance. Small figures ran about, the village children, employed to chase the birds off the crops and Paul could hear faint shrieks of laughter as they ran from one end of the field to the other, banging pots to keep the birds away.

"Are you angry with me?"

Paul turned to look at her in surprise. "Angry? Jesus, no, Nan. Why would I be angry?"

"I deliberately kept it from you."

"Well I forgot to tell you that I had once sexual relations with your new maidservant and that I'd bought us a house. I don't think I've much right to complain about this."

"I didn't know how it would go, Paul, and if it all went badly wrong, I didn't want you to be associated with it. They all say that you've no control over your wayward wife, so nobody would be able to blame you."

"You thought of everything, didn't you? How did you manage to coach Rory so well?"

"Sergeant Hammond managed to bribe the gaol guards to let him in with extra food for the prisoner a few times. And of course, Sally has been visiting regularly. I must say he's surprised me though, it's not easy for an enlisted man to get up and question officers in the way that he's done, and although he was well coached, some of that came from him. He did make a good impression, Paul, didn't he?"

"He made a very good impression, love."

"I was worried about Keren, but she insisted," Anne said. "I was afraid that somebody would raise the matter of the duel."

"They all know about the duel, girl of my heart, gossip spreads like the plague through this army. Most of them think Carl was mad to defend the honour of his mistress, but since he's married her, they're not going to say so openly. And in some ways it was good that Keren stood up and said what she did. Some of them will still turn their noses up at her, but a few of them will have been impressed by her, she's not what they'll have been expecting. I know it was the last thing on her mind, but she's actually just demonstrated very publicly that she's intelligent, presentable and very brave. I think she'll be accepted more easily because of it."

"I hope so. Paul, thank you for understanding."

"Thank you for doing it, I'd honestly no idea. I did think you were up to something a few weeks ago, but with everything else that's been going on, I forgot about it." Paul took her hand and raised it to his lips. "You're an extraordinary woman, Anne van Daan and I love you very much."

"There you are, I wondered where you'd wandered off to."

Paul turned to see Carl scrambling over the low wall to join them. "We're in hiding, come and join us. Where's your wife, is she all right?"

"Very much so, she's with Sally at the moment. Congratulations on a successful campaign, ma'am, it's one of the best concealed attacks I've ever seen."

"I'm sorry, Carl. I hope you're not angry with her."

"How could I be? I wish somebody had told me though."

"I'm sorry, if I'd known you would be in the courtroom, I would have spoken to you. I really didn't know how this would all work. Paul, will you excuse me, I should see how Sally is doing?"

Paul watched her go. "Are you all right, Carl? I don't think she should have done that without asking you."

"I'd have said yes, so where's the difference? Do you think it's going to help, sir? Rory, I mean."

"God knows." Paul thought about it. "It might. Certainly it's given them something to think about. This turned from a simple case which should have been decided in ten minutes to something a lot more complicated and that can only be good for Private Stewart. But I don't think they're going to believe the story of unidentified brigands in the area. Where the hell did that come from anyway?"

"It's true, as far as it goes. White told Manson, who informed your wife."

"Was my brigade major in on this as well?"

"You could ask him."

"I don't want to know."

"General! General van Daan, are you up here?"

Paul went to the wall and peered over. "What is it, Captain?"

"They're coming back," Manson said. "They've reached a verdict."

Paul took out his pocket watch and looked at it. "Twenty-five minutes," he said. "All right, Leo, we're coming down."

Word of the surprising events of the trial seemed to have spread through the officers billeted in Castelo Bom and the public area was much more crowded. There was an atmosphere of suppressed excitement in the courtroom. Anne was already in her chair and Paul joined her, taking her hand.

"You look worried."

"I am worried, Paul, but there's nothing more I can do now."

"Whatever the verdict, Nan, you helped him mount an extraordinary defence. I'm very proud of you."

"Do you think they'll convict him?"

"Yes," Paul said honestly. "But what matters, is what they do next."

Stewart was led in and took up his place at the bar. Larpent arrived, shuffling papers, and the members of the bench filed in. Anne's hand trembled a little in Paul's and he squeezed it reassuringly, although he felt far from confident. Stewart was very pale but looked composed, and Paul thought that he had never seen the Scot anything other than calm before a battle, no matter how dire the odds. The formalities of requesting the verdict passed in a blur of meaningless words, and then Larpent stepped forward.

"This court finds the defendant, Private Rory Stewart of the 110ᵗʰ Light Infantry, guilty as charged of the murder of Major Leonard Vane."

There was a collective murmur through the court. Sally Stewart, standing nearby, gave a sob and Keren and Teresa Carter both put their arms about her. Anne's hand tightened convulsively in Paul's, but she did not take her eyes from Judge Larpent.

"The court has asked for the following remarks to be read aloud before the sentence is given," Larpent said, and Paul's heart leaped with hope. It was not unusual for a court to accompany either verdict or sentence with a statement from the bench, but that was more common in the trial of an officer.

"The case of Major Leonard Vane and this unhappy solider appears simple, but this hearing has proved otherwise. No witnesses saw Private Stewart attack or kill Major Vane, and Stewart himself is unable to confirm or deny his guilt, due to his appalling state of inebriation on that night. Generally, this would have compounded his crime, but it is clear that this was no ordinary situation.

"Private Stewart believed, erroneously, that Major Vane had seduced his wife. This marriage was different to many army liaisons. This was no casual connection, born of lust or convenience, as are so many in these times. This was a true marriage, properly consecrated in church some ten years ago, and Private and Mrs Stewart raised two children, buried three others, and lived in a close and affectionate union for many years before Major Vane's arrival destroyed their happiness. The couple were separated and Private Stewart chose the unfortunate refuge of drink in his sorrow and anger.

"It is not difficult to imagine the shock and rage, when this man, a brave soldier of previously good character, discovered how badly he had misjudged and wronged his poor wife; that Mrs Stewart, far from being unfaithful to him, had been attacked and violated by one who should have been expected to show her the courtesy and respect befitting an officer and a

308

gentleman. It must have seemed to Stewart that there was no justice to be had. He could not know that his wife was not the only victim, that Leonard Vane's bestial nature and unbridled lusts had made more than one respectable female their target.

"The court does not believe that Private Stewart sought out Major Vane or made any plan to kill him. Their meeting that night was accidental and tragedy was the inevitable consequence. Drunk, angry and broken, Stewart can barely remember what was said or done that night, but has admitted with manly courage, that he might well have been responsible for the death of Leonard Vane. He did not seek to give excuses, but others have spoken for him. Four courageous women, one of them his wife, have overcome their natural modesty and shame to show the court what none knew; that Major Leonard Vane was a shocking reprobate, not worthy of holding an officer's commission.

"There can be no other verdict than guilty in this case, for guilt is certain, but the bench does not believe Private Stewart should die for his crime. Punishment there must be, and a severe one, but this court believes that there is hope for Private Stewart. The court, therefore, commutes the death sentence to that of one thousand lashes, to be administered in the presence of his entire battalion in the main square of Freineda at eight o'clock tomorrow."

Silence followed, and then Stewart saluted. The bench rose and filed out, with Larpent bringing up the rear and the deputy provost marshal came forward to escort Stewart back to his prison. A buzz of conversation filled the room. Paul sat very still, holding Anne's hand.

"You did it," he said finally.

"A thousand lashes is so much, Paul. It could kill him."

Paul stood up, caught her hand and pulled her to her feet. "It won't, I'll see to it. You did it. You bloody did it, you amazing, wonderful, astonishing woman. Come here."

Paul picked her up, swinging her around and then setting her back down on her feet. Anne had tears in her eyes but she was laughing too, as the officers of the 110th converged on them in a moment of shared celebration.

***

Floggings were rare in the 110th and there was grim silence in the neat ranks lined up in the main square of the village the following morning. It was compulsory for all officers as well as men to be present, and for some of the younger subalterns this would be the first flogging they had witnessed A number of officers from other battalions had chosen to be present. Rory Stewart had been seconded as sergeant under Michael O'Reilly in the 112th for two years and several officers and men from the 112th lined up alongside the 110th to support their former NCO.

Floggings were carried out by the regimental drummers under the supervision of the drum-major and Captain Forrester, the adjutant of the 110th. When the troops were fully assembled, Stewart was led forward to be bound by

309

his extended arms to three sergeants' halberds which had been planted in the ground in the shape of a triangle and lashed together at the top. There was complete silence in the square as Stewart was stripped to the waist and tied to the triangle. Drummer Edwards stood ready with the cat in his hand, and young Bates, the youngest of the drummers stood ready with his instrument to beat time. A flogging was a theatrical performance, designed to humiliate as well as punish the miscreant, as well as acting as a deterrent to the watching troops. Paul hated it, and stood stony-faced and silent.

As the drum-major stepped back, Captain Forrester read out the charges, then glanced over at Carl, who gave the order in a flat tone, and Edwards stepped forward, then paused uncertainly at a slight stir among the troops. Paul turned. Anne's Portuguese groom was lifting her down from the saddle. Anne thanked him gravely and walked forward to stand beside Paul. Paul glared at her.

"Did we not agree that you should not be present for this," he said very softly.

"No, General. You said that. I didn't answer."

"Nan, you don't need to see this."

"Yes, I do."

Paul sighed. Short of carrying her away, there was nothing more he could do, and he had no desire to quarrel with Anne. Grudgingly, he reached for her hand and raised it to his lips.

"All right. Let's get this over with."

Paul nodded to the drum-major, who gave the order. Edwards raised his arm, and the cat o'nine tails fell onto Stewart's bare back, leaving a long red weal. Paul felt his wife flinch beside him. As the cat fell again and again, Paul glanced at Anne. She was staring straight at Stewart, refusing to avert her gaze. Paul studied her for a moment, then felt her squeeze his fingers. She was pale but her expression was determined and Paul's exasperation melted into pride. Anne was right, she had fought for Stewart and should be here.

After twenty-five lashes, Edwards stepped back and handed the cat to the next man. Dr Oliver Daniels went to check on Stewart. The Scot had made no sound yet. Daniels spoke briefly to him then stepped back. The lash fell again. Stewart's back was a mass of scarlet raised stripes, and one or two were beginning to bleed. Once the skin was broken, the cat could inflict more damage and the pain got worse. Paul had been fourteen when he had been flogged, during his time below decks in the Royal Navy and he remembered the pain and shock and humiliation as if it was yesterday. He was not sure that a man ever forgot what it felt like to be flogged.

The drummers swapped over again, and then again. At one hundred and thirty strokes, Stewart's back was bloody and he could no longer keep silent, issuing a little groan at each stroke. Paul did not think the drummers were using full force with the cat, but the beating would cause bruising as well as lacerations, and the Scot must be in agony. Paul wanted to look away, but did not. He could do nothing to honour Stewart's stubborn courage other than to witness it.

310

At two hundred, Stewart was slumped forward and Paul nodded to Daniels, who went forward again. Paul had no intention of allowing Stewart to suffer the full one thousand lashes, but if he stopped it too soon, given the gravity of the crime, it was possible that the court would insist that the rest of the sentence be carried out once Stewart had recovered sufficiently. Paul had spoken to Daniels before the flogging to discuss how many lashes Stewart might be able to endure and whether Paul would be able to justify declaring the punishment over at that point.

There was another stirring in the crowd and Paul looked around. This time, men were coming to attention, saluting the figure in a plain blue coat who was walking across the square from the direction of headquarters. Paul waited until Lord Wellington drew level with him before saluting. Wellington stopped in front of him, but his eyes were on Anne.

"Mrs van Daan, I thought that my eyes were deceiving me. General, I cannot believe that you considered it appropriate to bring your wife to witness this awful spectacle."

Paul opened his mouth, but he knew that he was not going to get the opportunity to speak. Anne dropped a neat curtsey. "Forgive me, my Lord, but my husband did not bring me here. Indeed, he left me at home this morning. I waited until he had left then followed him."

Paul saw a flicker of amusement in the blue eyes. "That was unwise, ma'am. You should not be here."

"Every man of this battalion is obliged to witness this, my Lord. I cannot prevent this barbarity, but I will not hide at home and pretend that it is not happening, however upsetting I find it."

There was a long silence, and Paul realised he was holding his breath. Anne was looking steadily at Lord Wellington and Wellington looked back at her. Nobody else moved or spoke apart from Daniels, who was giving Stewart water, speaking to him in low tones as though the commander in chief had never arrived.

Abruptly, Wellington turned on his heel and strode over to the triangle. He inspected Stewart's bloody back, and spoke a few words to the surgeon, then turned and surveyed the lines of the 110th.

"Private Stewart was sentenced to one thousand lashes. As commander of the army, I am commuting his sentence by eight hundred lashes, in consideration of the tragic circumstances of his crime and his previous good character and excellent service. The punishment is therefore at an end. Take him down and tend to him, Doctor."

A collective murmur of relief ran through the lines. Paul called an order, and the battalion came to attention and saluted. Wellington returned the salute, glanced over at Stewart, who was being lifted down, then turned to return to headquarters.

Anne moved abruptly, running to join him. She put a hand on his arm and spoke to him, and Wellington replied. Paul could not hear the conversation, but he saw Wellington's austere face break into a reluctant smile. He bowed, and continued on his way and Anne whirled and ran to join Daniels,

311

who was kneeling beside Stewart. Paul gave the order to fall out and as the troops dispersed, Carl, Johnny, Michael and Leo Manson came to join Paul.

"Do you think she knew that would happen?" Johnny asked, his eyes on Anne, who was giving orders to lift Stewart into a waiting cart. "Wellington, I mean."

"I have no idea, Johnny. She planned that entire defence from start to finish, and I'll never know how she managed to persuade the two Spanish women to testify, they wouldn't even put in a complaint against Vane when I asked them. I have a strong suspicion that she rode in right past Wellington's window to make sure he knew she was here. Having said that, Wellington might have done that anyway, he's done it before. He's furious about Vane's behaviour, I'm reliably informed that there is a memorandum on its way to all officers giving them very specific instructions about their behaviour around the local women, with orders to speak to their men about the same thing. Which will give me a very good excuse to remind the men of my brigade what I'm going to do to them if any one of them steps out of line during this next campaign. Thank God this is over. I intend to collect my wife, go home and have a very large drink."

***

As Wellington's army made their final preparations for the new campaign, Giles Fenwick felt entirely detached from the whole process. Having made his report to Lord Wellington and handed over Sir Horace Grainger's precious documents, Giles was given leave and had no idea what to do about it. With no orders and no job to do, he spent most of his time out riding, or alone in his room. Giles cried when he was reunited with Boney, standing in the stable weeping into the horse's mane. It was ridiculous and Giles knew that the tears were not really about the horse. He cried for Antonio and Sir Horace Grainger, and the slaughtered people of Castro Urdiales and the things he had seen that he could never forget.

The tears seemed to be over now, but Giles could not shake off the feeling that he was drifting pointlessly in a world where he no longer belonged. Wellington had insisted that he take some furlough, but Giles longed for a message calling him back into service. At the same time he could not imagine how he would do his job without Antonio's reliable presence beside him. He missed the Spaniard's cheerful smile and laconic wit with an ache of loneliness.

Giles saw little of Michael during the first two weeks of their return, but he understood why, as Michael was wholly wrapped up in the trial of Private Stewart. With the exception of Ross Mackenzie, Giles avoided the rest of his fellow officers studiously. They would not understand his misery and he could not hide it and could not bear to explain it. He heard the news of Stewart's surprising sentence from Ross and on impulse, rode over to the village and stood quietly, well to the back of the battalion. Giles was not sure why he did so, he did not know Stewart, but Michael had spoken of him during

312

those many evenings by the camp fire, and it felt right, somehow, to share this moment with him, even at a distance.

As the battalion broke up, Giles made his way to where he had left Boney in the care of one of the village children. He was surprised to see Michael there, perched on the wooden rail, while Brat was stroking Boney's silky nose. The sight of them lifted Giles' spirits.

"Captain Fenwick, it's a pleasure to see you. I was beginning to think you'd either died or taken vows. Where the devil have you been?"

"Hiding from my fellow officers in Captain Mackenzie's cottage," Giles said frankly. "We spend the evenings weeping into our wine; he's missing his wife and I'm missing Antonio. What does that say about me, I wonder? Congratulations on the verdict. I can't believe he got away with that. How did he manage it?"

"He did not manage it at all," Brat said. "Mrs van Daan managed it. She is very, very clever."

Michael slid from the rail. "Come and have a drink and I will tell you the story," he said. "I have to warn you that that General van Daan has requested your presence at dinner in the mess this afternoon."

"I've nothing respectable enough to wear to dine in the mess," Giles said.

"He told me you'd say that. He wants to see you in the office first, and he's not accepting any excuses, Giles. Have a seat."

Giles sat, with a sudden sharp memory of the first time he had sat drinking with Michael. It seemed a very long time ago.

"This is good wine," he said, sipping it. "Have you come into some money, Michael?"

In response, Michael took a small bag from his pocket and pushed it across the table. Giles put down his glass, opened the bag and stared, then looked up, puzzled.

"Where did you get this from?"

"Looting," Michael said. "I took it from one of those bastards we killed in Castro Urdiales. I've shared it equally between the three of us."

Giles studied him and realised incredulously that his friend was completely serious. "Michael, if the general knew you'd taken this, you could get yourself cashiered. There's a tidy sum, here."

"What else was I going to do with it, give it to Alvarez? General van Daan wouldn't care, laddie. I gave a little to the priest, to say prayers for Antonio's soul. I hope you don't mind."

Giles felt his eyes fill with tears and he blinked them away. "Of course I don't. I wish I'd thought of it. Thank you, Michael."

"You're welcome. Put the purse in your pocket and raise your glass. To Antonio."

They drank the toast and Giles realised he was feeling better.

"Tell me about the trial," he said.

It felt good to be together again. The conversation moved on to other things; the condition of the troops ahead of the new campaign, army gossip

313

about which officers had managed promotion, who had transferred out and what was happening in other brigades. They talked on the ride back to the quinta and Giles was surprised to realise that he no longer dreaded the prospect of sitting down to dinner in the mess.

As they emerged from the stables, Michael clapped him on the shoulder. "Go and talk to him," he said. "I'll see you at dinner."

Giles looked back at the stables, where Brat was dealing with the horses. "Speaking of conversations, Michael, have you managed to have one with Brat?"

"No. And believe me, I've tried, she's impossible to pin down when she puts her mind to it. We have to do it soon, though, because we'll be marching out of here in a couple of weeks. We all have our troubles, Giles."

Giles grinned and made his way through to the office. The door was open and Giles paused. There was an odd grumbling sound from within, and Giles stood quietly, unexpectedly charmed at the sight of General van Daan engaged in an energetic tug of war with Craufurd, his wife's enormous shaggy dog. Paul held one end of a piece of short rope, while Craufurd held the other between his teeth. He was growling ferociously, and Paul was laughing, pulling the dog forward then letting him pull back.

"Come on, you oversized hound, you can do better than that."

Craufurd renewed his efforts and the contest continued for another minute, until the dog suddenly spotted Giles hovering in the doorway. Craufurd gave a yelp of excitement and let go of the rope, bounding over to greet Giles. Paul, unexpectedly released, staggered backwards and overbalanced, sitting down heavily on the wooden boards.

"Craufurd, you bloody menace! Get over here and stop jumping all over Captain Fenwick. Here, now."

Craufurd trotted apologetically back to Paul and sat, regarding him with an enquiring look. Paul got painfully to his feet, rubbing his backside, laughed and threw the rope to him. "Bloody dog. Craufurd, bed."

Craufurd ambled to a pile of elderly blankets in the corner and settled down, the rope held between his huge paws as he chewed on it happily. Paul beckoned to Giles to come in and went for wine as Giles saluted, closed the door and sat down. Paul sat opposite, wincing slightly.

"How are you? I feel horribly guilty, Giles, I've neglected everything because of Private Stewart trying to get himself hanged."

"I'm all right, sir. Just lacking in occupation."

"Don't talk bollocks to me, Giles. Michael has told me what happened up there, in more detail than I care to remember. I've no words to tell you how sorry I am."

"I'm not over it," Giles said. It was a relief to admit it. "I'm not going to get over it for a long time, I'm not sure I want to. But I'm all right. Ross and Michael have helped. And Brat, of course."

Paul laughed out loud. "Brat. Dear God, I am staying a long way away from that particular problem, I know my limitations."

"Me too, sir."

It felt good to laugh again, and Giles realised that he was ready to do so. He sipped his wine. "Thank you for the invitation, sir. You're right, I'm hiding."

"I do understand, Giles, and I'm sorry if I'm rushing you, but I'm expecting orders almost daily so I'm going to need an answer."

Giles was puzzled. "An answer to what, sir?"

"Didn't Michael tell you? Giles, I'm in need of a man to command the eighth company, Saunders has transferred to the cavalry, the bloody idiot. It's yours if you want it."

Giles sat very still, shocked. His mind had been wandering over new missions, on long rides alone through enemy territory, missing Antonio and wondering how soon he would join his friend. The idea of returning to the regiment, of taking up long abandoned duties had simply not occurred to him.

"Lord Wellington..."

"I've talked it through with Lord Wellington and he'll speak to you himself before we march. It's your choice, Giles. You're an exploring officer, that isn't going to change, but at present, Wellington isn't in desperate need of intelligence, you've all done very nicely this winter. At some point he might need you again, in which case you'll hand over to your juniors and do your job, if that's what you want. But right now I need reliable men to command my companies. I want you. Will you do it?"

Giles felt a sudden flood of relief. He had not realised until this moment how much he had dreaded the long hours of waiting for new orders, wondering where he would be sent and doubting his own capability to do this job without Antonio. The thought of standing at the head of a company, dredging up long dormant skills and trying to manage both officers and men was completely terrifying and he suspected it was exactly what he needed to lay the ghosts of Castro Urdiales.

"I don't know if I can," he said honestly.

"Of course you can. You've got two very good lieutenants and the men are steady and experienced. You've not forgotten anything Giles. I wanted you in command of one of my companies two and a half years ago and bloody Wellington snapped you up when you'd only been there five minutes. Come back. Come home. It will help, I promise you."

Giles nodded. He felt oddly shy, like a schoolboy being given his first taste of responsibility as a prefect or head of house. "I'll try," he said. "Sir - thank you. I wasn't expecting this."

"You will do very well, Captain Fenwick, I have total faith in you. Now finish that drink and come down to dinner. I may need to sit on a cushion to eat mine. That blasted dog."

Chapter Twenty-One

Keren was putting the finishing touches to her hair as Carl came into their room. She saw him watching her in the mirror and turned, smiling. "I'm nervous."

"Nonsense. You've dined in the mess many times, Mrs Swanson, and you look very lovely."

Keren moved to kiss him. "Not with the commander in chief and General Alten present."

"Don't worry about it, love, they both have very good table manners, I promise you. Better than Paul's, actually."

Keren tapped him lightly on the head with her fan. It was new, an elegant creation in Spanish lace that Anne had given her, and she had spent an hour before the mirror practicing how to manage it. After two years learning how to behave like a lady, Keren had discovered that it was often the little things that tripped her up.

"Do they know I'm going to be present?"

"Yes, Nan made sure of it. As a matter of fact, General Alten has asked that you be seated next to him so that he can get to know you better."

"Oh no…"

"Don't panic, darling girl. He is a very nice man, who will tell you all about his home in Hanover which he misses desperately. Oh, and he loves fishing."

"Fishing?" Keren stared at him and then began to laugh. "I can't believe I'm doing this, Carl."

"Well you are, and you'll get used to it very quickly. They'll both be very polite, I promise you, love. In the meantime, Jenson just handed me this, it's from my parents."

"Oh." Keren studied him. She had tried to conceal how much she had been dreading the response from Reverend and Mrs Swanson. Carl had laboured for a long time over his letter telling them of his marriage, trying to decide what to tell them. He was reluctant to lie, but he knew that his family would be upset at the idea of him living with a woman outside the bounds of matrimony. In the end, he had compromised and Keren read the letter before he sent it, and thought it was a masterpiece of tact, with only a few actual

316

untruths. Carl had described Keren as the widow of a Cornish rifleman, which was almost true, allowing for the fact that it had been a common law marriage. Wisely, he had omitted any mention of Keren's second, disastrous relationship with the surly Simmonds, but he had been honest about her taking employment with Anne van Daan and about their own growing attachment.

"Don't look so worried, Keren. They're happy for me, as I was sure they would be. My father has written a very long letter which you're welcome to read, but there is one enclosed for you, from my mother. I've not opened it, but I think you should."

Keren sat down, unfolding the letter and read it, tears welling up. She looked up. "She is so kind. And so welcoming. I didn't expect that."

"I did." Carl grinned. "I'll be honest with you, Keren, my mother was always going to welcome the woman who finally ended my bachelorhood, she's been dreaming of a daughter-in-law and hopefully grandchildren for years, and she was beginning to give up hope."

Keren stood up into his arms. Suddenly the spectre of sitting at table with Lord Wellington seemed less daunting.

"I hope we do, Carl."

"So do I. Is it the right time to confess I've spent all winter watching you with the children and dreaming?"

"Even before...?"

"Long before. It's been very confusing, love, you wouldn't believe the relief of having it settled. Now all I have to do is love you. We're going to be very happy and you're going to be a very good wife. Although not if you intend to go down to dinner with Lord Wellington in your petticoats. Get yourself dressed and I'll help you with the buttons."

***

When dinner was over, Carl remembered another duty and leaving Keren to drink tea with Anne, collected his horse and rode over to the convent which housed the regimental hospital of the 110th and 112th. Private Rory Stewart was the only patient in a small room at the back of the house, lying face down on a straw mattress with his back exposed to the air. A young hospital mate whom Carl did not recognise showed him in and Rory turned his head then moved to get up.

"At ease, Private Stewart. You can salute me when you can stand unaided. How is it?"

"Bloody hurts, sir, I feel like I've been kicked by a mule."

"That'll be Drummer Eliot, he's got a strong right arm. Here."

Carl passed his flask, but Stewart shook his head. "Thank you, sir, but I'm only drinking beer or ale just now. I promised Sal I'd give it a rest with the drink, it got me into a whole lot of trouble."

"It did, although it wasn't all your fault. Do you mind me asking how things are with Sally?"

"Much better, sir. She's been in every day, and she's brought the children. We're going to be together again, when we can, properly. I've sworn to her and to God that I'll never hit her again. I was that jealous, sir."

Carl thought about the horrible hours when he had believed that Keren had taken a lover, and remembered his own need to escape for fear of what he might do. He did not think he would ever have followed through on his murderous rage, but even feeling it had been terrifying. He wished, for a moment, that he could tell Stewart how well he understood.

"It's in the past," he said gently. "Make sure it stays there, Rory, you've been given a second chance in a way that few men ever are. I've been talking to General van Daan about you, he has an idea that he wants you to think about, while you're recovering. You know we've a new quartermaster but we've no assistant appointed. Would you be interested in the job?"

"In the quartermaster's department?"

"Yes, why not? You'd get your sergeant's stripes back. I was impressed with how you managed yourself in that courtroom, Rory. You're a quick learner and you've something to prove, which means you'll work hard. I've spoken to Captain Mackenzie and he's willing to give you a try. Think about it."

"I'll try it, sir," Stewart said quickly. "You can tell him now, I'll try it. Be better for Sal, I reckon, and better for me too. Not so much temptation to go drinking with the lads. And sergeant…I hated being demoted."

"I know you did. Good, I'll tell Captain Mackenzie and he can talk to you. We might have to march before you're fit, but if we can, we'll find you a space in the baggage wagons to start with. If you can't manage it, you can join us as soon as you're able."

Stewart pushed himself up into a sitting position, wincing. "Thank you, sir. Tell General van Daan as well. And his wife…what she did for me and Sal, there's no words. And your lady as well. Not many officers would let their wife do something like that. I'm that grateful."

Carl decided not to mention that neither Anne or Keren had actually asked for permission. He got up. "Make the most of it, Rory, and it will have been worthwhile."

"I mean to, sir. You're right about second chances. I thought I was going to hang. I'd be dead by now, and her a widow. Not many men come back from that. I'm not going to waste it."

"I'm glad to hear it. Welcome back to my battalion, Sergeant Stewart. Just to let you know that if I catch you drunk on duty one more time, I'm going to cut your bollocks off and feed them to Mrs van Daan's dog. Now get some rest."

***

With the army daily awaiting orders, Anne found herself frantically busy. She had coopted Sergeant Hammond to assist Ross Mackenzie with the myriad last minute details of preparing the battalion to march, and made a personal inspection of the baggage train to ensure that all animals were fit and ready and that wagons and carts were in good repair. On returning to the house with dreams of a hot bath, she was quickly embroiled with Oliver Daniels, furious about some medical supplies that had gone astray and complaining about two new hospital mates who seemed to be taking a casual approach to their duties. Anne listened sympathetically, suggested several ways of managing Fleming and Baker and took charge of the lists herself. She was sitting in the office checking off the list against the original orders in an attempt to work out what had gone wrong when there was a faint tap on the door.

"Come in."

The woman who entered was wearing a dark woollen gown which was a little too big for her, and a grey woollen shawl over her head. She closed the door and came forward, bobbing an awkward curtsey, and at that point, Anne realised in astonishment that it was Brat.

"Brat. Good heavens, I didn't recognise you."

Brat pushed the shawl back from unruly auburn curls. "Am I disturbing you, Señora? I can come back."

"No, come in. I am trying to work out if the transport board have lost half our medical supplies or if they were never sent in the first place. Either way, at some point I am going to have to write several very rude letters. I've no objection to putting that off. Won't you sit down?"

"I should not."

"Do so anyway," Anne said firmly. She had no idea what Michael's eccentric servant was doing here, dressed as a girl for once, and she was intrigued. "How may I help you?"

Brat took a deep breath. "I have talked today with Mrs Stewart," she said. "It is good that Private Stewart is not to be hanged, but may come back to the regiment. But she says she will not have time to act as your maidservant as it will take her away from him too much."

Anne regarded her in some surprise. "I know, she told me. I tried to talk her out of it, to tell you the truth. I hope that Stewart is sincere in his repentance, but I think she is being too hasty. She has decided though."

"Do you have a new maid?"

Anne was beginning to understand. "No. I often manage without, to be honest, although the general scolds me about it."

"Will you let me try?"

"As my maid?"

"Yes, Señora."

Anne studied her in astonishment. "Brat, this is something of a surprise. I thought you were employed by Captain O'Reilly."

"I cannot be so any more," Brat said. "He is trying to talk to me, and I am running away from him, because I do not want him to. He wishes to say to me that I can no longer be his servant, and if I can not be his servant, I cannot go with the army when you march out. It will be very soon, I know. He has arranged for me to work here, and if I cannot find work with the army, I must stay. But I do not want to stay."

Brat spoke very quickly, the words tumbling out. Her English had improved immensely over the past months, but she was clearly very nervous. Anne walked around the table and put her hands on Brat's shoulders. She steered her into a chair, and sat down opposite her.

"Brat, so far, every time Michael has told you to stay behind, you have simply followed him."

"I cannot do that any more."

"What has changed?"

"Everything," Brat said starkly, and Anne realised that underneath her attempted formality, she was very upset.

"Can you tell me?"

"I do not know what to tell, Señora."

"Start at the beginning. I'm not saying no to you, Brat, but I have to think of Michael as well. It's very clear that something has happened. If I am to consider employing you, I need to understand."

Brat took a very long breath and looked directly at Anne for the first time. She had extraordinarily pretty eyes, a mixture of blue and green which reminded Anne of a calm summer sea.

"I am nineteen," she said, apologetically. "Last year, when the captain found me and brought me to you, you thought I was younger and I allowed you to think it. You were kind, and I thought you would be more likely to help a child. Also, I did not want you to know that sometimes, when I was starving, I went with the soldiers. After the French came, and they did what they did to me, it did not seem to matter so much. But I was ashamed."

"Brat, I could not possibly blame you, you were trying to survive. And I don't care how old you are, but I'm guessing Michael does."

"He did not even think about it at first and nor did I. But these months, away from the army, things changed. I could not help it. I tried to keep everything the same, because I knew what he would do, but I could not."

Anne suspected that she understood. "Brat, I'm going to need to ask you…"

"No," Brat said quickly. "No, we have not. But it is different now, and I cannot pretend it is not. And nor can he. That is why, if I must stay behind, I will not follow him again. He will no longer see his little servant boy coming after him, which will make him smile. He will see a woman that he does not want, and it will make him uncomfortable. And I will not do that."

"Is that why you are wearing that dreadful gown?"

"It is all I have, Señora Palomo made me wear it in Castro Urdiales. I wanted you to see me as a girl. I wanted to show you that I can be a girl. I can do everything you need. I can sew, and do laundry and clean and even help with your horses. And if you will give me a little time, I will learn to do the other things, like your hair and helping you to dress. Mrs Carter can show me. I do not require payment, just food and somewhere to sleep, and a place. Please."

Brat's desperation tore at Anne's heart. Reaching out, she took one of the younger girl's hands in hers. "If you work for me, I will pay you for your labour, Brat. And I will replace that gown, it's dreadful. But there are other things to consider. Are you sure you're ready to be a girl again?"

"I am. I have to be. If I am to be your servant, I must be respectable. And I will be very loyal."

"I don't doubt that, Brat. But I also need to have Michael's agreement about this. I have no idea at all what has happened between you, but this cannot just be another way for you to follow him. You can't avoid that conversation any more, my dear. Go and talk to him and find out what he wants. If he agrees, the job is yours."

Brat scrambled to her feet, her face transformed. "Thank you," she said breathlessly. "You are so good. Now, I can talk to him. Now I know what to say. Thank you."

***

Michael was in the stable when Brat found him and he knew immediately that something had happened. He had been impressed at how well she had avoided any possibility of a personal conversation during these past weeks. Michael had tried, but he knew he had not tried hard enough. As the days passed, and the new campaign loomed ever closer, the thought of leaving Brat behind became harder and harder and cravenly, Michael put off the moment.

Brat stood in the stable doorway and Michael took in the gravity of her expression and the clothing she wore and felt suddenly sick. He wanted to find another excuse, but they could not go on this way, so he smiled and held out his hand. "Let's walk down to the orange grove, urchin, there'll be nobody there at present, and I've a feeling you've something to say to me."

It was shady under the trees, with the sun making dappled patterns on the grass beneath their feet. Michael held her hand and thought about all the girls he had met over these past years in Portugal and Spain. He had danced with them and flirted with them, and when he could, had gone to bed with them, and he remembered them with a fleeting fondness that had nothing to do with how he felt about this girl.

"I'm guessing this is not a scolding about the holes in my stockings," he said. "Are we finally about to have that conversation that we've been putting off?"

"We have to," Brat said. She withdrew her hand and turned to face him and Michael looked at her and could feel his resolve crumbling.

"Why are you wearing a gown?"

"Because I am a girl," Brat said. "I have been a boy for long enough, Michael. It is time for me to become accustomed to my skirts again."

Michael gave a faint smile. "You are so much braver than I am, urchin, I've always thought it. It would have taken me half an hour to say that."

"I cannot be your servant any more, Michael. I do not want to say this, but it must be said. When I first joined you, I was too much afraid to care about anything except that you seemed willing to take care of me and keep me safe. And you did that. I am so grateful to you."

"But…?"

"But I must learn to take care of myself. You do not need a servant, you have said it many times."

"I got very used to having one, so I did."

Brat stepped forward and reached up to caress his face, and Michael felt the familiar longing, coupled with an aching sadness for what he was about to lose. "If I remain with you in this way, Michael, one day I will not just be your servant. One day, very soon, you will forget that you did not mean to make love to me, and then we will be what so many of them already think we are."

"I know it, *mo gra*. I'm thinking about it right now, to tell you the truth. I wish it were otherwise, but I'm not that strong, and I want you so much that it fills me up and leaves no space for common sense. I should have said this weeks ago, but I couldn't bear the thought of letting you go."

"I could not bear the thought of going." Brat took a deep breath. "I have a job, but to do it, I must have your approval. Mrs van Daan is in need of a maidservant, since Mrs Stewart is going back to her husband. She will give me the job and pay me a proper wage to do it, but only if you agree. I will have my own tent and my own billet and my own place in the regiment."

Michael froze to the spot, staring at her. "You're coming with the army?"

"I do not wish to remain here, away from my friends. Jenson, and Sergeant Kelly and Charlie and Captain Fenwick. And you, Michael."

"Then what in God's name…?"

"If this happens, then it will happen properly," Brat said, and Michael heard steel in her tone. "I have seen you with your women, Captain O'Reilly. Me, I will not be one of them. I will not share your bed for a new gown or a pretty shawl or a few kind words, and I will not ever share it out of gratitude or because I have nowhere else to go."

"That isn't what I want either, Brat."

"We will have time to decide that. We will have time to get to know each other, Michael, not as master and servant, but as two people who care for each other. If you want that."

Michael could not speak for a long moment and when he could, his voice was thick with unshed tears. "I thought you were saying goodbye to me, Brat. And I just realised I couldn't bear it."

"I could not bear it either, Michael. But I will not be less than I am. I could not be happy that way, even for you."

They stood silent for a while, and Michael thought about what she had said and what it might mean. He was terrified and bewildered and happier than he could ever remember being in his life before.

"May I kiss you?" he asked.

"I would like that."

They remained for a long time, wrapped in each other's arms. With no expectation of anything more, it was somehow sweeter and more emotional, and Michael lost himself in the sheer joy of holding her and kissing her. It took him back many years to the green slopes of the Wicklow mountains and a different girl who had known him by another name. He had never told anybody about Sinead, but he suddenly wanted Brat to know. Another thought occurred to him, and he took her hand and raised it to his lips.

"What in God's name do I call you, now?" he asked.

She gave a gurgle of laughter and suddenly she was Brat again, the air of mystery vanished, the bright eyes mocking him. "Miss Ibanez? Ariana? I do not know, Captain. What did you call both of Mrs van Daan's other maids when you were trying to persuade them to go to bed with you?"

"Who the devil told you about that?" Michael said furiously. Brat was giggling uncontrollably.

"Corporal Browning. He thought I should know about your reputation. You look so cross."

Michael hovered between annoyance and laughter, but she was impossible to resist, and he began to laugh as well. "Bloody Ned Browning always did have a puritan streak. I called them by their given names, urchin, and a number of very flattering endearments. They both ignored all of them and went off with somebody else."

"I am glad to hear it. You may call me whatever you wish, Michael. But I like it when you call me Brat."

"So do I," Michael said. "I had better tell Mrs van Daan that your new job has my full approval."

"No, I shall do that myself."

"I'll miss you doing my laundry and mending."

"Oh, I will still do that for you, Captain. For the usual rate." Brat smiled up at him, stood on tiptoe and kissed him very gently on the lips. "Perhaps a small discount."

She was gone before he could respond, running lightly through the trees, her skirts caught up to avoid a fall and Michael watched her go, smiling, following at a more leisurely pace. He realised he had lost all urge to hurry, and it felt very peaceful and very good.

***

Wellington's orders to march were delayed by several weeks, and the commander-in-chief fretted irritably about difficulties over which he had no control. After the appallingly wet weather of the winter months, spring and early summer were unusually dry, which meant that it was difficult to find enough green forage for the horses. In addition, a combination of bad roads and dire weather meant that the pontoon train which was being secretly transported from the Tagus to the Douro was delayed. Wellington paced like a caged animal, poring over maps, snapping at his ADCs and writing long pages of orders. Receiving an appeal from Colonel Campbell, Paul gave his final instructions to his officers and rode to headquarters. He found Wellington staring at what appeared to be a wooden model of some kind of medieval siege weapon. Paul saluted, and when Wellington did not look up or respond, he walked across to the table to stand beside his chief.

"Very interesting idea, sir, but I'm not sure it's going to work all that well against a twelve pounder and a couple of howitzers. Is this London's solution to your request for more guns?"

Wellington looked up and fixed Paul with a ferocious glare. "Your attempts at being funny have seldom been more misplaced, General van Daan. This was sent to me by my wife. Apparently, it was constructed by my son, Arthur."

"Was it?" Paul studied the model more closely. "Yes, I can see the construction is a bit rough round the edges, but it's really very good. How on earth did it arrive in one piece?"

"It was packed in more sawdust than I have ever seen in my life," Wellington said irritably. "I will be brushing it from my clothing for weeks, I had no idea what I was opening. It is, however, quite a pleasing design. I thought, since I have absolutely nothing better to do, that I might write to him, telling him so."

Paul heard a question behind the words and was touched. Wellington was barely acquainted with his two sons and always seemed uncertain about how to behave as a father. Paul thought it a pity, since Wellington was good with children and had thoroughly enjoyed getting to know Paul's own children and the Mackenzie family during the winter months.

"I think it's a very good idea, sir," he said lightly. "Do you have time for a ride? I've barely seen you for the last few weeks, with Stewart's trial and the preparations for the campaign. We could take Pearl for a run."

Pearl, who was asleep in her basket, looked up at the sound of her name and trotted over to Lord Wellington, pushing her elegant head into his hand. Wellington caressed her absently, still looking at the model.

"Why not?" he said abruptly. "As it happens, I have several new horses I am trying out. One of them looks particularly promising, I'd like you to see him."

Jenson led Rufus back into the square and Pearl followed Lord Wellington, frisking excitedly around him, knowing that she was going out. After a few minutes, one of the grooms appeared from the stable, leading a horse that Paul did not recognise.

He was a stallion, not particularly tall but with a strong muscular frame, a very dark chestnut with two white heels. Wellington came forward and patted the horse's neck. Pearl jumped around and the horse sidestepped a little to avoid her. Paul came forward as his chief put a hand into his pocket and withdrew a treat. He fed the horse as his groom still held the reins, bent to check the girth then put one foot into the stirrup and mounted.

Unexpectedly, the horse pulled away from the grooms, backing up fast, his teeth bared in a grimace. Wellington hung on and the groom reached for the bridle. The horse bucked and then reared up with a squeal, his hooves lashing out. One caught the groom on the shoulder, and he fell back with a cry of pain. Wellington clung to the reins, displaying impressive reactions, fighting to bring the animal under control, while Jenson turned Rufus away and led him out of range before the horse's panic affected him.

As Paul tried to grasp the bridle, the horse kicked out hard with his back legs and Paul dodged, then moved in fast, and reached the horse, grabbing the bridle while taking care to avoid the animal's flying hooves. Wellington had regained his composure immediately and took a firm hold, pulling the horse in, talking to it in low tones. Paul met his chief's eyes and stepped back, releasing the horse. With another man he might have held on until he was certain that the horse was calm, but he was not afraid for Wellington, who was a superb rider and more than capable of managing the most difficult mount. Paul stood watching for a moment, to be sure, but Wellington had the animal well under control. Paul turned to the groom, who was being helped to his feet by Wellington's orderly.

"Are you all right, Brett?"

"I think so, sir." Brett was cautiously moving his arm. "Winded me a bit."

"You should see the surgeon, just to get him to have a look at that, it was a hell of a kick."

"I'll be all right, sir. I'm sorry, my Lord, he caught me off guard. Shall I take him…?"

"Do not be stupid, Brett, if you are injured, you may not be able to control him, and besides he will settle down now that he knows who is in charge. Morrison, escort Brett to see a surgeon. General van Daan, stop fussing over the poor man like a mother hen, you are making him uncomfortable."

"I think it was the kick in the shoulder from that ungainly brute that has made him uncomfortable, sir. Where in God's name did you get him from?"

"He has recently arrived from Lisbon. I am in need of one or two new mounts and Gordon heard that Charles Stewart had two to sell prior to his departure."

"Charles Stewart sold you that horse? I'd ask for my money back, sir, you've been robbed."

"Nonsense," Wellington said. He was stroking the smooth chestnut coat. "He rides well, he is very strong and he doesn't seem to tire easily. He is a little testy, it is true…"

"A little testy?" Paul surveyed the horse in disgust. The horse returned his stare with a baleful eye. "If you want my opinion, he's a cross-gained, bad-tempered brute who is likely to throw you in the middle of a battle."

"He will settle down once he is accustomed to me, and understands that I will brook no defiance, General," Wellington said, watching as Paul retrieved his own horse and swung himself into the saddle.

"Like the rest of the army then, sir."

"With one notable exception. Brett, why are you standing with your mouth hanging open, when I am sure I instructed you to visit the surgeon?"

"Yes, my Lord. Very sorry."

Paul eyed the horse as they rode out of the village. "What's his name?"

"Copenhagen."

"He's Danish?"

"No, but he was foaled in '07. Probably just about the time you were getting yourself court-martialled for insubordination towards senior officers of the Royal Navy. It is a pity he is already named, I would have liked to have come up with something in memory of such a significant event."

"What an excellent idea, sir. You could have called him Popham, he's got that smug expression, with a strong look of being up to no good behind the eyes. I just hope that when he throws you, it's not in the middle of a fight. I'll tell Fitzroy to look out for the eye-rolling and bared teeth just in case."

"If he proves too troublesome, General, you could take him off my hands. Perhaps you would like to exchange him for that black you bought in Denmark? I have always liked the look of him, he is far too good a horse for your orderly to be riding."

"Felix? Not a chance. If you think I'd put Jenson up on this bad-tempered bastard, sir, you must be all about in your head. Send him back to Stewart and ask for your money back."

"Knowing Charles Stewart, I imagine that the money has already been spent on expensive Madeira and port for the voyage home. Besides, I have no desire to send Copenhagen back. I will offer you a wager, if you like, that within the year, he will have proved his worth. I am tired of horses blowing up halfway through a fast journey. I think I may have found the mount I have been looking for."

"If you like, sir. I'll happily stake a case of good port that you'll be looking to get rid of him in a year. What's your stake?"

Wellington touched his white neckcloth. "A broken neck, if you prove to be right, General."

"That's not funny, sir."

The incident seemed to have improved Wellington's mood. They rode through the sunny afternoon, between spreading olive groves and dusty villages, often partly ruined. People stood on doorsteps to watch them pass and occasionally barefooted children ran out and kept pace with the horses for a while, with Pearl running joyously between their feet threatening to trip them up until Wellington put his hand into his pocket and threw them wrapped sweets. It was clearly a familiar ritual, and Paul watched him and wished his commander could find a way to reach the same uncomplicated understanding with his own sons that he had with these village brats.

As they arrived back at headquarters, there was unusual activity for a sleepy afternoon. Paul dismounted but did not send Jenson to the stable with the horses. Lord Fitzroy Somerset handed a letter to Wellington as soon as he dismounted, and two grooms led the bad-tempered chestnut away as

Wellington read. After a moment he looked up, and Paul knew immediately the news it contained.

"We are ready," Wellington said softly. "By God, we're finally ready. Fitzroy, get Murray. Have the orders I have already written copied and..."

Wellington paused, apparently suddenly remembering Paul, and turned. Paul met his gaze. There was a jumble of conflicting emotions at the beginning of any new campaign, but predominantly he felt a familiar rush of excitement at the prospect of action, and he knew that Wellington was feeling exactly the same thing. Paul saluted.

"I'll await orders then, sir. Good luck."

"Good luck, General."

Paul mounted and waited for Jenson to collect his own horse. Wellington was still in the square outside his headquarters, issuing a stream of instructions, but as Paul turned his horse, he called:

"Paul."

"Sir?"

"It was a good afternoon. Thank you."

"It was sir. Thank you, too."

Wellington disappeared into the house, and Paul sat his horse, looking after him. Already his mind was running over last-minute preparations for the march, but he took a moment to look around the dusty village square which had been home to headquarters for two winters. Paul did not think they would be back; there was a new sense of purpose to Wellington's preparations. Bonaparte's disastrous Russian venture had weakened the French armies, while Wellington's men were better equipped, better trained and better prepared for the new campaign.

A flock of crows flew up from the dusty roadside, startling the horses a little as Paul set Rufus to a canter. He rode in as the sun settled lower into the sky and the white, peeling walls and red tiled roof of the Quinta de Santo Antonio stood out against a cloudless blue sky. Anne must have seen him approach, because she was waiting for him on the steps. Paul tried to imagine how he would have felt if she had decided to board the ship with the children and felt extraordinarily lucky.

"Are you ready to come to Spain with me, girl of my heart?"

"I'd rather like to see France actually, General."

Paul was surprised into a laugh. "That may take a little longer, Mrs van Daan, but why not? I will take you to Paris, I give you my word."

"See that you keep it, Paul."

Paul put his arm about her and kissed her then walked with her into the house, to give the news to his officers.

Author's Thanks

Many thanks for reading this book and I hope you enjoyed it. If you did, I would be very grateful if you would consider leaving a short review on Amazon or Goodreads or both. One or two lines is all that's needed. Good reviews help get books in front of new readers, which in turn, encourages authors to carry on writing the books. They also make me very, very happy.

Thank you.

Author's Notes (may contain spoilers)

I chose to set this book during winter quarters because sometimes it helps to remember that for huge chunks of their time in the Peninsula, Wellington's army wasn't fighting at all. It gave me an opportunity to look at other aspects of military life, especially discipline. But I also wanted to draw attention to the other aspect of this war, where the Spanish irregular forces were fighting for their lives in northern Spain.

The siege of Castro Urdiales was a real event, and is very well documented in Spanish sources. In 1818 the Spanish government held an official inquiry to investigate complaints by the survivors of the massacre that Alvarez had abandoned them to the mercy of the French and Italian troops. Alvarez was exonerated, but the inquiry has left us with unusually detailed reports of what actually happened to the people of Castro Urdiales in May 1813, and the reports are horrifying. As far as I know, there were no British officers present, but the role of the Royal Navy is well documented, although I have given them an extra ship, the *Iris*, to assist with the evacuation. Writing some of the scenes in Castro Urdiales was very upsetting, and there were some that I could not bring myself to include.

I have used author's licence a little, when it comes to dates. It would have been impossible for Giles' party to get back to the Portuguese border from Castro Urdiales in time to march out with Wellington's army, but for the sake of my story, I have left out the actual dates of some historical events and stretched time a bit to allow my actors to be where I wanted them to be. It is only out by a week or so, and I'm sure they'll catch up, so I hope my readers will forgive me.

The third brigade of the light division is well rested, with one or two exceptions, and I think they're ready to march back into Spain for the campaign of 1813. Next stop, Vitoria.

To celebrate the paperback editions of these books, I've decided to include one of my free short stories at the end of each book. All these stories are available on my website, but not all my readers spend their time online. A Winter Idyll was my Valentine's Day story in 2019 and tells the story of what Colonel Johnny Wheeler got up to during his visit to England in January 1813. I hope you enjoy it.

A Winter Idyll

The lawyer's office was stuffy, a blazing fire heating the room. It had been a relief at first, after the freezing air of the street outside, but after ten minutes, Colonel Johnny Wheeler was beginning to feel as though he was quietly roasting. His host, sitting across the table with an impressive array of papers set out before him, seemed unaffected.

"Very good to see you looking so well, Colonel," Mr Langley said. Johnny found himself smiling inwardly at the words, since Langley's cadaverous face and gloomy tones gave the impression that Johnny's well-being depressed him.

"Thank you, I'm recovering well. I probably won't need this for much longer." Johnny touched the sturdy cane which he had been using, since a serious leg wound at San Munoz several months ago had left him close to death during the miserable retreat from Burgos. "I was surprised to receive your letter, Mr Langley, but it came at a good time, since we're in winter quarters so I'm not needed."

"Indeed. I believe it is a long time since you were in England, Colonel?"

"Four years, I suppose," Johnny said, thinking about it. "I came out in 1808, went back briefly at the end of that year, and then returned with Wellington – Wellesley as he was then – the following year. There's little leave granted and I've not applied, since apart from my uncle, I've no family to visit. The last time I saw him was the Christmas before I left, and he was already very frail. I've written from time to time but he stopped replying a couple of years ago. To be honest, I wondered if he'd died and nobody knew to inform me."

"Surely you realised that your cousin would have written?" Langley said, somewhat repressively.

"I hope she would have, sir, but there's no real obligation. I've not seen Susan since I joined the army and we were never close. I was very sorry to hear of her death, though, she was so young."

"It was very quick and very unexpected – a fever epidemic which swept through a number of towns and cities. Both Mrs Fletcher and her

331

husband died within a week of each other. I think the shock probably hastened your uncle's death."

"How old is the child now?" Johnny asked. "I'm ashamed to say I've no idea."

Langley peered at him blankly over the top of his spectacles. "Child?" he asked. "Colonel Wheeler, there is no child."

Johnny stared back, bewildered. "What do you mean? I remember my uncle writing to me to tell me how happy he was. A grandson."

"Mrs Fletcher's son died in infancy, Colonel, and she had no others, although I know your uncle hoped that she would. I'm sorry, I thought you understood from my letter, when I explained that there were business matters to attend to."

Johnny reflected that the lawyer's letter had been so verbose and full of over-elaborate periods that he had never given it a second reading. He wondered if Mr Langley had failed to be clear or if he had simply skipped the boring parts.

"I rather assumed that you were telling me that I was going to be appointed guardian and trustee for my nephew," Johnny said.

"Not at all, Colonel. You are in fact, your uncle's heir."

Johnny sat still, thinking about Charles Wheeler. He had always liked his uncle, although he had not seen him regularly since joining the army. Charles had taken a kindly interest in his early career and had funded both his first commission and his promotion to lieutenant, since Johnny's father had not been able to afford either. When Charles' only daughter grew old enough to be presented, he had focused his energy and his money on seeing her well-established, and Johnny had not expected more and been grateful for his generosity. He realised now that he had missed their desultory correspondence since it died away, more than he had realised.

"Where is he buried?" he asked. "My uncle."

"In the churchyard at Aberly. Your cousin and her husband are buried with their son in Derby."

"And there's no other heir?"

"No," Langley said. "Forgive me, Colonel, but I had expected that this would be good tidings for you. I am aware that you have risen in your profession, but Limm Abbey is a fine property. A little neglected in recent years, but I am told that the tenancies are in good order."

"It's a shock to be honest," Johnny said bluntly. "I thought I was coming home for a few weeks to settle my uncle's affairs and to make the acquaintance of my nephew. This rather feels like a lot more work than that, and it bothers me, because I can't stay for too long."

Langley made a sound which sounded suspiciously like a snort. "I rather assumed that you would choose to sell out, Colonel. With your recent wound, nobody would think worse of you, and you have responsibilities here..."

"I have responsibilities there as well, Mr Langley, and while this war continues, they come first," Johnny said inexorably. "I imagine my uncle must have had an agent?"

"He did, but you will not wish to continue with him," Langley said, somewhat shortly. "He is elderly, and I would not place the whole care of the estate on a man of his age. I suggest..."

"It's good of you, Mr Langley, but I think I need to speak to him myself, and to have a look around, to find out how things stand. If I need to find a new agent, may I write to you for help with that? As I said, I've limited time."

"Of course," Langley said stiffly. "Will you be going directly to Aberly?"

"Yes, I'll arrange to post up."

"Where are you staying in town?"

"In Curzon Street, with the family of my commanding officer. I'll make the travel arrangements. In the meantime, perhaps you could take me through the rest of the paperwork. As far as I'm aware, Limm Abbey was the only property."

"It was. There is some money, however, and some investments, mostly in government bonds. I have a copy of your uncle's will here and a list of all his assets." Langley passed several sheets of paper over to Johnny. "His bankers will want to see you before you leave town, I imagine. It isn't a vast fortune, Colonel, but it's a comfortable living."

Johnny stared at the lawyer for some moments. "A comfortable living," he said softly. "Jesus, what in God's name am I going to do with that?"

■■

It had been some years since Johnny had visited his uncle's home at Limm Abbey, on the edge of the Derbyshire village of Aberly. Arriving in the chill of a January afternoon, he was grateful to find that Mr Langley's letter had reached the house ahead of him, and the housekeeper was ready to welcome him with a roaring fire and a hot meal.

The original buildings at Limm Abbey dated from a twelfth century Benedictine foundation, and as a boy, Johnny had loved playing among the graceful ruins. The current house had been part of the Abbey great hall, extended and rebuilt over the centuries to form an attractive manor house built in mellow local stone, set in the middle of well laid out gardens and surrounded by a home farm and half a dozen tenant farms. There was no lake, but a river ran through the grounds and as his hired chaise rattled over the old monks' bridge and up the short driveway to the house, Johnny could remember his uncle teaching him to fish off the bridge.

He knew none of the staff. His uncle had been an invalid for several years and had kept only a minimal number of servants; a housekeeper, a cook, a parlour maid and kitchen maid, one manservant and a groom to manage his uncle's horses.

"We've not needed more, sir, with the master not entertaining," Mrs Green said, as she showed Johnny to the master bedroom. "Especially after Miss Susan died. He never really got over it."

"I'm not surprised, he adored her," Johnny said, looking around the room. He could not remember ever coming up here, but it was not hard to imagine his uncle's last days in this dark panelled room. The windows were long, hung with faded green drapes, and Johnny walked over and threw them open to let in the weak winter sunlight, noticing the absence of dust and the sparkling panes. He looked around. "You've worked hard," he commented, and the housekeeper, a trim woman of about his own age, blushed slightly.

"I had some of the women up from the village when we knew you were coming, sir. It just needed a good turning out, we'd not wanted to disturb the master in those last months."

"Thank you, I'm grateful. I'm afraid I'm likely to prove a very absentee master for a year or two; I've already explained to Mr Langley that I've no intention of abandoning my career in the army just yet, I've men who rely on me. To be honest, Mrs Green, I need to spend a few weeks setting my affairs and then I'll be relying on you to keep the house in order while I'm away."

The housekeeper bobbed a curtsey. "Of course, sir."

"I'd like to speak to all the staff before dinner, to introduce myself; will you arrange it, please? And I need to see Mr Ludlow, the agent. I understand he doesn't live here?"

"No, sir, he has a small house at the edge of the village. I can send Hanson with a message."

"No, don't worry. I'll visit him tomorrow. I've not looked at the stables, but I understand my uncle kept a couple of horses?"

"Three, sir. The carriage horses are both elderly, they can pull the small barouche if needed, but not that far and not that fast. Star is in better condition; Hanson keeps her exercised."

"Excellent, I'll ride over then."

"I'll send your man up to unpack for you, sir."

■■

The village of Aberly was a mile from Limm, a picturesque Derbyshire village set around a small grass square. There were two inns on opposite sides of the village green and on the fourth side was the imposing tower of St Peter's Church. Johnny stabled his horse at the Plough and walked first over to the churchyard in search of information about his uncle's grave. He found the parson who led him to the newly erected stone, the turf still raw about it. Johnny stood for a long time, looking down at the name of the man who had allowed him to be where he was. He had always been conscious, through his long years in the army, of how much he owed Charles Wheeler, but he had never expected to step into his shoes and it brought a new closeness to the man as well as a pang of sorrow that he had not managed to see him before he died. He made his apologies silently, knowing that Charles would have understood that duty came first.

Afterwards he followed the parson's directions uphill through the village to the old mill house at the far end. The mill was long disused, although Johnny could see the remains of the old wooden wheel against the side of the crumbling mill building. But the cottage beside it, set in a well tended garden, was trim and neat and Johnny went through the wooden gate and knocked on the door.

It was opened by a maid in a dark dress, who conducted him through to a dim parlour. The girl lit several lamps and stoked up the fire then disappeared. After only a moment, the door opened and a young woman came in.

"Colonel Wheeler? My apologies, sir, we were not expecting you today. My father will be with you shortly. A winter cough has him laid up, but he will want to see you."

"I am sorry, I should have sent a message first," Johnny said, studying the girl. She was probably in her mid-twenties, perhaps a little more, dressed with propriety rather than elegance in a long sleeved green gown. It suited her colouring; she had bright red hair which could not have been called anything other than ginger, confined firmly under a lacy cap.

"Miss Ludlow?" Johnny guessed. The girl blushed a little and curtseyed politely.

"Yes, sir, I'm sorry, I should have introduced myself first. We aren't accustomed to many visitors; I am out of the habit of society."

"I've just come from an army camp, ma'am, you're not going to get much in the way of grand manners from me," Johnny said gravely, and surprised a laugh out of her. The smile transformed her; she had the pointed face of a woodland elf, with grey-green eyes and too many freckles to be considered pretty, but when she smiled she lit up the room and Johnny was conscious of a surprising wish to see her do it again.

"I suppose not," she said. "There is no sign of it so far, though, Colonel. Please sit down, I will ask Maggie to bring you some refreshment. Some wine, perhaps?"

"I'd prefer tea," Johnny said, and she looked surprised and slightly relieved.

"Certainly. I'll check on my father and be with you shortly."

Johnny had been prepared for an elderly man, but he was slightly shocked at how frail Arthur Ludlow seemed to be. He was neatly dressed in a dark suit, his sparse white hair tidy and his linen clean, but he came into the room on the arm of his daughter looking like a very sick man. Johnny rose and shook his hand, making civil enquiries about his health.

"Just a cold. A winter cold. The place is draughty," Ludlow said, sinking gratefully into the chair. "Is that tea, m'dear? I'll take a cup, thank you." He looked at Johnny. "You've met my daughter, Mary, haven't you?"

"Miss Ludlow introduced herself when I arrived," Johnny said. "I am sorry to arrive like this, Mr Ludlow, especially since you are unwell. Did you receive Mr Langley's letter explaining the circumstances?"

Ludlow did not immediately reply and Johnny wondered if he had not heard him. Before he could repeat himself, Miss Ludlow said:

"You told me that it arrived last week, Father. Before your cough got so much worse."

"Yes. Yes, of course. Of course."

"If I had more time, we could delay this. And I'm absolutely not willing to keep you from your bed too long today. I'm wondering about the estate books. I could see no sign of them up in the estate office, at least not the recent ones. Do you...?"

"They're all here, Colonel," Miss Ludlow said. "My father asked them to be brought down so that he could continue to work. When he heard you were coming, he made extensive notes for you. In case he was not well enough to see you."

"Thank you, that's very good of you," Johnny said. He was aware of a sudden tingling sense that something was slightly amiss. There was nothing but warm welcome and co-operation from these people, and he had no intention of forcing Ludlow into a lengthy session with the books given his obvious state of ill-health, but he had a strong sense that there was something he did not know. "I'd like to take them back with me today, if I may. If the weather holds, I'll do a tour of the estate over the next few days and meet the tenants. I hope by the end of the week to have a much better sense of what I'll need to do before I have to return to Portugal. As you'll not be well enough yourself, sir, I'll get the groom to show me around."

"I can do it," Miss Ludlow said. Johnny stared at her and she flushed slightly. "I mean...if you would like, sir. I grew up here, I know the estate as well as Hanson. And I might be able to help with any questions. My father has been accustomed to talk to me about his work."

"Thank you, I'd be delighted," Johnny said pleasantly. "I'm concerned that I'm keeping you up and around when you shouldn't be, Mr Ludlow. If you can tell me where the books are..."

"I'll bring them for you," Miss Ludlow said, getting up. "I know where my father keeps them."

The library at Limm Abbey had a faintly musty smell about it, as though it had been little used, but like the rest of the house it was spotlessly clean. Johnny asked for a fire to be lit and as the early winter darkness drew in, he sat with the ledgers and files Miss Ludlow had given him and pored over them. Molly, the housemaid, brought candles and lit the oil lamps and Johnny moved one of them onto the big table he was using as a desk and continued to read. He was frankly astonished at Ludlow's meticulous book-keeping and copious explanatory notes. The running of the estate was laid out before him in more detail than he could have hoped, and he was beginning to think that he had completely misjudged the agent. He was obviously currently very unwell, and must be approaching seventy, but clearly he still had a razor sharp brain and was a good organiser.

The thought was confirmed during the following week, as Johnny rode his lands beside Mary Ludlow and inspected farms, met tenants and looked at drainage and fencing and cottages. Johnny did not come from a landowning family and had no experience of running an estate. He had considerable experience, however, of running a regiment, and he could see that Limm Abbey and its lands were not neglected. Nor could he see any sign of dishonesty or peculation in the accounts, and he was beginning to think that he had imagined the slight sense of something wrong that he had felt in the company of the agent.

He did not see Ludlow again. Mary was his connection to her father. She left him each day with a list of questions and would return the following morning with detailed answers. Johnny was concerned that his irritating persistence would tire the older man, but he had so much to do and so little time.

"I hope your father is a little better?" he said, setting out to inspect the home farm flock, which already had one or two early lambs in their winter pens. "I'm afraid I've been a good deal of trouble to him this week."

"No, he does not mind at all," Mary said. "I promise you, he is very glad to see the estate has passed into such capable hands. He will be well again in the spring, it is the cold and damp that makes this hard to shake off."

"I can see that he's managed to stay on top of his work, his ledgers are immaculate. But, forgive me, Miss Ludlow, I am a little concerned about him being able to continue to ride about the lands. May I be frank with you?"

"Please do," Mary said, and her tone was slightly cooler.

"Mr Langley, the lawyer in London, has advised me to look about for a new agent, given your father's age and the state of his health. I came here prepared to find the estate in some disarray, but it isn't. It's clear he's been doing his job, and doing it well, but I'm worried that it's running him into the ground. If I were here full-time, I think it would work very well. I could undertake some of the work and he could teach me what I need to know without exhausting himself too much. But I cannot do it. We're in winter quarters just now, but I need to get back before spring."

"I thought you were wounded."

"I was, but it's healed very well, apart from this limp. And that will go. I have to go back and I have no idea when I can return. In the meantime, I need to be very sure that the man I leave in charge is capable. And fit enough to do the job."

Mary Ludlow turned cat eyes towards him. "Are you dismissing him, Colonel Wheeler?"

"Of course I'm not dismissing him," Johnny said, slightly irritably. "Aside from the ingratitude of it, after his excellent service, I'd have to be a fool to dismiss a man who knows the estate as he does. I need him here. But I'm wondering if I should appoint an assistant."

Mary did not reply for a long time. Eventually, she said in a colourless voice:

"You must do as you think best, Colonel. It is your estate. Come and see the newborns."

Johnny did not speak of it again. Back at the house, he returned to his desk and once more ran through the notes Ludlow had left for him. He sensed that Mary was worried that her father would be hurt if a junior agent was appointed, and Johnny understood. The man seemed to have devoted his life to the estate.

Johnny went to his solitary dinner, wondering if the girl was worried about the Mill House. The cottage was part of the estate, and it occurred to him that she might be afraid of losing their home. Johnny had no intention of evicting the Ludlows; they had earned the right to stay. A new, younger agent could occupy rooms in the house while Johnny was in Spain, and Ludlow could enjoy an honourable and comfortable semi-retirement, training up the new man. There was money for a pension for him and he could recover his health without having to shoulder the entire burden of responsibility alone.

Johnny decided that he would write to Langley, asking him to look about for a junior who might be suitable for the post, and would talk to the Ludlows. Mary might be upset, but he hoped that he could reassure her, and he wondered if it might be a relief to her father.

He woke the following morning to a curious light shining through the chink in the long curtains. Getting up, he went to the window to look out and found his suspicions confirmed. It must have snowed all night to blanket the lawns and gardens so thoroughly, and it was snowing still, great heavy flakes swirling so thickly that he could barely see the trees at the end of the back lawn. Johnny shivered and went to find his robe. He rang for his orderly to bring hot water and found Private Thompson in gloomy mood.

"Cold this morning, Thompson."

"Bleeding freezing, sir. Can't wait to get back to Portugal."

Johnny turned to stare at his orderly. "Thompson, where did you get that wound to your shoulder?"

"San Munoz, sir, same as you."

"I was just checking your memory, I thought you might have had a blow to the head at the same time. My memories of the sheer misery of staggering through freezing rain in November with no food and no chance of getting dry and warm are very clear. You're living in luxury here. Stop moaning or I'll bring somebody else next time. Or nobody, I can manage perfectly well without a valet, I've done it for years."

Thompson grinned. "Yes, sir. Want me to shave you?"

"If it's not too much trouble, Thompson, I wouldn't want to put you out," Johnny said gravely, and the other man laughed aloud.

"You sound like the colonel, sir."

"That's bad. I need to improve." Johnny smiled. "Missing your mates, Thompson?"

338

"Yes, sir. Dead quiet here, it is. I've not slept without Jonesy and Wickes snoring in my ear for about ten years, I can't get a wink without it."

Johnny laughed aloud. "I'm missing it too," he said. "What's wrong with us?"

"Army men, sir, through and through. Mind, I don't think we'll be travelling far for a few days, do you?"

Johnny looked out of the window. "Not if I can help it. I only march in the snow when Lord Wellington says I have to. I'm staying by the fire and catching up on some letter writing today, trust me. Although it looks as though someone is out and about. Is that Miss Ludlow I can see? Where the devil is she off to in this weather?"

Thompson came to stand beside him. "Not sure, sir. The home farm, maybe, it's out that way."

"Well she bloody shouldn't be," Johnny said, exasperated. "What is it with females, Thompson, they've no sense at times? The likes of you and I, know the sense of staying home and staying warm on a day like this. Look, forget the shave, get my boots, will you? I want to find out what's going on."

Thompson moved away, grinning. "D'you know, sir, I've never heard you speak of women that way before, in all the years you've served under General van Daan. Wonder why that is?"

"Because his wife would hit me with a blunt instrument if I did, Thompson, and I am terrified of her. And she, let me tell you, is a prime example of a woman who can't sit still for five minutes. But don't tell her I said that either."

Wrapped warmly in his shabby army great coat, his hat pulled firmly down, Johnny ploughed his way up the drive and followed Mary's footprints across the lawn. He cut down behind a small row of tenants' cottages, most of them with smoke curling from the chimneys. He could see her now, with three men dressed in working clothes, surveying the wreckage of the fence surrounding one of the sheep paddocks. Johnny went to join them.

"Morning, Colonel." Webster, who ran the home farm, was so wrapped up in scarves and coat that only his nose and eyes were visible and his voice was muffled. "Must have been windy last night, lost this section of the fence."

"Did we lose many?"

"A few, but we've got most of them back. Miss Ludlow says there's enough wood in the lumber shed back at the Mill to patch this up until we can do a proper job so I've sent two of the men over to get it, along with the tool bag. We're putting them in the barn anyway today, they can't be out in this."

"No. This came out of nowhere."

"Often does up here, sir."

"How many still missing?" Johnny asked.

"Four. But one's a lamb, he'll not survive this, need to find him. Just about to spread out and look. They can't have made it far."

"No. Get the rest of the men out, then, but tell them to stay in pairs. If someone goes over in a rabbit hole they can't see, we'll be searching for them as well. Meet back at the barn when you've found them – or at noon, if you've not. And don't get too cold. I don't want to lose a sheep, but I've more value for a man."

Johnny had spoken without thinking, as if to a man of his regiment. As he turned to begin the descent down the hill towards the river, the men moved away and Mary Ludlow fell in beside him.

"You'll be a good landlord."

Johnny glanced at her, surprised. "Why?"

"A man above a valuable sheep? There's a few around here would disagree."

"Don't tell me who they are, I've no wish to be at outs with my neighbours. You shouldn't be here, Miss Ludlow. Why did they come to the Mill instead of to me?"

The girl smiled. "Habit, I expect. They always come to me. Or my father, of course, when he's well."

"Well while I'm here, I expect them to come to me. But we'll talk of it later. Since you're here, where are you taking me?"

"There's a copse of trees further down, which will be sheltered. I'm guessing this ewe wandered with her lamb before the snow really took hold. They're not wholly stupid, she'll be looking for somewhere to hide."

"She has my sympathy," Johnny said, pulling his hat further down to shield his face better.

Mary turned to study him. "Should you be doing this, with your leg? I don't want you to hurt yourself."

"I'll be fine, I've abandoned the cane now. Although if I'm not, I warn you, it will be your job to scramble back up and get help for me. I'm not that much of a hero."

The girl studied him from those interesting eyes. "I'd heard that you were," she said, in matter of fact tones.

"Really? From whom?"

"Your uncle. I used to go up most days, when he was failing, to spend some time with him. He liked me to read to him, and to talk. Listen, really. He talked of his daughter and of you, a good deal. I think he missed both of you. He told me a lot about your career. He always wished he had managed to do more for you, but he was so proud of what you'd achieved on your own."

Johnny felt a rush of emotion, and with it, a passionate gratitude to this woman. "I'm so glad you were here for him," he said. "I feel terrible not knowing how ill he was, I'd have come home no matter what, to see him."

"You shouldn't feel bad; it was what he wanted. He used to say that it had been his privilege to get you started and it wasn't his job to hold you back now. He didn't want you told. I feel guilty though, I should have overridden him and written to you. I didn't know you then, or I'd have done so. Some men would have been angry at a woman taking such a thing upon herself, but I don't think you would."

"What about..." Johnny stopped suddenly and put his hand on her shoulder. "Wait, what's that?"

"I hear it." The bleating was loud and persistent.

"I think we've found our strays. This way."

It was a scramble through a thick drift down to the edge of the trees and Johnny took her hand to steady her, thinking not for the first time how frustrating it must be to be a woman and have to manage through difficult conditions in skirts. She managed well, though, and they made it through the drift to find two bedraggled creatures huddled under the trees. Mary went towards them, making soothing noises and Johnny stayed back, recognising an expert when he saw one. The woman ran her hands over their legs and looked back over her shoulder.

"They're both well, but very cold. We need to get the men down here, there's a wooden sledge we use for this, we'll never get her back up that hill through those drifts. I can go back up..."

"I'll go," Johnny said firmly. "Livestock is not my forte, they'll stay still with you. But you're going to freeze in that cloak. Here, put this on, I'll move faster without it."

Mary hesitated and then allowed him to help her into his heavy army great coat. Johnny draped her cloak over the top of it and then set off grimly back up the hill.

Johnny's leg was aching and he did not return with the men but watched from a window as they towed the ewe and her lamb back up the hill to the warmth of the barns. He went down to the library where a roaring fire was burning in the grate, and poured a glass of wine, reflecting with sudden amusement, that he was beginning to get used to the life of a country gentleman, and that he should probably get himself back where he belonged before it made him soft.

There was a tap at the door, and it opened.

"Miss Ludlow to see you, sir."

"Come in, Miss Ludlow." Johnny came forward quickly. "Christ, you're soaked. And freezing. I'm sorry, I shouldn't have left you down there. Here."

He removed both cloak and coat and turned to Molly. "Molly, do you think..."

"I'll take them to the kitchen, sir, we'll get them dry there."

"Thank you. Come and sit down by the fire, Miss Ludlow, and have some wine. I've just about thawed out myself."

Mary Ludlow accepted the glass tentatively and sipped it. Johnny sat in the opposite chair and studied her. "Would you forgive me if I asked a very impertinent question, ma'am?"

"That depends on what it is, Colonel."

"How old are you? I've been trying to guess."

Mary smiled. "I'm twenty-seven," she said.

"Why haven't you married?"

The pointed chin lifted a little. "Nobody has offered for me, Colonel. Why haven't you?"

Johnny laughed aloud. "Touché. That was two impertinent questions. I am ten years older than you, and I've not married because for most of my career I couldn't afford to. And also, I had no time."

Unexpectedly, Mary's face softened into her lovely smile. "I'm sorry, I've no reason to be snappish. I'm not unhappy on the shelf. I take care of my father and have one or two friends locally, who kindly invite me to supper sometimes. There is no money for a dowry and I am not pretty enough for a man to overlook the lack."

Johnny wanted to argue with her, but he realised suddenly that it would sound condescending, so he said nothing. After a moment, she looked up with a sudden and completely unexpected imp of mischief dancing in her eyes.

"I am sorry about that, Colonel. How very awkward for you. I truly wasn't fishing for compliments. But you managed it beautifully."

Johnny grinned. "I'm glad you think so, I couldn't decide. I think you're wrong, mind. You have glorious hair and very lovely eyes, and when you smile it makes me feel immediately happy. Is it the freckles that bother you?"

"They don't bother me at all, Colonel, but they bother other people. I once heard a very fashionable young gentleman at a public assembly say loudly that he could see why I hadn't a partner as it would be like dancing with a milkmaid."

"Clearly the youth had very limited life experience, ma'am. During my time in the army, I have danced with a varied collection of females, including several milkmaids, and they often dance very well. I'm sorry he was so rude to you; men often are when nobody has beaten the manners into them."

She was smiling broadly. "And who beat the manners into you, Colonel Wheeler? Somebody did a very good job of it, I've never come across a man with such excellent address. Literally nothing throws you off. Your servants are already devoted to you, and I am told that at least two local ladies with hopeful daughters are trying to work out how to manage an introduction so that they can invite you to dinner. You have made no calls on the neighbours, you know."

"Dear God, I'd forgotten about all these rules. Which is a good thing on this occasion, since I've such a short time here and so much to do, I don't have time to be social."

"Do you think you will settle here?" Mary asked unexpectedly.

"Yes," Johnny said. He had not thought about it at all, but the answer came very easily. "If I survive this war, I'd like to come back here and live. I've never allowed myself to look ahead that much. Over the years I've saved what prize money I could. I suppose one day I hoped to be able to marry and have a family. But I'd no home to come to. This...I can't believe this is mine."

"You could sell out," Mary said. "Nobody would think ill of you. You've responsibilities here now."

Johnny thought about it. He tried to imagine himself out of uniform, going about the daily chores of a landowner. He would get to know the neighbours and attend social events and join the local hunt. The picture was surprisingly appealing. Perhaps, one day, he might even meet a woman who would drive the smiling ghost of Caroline Longford from his heart, although Johnny was not sure he even wanted that to happen. While Caroline lived, even though she was married to another man, he suspected he would never feel free to offer his hand or heart to another woman. Still, a man could live here very happily alone.

The voice in his head was not Caroline's, but that of his brigade commander. "Just do it, Johnny. You've bloody earned it, you almost died last year. You've served all your adult life; you don't owe the army anything. I'll promote Carl. Get on with it."

Johnny sipped his wine and wished that Paul van Daan was sitting on the opposite side of this fire with him. He realised how much he was already missing his friends in the regiment and the brigade. He knew them safe in winter quarters at present, but within a few months they would be marching again, and he could not contemplate allowing them to do so without him.

"I don't belong here," Johnny said. "Not yet. I belong with my men. But I like the idea that one day I can come back here. Although I suppose I ought to think about making a will before I leave. I've never had anything to worry about before. God knows who I'd leave it to, I should ask Mr Langley who the heir would have been if I'd got myself killed last month."

Unexpectedly the woman shivered. "I hope you don't."

"So do I, it would be a waste now. Let's talk of something else, I'm giving you the horrors here. While I have you, would you mind going over a few things with me, to take back to your father if he's well enough? I've been looking over the cottages, and there are some repairs I'd like to set in motion before I leave. I made a list somewhere."

They moved to the table with their wine, and he read out the list he had made then handed it to her. Mary skimmed through it quickly, nodding. Johnny wondered what she would do when her father finally died and she was left alone without an income. He supposed she could apply for a post as a teacher or a governess, or perhaps as companion to some elderly lady. He found the thought vaguely depressing, and thought again how difficult it must be for a woman, with so few respectable ways of supporting themselves.

He was still thinking about it as she reached for a sheet of paper. "I'll send Hanson over with a note to the thatcher, he can come out when the weather lifts. Our men can manage most of the rest of these, but we'll need more timber properly cut for the fences, and the carpenter from Eyam should really see to those windows in Granby's cottage."

Johnny watched the quill flying across the paper and finally understood. He could not believe he had not worked it out before. His commander's wife would have scoffed at him for missing the obvious, but then she was a woman very accustomed to taking on work which was not rightfully hers and would have understood Miss Mary Ludlow very well.

"It was you, wasn't it?" he said quietly.

Mary stopped, the pen poised above the paper. She stared down at her own handwriting for a long frozen moment and then over at the open ledger nearby. The hand was identical.

"No," she said quickly. "Oh no. Only, my father gets rheumatism, his hands aren't good, sometimes he dictates to me..."

"Stop it," Johnny said firmly, removing the quill from her hand and setting it down. "What is wrong with him, Mary? Other than a winter chest."

Suddenly he was horrified to see tears in her eyes. "He gets confused," she whispered. "Forgets things. Can't add up the figures. It's been coming on for a year or more, but it's getting worse. He doesn't always realise it, but when he does, it upsets him so. Sometimes he doesn't even seem to know it's me, he calls me by my mother's name."

Johnny stared at her in silence for a long time. "I already have a junior land agent, don't I, Mary?" he asked quietly.

"Yes," the woman said baldly. "But I can't be. We both know that. It has to be a man. They know, most of them. The workers. But I've been going out with him around the lands all my life. I know the farms and the stock and the people. I can do everything he did, just as well."

"That's why they went to the Mill House first today, about the fences down. Not to see your father, but to see you."

"Yes. And I've told them that while you're here..." Mary broke off and folded her hands very neatly into her lap. "Are you going to dismiss us?" she asked.

Her taut misery wrung Johnny's heart. "I was never going to dismiss you, lass, what do you think I am, to throw aside all those years of good service to my uncle? He's due a pension and the house is yours for as long as you need it. That was always the case."

She lifted startled eyes to his face, her pale skin streaked with tears. "Truly?"

"Yes, I was going to come over to speak to him about it. I do need to employ somebody else; he's clearly not fit enough to be going out and about."

"I am," Mary said quickly. "I can do it, Colonel, I swear it. It's so good of you to say that we can stay, but I've no wish to take charity."

"Mary, I cannot employ you as my land agent. It wouldn't reflect well on either of us, and you know it. Although I wish I could, you're very good at it."

"Then continue to employ him," Mary said. Johnny could hear, beneath the calm reason of her tone, how desperate she was. "If you bring in another agent now, it will finish him. He can't give the training he should be able to and no man is going to take instruction from a woman. My father will see it happening and it will kill him. And with him gone, I have no place here."

It was what Johnny had been thinking. He sat looking at her, deeply troubled. After just over a week of being in her company every day, he realised how much he had come to like this self-effacing young woman and he could not bear the thought of her out in the world alone. She had spent all her life on this land, had given it her time and energy and devotion, and by an accident of

344

birth she could have no place here once her father died. Even if he gave instructions that she was to be allowed to remain in the cottage, there would be gossip about a young woman living alone; it was simply not done. He supposed that he could help her to find a post somewhere as a companion or governess, but he suspected she would be miserable so far from home and he knew that employers were often not kind to such women.

There was another danger that Johnny was very well aware of. Mary Ludlow spoke dismissively of her lack of beauty, as though a plain woman need have no concern in a world of predatory men, but Johnny had been out in the world all his life and had seen and heard of things he wished he could forget. Any young woman without a male relative to protect her and lend her respectability was vulnerable, and Johnny was under no illusion that she would not find herself prey to impertinence and embarrassment at best and a good deal worse.

And she was not plain. Johnny's enduring devotion to a woman he could not have, did not blind him to Miss Ludlow's very good figure and glorious hair. She had the shy charm of some woodland creature, disguised in her mundane setting but with a hint of pure beauty in her pointed face and grey-green eyes. As for the pale freckled skin, it might have drawn the scorn of some jumped-up dandy at a country ball, but Johnny could very easily imagine a set of circumstances in which it could seem very attractive indeed and he was sure he would not be the only man to find himself imagining how lovely that face might look framed by loose hair around bare shoulders and breasts.

Johnny caught himself and dragged his mind back to the problem with an effort. She had found a handkerchief and was drying her tears.

"Let's not jump so far ahead, lass," he said very gently. "Your father will probably recover well enough from his cough, although I want to add some work to the Mill House to that list of yours; it's too cold for him there and I want the chimney looked at, it smokes. I also think that you need a housekeeper."

The pointed chin lifted. "I can manage with a maid, sir. I'm used to..."

"Don't be dense, Mary, it isn't like you. This is going to get worse, I've seen it before. It happened to a friend of my father's. He developed a tendency to wander off. You can't spend your life watching him. I'm going to find a nice motherly woman who can tend the house, and take care of your father. Her wages will come off the estate, your father has earned it after all that he's done. And it will free you to continue to take care of my lands for me, since you do it so well."

"Sir?"

"I can't pay you as my land agent, but I can continue to pay him for as long as he lives. It might be for years; I hope it is. If I survive the war and come home to Limm Abbey – and I really hope I do – we'll talk again about your future. If something happens to him in the meantime, you will have a home, and his pension will continue to be paid to you, with all the expenses of your servants coming off the estate. I'll set it up before I leave. That way, you'll have a respectable woman living with you, which should silence any gossip about you living alone."

"You can't do this," Mary said.

"I can do whatever I like, I'm your employer. Stop arguing with me, it's a bad habit and I'm a very conventional man. I like a girl to look pretty and agree with me."

"No, you don't. I have never come across a man so outrageous."

"Believe me, lass, beside my commanding officer, I am a pattern card of rectitude. Although I've realised over the years that I am far less staid than I used to be; I think he's been a bad influence. If I'm killed..."

"You won't be."

"I might be. It happens. If I die out there, the Mill House and a small annuity will keep you safe and comfortable. I hope I don't. I'd like to come back and see you again."

"I'd like that too," Mary said.

Johnny was aware, suddenly, that the atmosphere between them had changed. He sat thinking about it, looking at her, and he wanted suddenly to tell her the truth.

"I'm not free," he said quietly.

"Are you betrothed?"

"No. And I'm not likely to be. I fell in love, very unsuitably, with another man's wife. Fool of a thing to do, but I couldn't help it. I'm not sure I'll ever get over loving her and I'm not sure I want to try."

Mary's eyes met his and held them. "Why did you tell me that, Colonel?"

"Because I really needed you to know, lass. Just in case I forget myself and do something stupid here. It's time I got you home, it'll be dark soon. I'll walk you back. Wait here and I'll send Molly for your cloak."

The men had been out for most of the day with spades and there was a clear path through the drifts down to the village. The snow had stopped finally although looking at the sky, Johnny suspected that more might fall tonight. He would need to put off all intention of travelling until this had cleared. Curiously, he was glad of it, it would give him time to get his affairs in order so that the people who had unexpectedly become his responsibility with this inheritance would be taken care of if he were to die.

It was a walk of a mile or so to the Mill House. The village was quiet, with people staying warm within doors, and as they approached, Johnny reached out and took her hand. He had no idea why he did it; he had wanted to see how it would feel. She did not pull away and they walked hand in hand past the village green to her door.

They stopped and Mary turned to look up at him. "Thank you," she said simply, and he knew that she was not referring to his escort home, although if he chose, he could easily pretend that she was and she would not mind. It was what she did best, managing herself and any difficulties quietly and without demands on other people and he realised unexpectedly how much he valued that.

346

Johnny knew that he should go, but he was conscious suddenly of a warmth of feeling and he wondered if she felt it too. Still holding her hand, he stepped closer to her and put his other hand under her chin, tilting her face up towards his. She did not flinch away although he saw her eyes widen in surprise. He had not really thought before about how tall she was; he only had to bend a little to kiss her.

She leaned towards him, and Johnny let go of her hand and put his arm about her, drawing her closer very gently. He could tell how nervous she was, and he was not surprised; nothing in Mary Ludlow's sheltered life suggested that she had been kissed before. He found her shyness very endearing and was deliberately gentle, not wanting to frighten her.

Eventually, after a long time, Johnny raised his head. Mary looked up at him, wide-eyed and startled as a young doe, and Johnny felt a sudden surge of desire, so strong that it shocked him a little. He wanted, for one insane moment, to pick her up and carry her into the house, and he took a deep breath and brought himself firmly under control. After all his careful concern about her future, he had no intention of hurting her so badly.

"Why did you do that?" Mary asked.

Johnny cupped her cheek with his hand and kissed her again, very lightly, just a brush of his lips to hers. "Because I wanted to, and I really hoped you did too. I'm sorry. I should..."

"I did want you to. And I do understand, Colonel, what you told me earlier. But I'm glad you did it anyway. It was nice."

It was not a word Johnny would have used for that kiss, but he was not going to tell her so. "It was. Go on, get yourself inside before you freeze. Have you time tomorrow?"

"Yes."

"Will you come up early? I need some lessons in farming, Webster has been talking seed drills and crop rotation until my brain dribbles out of my ears, and I've no idea what he's talking about, but I suspect you have. I'll write to Langley to set everything in order tomorrow as well. I'm not attempting to travel in this weather. And they can manage without me for a few weeks anyway, it'll do them good. Miss Ludlow..."

"Mary. You cannot change back now, no matter how unsuitable it is."

"Mary – would you be very shocked if I asked you to dine with me tomorrow? Country hours, I swear I'll have you home early."

Mary regarded him steadily. "It would be very improper, Colonel, as I am sure you know. And the servants would talk."

"You're probably right."

"However, if we are to spend the day working in the library, it would not be at all improper for me to invite you to dine here, with my father and I. And we have no live-in servants, so nobody will have any idea if my father makes it to the dinner table or not. I think it's unlikely he will, he sleeps a good deal at the moment."

Johnny felt an unaccustomed lift of his heart. "I would love to dine with you and your father," he said seriously.

347

"I shall make a steak and kidney pudding then. I am a very good cook, if you like plain food."

Johnny stared at her for a long moment. "I cannot remember the last time I ate a steak and kidney pudding, and that does not count as plain food," he said. "If you saw what I live on sometimes on campaign..."

"I'd like to ask you about your service, but I wasn't sure if it was my place. May I?"

Johnny nodded. "You may ask me anything you wish. Once I have mastered crop rotation. Did you hear anything just then?"

Mary shook her head. "No."

"No, you wouldn't. I think I just heard the sound of my commanding officer laughing inside my head. Good night, Mary, I'll see you tomorrow. Come early and have breakfast with me."

She was laughing now. "Breakfast is even more unsuitable than dinner. I will be with you just after. Good night, Colonel Wheeler."

Johnny stood watching her as she picked her way carefully up the slippery path to her door and went inside, flashing him that smile over her shoulder. He turned and walked back up to the Abbey, not really noticing the cold. He found himself thinking about Caroline, seeing her golden loveliness as though she was walking beside him, but she was smiling at him, and there was no hint of anger in the smile. Johnny reflected that he might well continue to love her until the end of his days, but for some reason there was no sadness in him tonight. Turning at the top of the street, he looked back down towards the Mill House, its bulk outlined against a darkening sky.

Snow was beginning to fall again, and Johnny pulled up the collar of his coat and quickened his step, eager to be home. Lights were already burning and he could almost feel the warmth reaching out and drawing him in. Despite the cold, he stopped for a moment to look at the house, appreciating it. He thought of Charles Wheeler with immense gratitude, for giving him so much; a start in life, a career he loved and now a home to come back to. Suddenly he felt very close to the old man, and could hear his voice clearly in his head for the first time since arriving at the Abbey, the familiar Derbyshire accent making Johnny smile.

"Aye, lad, and if you'd the sense you were born with you'd get inside and enjoy it before you freeze to death out here."

Acting on excellent advice from beyond the grave, Johnny walked up the front steps and into the brightly lit hallway, allowing the house to welcome him into comfort and familiarity and an unexpected promise of a very different future.

By the Same Author

The Peninsular War Saga

An Unconventional Officer (Book 1)

An Irregular Regiment (Book 2)

An Uncommon Campaign (Book 3)

A Redoubtable Citadel (Book 4)

An Untrustworthy Army (Book 5)

An Unmerciful Incursion (Book 6)

An Indomitable Brigade (Book 7)

The Manxman

An Unwilling Alliance (Book 1)

This Blighted Expedition (Book 2)

Regency Romances

A Regrettable Reputation (Book 1)

The Reluctant Debutante (Book 2)

Other Books

A Respectable Woman

A Marcher Lord

Printed in Great Britain
by Amazon